RAVES FOR
JAMES PATTERSON

"Patterson knows where our deepest fears are buried...There's no stopping his imagination."

—New York Times Book Review

"James Patterson writes his thrillers as if he were building roller coasters." —Associated Press

"No one gets this big without natural storytelling talent—which is what James Patterson has, in spades."

—Lee Child, #1 *New York Times* bestselling
author of the Jack Reacher series

"James Patterson knows how to sell thrills and suspense in clear, unwavering prose." *—People*

"Patterson boils a scene down to a single, telling detail, the element that defines a character or moves a plot along. It's what fires off the movie projector in the reader's mind."

—Michael Connelly

THE MURDER INN

For a complete list of books, visit JamesPatterson.com

THE MURDER INN

JAMES PATTERSON AND CANDICE FOX

GRAND
CENTRAL

New York   Boston

The Murder Inn copyright © 2024 by James Patterson
Black & Blue copyright © 2016 by James Patterson

Cover design by James T. Egan of Bookfly Design. Cover images by Shutterstock. Cover copyright © 2024 by Hachette Book Group, Inc.

Grand Central Publishing
Hachette Book Group
1290 Avenue of the Americas, New York, NY 10104
grandcentralpublishing.com
twitter.com/grandcentralpub

First Edition: March 2024

Grand Central Publishing is a division of Hachette Book Group, Inc.
The Grand Central Publishing name and logo are trademarks of Hachette Book Group, Inc.

The publisher is not responsible for websites (or their content) that are not owned by the publisher.

The Hachette Speakers Bureau provides a wide range of authors for speaking events. To find out more, go to hachettespeakersbureau.com or email HachetteSpeakers@hbgusa.com.

Grand Central Publishing books may be purchased in bulk for business, educational, or promotional use. For information, please contact your local bookseller or the Hachette Book Group Special Markets Department at special.markets@hbgusa.com.

LCCN: 2023946032

ISBNs: 9781538710944 (trade paperback), 9781538766460 (large print), 9781538710951 (hardcover library), 9781538710975 (ebook)

Printed in the United States of America

LSC-C

Printing 1, 2024

DESERT OUTSIDE BAGRAM, AFGHANISTAN, 2010

NICK JONES'S FELLOW soldiers were lying to him. They'd never done it before, and Nick knew that for one simple reason: because he wasn't dead. He could rely on one thing out there in the desert in Afghanistan, and that was the word of his teammates. Without that trust, without a team behind him, promising to protect him, Nick was alone. And a soldier alone was just waiting to catch a bullet in the brain.

On a dark roadside somewhere between Bagram City, the US Army outpost, and the distant ceiling of a billion stars, Nick stood and watched Staff Sergeant Roger Dorrich draw a map on the dusty hood of the tactical vehicle with his stubby finger. As he spoke, the older soldier shattered Nick's trust one word at a time.

"We're abandoning tonight's routine quadrant patrol for a quick mission into a village just ten clicks past that hill," Dorrich said as he drew vast, confident lines in the dust of the JLTV.

Three large boxes, a smaller box, a snaking boundary. "We're going for the third house on the right, here, after the goat pen."

It was around the time Dorrich took out his cigarette that Nick realized what he was hearing was deception. Just like when he was trying to bluff a good hand at poker, Dorrich put the cigarette between his lips and bit down on the tip, chewing it flat, so it was impossible to draw through.

Nick had started to feel uneasy the second Dorrich said "Change of plans, team," and pulled off the side of the road. Now he was downright scared. That useless cigarette jutting from between Dorrich's lips bobbed up and down as he lied.

"We got two entry points," Dorrich continued. "Front and back. Two expected hostiles inside the dwelling. This is not a grab-up, ladies and gentlemen. We neutralize the targets and exit immediately. Back on patrol by 2300."

Nick waited for his two other teammates to ask one of the dozens of questions that immediately rose in his mind. Neither did.

"Sir, who's got eyes on the site right now?" Nick ventured.

"Nobody. It'll be just us out there," Dorrich said.

"But..." Nick shook his head, tried to comprehend. "Sir, how do we know...I mean, what's the situation? Are they hot?"

"We're going into this blind, Jones." Dorrich narrowed his eyes at Nick, challenging. "You got a problem with that?"

"Sir. No, sir. But—"

"You want to know something about the targets. Should I break them down for you? What they ate for breakfast? Where they went to school? Boxers or briefs? Should we sit down, have a little discussion about whether they deserve to die or not?"

"Sir. No, sir."

"Maybe we'll just get on with it then, huh?"

"Sir. Yes, sir."

Nick felt a tingling sensation creep over his scalp. This wasn't right. He glanced at Karli Breecher, who was tightening the straps of her helmet over her closely shaved skull, eyes on the map, nodding like she'd done a hundred spur-of-the-moment, blind, completely solo kill runs before. All routine. Rick Master, the fourth member of their team, was shuffling from foot to foot, blank-faced. It seemed to Nick suddenly that nobody would look at him. That nobody else smelled the lies in the air.

And that was a problem. That was deadly.

Because on deployment, Nick couldn't be sure that setting out on any road meant he was going to arrive where he intended. The yawning, searing desert was inclined to throw something at him. IEDs. Bandits. Sandstorms. Goddamn locust plagues. On any given day, Nick couldn't trust that he'd get food. Or water. Or ammo. Or sleep. Hell, sometimes it even surprised him that the sun came up in the morning out here.

But he could rely on Dorrich, Master, and Breecher.

At least, he'd thought he could.

Nick climbed into the JLTV anyway. He had no choice. They rolled out into the blackness, silent.

Just following orders, Nick thought.

Master must have felt his anxiety, because he reached over and slapped Nick's arm.

"Cool it, man. The hajjis hit Romeo 12 company last night," Master said. "It's got to do with that, for sure."

"What?" Nick said. "R12 got hit? When?"

"About 0100," Breecher said. "Northwest of the outpost. R12 went out alone to recover a piece of drone that fell into a valley out there. Two local idiots stopped them, took their weapons and the piece of drone."

"Why didn't I hear about this?" Nick asked.

"Gee, I don't know—because it's embarrassing as all hell?" She smirked. "Romeo 12 getting their asses handed to them by a couple of teenage goat farmers? No wonder they're keeping it low-key. And they're sending in the professionals to clean up." Breecher bumped Nick with her shoulder. "Now stop chewing your nails. You're making me nervous."

Nick fell quiet again. His gear was hanging off him. In the front, Dorrich's cigarette had become a cylinder of ash. Nick let the vehicle rock and jostle him on the desert. It was pure craziness to think that Romeo 12 would ever go into a recovery mission like that without air support and a convoy. Crazier still that the outpost's best and deadliest team could possibly be held up by two kids. Beyond crazy that Nick, Dorrich, Breecher, and Master would be sent in without a brief and also without backup, as a response.

They stopped in the moon shade of a rocky outcrop and slid out of the vehicle. The uneven ground on the run to the village boundary felt to Nick like it was moving. He crouched in the spiny grass by a low mud-brick wall and waited while Breecher and Master got into position. There were lights on in the tiny, sun-scorched house. Nick was close enough that he could see the outline of blue flowers on the faded curtains in the windows. Goat shit tainted the breeze.

Breecher signaled him from the road at the front of the house. Nick rushed forward, felt Dorrich at his heels, the shorter, thicker man's footfall louder than his own. He flattened against the side of the house and shouldered his rifle, winced as Dorrich kicked in the door.

Nick inhaled.

At first, he thought a bomb had gone off. Nick's bootcamp company leader had detonated an IED in front of his platoon once, just to show them how much damage a school lunchbox packed with ammonium nitrate and fuel and roofing nails could do. The same sudden white light burst against his eyelids now as he rounded the doorway into the little house in the desert. His eardrums pulsed. His brain rattled in his skull. But the noise and light and vibration didn't stop, and Nick soon realized that it was Dorrich's gun, not a bomb, ringing out in the night.

Nick stood stricken in the doorway as Dorrich sprayed the family sitting on the rugs on the floor with bullets. He looked up from the carnage in time to see a woman running across the doorway to the dwelling's second room. She was just a flash of black hair and thin arms, before Master passed after her, his gun out in front of him. Nick felt the percussion of the gunshot in the other room reverberate through the center of his chest.

The whole family was dead before Nick could exhale.

CHAPTER ONE

Gloucester, Massachusetts, 2022

MY BEST FRIEND was going to hurt someone.

I sat at the dining room table and watched Nick Jones out of the corner of my eye. He tapped the screen of his phone again, redialing a number that hadn't connected once across the seven calls he'd made to it in the previous two minutes. Nick didn't know it, but I could see his phone screen in the reflection in a framed picture sitting on the bookshelf behind him. I did a lot of that; watching my buddy carefully. The traumatized army veteran, one of the residents of the inn I owned by the seaside, was on the ropes again with his schizophrenia. It was typically up to me to throw in the towel for him. I knew that the moment was coming. It was usually heralded by a single thought, the instinct pushing to the forefront of my mind—that Nick was going to hurt someone. A stranger; himself; me.

Maybe another resident of the inn.

That would be the worst-case scenario. I could take a hit,

and I knew Nick could too, but the people who resided with us in the ramshackle house by the water were our family. They'd saved the both of us—Nick after he returned from war, and me after I lost my wife to a road accident shortly after we moved to this place.

Buying the inn had been Siobhan's idea, and I'd reluctantly gone along with it after losing my job as a detective in the Boston PD five years ago. While I'd been sulking over my termination, she'd handled the purchase and set-up of our New England bed-and-breakfast.

"It'll be great, Bill," she'd told me. "I've found the perfect fixer-upper."

I was unconvinced but let Siobhan's enthusiasm pull me along. She'd always had a knack for seeing potential.

The Inn by the Sea was a simple construction: its weatherboard exterior, recently painted sunflower-yellow, did little to shut out the freezing Gloucester winters, and its mismatched steel and wood bones, rambling with poorly thought-out extensions and adjustments, creaked as the people inside it moved. But it was those people and their stories that give the house a heartbeat. We had a collection of mystery men and women among our permanent residents: gangsters, law enforcers, runaways, and ex-criminals. You couldn't put those kinds of souls together without creating fireworks, but for every dangerous spark there was also a good helping of warm glow.

At night the inn hummed and thrummed with people coming and going, whispering in the kitchen, singing in the shower, yelling across the halls. By day it practically vibrated as people jogged down the stairs, screamed at the television in the living room, drank wine and danced on one of the large porches. Short-term guests bustled in and out, battering the walls with suitcases, and occasionally the house pattered with little feet or thumped with the bedroom activities of lovers on cheap getaways.

It was my job as innkeeper to make sure that none of the darkness that swirled and twirled through the pasts and presents of our guests here threatened what we had: a big, beautiful, crazy home. And whatever was troubling Nick was gathering energy like a storm cloud around the guy's head.

I needed to do something about it soon because I was headed out the door for an old colleague's funeral. Needham was only about an hour's drive away, but I'd booked a hotel for the night. I didn't want to leave Nick alone at the inn in his present state.

My careful monitoring of my friend was interrupted by a rise in volume in the argument carrying on at the end of the table.

"Bill?" Susan Solie called over to me.

I'd been lucky enough to call Susan, a gorgeous blond former FBI agent, my girlfriend these last couple of years. But she was currently in a standoff between Effie Johnson, the inn's unofficial handywoman, and fellow resident Angelica Grace Thomas-Lowell—internationally bestselling novelist, vegan, activist, humanitarian.

Susan had a hand on the ironing board that was acting as a bench dividing me from her and the other two inn residents. "If you don't step in here, Bill, you're never going to get your shirt ironed. You're going to end up at the funeral in a sweatshirt. Or bare-chested."

"Now that would be awkward," I quipped. "There's a rule about that, I think. Don't wear white to a wedding. Don't go half-naked to a funeral."

"Bill."

"Hey, I tried to avoid this altogether." I held my hands up. "I tried to iron the shirt myself. Before I knew what was happening, ironing experts pounced from outta nowhere like ninjas. I was overcome."

The three experts in question each had a seemingly unmovable stance regarding the correct way to remove wrinkles. Angelica had command of the stark white dress shirt I'd selected for the funeral and was pinning it to the ironing board with her hand. Effie held the iron, but Susan had the iron's cord and was refusing to plug it into the wall socket. The shirt-ironing turf war between the three women had been carrying on for ten minutes now and no one had made or lost a square inch of ground.

"I only offered my opinion because you were beginning with the collar," Susan said, turning her slim gold watch around and around on her wrist, something she does when agitated. "And that's not where you start. Not even close."

"Please just let me explain *my* position," Angelica said. She tried unsuccessfully to swipe the iron from Effie. "I understand, Effie, you have some mysterious military or government or guerilla warfare–type experience that makes you think you know how best to iron a shirt. And I understand, Susan, that you have good intentions. But the fact is simply that this is not a *uniform* shirt. It's a man's *dress* shirt, and thus one must consider the garment's stylistic nuances in preparing it for wear."

"Oh Jesus," I sighed.

Effie, mute from a near-decapitation sustained in the aforementioned mysterious personal history, slapped her free hand over her eyes in dismay.

"As research for my third novel," Angelica said as she yanked the iron from Effie's other hand while she was blinded, "I spent six months living in Powai serving as a house manager for a high-ranking minister in India's parliament."

Angelica waited for everyone to be impressed. We weren't.

"It was my duty," she carried on, regardless. "One of my *many* entrusted duties, to ensure that the minister's substantial collection of house staff, including the staff who ironed and pressed his clothes, respected the—"

"Angelica, I'm not plugging this iron in until you—" Susan began.

"Respected the deeply nuanced traditions of fabric care established during India's long and rich history of—"

"Angelica! Angelica!" Susan barked. "We have five minutes to get this done! If Bill's not dressed and on the road by—"

Effie had wrestled back the iron from Angelica. I looked over at Nick again. The muscular Black man continued dialing the unresponsive number. In the reflection, I saw that the contact's name was Dorrich.

Whoever Dorrich was, there was only one reason for Nick to be calling him every fifteen seconds: because Nick was desperate. During the years that Nick had resided at the inn, I'd learned that his desperation preceded his fear, and after the fear stage it was just a hop, skip, and a jump before my friend was either wading into the freezing waters of the bay chasing ghosts, hunting perfect strangers with guns, or rambling on with stories about people coming to get him. I needed to break the cycle, find out who Dorrich was and why getting in touch with him seemed to be Nick's only priority. And that wasn't going to happen if Nick stayed at the inn with his demons while I went to Boston.

I reached over and tapped the table near his hands. Nick was startled by the noise, the movement. Too startled.

"Hey," I said when I had his attention. "Why don't you come with me?"

"Where?"

"The funeral," I said. "Come on. It'll be fun."

"It'll be *fun*?" Nick raised a thick eyebrow.

"Not the ceremony. The reception. The after-party."

Nick looked unconvinced.

"You ever been to a cop funeral?" I asked. "We go all out. The bigger and better the cop, the larger the send-off. And these aren't just any cops. They're Boston cops. Boston *Irish*. I promise you: you've never been this drunk in your life."

"I don't think you're supposed to just bring friends along to a thing like that," Nick said and went back to his phone. His voice was casual, but his eyes were dancing over the screen, his big hands trembly.

"I'll tell them you're my emotional support animal. Like the dogs people take on planes."

Nick gave a half-smile. I was winning. Slowly, carefully. I pressed on.

"We'll stand at the back," I said. "Or you hang out at a bar down the road while we get the boring part of the day done, then meet me after."

"Man, you ain't going anywhere." Nick nodded at the three women still scuffling at the end of the table. "Except a hospital, maybe. You'll be sittin' in the waiting room an hour from now while Angelica gets a CT scan after Effie beats her brains in with that iron."

"Effie or Susan." I nodded in agreement, watching the vein

in Susan's temple starting to tick. "I know better than to argue with Susan when she's got something in her hands she could strangle me with."

"As you should."

The doorbell rang. I spied another resident of the inn, Clay Spears, standing at the hallway mirror, adjusting the tie on his sheriff's uniform.

"Clay, can you get that?" I called.

"Yeah, Bill," Clay called back.

I got up and tugged my unpressed shirt off the ironing board and whipped it over my shoulders. The women gave a unified gasp of horror and outrage.

"It's fine, really," I said. "I'll keep my jacket on."

Over the sound of their protests, I walked past Nick and grabbed a handful of his huge biceps before he could dial the mystery number again.

"You're coming to Boston," I told him, pulling him up. "That's an order."

CHAPTER TWO

SHERIFF CLAYTON SPEARS was having one of those mornings, directly following one of those nights. The previous evening had been spent in Manchester-by-the-Sea, wining and dining a woman he'd met on an online dating app. Though she'd kissed him on the cheek and let her fingers trail across the back of his thick, hairy hand before she slid into the cab he'd hailed her, he'd awakened this morning to the inevitable "It's not you, it's me" text. Clay was well-acquainted with that text. The one that cited her hesitation at leaping back into the romance game after a long and serious relationship, her feeling that he was a nice guy but that they just didn't "click," her need to "listen to her heart" or "find out who she really was" before "getting serious" with a man again. He'd known just by the length of it what the text was going to say. It sat like an angry green block of rejection on his screen, waiting for him to wake in his little room on the first floor.

Now he looked at all 280 pounds of himself in the hall mirror—his wild sandy hair, his crooked nameplate and lopsided tie—and tried to access some deep reserve of courage and energy so that he could go out on duty in Gloucester. The town's head lawman was a brave man. A confident man. Someone who shrugged off the fact that he was too fat, that his laugh was too loud, that he bored his dates into a stupor talking about the Red Sox, that everybody in town knew his ex-wife had left him for a male model she'd known for a total of forty-eight hours. Clay pushed his shoulders back, looked into his own eyes, and tried to be that man.

The doorbell rang. Bill called for him to get it.

Clay pulled open the door and saw the love of his life standing there on the stoop.

She was a brunette beauty, bathed in that icy New England morning light that seemed to only want to dance upon natural, unspoiled things. Forest floors and ocean cliffs. She had girl-next-door freckles and doe eyes (which would have been exactly what Clay would have written that he was partial to in his online dating profile, had he been so bold).

And she wasn't alone. Out of the corner of his eye, Clay also spotted for a fleeting moment a small blond boy about five years old at the woman's side. Both woman and child held backpacks; she held hers by the strap, and the boy clutched his blue backpack against his chest.

Clay choked on a greeting and simply stood there clutching the doorframe in one clumsy mitt and his belt buckle in the other and looking at the beautiful woman and her child.

The woman took in the sight of Clay in his uniform and her mouth dropped open like a mailbox door.

"Oh," she said. "Um. I think we must have the wrong place."

Clay realized his mouth was open. He slammed it shut with an audible clack of his molars.

"You don't," he said. The pair in the doorway paused, confused.

"But we—"

"The Inn by the Sea." Clay pointed to the awning overhanging the porch, where there might have been a sign if Bill had ever bothered to have one made. "This is it. You must be guests."

"We are." The little boy grinned. "Are you the cops?"

"Ah, well, I—sort of—" Clay stammered. "I'm sort of a cop. The sheriff's department does a lot of the same, uh. Our jurisdiction is—anyway, hello! Welcome!"

"Hello," the woman said. "I'm April and this is Joe."

April stuck out her hand. Clay's brain spasmed and he reached for the backpack in her other hand, for some reason. There was a midair fumbling. April dropped the backpack, and Clay caught her hands suddenly and harshly like a kid trapping a firefly. His joy at feeling her skin against his clashed violently with horror at the bungled handshake. He pumped her hands twice and let them go. He chanced a wave at the kid.

"We have a room booked here? I think?" April said, as though the entire encounter thus far had left her believing nothing was certain in the world anymore.

"You do," Clay said, stepping back. "I mean. I don't know if you do. I haven't looked at the book. I just heard the bell and answered the, uh, the door."

He turned away, grimaced.

Stop talking! his mind screamed.

"I don't run this place, I just. You know. I just live here—have been living here—for some time, but it's temporary," Clay said. He looked into the dining room where it seemed a dozen people had been only seconds earlier. He found no one. Clay's voice boomed down the hall in the other direction. "Bill! Nick! Someone? Anyone?"

April and Joe waited in the hall with their backpacks, watching him mess up the simplest of all tasks. Something he had done a bunch of times: welcoming short-term guests into the inn.

"I'm hungry," Joe announced.

"Just wait, baby," April said and ran a hand over Joe's close-cropped hair. Clay noticed for the first time how tired they both looked. He grabbed up the ledger sitting on the hall table and saw her name written in Bill's handwriting. *Leeler, April. Plus kid. 3 days. Pay cash on arrival. Room 3.*

"OK, I've got this. I've got this." Clay snatched the bags from the mother and son. "Follow me. Room three. It's right this way."

"Hooray!" The boy skipped after him.

"Thank you so much," April said.

Clay saw them to one of the two rooms Bill kept for overnight guests. It was the sunnier of the two rooms, which made Clay wonder if light simply followed April Leeler everywhere, if wherever she went she would touch people with that golden warmth. The little boy swirled the dust motes caught in that sunlight with his hands while his mother immediately went to the window and tried to open it. Clay thought about that. About how April's first concern in the room seemed to be how she could escape it. Or open another portal out of it. Something fluttered in his cop brain, the deeply embedded intuition that had served him so well on the job. But he didn't have time to pursue the thought before the little boy was tugging on his sleeve.

"I'm hungry," Joe repeated. "Do you have pancakes here? I need pancakes."

"Young man, you are a child after my own heart," Clay said. "*I need pancakes* is on my family crest."

"What's a family crest?"

"Let me show you to the kitchen," Clay said. "I'd rustle you up something myself but I'm headed out the door to serve and protect. But anything in the fridge is up for grabs. I'm sure we've got fixings for—"

"We're fine," April interrupted. She laid her hand on the little boy's shoulder and scooped him back against her legs. "We just want to keep to ourselves. We've come a long way and we're tired."

Clay's mind flickered again.

Something is wrong here, he thought.

He said his goodbyes and promised himself that he would find out what it was.

CHAPTER THREE

NORMAN DRIVER STOOD leaning against the steel fencing surrounding a building site. He could remember a time when the sight of a law enforcement officer's car pulling up anywhere near him would make the hairs on the back of his neck stand on end. Yet now he felt barely a rise in interest as a deputy sheriff's squad car pulled over to the curb, the officer eyeing him for a moment before popping the door.

Driver had spent most of his twenties feeling the cold hand of Lady Disaster on his shoulder whenever an officer stepped into a diner he was sitting in, or when a police squad car stopped beside him at a traffic light. Pushing sixty now, he simply smiled and nodded.

The jangling of equipment on the officer's belt was lost in the sounds coming from behind Driver. The ripping and tearing of sheets of cladding, the slam of hammers and buzz of saws. Driver lit a cigarette and tried to get a measure of the man.

There wasn't much to go by. Tall, streak of Hispanic, all muscle, in a tight-fitting uniform. Driver knew some of the Gloucester cops. This guy wasn't on his radar.

"What's the trouble, officer?" Driver asked.

"You tell me," the guy said. "Got a noise complaint. Resident nearby tells me you and your crew have been starting work early the past two days, making all that racket. Fifteen minutes to eight, or worse."

"No kiddin'?" Driver said. He gave another smile and exhaled smoke politely over his shoulder. "I'm surprised the response isn't bigger. But maybe there's a chopper overhead that I don't know about." He glanced skyward. The joke paid off. The sheriff cracked a grin.

"You can't start making serious noise around here until at least 8 a.m." The deputy shrugged. "Sleepy seaside town. You know how it is."

"I know how it is."

"You guys new in town?" The officer eyed the nearest truck, the red lettering on the side. DRIVER CONSTRUCTION SERVICES.

"Relatively," Driver said. "Whose shut-eye were we disturbing? I'll make sure to send over a fruit basket or something."

"You know I can't tell you a thing like that."

"Just trying to be neighborly."

Driver watched the deputy sheriff step off the curb, saw him glance up at the house across the street. Driver followed his gaze over there and saw a lace curtain fall back into place. A mean quiver wanted to start in his lip, so he shoved his cigarette back in his mouth.

"Try to keep to the allowed times," the deputy said. He returned to the squad car and raised his hand in a wave. As the officer grabbed the door handle, Driver thought he was home free. Then the officer paused and came back, his face pinched with an afterthought.

"The resident also said she'd seen workmen on the site at night," the officer said and cocked his head, curious. Driver hid his taut upper lip behind his knuckles.

"That's a strange accusation," Driver said. "Pretty tough to do this gig by flashlight. And silently."

"That's just what I was thinking," the deputy said. "So what would your guys be doing here at night?"

"Beats me. Maybe that neighbor needs to get her eyes checked."

"What's all this about, anyway?" The officer leaned around Driver to look at the site.

"We're removing the cladding from this old house. Replacing it with pine weatherboard. Suits the scenery better," Driver said.

The two men took in the view of the little house, its exposed sides, with its dark hardwood framing and pink insulation foam, dusty with age. On the ground by the porch, guys in white suits and masks were folding shattered pieces of fiberboard into large sheets of black plastic. They watched as one of the men ripped a strip of duct tape from a roll and began sealing the package of fiberboard shards tightly at the seams.

"What's with all the protective equipment?" The deputy smirked. "They look like they're handling radioactive waste."

"It's not radioactive, but it's nasty," Driver said. "Asbestos. You know much about it?"

"Nah, man. My dad was a cop. I played with guns as a kid, not hammers."

"Well, you don't want to know much about this stuff," Driver said and drew on his cigarette. "It's an old building material from the fifties. Pretty popular because it was cheap. Lot of houses around here were wrapped in it, top to bottom, inside and out. It's not a problem if it stays intact. But maybe you scratch it. Bump it. Drill into it without knowing it's there. Maybe some gets torn down and scattered everywhere in a storm. Before you know it, the fibers get into your lungs and start eating their way through you like worms in an apple."

"Jeez." The officer took a step back from the fence. "I think I've seen those late-night ads about it. Meso...Meso—"

"Mesothelioma," Driver said.

"Right."

"Yeah. A single breath of it could be all it takes," Driver said. "Anyway. You can go in and talk to some of the boys if you want. Have a look around. See for yourself that there's no funny business going on here, day or night."

"No thanks." The deputy held his hands up, gave Driver a friendly tip of his hat. "Really. I appreciate the offer."

"I bet." Driver shared a sarcastic smile. The two men parted. Driver even waved as the guy pulled away from the curb.

The smile twisted as that evil feeling snagged his upper lip like a fishhook. The house across the street was still now, silent. Driver stubbed out his cigarette and headed across the road.

CHAPTER FOUR

NICK WAS GRIPPING the seat belt with both hands, eyes fixed on the highway ahead of us, one long leg jangling up and down as I drove. He was wearing a powder-blue dress shirt he'd pulled from his closet immaculately ironed, and I figured it had probably been that way for months. The guy was all about control. Order. Process. Above the collar I could see his jugular vein, taut and thrumming.

"So what's going on?" I asked.

"Huh?" He looked at me, unseeing, still captive to his thoughts.

"Who's Dorrich?"

Nick gave a quick laugh, but there was no humor in it.

"Man, you are like some all-seeing eye," he said. "I knew there was something hinky about this." He sighed. "There is no funeral, is there? You're taking me back to the shrink. I really am your emotional support dog, only you've tricked me into a ride to the vet when you promised me the park."

"There really is a funeral, Nick. Old boss of mine, Mark Bulger. He retired. Kicked the bucket. I didn't like the guy but I liked his wife, Shauna. She used to bring this amazing home-made soda bread with raisins into the station sometimes. That stuff could make grown men weep."

"How do you know about Dorrich?"

"I'm the innkeeper. Nothing gets by me."

"That right?"

"Yeah. And you're lucky that's true," I said. "Because you seem to me like you're about to run off with the ghosts of your past again. So I'm your friend, and I'm here, and I'm asking you to talk to me. Tell me what's making you want to do that."

"I'm fine, Cap." Nick sometimes called me Cap, for Captain. He considered me a guiding and commanding force in his life, and had for some time.

"Come on. Just give it to me. Who's Dorrich? Why do you need to get a hold of him so bad?"

The forest scrolled past us, undulating hills of leafless winter trees. Nick's gaze was fixed on the horizon.

"Is Dorrich real?" I asked.

"Yes, he's real," Nick snapped. I let it go. We both knew Nick's schizophrenia had caused him to come up with imaginary people before, or to assign imaginary intentions to people. But there was no need to rub it in his face. "He was my staff sergeant on my second deployment."

"OK, so why isn't he answering your calls?"

"I don't know."

"Have you talked to him since you came home?"

"We check in now and then," Nick said. He tapped his phone against his knee. "You know. Say hi."

I let the silence build in the car. When Nick didn't break it, I did.

"You're not giving me the full picture here."

"I know," Nick said.

"Why not?"

"Because it's bad," Nick said. I looked over and he met my eyes properly for the first time that morning, and what I saw in them was something dark and desperate. Something only barely contained. "It's bad, OK? Worse than you could imagine."

"It can't be," I said. "Because I know you, OK? I was a Boston cop for twenty years, for God's sake. I've seen some stuff. And you? You're not like that."

Nick said nothing. He was listening to my speech, his jaw locked.

"So whatever it is, whatever you and this Dorrich guy went through together," I continued, "it's in the past. It's over."

"It's not over. Something's changed."

"How do you know?" I asked.

"Because all these years since I've been home, checking in every couple of months with Dorrich and Breecher and Master has been like . . . my way of sniffing the wind for smoke," Nick said.

"And now you think that because he's not answering, it means a forest fire is coming," I said. "Jesus, maybe the guy's on vacation. A man can't take a vacation?"

"None of them are answering," Nick said.

I gripped the wheel and tried to organize my thoughts. It seemed impossible to comfort Nick without being drawn into his terrible, dark world. Without him showing me the monsters he so deeply feared. All I had to offer were vague words of reassurance, that he was safe, that whatever horrors he had seen weren't going to reemerge here. That New England was about as far from Afghanistan as a person could get—both literally and metaphorically. The words seemed empty. But I said them anyway.

"There's no forest fire coming, Nick," I said. "I promise you."

He shook his head. "No. There's not. What's coming is hellfire."

CHAPTER FIVE

THE ONE THING Norman Driver had never been able to get right was a convincing smile he didn't mean. As soon as the young woman opened the door to the little house across the road from his construction site, Driver knew he was giving her a pretty flimsy smile, something completely lacking in warmth, something that failed to disguise the monstrousness in his being. A crocodile grin. She was unnerved by it. People usually were. She was a pretty young thing in her late twenties just starting to play housewife, and the noise complaint, he knew, had probably come from her desire to fit into the perfect new mommy role. A good mommy made noise complaints. She called the manager. She spoke to the principal. She posted the review and comments. Calling and complaining and commenting spoke of care and vigilance, of self-respect and family pride. Driver smiled and leaned a thick forearm on the doorframe.

"Mornin', ma'am."

"Can I help you?" The woman swiped her bangs in a way that was supposed to communicate that she was busy—there was laundry to be done, cookies to be made, Instagram posts to be scheduled. Somewhere in the house, a tub of toys was being emptied, the sound of small, hard parts cascading and clattering.

"I'm from the site across the street," Driver said. "I understand we may have ruffled some feathers in the neighborhood by starting early this morning."

"And yesterday morning," the woman said.

"Yeah," Driver said. "We're so sorry to have disturbed you."

"Well—"

"Disturbed you so bad, in fact, that you brought in the law," Driver said. He let the words hang in the air, heavy with menace. "We must have really punctured your beauty sleep for you to have done that; breezed right by us and went direct to the sheriff. Didn't even think to just wander over the road and speak to us yourself."

"There's no—I mean—" The woman gave a nervous laugh. "Who's saying I'm the one who complained?"

"Me," Driver said. "Call me psychic."

"Well...well, you're wrong," the woman said and drew in a sharp breath, trying to steel herself. "I didn't appreciate the noise but I—I would have just gone over there and told you guys how I felt, just like you said."

"Good." Driver grinned. "Good. Because going to the law like that without even giving us a warning, without even asking for an explanation...It's almost aggressive."

"Right." The woman nodded.

"And when people are openly aggressive with me"—Driver shrugged—"I tend to get aggressive back. It's just in my nature."

A fat toddler rounded the corner to the tiled living room beyond and paused in the hallway. The child was long-lashed, wild-haired, and full-lipped in a way that made it completely androgenous. The T-shirt stretching taut over its belly read *Feelin' cute, might throw a tantrum later.*

"Hey, little buddy," Driver said.

The woman pulled the door closed a little, an automatic reaction, trying to protect her cub from the predator on the porch.

"I didn't realize there were kids living on the street," Driver said. "We've kept an eye out, but I'll make sure the guys are aware. You know how construction sites can get. There's a lot of noise, a lot of distraction, a lot of big trucks *backing in* and *backing out.*"

Driver saw his words register in the woman's face. Her mouth puckered, her jaw locked.

"You wouldn't want somebody small to go wandering," Driver said. "And one of the guys doesn't see. Those big trucks have terrible reversing vision." He bent and put his hands on his knees, waved at the toddler in the hallway. "You like big trucks, little buddy?"

The woman shut the door on him. Driver's icy, phony smile turned genuine as he headed back to the work site.

CHAPTER SIX

THE PLASTIC SHEETING covering the doorway to the living room rustled as Driver shoved it aside. The precautions he and his crew had to take with the interior of the house were tedious. On the fold-out tables stretched along the length of the room, Pooney and Marris, two of Driver's crew, were suited up and masked—like the men outside, except these two were pouring an even deadlier powder into storage containers marked with labels. Driver liked accuracy, so he couldn't call what they had been producing "fentanyl." That was a legal prescription drug, a thing made in medical labs, prepared with care and consideration. Whatever Pooney and Marris were making here followed a similar recipe, but tweaked with substitutes easily stolen from chemical storage warehouses or hardware stores.

Every surface in the living room, the "cook" room, was swathed in plastic. It crumpled under his boots and the fabric booties of the workers. The danger was that if Driver's people left a single trace of their drug on a rug or counter, even just a few specks, it could bring down his entire operation. More than a hundred times more powerful than heroin, their mix might be snuffled up by the curious and beloved family dog when the owners of the house returned after the job was done. It would not chew through the animal slowly like a worm in an apple. It would make the creature shrivel up and die like a spider in a flame.

And then there would be questions. Questions that Driver couldn't afford to have answered.

Pooney pulled his mask off and stepped away from the equipment on the tables when he noticed Driver. Pooney was a typical meth cook; hollow-cheeked and rail-thin, blessed with just enough intellect to cook drugs, steal cars, write bad checks, and say "Lawyer" and nothing else when he found himself in a police interrogation room. So many of the skinny drug cook's available brain cells had been exhausted learning those things, he was now hard-pressed to remember much beyond how to dress himself in the morning. He had taken up the position of meth cook after Driver's former employee OD'd on his own product.

Marris, Pooney's narcotic sous-chef, was a typical meth cook's girlfriend. The parasitic prostitute had lost enough body fat and teeth to the drug that the price of her sexual services plummeted and she had to charm her way into the life of a man like Pooney, where she would remain, hooks embedded, until she sucked him dry.

"One more day," Pooney said, before Driver could ask. He held his hands up in surrender. "Sorry, boss. It's the salty air around here. It's messin' with the levels."

"Let me ask you a question, Pooney," Driver said. "What did Cline do to you when you went over deadline?"

Pooney thought about it. Driver waited. Across the table, Marris was picking at an angry sore on her neck.

"One time he stuck my head in a car door and slammed it," Pooney volunteered.

"You think I'd do better or worse than that, Poon?" Driver asked.

"I don't know," Pooney said.

"You want to find out?"

"No, boss."

Driver jutted his chin at the table, and Pooney and the woman masked up again and got back to work. Mitchell Cline was Pooney's former boss. The last drug kingpin in Gloucester, Cline had been a professional gangster, until he was thrown off a building in Boston, or so Driver heard. Driver had been sniffing around the cute little coastal town, interested in its relative proximity to the Canadian border and the lack of serious monitoring of the ports around Cape Ann, and had found a bunch of deadbeats left over from Cline's reign, popping each other on street corners as they tried to decide who would step up as the new boss. There'd been almost a sense of relief when Driver arrived— like a pit bull arriving at a scuffle between Chihuahuas. On his first night in town, his crew murdered eight random dopers and dealers, as a show of power. Once he'd made his display, Driver invited all Cline's former men to either join his ranks or scram. He kept his original construction crew for his inner-circle team, the men who guarded him and the houses he was hired to reclad, which he used as cover for his pop-up drug labs. Driver tapped Cline's former guys for distribution and dealing, keeping them at arm's length until he got to know them.

It wasn't an easy takeover, showing the local boys who was

boss without the resident law enforcers knowing about it. Disappearing men while making it obvious where they'd gone to certain people and not others. But Driver had been doing this a long time. He had the sleight of hand down pat.

Driver was considering making himself a coffee in the family's kitchen when Pooney suddenly pulled his mask off again, marched over to Driver, and puffed up his chest. "Boss? Marris and me: we have a proposal for you." He blasted out the words like he'd been building up the pressure of the announcement for some time.

"Oh Jesus." Driver turned away and headed for the kitchen.

"Check it: We're doing pretty good here. You're happy with our recipe. The skells are happy. People are buying like crazy. I know we're a little late on this batch but that's our first slipup since we started working for you, yeah?"

"What do you want, Poon?" Driver rummaged through the family's cupboards for the coffee. He found a tin of matcha powder and felt hopeless despair. "You want a raise? You want the night off? You gonna take your gal there to the drive-in and get a couple of malts?"

"What's a malt?" Marris asked through her mask.

"We want our own slice of the business, you know?" Pooney puffed his chest even further. He looked like an underfed rooster. "We want to hire a couple more cooks, train them up, expand the output and take a bigger share of the profits for doing that."

Driver rubbed his eyes. After the complainer across the street with the kid and the near-miss with the sheriff's deputy, he didn't need this. He gave up on the coffee and locked eyes with Pooney.

"Pooney," Driver said, "if you think I'm going to give you and that walking, talking tapeworm you call a girlfriend any more responsibility than you already have, you're out of your peanut-sized mind. I am honestly shocked that you haven't already brought this whole business to a grinding halt by screwing up the recipe and serving every addict in Eastern New England with hotshots."

"Boss." Pooney tried to laugh off the insult but his face was hangdog.

Driver pointed to the tables. "If I was a zombie skell out there living off this stuff, and I found out *you* were the one cooking it? Man. It would send me straight. It would send me so straight so fast I'd have a job within a week, a family and a mortgage within a month, and a healthy 401K within a year."

The two cooks looked at each other; Marris was trying to figure out how to respond to the tapeworm comparison, and Pooney just trying to follow Driver's multipart sentences.

"You just stick to your job, Poon," Driver said and held out a reassuring hand. "Those guys clad the house. You two cook the crank. I manage the business side of things. There's no need for anybody to start changing lanes."

Pooney started nodding, which made Driver feel queasy inside. The meth cook had the look of someone with a plan. And Pooney with a plan was like a toddler with a handgun.

"You just need a demonstration," Pooney said. "Well, we got one coming. We're gonna show you how useful we are, Marris and me."

"Get out of my face, Pooney," Driver said, finally seizing on a jar of coffee in a cupboard over the oven. "I can't afford to keep listening to you. I'm getting dumber by the second."

CHAPTER SEVEN

THE LAWN AT the house in Needham was full of people. Newly widowed Shauna Bulger had to strain to remember a time the house had been this loud. Maybe at Henry's christening, more than forty years earlier. She remembered being as concerned then as she was now about guests encountering dusty bookshelves or bare patches in the lawn, about cups running empty and not being refilled.

She'd sat quietly this morning on the end of the bed in her funeral outfit, smoothing the coverlet, trying to think of everything that needed doing. Everything she would be allowed to do. A couple of busybodies from her craft circle had taken over the kitchen and insisted on cooking everything, which gave her absolutely nothing to do with herself now that everyone had arrived at the house. Shauna had wanted to bury herself in jobs, to avoid all the earnest clutching of her hands. All the repetitions of "I'm sorry for your loss" and kind words about her late husband, Mark.

She stood behind the lace curtains at the window of the sitting room, literally hiding from them all, chastising herself for every second that passed. She saw Mary McKinnon out there talking to someone, pointing into a garden bed. Probably at Shauna's wilted asters, or a weed that had slipped under her radar.

When her gaze fell on Bill Robinson, Shauna felt a slight lift in her mood. Here was someone who might understand. She remembered that Bill had lost his wife to a terrible accident a few years ago, though the specifics escaped her. Memory was funny like that. Sorting, picking, discarding. For instance, Shauna couldn't remember where exactly she'd first met Mary McKinnon. Or the name of the short woman in her knitting circle. But her mind was flooded with details about her late husband, Mark. His crimes. They'd all come rushing back to her as she sat rigidly in the front pew of the church during the funeral service, listening to speeches about what a hero the man had been.

A female cop had stood and talked through sniffles about being taken under Mark's wing as a rookie, how he'd molded her patiently and gently into the law-enforcing dynamo that she was now.

Shauna remembered that particular rookie. How Mark had spoken about her. How the girl had turned up late one night to bang on the front door of their house and argue with Mark in the driveway. Throwing her phone at him. Mark telling his wife that the rookie's dramatics were over a case, and Shauna choosing to believe him, because she had no choice.

A superintendent talked to the church gathering about Mark being a stickler for his officers taking witness reports, how he spot-checked patrol cops' notebooks for the quality of their handwriting. Smatterings of gentle laughter. Ah, Mark.

Shauna recalled emptying the pockets of Mark's uniform and finding notes—scribbles made not on official police notebooks but on scraps of battered and sometimes blood-speckled paper. How the content of some of those notes had made her stomach clench. Lists of debts, late payments, vigs. Names and ages of family members. Maps without annotations, and once, just a single line on the back of a coaster: "Bury girl under big tree. No flooding."

Bill Robinson was in the doorway now, almost as though she'd called him in from the yard. Shauna had to shake herself out of her reverie to acknowledge him.

"You OK?"

"Sure, yeah," she said. She beckoned him in, eased herself into an armchair by the window, tried to give him a smile. "Just trying to keep out of the way."

"Out of sight, more like it."

"Guilty as charged."

"I don't blame you," Bill said. He came and took the armchair across from her, looked like he was going to reach over and do some of that awful hand-clasping. Shauna was grateful when he didn't. "Who invented the funeral, anyway? What a weird thing. Somebody dies, the last thing you want to do is have cake and talk to everybody you ever met about it."

Shauna laughed. Her face felt stiff, tired. "Yes. Exactly. But how are you? It's been years. You look like you have a woman in your life again."

"How do you figure that?"

"Somebody's been feeding you up and reminding you to get your hair cut," Shauna said. "Although doesn't look like she insists on ironing your shirts."

"Oh. Wow. Don't even go there," Bill sighed. "That's a story in itself."

They looked out at the gardens, the sunlight on the lawn, the people laughing with their little plates held out between them. A tall, muscular man Shauna had seen arrive with Bill was perusing the cake table, loading a plate high with cookies and sandwich slices.

"That service was such a crock," Shauna said suddenly. Her words seemed to fall out of her. She looked up in horror, expecting to see that Bill shared the mortification at her candor. But there was only understanding in his eyes. It was a look the two had shared silently before, back in the years when Bill was on patrol in the Sixth and Shauna would drop into the station while Mark was holed up at the station. Her big Irish-American husband had made captain and became too important to be out on the street, where he'd been happy roughing up criminals and bullying drug dealers. But the promotion had made him sloppy. He'd held meetings with crime lords in his own office. He'd harassed the female desk cops until they transferred out just to get away from him. Bill had been someone Shauna could trust to intercept her on the station steps and tell her with just a look whether now was a "good time" to drop in, or whether she should leave whatever she'd baked for the station staff and go home.

"Everybody looks great in a eulogy," Bill said. "But listen, Shauna, none of that matters now. What matters now is you.

What are you gonna do? Are you going to have Henry move in here? He's got a new girlfriend, right? I saw them out there in the gazebo lookin' pretty friendly."

"I don't need anybody to move in here," Shauna said.

"No, no, of course not. I'm just saying—"

"What? That now that I've done my last load of Mark's laundry I'll need to find a replacement?" Shauna flared up then sighed. "You're right. I'll get bored. Restless. I feel it already. It's been ten days and I'm going out of my mind. But I can't go back to being a mother. Henry's in his forties. He doesn't need me. And I can't go back to teaching. I'm too old. I guess I just have to figure out who I am now."

"And that's a scary concept," Bill said.

"You would know, I suppose." Shauna looked at him. "You lost being a cop and being a husband all in one year."

"Yeah, I did. And you know what? By the time I figured myself out, I was the keeper of an inn full of loveable nutjobs," Bill said.

"I heard that." Shauna smiled. "Rumor is you've got your hands full."

"It's a free-range asylum."

"What makes it so crazy there?"

"Oh, you know." Bill shrugged. "The house is a sort of vortex that sucks in trouble. We've had to deal with residents... dying. There was a drive-by shooting, too. A dead body was dumped there, and a wild rat turned up to live with us as a pet. It's kind of the house mascot now. It wears a little collar so that we can tell it apart from all the other rats that are around."

Shauna had no words.

"It's never boring, at least," Bill said. "It was Siobhan's plan for me. For us. I was pretty skeptical at first. But to be honest? I've never been happier. So I'm telling you, whatever your future looks like, it's—"

Bill's words were interrupted by a squeal and a giggle from just outside the window. "Henry, come on, you can't talk about her like that!"

Shauna and Bill froze in their seats.

"I'm telling you, the old woman will be dead in three years."

CHAPTER EIGHT

I LEANED OUT of my seat a little to look through the lace curtains hanging on the sitting room window beside us. Shauna
Bulger had withered in her seat. We both knew who was
standing out there in the garden. I could smell her son Henry's
cologne through the window, and his new girlfriend's cackle
was unmistakable.

"Without Dad around, she'll be hopeless," Henry continued.
"The man decided everything for her. She was like a little bar-
nacle stuck to the side of a whale. Now the whale's dead. She'll
float for a while but eventually she'll sink."

"Oh maaaaan. You're *so* bad, Henry."

"What? You know it's true."

"Maybe I should—" I started to get up. Shauna flicked a thin
hand toward me, locked me in place with her hard eyes.

"Sit, Bill," she said.

I sat. We listened.

"In two years, Mom will be crazy," Henry went on. "Inactivity messes with old people's brains. Starts flicking the light switches off one by one. I've seen it before. When she's crazy enough, we'll stuff her in a home and she'll be dead by Christmas."

I felt my nostrils flare. My nails bit into the fabric of the armchair.

"We'll put a home gym in the garage," Henry said. "This can be your studio. We'll have to leave the windows open for a while. Get the old-woman stink out."

I shot up in my chair.

"Don't." Shauna shook her head at me. "It's not worth it."

"The little prick's got some attitude on him," I managed. I just about had to cough the words up through my throat, which was tightened with sudden rage.

"He's just being an idiot." Shauna looked suddenly tired, her chin resting on her palm. "Nobody's going to stuff me any-where, Bill."

I'll make sure of that, I thought. I made my excuses, slipped out to leave Shauna with her understandably dark thoughts. On the back porch of the house I ran into Nick, who was balancing a stack of food on a plate that would have been a polite amount for three or four people. "You were right about the food, Bill," he mumbled through a mouthful of cookies. "Those Irish, huh?"

"Come with me," I said. Nick must have understood my tone, because he put the plate down and was at my heels as I headed out and rounded the corner to the sitting-room windows. Henry Bulger had his arm around a fish-lipped blond girl with a tan no one could conceivably get in Boston or anywhere near it. I grabbed Henry and tugged him away from the girlfriend just as Nick stepped in to distract her.

"Hey! Henry! Look at you! All grown up! Come over here, would ya? I want to have a little chat with you!"

Henry grabbed at my hand as I gripped his arm. "Whoa, Bill, slow down a minute!"

I marched the jerk around the back of the house and slammed him into the wall of the brick garage. I gave him a slap upside the head that made him yowl with pain and humiliation like an angry teenager.

"Ow! What the *fuuuuu*—"

"I was just listening to you filling the girlfriend in on your little string of predictions," I seethed. Henry tried to push past me, but I shoved him hard into the bricks again. "You were just saying your mom's lights are going to start flicking off one by one now that Pop's not around. Tell me more about that!"

"Oh shit," Henry said. He put his hands up, gave me his father's grin full of big, square teeth. "Bill, come on. I was only joking."

"That's good! That's good!" I nodded. "Because I'd hate to have to put *your* lights out. And believe me, that's exactly what I'd do if I believed what you said back there. Those weren't the words of a loving son. You sounded more like a vulture circling above a wounded deer, waiting for it to roll over and die."

"Jesus." Henry's grin was ugly and hard now, his eyes everywhere but on mine. "Look, man, I'm here with my new lady. I was trying to impress her."

"Yeah, she looks like a real catch. Better keep an eye on that one."

We looked over to where Nick was distracting Henry's girlfriend from our little meeting. Nick was pointing to the trees at the end of the long driveway, sweeping his hand over the horizon. The girl was nodding, now and then glancing at Nick's biceps straining against the sleeves of his shirt.

"Bill, Bill. I'm just emotional, OK?" Henry put his hand on my shoulder. I slapped it off. "My dad just died. I didn't mean any of that stuff! There's no need to spread this around, OK? I'm just talking trash. And this girl's different from the rest of them, OK? She's an artist."

"Henry, let me just leave you with a prediction of my own," I said and poked Henry hard in the chest. "Right now, your priority is charming the kind of woman who'd let you talk about your own mother like that. Like she's an old dog you're getting ready to abandon on the side of the highway. Well guess what? You keep going down this path, and you're going to arrive in a world of hurt, my friend."

I saw the truth of my words flicker behind Henry's eyes. All his arguments and defenses faltered on his lips.

"Let's see if I'm wrong, huh?" I said, as I walked away.

CHAPTER NINE

THERE WERE PEOPLE singing in the kitchen of the inn when Sheriff Clay Spears got home from duty. The setting sun made rainbow patterns through the stained-glass panels in the front door as he pushed it open, and his ears were filled with "Love Is in the Air," by John Paul Young, coming from the back of the house. The inn's residents always sang in the kitchen. Bill's wife, Siobhan, had been the worst offender. Maybe, after her death, there was some unconscious effort to honor her by carrying on that joyful practice. Clay had passed by and seen even the grumpiest of residents participating, even ex–criminal overlord Vinny Robetti sitting in his wheelchair peeling potatoes and humming Sinatra.

Susan and Angelica got to the big bursting chorus just as Clay came in and dumped his bag in the corner.

Vinny was at his usual station at the little table and chairs, chopping carrots.

"You wanna sit here, you gotta work," Vinny said, pushing a chopping board toward the sheriff without looking up.

"Can I join the choir?" Clay asked.

"No. Any more of this and you'll get my ears bleeding."

Clay took up a knife reluctantly and started chopping. Susan put a beer in front of him.

"How's crime in Gloucester?" Susan asked. "Anything you can give me to beef up my contribution to the local rag? I'm sitting on a wild story about the anniversary of a flagpole installed in the town square."

"It's quiet," Clay answered. "Just how I like it. Tonight's game night, and for once it's my night off. So everybody get out your lucky turtle's foot, or touch wood, or drink holy water, or do whatever it is that you do when you want the universe to behave itself. Because if I get called out to a major case before the seventh-inning stretch, I'm gonna..."

Everyone waited for Clay to issue some violent threat. He searched his mind for something these people might believe him capable of, but nothing presented itself. Everyone knew he had been violent approximately once in his entire life, and that was in response to two men trying to kill him and bury him in the woods.

"Well, I'm gonna get really upset," he said eventually.

"Can we go back to the turtle's foot?" Susan paused by the oven, a saucepan in hand. "You mean rabbit's foot, right?"

"Whatever," Clay said.

"In Lithuania, particularly in rural households where tradition holds strong, it is forbidden to whistle indoors," Angelica proclaimed as she delicately peeled an onion. "It's bad luck."

"OK, so no whistling. Not until the game's over," Clay said.

"The practice is said to summon demons," Angelica went on. "I know this because—"

"You're doomed, pal," Vinny said and nudged Clay. "You can't go an hour without whistling. You whistle in the bathroom like a goddamn canary."

"A dozen canaries," Susan agreed.

"Because as a young girl I spent my formative years in—"

"We got birdwatchers scaling the side of the house with binoculars, trying to get a look in at all these goddamn canaries." Vinny smirked.

"I was enrolled in a school in which—"

Susan was reddening with giggles. "They're all like *Holy crap! It's a flock of rare, endangered Bostonian canaries all converging on this one modest bathroom.*"

"I don't whistle that loud," Clay sighed.

"Yes, you do."

"You actually really do."

"The school in which I—"

"There's whistling to yourself, like you don't even know you're doing it," Vinny said, "and then there's what *you* do. You whistle like you're trying to call ships in from the sea. Like you want people to notice that you're whistling and comment on it. Like *Jesus, can this guy whistle or what?*"

Susan was laughing hard now. "*Is he classically trained? Did he study for that?*"

"DOESN'T ANYONE WANT TO HEAR ABOUT MY EXPERIENCES IN RURAL LITHUANIA?" Angelica roared.

The room fell silent. It was in the hush that Clay noticed the boy, Joe, standing in the doorway.

"I'm hungry," the child announced.

"Come here, kid." Clay pulled out the third chair at the little table. "Take a seat. We'll get you a snack."

"You wanna sit here, you gotta work," Vinny said, pointing his knife tip at the child.

"You can keep us entertained with conversation," Clay said and put a hand on the tiny boy's shoulder. "That can be your work. Where's your mom?"

"Still sleeping." Joe kicked his legs under the table, his blue eyes following Vinny's gnarled, scarred hand as he moved the blade. "We've been driving a long way, sometimes at night. She's tired."

"I bet."

"What are you guys making?" Joe asked.

"Personal pies," said Susan as she fished around in the cupboard, examining boxes of crackers. She put a stack in front of Joe. "We've counted you and your mom in."

"What's a personal pie?" the boy asked.

"Once a week somebody's in charge of making dinner here," Clay explained. "Susan makes these great beef pies. Only, when she did it the first time, she figured three big pies would be enough for all the residents to share. But—"

"But it's nearly impossible to divide a circular pie equally," Angelica sniffed. "Particularly three large pies being divided between seven people by someone with an obvious bias toward male diners *and* diners toward whom she has an established romantic affection."

"So now everybody gets their own personal pie." Susan rolled her eyes. "No dividing necessary, no bias possible. It's a lot more work but a lot less drama. I bet they teach you in school how important it is to share, don't they, Joe?"

"I don't go to school anymore," Joe said.

"Oh, why not?" Clay asked.

"School is stupid and boring." He gave a wide grin. "It sucks big time!"

A wave of laughter swept over the room. Vinny pointed his knife at the child again.

"I like this kid. What did you say your name was?"

"Joe," the boy replied. "You can call me Joey if you want."

"Zoe, was it?" Vinny tapped the blade against his ear.

"Joe, Vinny," Clay said. "It's *Joe*."

"I can't go back to my school because there's no time," the boy continued. "We're going on an adventure now and we're miles and miles away. It would take so long to get back, probably school would be over by the time I got there and all the teachers would be going home."

"Where did you come from?" Angelica asked.

The boy tucked his chin into his chest suddenly, stared at the floor. Behind his back, Angelica shrugged at Susan.

"So you're on a road trip," Susan said. "A vacation. That's exciting, right?"

"Kind of. But it can be scary sometimes," Joe said.

"Scary?" Vinny squinted. "You kiddin'? What's scary about a vacation? Maybe you'll get some fresh air and sunshine. Maybe you'll make a friend. How terrifying."

Joe shrugged. "It's fun if no one's following you. But maybe, you know…Maybe someone is. So you've got to keep a look out. You've got to be careful."

There was a heavy pause in the room.

"What are you talking about, buddy?" Clay asked. "Who would be following you?"

"Nobody." Joe stopped kicking his legs under the table.

"Then why did you say someone might be?" Susan asked.

"I don't know." Joe shrugged again.

"Joe?" came a voice from the hall. The child's head snapped up and he flew off his chair and disappeared through the door. The silence that lingered after him hummed with tension as the residents returned to their work.

CHAPTER TEN

THE CLOCK CHIMED midnight somewhere out there in the house. Shauna Bulger stared at the ceiling and counted the *bongs* echoing up the hall. There were so many new night sounds that registered with her only now, since Mark was gone. She'd worn earplugs at night to mask the sound of her husband's snoring since she was forty. He'd been two days dead before she realized she didn't have to do that anymore.

Some of the night sounds, she liked. The patter of rain on the roof. The rattle and groan of hot-water pipes. But there were others that she couldn't identify. Pops and creaks and whispers that made her huddle under the blankets. She refused to sleep with a light on, though her mind screamed for her to expel the blackness that swirled in every corner. She also refused to indulge her impulses to double-check all the window locks, to rattle the deadbolts on the front and back doors. She forced herself to ignore the mystery sounds. They gave way only to icy, ringing silence.

It was in the silence that her mind drifted, and she wondered how long she would be able to defy Henry's plan for her. She told herself that if she was stuffed into a home, there would be plenty of noise from the other residents, at least. Friendly, identifiable sounds. People shuffling about in their rooms, chatting, visiting, playing music. Nurses knocking on doors. Phones ringing. Life sounds. She would be enveloped in a community. Safety in numbers. Life in a nursing home seemed like it could be comfortable and predictable. There would be routines, of course. Wake-up times, lights-out times, familiar carers and staff who would listen patiently to her stories and requests. Shauna would be able to adapt easily to the new identity, would probably have one assigned to her on arrival. She would be Mrs. Bulger of Room 17, Pleasant Meadows Nursing Home. Knitting enthusiast. Avid reader. Permanent resident.

A nursing home, and then a grave, Shauna thought.

That's all that was left in her future.

She was just beginning to turn wilder fantasies over in her mind when she heard the sound. She was imagining herself selling the house and buying a yacht, running breakfast tours along the coast, something like what Bill Robinson was doing. Except her patrons wouldn't be the weirdos and dropouts Bill described as populating his inn. They'd be adventurers full of stories, foreigners, wistful people drawn to the horizon and the salt air and rumors of good food and coffee.

A boot squeaked on the floorboards in the hall. Her mind identified the sound perfectly and immediately. A footfall in her empty house. Shauna sat bolt upright and looked at the depth-less black outline of the open doorway. She watched the shape widen, then split as two people entered her room.

She was blinded by an explosion of light.

"Get up, bitch," a voice said.

CHAPTER ELEVEN

SHAUNA WAS GRABBED by the back of her neck and yanked out of the bed. She hit the floorboards in a painful heap, elbows and knees and shoulders knocking, her nightgown slipping humiliatingly up over her hips. There wasn't time to scream. She rolled over, and a boot clamped down on her chest, pinning her, and that searing light whipped up again into her eyes, bursting blood-red through her scrunched eyelids.

"Where's the safe?"

"Help!" she cried. It was barely enough for the two intruders to hear, she was sure. A frightened rasp. The boot crushed down for a moment and then eased off.

"Chill, chill, chill. She's pretty old, babe."

"Let me go. I've got this."

A man and a woman. It was unmistakably a man's hand that encircled Shauna's thin wrist and dragged her up, shoved her down again on the floor by the end of the bed. She noticed blood on her fingers as she tried to push herself upright, but she couldn't tell where it was coming from.

"Tell us where the safe is, old bag. Quick, so we can get out of here."

"The what?" Shauna managed.

A kick to the chest. For a second, she was lifted completely off the ground from the force of it. The pain made her eyes bulge, seized her breath. She saw slices of the intruders in the green and red clouds that were exploding against her vision. Skinny, both of them. Sharp-angled faces hollowed out around the eyes, cheeks, and mouth. Skeleton people. In the terror swirling through her brain and limbs, Shauna tried to understand what they wanted, but she was flailing through darkness, emptiness. The woman grabbed a chunk of Shauna's hair. Shauna smelled cigarette smoke in the hot breath on her face.

A cold, metal edge touched the corner of her mouth, then jammed into her cheek. Shauna couldn't bear to look at the weapon. She felt it shudder as the hammer clicked back.

"Don't be stupid, bitch."

"I really don't know what you're talking about," Shauna said. The words were suddenly there, and she felt a surge of confidence. She could talk her way out of this. Reason with them. "There's n-n-no safe. There's money in my bag by the door. You c-can take the jewelry. I'll show you where it is."

"The safe. The fucking safe. That's what we want."

"There is no safe!" Shauna pleaded.

"I will put a bullet in your goddamn knee, woman."

"Don't!" Shauna cried.

"Where is it? Where is it? *Where is it?*"

"There! Is! No! Safe!"

Silence. Shauna wiped the blood dribbling from her mouth on the sleeve of her nightgown. Her breath was rattling in her throat.

"Babe," the woman ventured to the man. "Maybe she doesn't know about it."

"She fucking knows."

"But—"

"Go take another look around," the man said. "I'll stay on her."

"All right but just chill, OK?"

"Don't tell me what to do!"

"You kick her again and you'll probably kill her, Poon!"

Shauna looked up. They were turned toward each other. The male one, Poon, was holding a flashlight in one hand and a gun in the other. The woman was standing closer to Shauna, her revolver gleaming in the light. Shauna could see the frustration in their eyes. The fear. Their plan had unraveled. *If the old woman knew where the safe was in the house, she'd have given it up as soon as that steel-capped boot collided with her birdcage chest.* They were restless on their feet, poised to give up and run, locked in a wordless negotiation in which they weighed the merits of a full-house search, more torture of the old crow on the floor, the possibility that a neighbor might have heard the commotion and called the police. Flicking over to Plan B.

Shauna knew this was her moment. She slid a hand under the mattress on the bed beside her and gripped the handle of Mark's shotgun, lying there as it had been for years, a sleeping snake that she tugged out of hibernation by the tail.

Shauna lifted the gun and pumped it once.

The intruders turned at the sound.

Shauna blew the woman's head off.

CHAPTER TWELVE

THE CONFRONTATION WITH Henry Bulger at the house in Needham brought a tension into my neck that lingered all the way through the rest of the wake and into Boston. I carried it through two pubs and into a third—Durty Nelly's, the Black Rose, and Biddy Early's. No amount of stretching or rubbing the muscle would ease it.

For some officers of the Boston PD, my murky involvement in my partner's rip-off of a drug dealer, and his spectacular death from a high-rise building in the company of yet another drug dealer, was a passing and forgivable curiosity, trumped by pity over my wife's death. I was granted leave to stand at the edge of small groups of men I'd once known well while surface-level conversations played out. There was shop talk that flew right over my head—policy and management changes I hadn't kept up with since I left, bitching about hopeless young rookies I'd never meet. I felt stressed and tired and excluded, staring at colorful lanterns behind the cluttered bar and the old dark wood finishing of the poky little bar by the water.

Nick wasn't helping my stress levels: still obsessed with his phone and too jumpy for my liking. Around midnight I was starting to reach my limit with the sidelong glances I was getting from certain former colleagues of mine. Boston had a long history of cops bending and twisting the law, and the man of the hour, Mark Bulger, had certainly outshone me in that department. But for others, it was an opportunity for a bit of teasing.

I was squeezing past a group of men playing darts when a guy I'd known in the academy but whose name I couldn't remember reached out from the huddle he was in and grabbed my arm.

"Next round's on you, huh, Robinson?" He grinned. The guys standing around him, none of whom I recognized, had eyes bright with mean-spirited intrigue.

"Is it?" I asked.

"Sure," the guy said. "You can afford it, right? What with all your extracurricular activities over the past few years."

"Oh yeah? And what activities were those?" I asked, turned square to him. The huddle of men stepped back, anticipating a swing, maybe a shove, something to light up their evening. Around us men were singing and spilling beer on the peanut shells on the floor and yelling at the Red Sox game playing on a set behind the bar. The muscle in my neck was taut as a wire. The guy sized me up and seemed to lose interest in the idea of a fight.

"You—you know—you've been running a hotel or whatever it is you do now." The guy swirled his beer dismissively at me. "Forget about it."

"Yeah," I said. "Let's hope I just forget about it."

At the bar, I pulled out my phone and saw Susan was already calling me. Synchronicity. I slipped through a door into the alleyway and stood looking up at the gold lights of apartment blocks reaching for the sky.

"I know exactly where you are," I said in answering.

"Oh yeah?" she said. I could hear the smile in her voice. "Tell me."

"You're in that bed of ours," I said. "Only, you're on my side because you like the smell of my pillow. You got all the blankets piled up. Even the gray one from the cupboard. Soon you'll get too hot and dump them all on the floor. You got your book, laptop, glass of wine. Bag of chips. You started in on the book but you got bored and Netflix lured you away, so instead you've been watching bad reality TV shows."

She laughed. I pictured her in the attic room we'd renovated together, the one with the round window looking out to the sea. The window had been boarded up when we moved in, Siobhan and I. Breaking it open had been a big step for me. Lying there that first night with Susan, and not with my wife, had felt less like a betrayal than I'd imagined. There was a rightness and an easiness to being around Susan, a security, the kind a boat feels when its anchor hooks on to a big, steady rock.

"I tried. I really tried." I heard the thunk of her tossing the book onto the nightstand. "I want to be literary but I'm just not. I'm on page 200 and nobody's dead."

"No grisly injuries, even?"

"Not so much as a stubbed toe."

"Might as well be reading a gardening manual."

"How's the crowd? Have they sung 'Body of an American' yet?"

"Only fifty-six times."

"And Nick?" she asked.

"The guy's still worrying me." I looked through the bar's windows. Nick was leaning against a pillar, pretending to listen to a woman who was jabbering at him animatedly, and waving a Budweiser around. There was no mistaking it—my best buddy was a good-looking man. Women got sucked into his presence, clung to him sometimes like lint on an old mohair cardigan, particularly in bars. He looked like he worked out for three hours a day every day—because he actually did—and the scars and the soulful eyes did all the right things to drunk ladies searching for a fixer-upper. But this woman was getting nowhere with him. She gave up and walked away.

"I'm watching him right now completely ignore the third woman tonight who's tried to get eye contact with him," I told Susan.

"Maybe he needs to see somebody," she said.

"You're telling me. He hasn't had a proper girlfriend in all the time I've known him."

"No, I mean a better psychologist," Susan said. "Somebody big-city. Nobody in Gloucester has the resources to deal with what happened to him."

"It might help if we had any idea at all what that actually was," I said. I left a pause for her to fill with information, but all I got was a gentle sigh.

"Come on," I said. "I know you used your contacts at the Bureau to screen everybody in the house before you moved in. You must know Nick's story."

"I know he served. I don't know what went so wrong over there."

"So look it up," I said.

"You say that very casually," Susan said. Her words were getting short, clipped, defensive. "But it's not a casual thing to do. My departure from the Bureau was problematic. And I have my own reasons for not going further into that. But Bill: I only looked up everybody in the house because I wanted to protect myself. It was wrong, and I won't be doing it again. I can't just fish around in someone's past for my own entertainment."

"It wouldn't be for your own entertainment," I said. "It's to help him. Nick's on the edge. He thinks people are coming for him. If we knew who these people are and why he thinks that, maybe—"

"No, I'm not doing it," Susan said. "I love you but I'm not doing it. Nick will be OK. With some help from a professional. I promise you, he will be OK."

I didn't have a chance to respond. The door to the bar beside me burst open and a guy flew out so hard he hit the street between two parked cars and rolled twice. A taxi that was cruising for patrons had to swerve to avoid hitting him. Nick came storming out after the guy, his fists balled and murder in his eyes.

CHAPTER THIRTEEN

I DROPPED THE phone and went after my friend. It was a mistake. My body reacted without thought, without reason. I reached for Nick, forgetting the painful education I'd already had of how he operated in this state.

Over the two years I'd known him, Nick had been "episodic" a bunch of times. When he was in an episode, he was psychotic, and I seemed to him just as likely an enemy as a friend. I didn't know if Nick was imagining he was in battle, or on a distant army base, or on the mean streets of Baltimore, where he grew up. He could have been imagining he was on the moon, for all I knew. But it was immediately clear that whatever fantasy we were in, as soon as I grabbed Nick's shoulder and tried to drag him off the guy on the asphalt, I marked myself as a threat.

Nick whirled around, his hand as wide and lethal as a grizzly paw as it smacked me sideways and onto the ground. My head hit the pavement. I saw black for an instant, heard a buzzing sound between my eardrums. Nick dragged me up, and threw me against a car, and pinned me there by my coat.

"Whoa! Jesus! Nick!" I yelled. "It's me! It's me! It's Bill!"

"Where is it?" Nick roared, his fist bunched and raised behind him, like a hammer lining up a nail.

"Where's what?"

"The microphone! I know you're wired up, you traitorous piece of shit!"

"It's—" I scrambled to collect my thoughts. I knew it was better to go with the fantasy rather than try to counteract it. I fished desperately in my pockets and handed him the first thing I found. "It's here! Take it. Take it. Take it."

Nick snatched my car keys, threw them on the ground, and crushed the key fob under the heel of his boot. People were gathering around us at a safe distance now, officers from the bar spilling out to see what all the fuss was. The guy Nick had thrown out the door was scrambling to his feet.

"Hey, Bill, what the hell's wrong with this dude?"

Nick crouched at my feet and started to gather up all the pieces of the crushed key fob carefully in his palm.

"This should do it," Nick was muttering. "As long as there isn't another copy, we'll be fine."

"The guy's crazy," someone in the crowd said. "He was talking all sorts of weird stuff in the bar about conspiracies and recordings."

"He's just, uh." I shook my head. "He's unwell, OK? He didn't mean anything by it."

"I didn't even say anything to him! He just walked up and started swinging!" the guy from the street said.

"I'm sorry." I put my hands up. "I'm sorry on his behalf, all right?"

My face and neck were burning. Nick was muttering to himself, examining little crushed pieces of a plastic keychain with a Boston terrier on it that Susan had given me for my birthday.

"Just—everybody go back inside," I told the crowd. "I'll handle this."

I crouched beside Nick, hearing murmurs from the men and women around me. The words "psycho" and "lunatic" drifted on the wind. Nick's eyes were wild, his hands shaking as he swept the asphalt for more pieces of cracked black plastic.

"There can't be any evidence left behind," he said. "If we can just contain it, then maybe...maybe no one will know."

"Know what?" I asked.

"We've lasted this long," Nick said, ignoring me. "We can keep going."

I slid down against the parked car beside us and watched my friend. When Nick's phone started ringing in his coat, he seemed not to even notice. I saw the device poking out from the pocket, the screen flashing, and despite the danger I reached forward and pulled it out.

The name of the caller was BREECHER.

It took all of my resolve not to answer. But Susan's voice was ringing in my head, her words about diving into someone else's past uninvited, opening locked doors with stolen keys. Maybe, whoever Breecher was, it was better for Nick that they didn't get in contact. Maybe, despite what he'd said, speaking to this person wouldn't make matters better, but worse. I took the phone and slipped it into my own pocket, and Nick stood and brushed himself off. For the first time that night, he looked down at me with clear, calm, familiar eyes.

"Bill, what're you doing down there?" he asked. "Is your head bleeding?"

I swiped at my temple, looked at the blood on my fingers. There was asphalt in my hair. I thought about telling Nick the truth about what he'd done and the call he'd missed, but it was late, and we were far from home, and all that had happened made me exhausted at the thought of pursuing anything more than a shower and a clean hotel bed.

"I fell," I lied. "You gonna help me up, or just stand there looking pretty?"

CHAPTER FOURTEEN

SHAUNA SWUNG THE gun toward the other intruder. He dropped his pistol and cowered.

"Oh Jesus, no! Please! Please! Please no!"

"Who the hell are you people?" Shauna snarled. Her own voice sounded completely unfamiliar to her, as if someone had entered her body and was moving her mouth like a puppet. "What do you want?"

"Oh God, don't kill me," said the one named Poon. He was sobbing openly now, his head on a swivel between his partner's crumpled body and the gun pointed at his face. "I don't wanna die. I don't wanna—"

"Who *are* you?"

"I'm Peter Sallers. People call me Poon. And that was—she was—Oh Jesus! She's dead!"

"What are you doing here?"

"We were just trying to—"

The doorbell rang. Shauna was caught off guard by the cheerful melody bellowing out from the hall. When she looked back, Poon was gone. She heard the window in the en suite bathroom grind open, and then silence.

Shaking from head to foot, Shauna put the gun on the bed and took her fluffy robe from the hook on the door. She wrapped it around herself and looked in the mirror. Blood was running from her nose and mouth. She had to step over the body of the woman whose name she had never learned, as she went to the en suite to get a hand towel. The doorbell rang once again, and then the knocking began. Shauna stepped in a chunk of something warm and wet as she crossed over the body again—a piece of brain, or face, or who-knew-what—as she made for the front door.

She put her hand on the knob, seeing the familiar outlines of her young neighbors Kylie and Don on the other side of the frosted glass. It was as she stood there preparing to let the tears and sobs of horror take control of her body, to finally release the death grip that adrenaline had on her soul, that she realized something else was taking the place of survival mode. It was a white-hot rage. The voice pounding in her brain wasn't her own cries of mortification. Instead, her son's voice rang there in the gaping darkness.

The old woman will be dead in three years.

Shauna pulled the door open a crack, standing back so that her bloody feet weren't visible. That voice still pounded in her head.

We'll stuff her in a home.

"Oh my God, Mrs. Bulger, are you OK?" Kylie was hugging a big fluffy pink jacket around her small shoulders, her hulking husband shivering in a T-shirt and boxers. "We heard a massive bang! What happened?"

"A bang?" Shauna murmured. She held a hand up against the moonlight. "Oh. Uh."

She looked behind her, at her own bloody footprints on the floorboards. She thought of the blood in the bedroom running down the walls in rivulets, spattered on the ceiling. She saw herself sitting wrapped in a blanket in some blaringly lit hospital, having her vitals taken "just in case," Henry murmuring to his girlfriend that it was clear now his mother couldn't handle herself, shouldn't be left alone. She'd overreacted. Panicked. Killed someone. She couldn't be trusted with guns, knives, flames, her own credit card. She needed to be stuffed somewhere immediately. Had she slept in her own bed for the last time, made her last adult decision, without even knowing it?

She looked at her big-eyed neighbors and made a decision, because she still could.

"Mark's car," Shauna said, straightening. "I was lying awake thinking about it. You know, I'm having trouble sleeping, since he's been gone. You, uh, you have to run the Corvette every now and then, just turn the engine over, keep everything lubricated. It hasn't been run since he died, so I decided to switch it on. I guess it must have backfired."

"You *guess* it must have?" Don grinned, threw Kylie a look. "Damn, the sound of it shook our house."

"Oh well, you know, my hearing's not great these days, and I was inside the car." Shauna gave a thin smile. "I thought I heard something, now that I recall."

"But everything's OK?" Kylie's eyes were huge and earnest, the girl desperate to help in some way, probably so she could report what a good person she was to her thousands of friends on social media. "Do you need us to come in and sit with you? Can we make you a cup of tea or something?"

"I can make my own tea, thank you," Shauna said. "Sorry to have made a racket."

She shut the door. The words had given her a giddy feeling, a kind of lightness, like all of this wasn't real, like she was reading lines for a play. She went back to the bedroom and looked at the headless body on the floor. Then she went to the laundry and pulled out a bucket and mop.

CHAPTER FIFTEEN

I WOKE NICK up by throwing a cup of cold water in his face. The big guy was sprawled diagonally and face up over the bed in our small hotel room, one leg hanging over the side, foot flat on the floor. He leaped up when the water hit his face and yowled in shock.

"What the hell, man?"

"Least I could do to pay you back for bopping me in the head last night," I said, pointing to the giant lump at my hairline that had come from my skull bouncing off the road. "Get up. Get dressed. We're going back to Gloucester."

"Did I . . ." Nick began, his face filled with dread.

"Yeah, you did," I said. He shook his head, the way he always does after an episode, full of anger and resentment, like his body had been stolen for a night by a serial possessor. Which, I guessed, was kind of what it *was* like.

"Damn. I thought I had it all under control."

"Nope," I said. "So I've done something."

"You've 'done something'?"

"Yeah." I tossed his bag at him. "I texted Breecher last night while you were asleep and set up a meeting with him for today."

"She *answered*?" Nick's eyes were wild.

"Breecher's a lady?" I asked.

"Yes."

"Well, yes," I said. "She answered. We're meeting her at an IHOP off the highway in half an hour. Better hurry."

The parking lot of the roadside restaurant between Gloucester and Boston smelled of pancake batter and the almost sickly-sweet tang of flavored syrup. A weird little part of my mind told me that Nick jumped out of the car and went trudging off toward the door to the IHOP because he could smell pancakes. The guy loved them.

But when my friend tore open the door and rushed inside, with me at his heels, he made a beeline for a lean Hispanic woman wearing a black ball cap. She was sitting in a booth by the windows. The woman got up and she and Nick fell into each other's arms. I stood awkwardly by as she cried, her face buried against his shoulder. When he released her, she gripped his face in both her hands, and I saw them exchange a look that only two people who have been at war together can ever share. It was a look of love, anger, regret. I didn't understand it, but I could feel it, the rawness passing between them, countless terrible memories exchanged in a single glance.

"Dorrich is dead," she said.

CHAPTER SIXTEEN

NICK SLID HEAVILY into the nearest booth. I got in beside him, the woman named Breecher numbly taking the seat directly across from me. She looked at me with the detached aloofness I'd seen in Nick plenty of times when he met new people, a distrust born of the scars of war.

You weren't there. You couldn't know.

"Who the hell is this?" she asked Nick.

"I'm Bill Robinson." I put out my hand. Her shake was hard and fast, noncommittal. "Nick's buddy."

"Karli Breecher."

"You should know I'm former Boston PD," I said.

Breecher glanced at Nick so quickly I might have missed the gesture if I hadn't been looking for it, but Nick was holding his head in his hands.

"Jones didn't tell me he was bringing a friend," Breecher said.

"It was me texting you last night. I used his phone to set this up," I said. "But let me save you some time and concern. I don't know what happened over there between you two and Dorrich. But Nick's got some worries that whatever it is, it's about to blow up, big time. And that's a problem, both for him and for me."

"Oh yeah?"

"Yeah," I went on. "Because while you army people have got your policies about looking out for each other and leaving no man behind, us Boston cops have similar ideas."

"I thought you said you were a *former* cop," Breecher said.

"It never really leaves you," I said.

"I know the feeling." Breecher gave her first smile of the meeting, a small, careful one. I could see from the way her cheek dimpled that her usual smile was broad and generous. I had a desire to see more of it, and I got the feeling most people who met her did. "Look. No offense, Bill. But you being a lawman doesn't give you the right to just barge in on our business."

"Maybe. Let me tell you a little story," I said. I could feel Nick's eyes on me now. "My best buddy in grade school was this kid named Max. He lived three doors down. We used to ride our bikes to school together every day, take a detour to throw rocks off a bridge. This was Revere in the 1960s. Not the best neighborhood in the world but not the worst."

The waitress came and put down mugs and a coffee pot for us, unnerved enough by the weird vibe at the table to forgo pouring the drinks. She practically flung the menus at us as she turned away.

"Max's dad was a real deadbeat," I continued. "There'd be bruises on Max and his mother now and then. I'd see them, but I wouldn't say anything, because my dad was a cop too and I knew it would cause trouble. Maybe my folks would stop me going around there. Anyway, this one day, Max gets on his bike but he doesn't want to go to the bridge, like usual. We go to the general store instead and buy a bunch of comic books. When I asked Max where he got the money, he went all quiet. And he stayed quiet all day at school. Distant. Troubled. Couldn't focus. Wouldn't tell me what was up. We went to the bridge after school that day, which we never did, because we were always starving and my mother would put cookies and juice out for us. We stayed out until it was dark. He didn't want to go home."

Breecher and Nick were watching me. I poured the coffees and held mine, let it warm my hands.

"I was a kid. I couldn't put the signs together and predict what was going to happen that night after Max got home," I said. "I tell myself that, and I believe it, but I don't really *feel* it, you know?"

"What happened?" Nick asked.

"Max's dad beat him to death," I said. "He told the court it was just supposed to be a regular old whooping because Max stole money out of his wallet. But Max hit his head on the coffee table accidentally and he just never woke up."

"Jesus," Breecher said.

"The dad did three years. Got out on good behavior."

"Man," Nick said and shook his head.

"The thing that sticks with me about it all is that Max stole five dollars," I said. "I *had* five dollars I could have given him to cover for what he did. My grandmother had just given it to me the day before, for my birthday. My point is that I knew my friend had a problem and I didn't get involved. I could have pushed for answers, but I didn't. And Max didn't want to tell me what was going on, probably, because I was pretty rigid about that sort of stuff: stealing and lying. I was from a family of cops. Max probably thought I would think less of him."

I turned to Nick.

"Sound familiar?"

"You wouldn't think less of me if you heard what we did," Nick said. "You wouldn't think anything of me at all, Bill. I'm not a kid. I didn't steal five bucks."

"We can't tell him." Breecher reached over and gripped Nick's hand. "We just can't."

Nick and Breecher watched each other.

"Is it what I think it is?" Nick asked her. "With Dorrich?" She nodded gravely. I waited, but they still wouldn't let me in.

"Listen, you're in trouble," I said finally. "I can see it in your eyes, both of you. You need an ally, and I am one. Whatever it is, however bad, I'm with you on it, OK?"

They struggled in their own way, each of them. Breecher was focused on her hands, her mouth twisted; Nick was watching the waitress making her rounds, his eyes hollow.

Silence enveloped us. Nick put his hands flat on the table, his decision made.

"He's right," Nick said. "We need an ally. We've tried to do this alone and I for one can't carry it anymore. Breecher, we need to get some help on this thing."

Breecher looked at me, defeated. The diner bustled with noise and warmth and smells all around us, happy people enjoying their breakfast, going about their business, immune to the darkness we were dealing with at our table. Nick and Breecher seemed to decide wordlessly who would give me the key to Pandora's box.

It was Nick who spoke. Nick who, with his words, tore to shreds the image of the man I thought I knew.

"We killed a family," Nick said. "A big, innocent family."

CHAPTER SEVENTEEN

I SAT BACK in my seat and let it wash over me, the story Nick told me about the night in the desert, the little house two down from the goat pen. I saw Nick crouching in the dark while Dorrich smashed in the door. The gunshots pulsed in my ears. I saw children sitting on the floor, mixed in among the adults; three generations of a family lounging together, reading, talking, safe and secure in their home in the desert until they were unceremoniously blown apart, all eight of them.

The IHOP waitress avoided us and no one moved in our booth as the story trailed off, dread weighing heavy on us, keeping us still and silent as the diner buzzed and bustled with activity.

I knew Nick and Breecher were waiting for a response from me, but for a long time I didn't have one. I had to swallow the horror and disgust that captured my mind first, because I knew those feelings were valid but not useful to me right now. I needed to know more. During my time as a cop, I'd sat with dozens of confessed killers around tiny tables like this, trying to set aside my human response before it interfered with my real job. I was the investigator. The listener. The consumer of secrets. I would decide what to do with what I was hearing later.

"It sounds to me," I said carefully, drawing both their gazes, "like *Dorrich and Master* killed a bunch of innocent people. Not you two."

"Doesn't matter. We were there," Breecher said.

"Yes, but the way you tell it," I said, "you couldn't have stopped those two from—"

"There's no putting a good spin on this, Bill," Nick said. "We were there that night, and we kept quiet about it afterward. We're complicit."

"But you didn't *know*," I insisted.

"I knew something wasn't right about the situation." Breecher swallowed hard. "And I went along anyway. You knew the whole thing was off as well, right, Jones?"

"It was very out of the ordinary," Nick said. "How it was planned. How we got there. You don't just suddenly dump your routine patrol for a side mission. And we would never have been sent to do something like that alone."

"So the story about the missing piece of drone, and the two kids who'd stolen it," I said. "Romeo 12, was it?"

"Yeah," Breecher said.

"Was that all a lie?"

"Not completely," Nick answered. "Some local kids really did hold up another company that was on a mission from our base. They did steal a piece of drone from them, and some weapons. But nobody ever found those kids. They disappeared into the hills."

"So why *did* Dorrich and Master cook the story up? Why did they kill that family?" I asked. "And why did they sucker you two into coming along?"

"Man, isn't it enough just telling you this?" Nick suddenly snapped. The tables around us fell into shocked silence. He lowered his voice to a growl. "You want to know more? You want me to draw you a goddamn sketch?"

"You're right." I put my hands up. "You're right. I'm trying not to overwhelm you, I'm just . . . I'm a little overwhelmed myself."

"All you need to know is, we *killed a family.*" Nick's eyes were fierce, full of tears, skewering me in my seat. "Yeah, Master and Dorrich pulled the triggers, but Breecher and I, we covered it up."

"We were scared," Breecher said, under her breath. "That night. It all unfolded so . . . so quickly. We just did what Dorrich and Master told us to. But then the next day, we didn't come clean to our superiors about what really happened. And then we still didn't the day after that. And now . . ."

"If anybody finds out about this, we're going to prison for the rest of our lives," Nick said. "Master and Dorrich for doing it, Breecher and me for protecting them. There. Are you satisfied? Are you involved enough now, Bill?"

"I'm sorry." I shook my head. "I just don't know what to say."

"There's nothing you can say," Breecher said.

I wasn't there, I thought. *I couldn't know.*

We fell silent again. I remembered Nick from last night, his paranoia about being betrayed, recorded, about someone finding out what he had done.

"What happened to Dorrich?" I ventured carefully.

"Suicide," Breecher said.

"Why?" I asked. "Was he depressed?"

"It's worse than that."

She took out her phone and put it on the table in front of us.

"Dorrich called me the night before he killed himself," Breecher said. "My phone was in the shop. I'd dropped it and the microphone was broken. When I didn't get back to him by morning, he left me a message and ate a bullet."

For the first time, I saw Breecher's hard exterior crack. Her lip trembled. "I'm kicking myself. The one night that I wasn't available. Maybe I could have talked him out of it."

"Play the message," Nick said.

Breecher woke the phone screen, found the message, and put the phone on speaker. The recording was silent for a few seconds, like the caller was thinking about what they wanted to say. We all leaned in.

"Breecher, it's me," a deep male voice said. "I need to talk to you. They know what we did. OK? Somebody knows. And they're coming for payback."

CHAPTER EIGHTEEN

THE WAITRESS COULDN'T hold off any longer. We all ordered something we knew we wouldn't eat, and with the weight of all that I now knew hanging on my shoulders, I hardly noticed Nick leave to get some air. Karli Breecher and I sat ignoring each other and our coffees, taking some solace in watching two small kids racing each other up and down the aisle beside the booth in which we sat.

"Nick said you guys were checking in with each other every couple of months," I said eventually.

"Right." Breecher nodded. "That was something Master and Dorrich insisted on. They wanted to make sure no one was going to talk. After a while, I found myself checking in on them too."

"Why?"

Breecher eased air through her lungs.

"Because they were my teammates," she said. "Yes, they did

a terrible, terrible thing. But I can't just shake off what we went through together. It does something to you. Fuses you together. I don't know. Maybe I wanted to understand what they did, or...see if it had any effect on them."

She held her head the same way Nick had, like the sheer burden of her troubles was weighing down her skull.

"I guess I just didn't see that Dorrich was on the edge."

"What do you think his message means?" I asked. "Who do you think he means has found out? And why didn't he give Nick a heads-up, too?"

"I don't know. And it could be anyone." Breecher shrugged. "A journalist? The *New York Times* is always looking for stories like this, trying to undermine the whole deployment. This would be an international sensation. And then the trial. A trial would be..." Words failed her. "But maybe it's someone inside the army. Or maybe one of the relatives."

"How did the killings play out to the people over there when it happened?" I asked. "Surely something like that didn't go unnoticed."

"We made the whole thing look legitimate," Breecher said. "Dorrich and Master instructed us on what to do. After the family was...when there was no one left alive, we took the farmers' old rifles and shot up our own vehicle. Then we fired on the house from the outside. When it came to explaining what had happened, we told our superiors that two men from the house had fired on us out in the desert. We said it was a random act. Unprovoked."

Breecher paused to wipe at her eyes.

"We told them we did what any other company would do. What we were trained to do," she continued. "We pursued the men to a small farmhouse and engaged them there. We said we didn't know there was a family inside until it was too late."

"I don't understand." I shook my head. "Why would Dorrich and Master do something like this? Was it for kicks? Was this a game to them? Why did they take you two along? They must have told you something."

Breecher wouldn't look at me. I gave up on getting an answer for now, while everything was so raw. Her face had become aloof and stiff again, like a wall.

"Where's Master?" I asked. "He might know what Dorrich was talking about in the message."

"He's not answering his calls," Breecher said. "I went to his house and it's locked up tight. If he knew we were in danger, he'd have told us. Rick probably heard Dorrich was dead and did what I did: went to ground until he could figure out what the situation is. I was hoping Nick would know more, or be able to help me track Master down so we could ask him together."

I saw Nick through the glass front doors of the IHOP, standing with his back to us, watching cars roll in and out of the lot, his breath making mist in the cold air.

"What's his situation like?" Breecher asked, nodding toward my friend. "It's been a few months since Jones and I talked. He sounded strange last time. Like he was distracted."

"He's been surviving," I said.

"Jones told me he's had some mental health issues," Breecher said. "Last year. Starting to hear voices, get paranoid. It's probably natural for us all to feel a little paranoid, knowing what we did. But is it serious?"

I explained a little about how Nick had fled Baltimore wanting a reprieve from violence in his life. I talked a bit about the

Inn on the Sea, the town of Gloucester, how I watched out for Nick, tried to read his moods and head off any episodes. I held off on the more serious details of Nick's mental health—his violence, his delusions, his ability to lose all sense of time and place, finding himself lost in memories or newly created dreams, and waking with no recollection of his behavior during those times. Those were not my tales to tell. "When Nick starts to flounder, me and the other people at the inn, we help him out."

"What's he been doing for work?" Breecher asked.

"He has his benefits," I said. "And I pay him to fix things around the inn now and then."

"So that's all he does?" she asked. "He's just been hanging around? Living on his benefits?"

"Yes." I felt an awkward flutter in my chest. "Why? Are you worried about his financial situation? Has he said something?"

"No, no," Breecher said and shifted in her seat as Nick slipped back through the doors of the IHOP and headed toward us. "I just want to know he's OK. He's not the most forthcoming guy in the world, as you can imagine. And I think he's better when he's busy. We all are. Veterans. We need a mission."

"We should go," Nick said when he got to the table. He flopped a couple of bills onto the table, for the uneaten food. "We can sit here and talk about this all day long, but the reality is that we're not safe here. And until we figure out what's coming for us, we need to do the smartest thing we can in a situation like this."

"What?" I asked.

"Return to base," Nick said.

CHAPTER NINETEEN

NORMAN DRIVER STOOD with two of his men at his side, his arms folded against the wind and his chin tucked against his flannelette jacket, listening to Pooney, who was staring at the gravel at his feet. Beyond their little pocket of solitude bounded by boat sheds and their trucks, the marina was loud with early morning life. Fishermen were bringing in catches made in the darkness before dawn. There was sawing and grinding coming from the dry dock, and the distant whistle of boats passing the breakwater. Half of Pooney's face was still dusted by a fine blood mist that looked like brown freckles.

"She-she came out of nowhere with this gun and just-just-just…" Pooney struggled, running his hands through his greasy hair and gripping at his throat as though to wring the words out. "She's dead. I can't believe Marris is dead. Aw, boss, we were just trying to do a good thing."

"Did she tell you where the safe was, in the end?" Driver asked.

"No. I ran, man. I just got the hell out of there."

"What's your best guess. Is she alive? You said you kicked her pretty hard."

"I don't know. I honestly d-d-don't know."

Driver closed his eyes. He'd been angry in his life, plenty of times. Sweating, seething, shakingly mad. Murderously so. But there was a rare kind of fury Driver sometimes felt that was so deep in his core, so dark, it created only stillness and silence as it spread throughout him. Because as he stood there, Pooney before him quivering and quaking and blubbering like a pathetic, emaciated child, Driver's mind was hopping from one aspect of this disaster to another and never finding an end point.

His secondary drug cook was dead. Her phone was at the crime scene, a phone that almost certainly contained all manner of incriminating messages and calls that directly identified Pooney and Driver and his men, and everything they had been building since they arrived in Gloucester. And nightmare of all nightmares: the safe. If Mark Bulger's widow had survived the attack, she now knew what Pooney and Marris had been after when they broke into the house. And if she didn't already know about Mark Bulger's precious little collection, his private box of secrets, she would soon. And so would the cops who responded to the incident and conducted a search of the house. Driver pinched the bridge of his nose and felt the quiet fury consuming his insides like a fast-acting acid.

"Get down there," he finally said to the men at his side. "I'll call ahead and try to get some Boston cops I have on the hook to weasel in on the crime scene. Maybe we can head this off. If we can just get a hold of Marris's phone, we can protect the business. If we got the contents of the safe, that would be even better. But that might be too much to hope for. See what you can do and keep me updated."

"What about him?" The guy nearest to Driver pointed at Pooney. Driver just waved the men away, and they turned and went, because they had enough brain cells to rub together to know that a boss like Driver wasn't someone you stood around questioning. Driver took Pooney by the arm and led him over to Pooney's pickup truck. A pair of curious seagulls fluttered down and stood on the gravel watching as Driver guided Pooney silently into the driver's seat.

"Listen, boss," Pooney said as Driver rummaged in the back of the cluttered, dusty truck. "I was just trying to m-m-make an impression, you know? I was trying to show you how valuable I can be, so that maybe you'd trust me with a bigger stake in the business. When I heard Mark Bulger was dead, I remembered what you told me about h-h-his collection. I thought maybe this was a chance for someone to step up and—"

"See. That's the problem," Driver said calmly. "You thought. You heard Bulger was dead and you *thought*. You made a plan. You made a decision. And that's never been good for you, Pooney. If you had just *told me* that the man had died, I might have sent someone capable down there. Someone whose mind isn't so addled by drugs he can hardly string a sentence together."

Driver found what he was looking for. He ripped a strip of duct tape from the roll and wound it around Pooney's hands. The drug cook sat numbly in the driver's seat as Driver bound his hands to the steering wheel. He was too paralyzed by fear, or too shell-shocked from the night's events, to conceive of what was happening to him.

"It's my fault," Driver said as he bent and jammed the roll of tape under the brake pedal. "When you said you were planning something, I should have known then that there was only trouble on the horizon."

"Boss," Pooney pleaded. He was starting to struggle now, the numbness wearing off. "Boss. Boss. Boss. Wait—just—hear me out—just—"

"Don't worry, Pooney," Driver said as he rolled down the window. He reached over, put the car into neutral, and let off the hand brake, then leaned back and slammed the driver's door.

"You don't have to think any more," Driver said.

He went to the front of the vehicle, put his hands on the bumper and pushed. The car rolled backward, down the boat ramp, into the icy water, gathering speed as it went. It slid gently under the surface, the freezing waters of the bay swallowing Pooney's screams as the gulls took flight again.

CHAPTER TWENTY

THE DEAD WOMAN'S phone rang six separate times. Shauna had counted them off as she worked through the wee hours, scrubbing, brushing, bleaching the mess in the bedroom of the big, empty house, scraping up bits of human from between the old floorboards and from the cornices. The phone's ringtone was the mock sound of an antique telephone, high and musical. It pealed and pealed, and the silence that followed it rattled Shauna's frantic mind. She eventually put the device on silent and slipped it into her handbag. She knew the dead woman's phone would be full of clues pointing to where the intruders had come from, who they had been. But there was time for that, later.

When she was done with the mess and she had swaddled the pale, headless body in bedsheets, Shauna went to the kitchen. She opened the fridge and took out one of the food platters lovingly wrapped by the bossy women of her knitting circle. She brewed herself a strong coffee, then sat at the counter and ate seven sandwich fingerlings in a row, end to tip, like she was chain-smoking cigarettes. The food gave her strength. The shaking that had infected her body finally stopped, and all that was left—after the break-in, the beating, the murder, and the cleanup—was pure exhaustion. The sun rose, yet Shauna pushed on, showering, and scrubbing the blood from under her fingernails. She surveyed the huge red and blue marks blossoming everywhere on her body, the split lip, the grazes on her elbows and knees. She dressed, ignoring all of them. She went to the cupboard to get a suitcase and spied her summer duvet on the top shelf, sealed and shrunken into a wrinkled pancake in a vacuum-sealed storage bag.

By the time she'd rolled and wrestled and crammed the woman's body into the vacuum-sealed bag, then into the zippered suitcase, Shauna was ready to collapse into the bed. She spied a silver necklace on the floor, covered in the woman's blood. She rinsed it and put it into the pocket of her coat, deciding she would get rid of it later. Sleep was barreling into her, sucking her downward into a black and silent sea.

She woke on the bed after only an hour. She rose around eight, gasping for air.

She wheeled the suitcase to the hallway outside the garage, where the Corvette, Mark's pale-blue truck, and her own Honda stood waiting. She chose the truck.

As Shauna was pulling down the tailgate, she realized she couldn't lift the suitcase high enough to get it onto the truck bed. As she considered making a ramp out of some of the two-by-fours Mark kept stacked against one wall, she heard a man's voice. She left the suitcase where it was and tucked herself into the small space behind the open door to the hall.

"Boss, I don't know what to tell you. We're seein' nothing. No crime scene. No squad cars. There's just nobody here. It's quiet as a goddamn graveyard."

Shauna gripped the door handle in front of her, listening to two sets of footsteps on the driveway outside the automatic garage door. She saw shadows pass on the polished concrete at her feet as the people moved around the side of the garage to the windows there.

"Yeah, of course," the man said. Shauna knew from the intermittent silences that he was talking on a phone. "But we've looked in every window of the house. There's no body in the bedroom. There's no . . . no old lady. If she was here, she's gone, or Poon was trippin' on some pretty good shit. There are three cars in the garage. I'm taking a picture of them now."

Shauna looked down, saw the tiny hairs on her arm rise.

"Do we go in?"

Shauna held her breath.

"OK. OK, sure. And this safe, do you know what it looks like?"

Another mention of a safe. What safe? Was Mark keeping a secret from Shauna?

Shauna almost screamed in surprise when the doorbell at the other end of the house chimed down the hall. She clapped a hand over her mouth.

"Mrs. Bulger? Are you there?"

"Hang on, hang on." The man on the phone dropped his voice so low Shauna could barely hear it. "We got visitors. We gotta pull back."

Shauna waited until she heard the men's footsteps receding, then slipped out from behind the door. She walked to the foyer and saw the familiar outlines of Kylie and Don, the young do-gooders from next door.

"Mrs. Bulger—oh wow," Kylie said. Her hands flew to her mouth when Shauna opened the door and revealed the bruises it had been too dark to see the night before. "What *happened?*"

"I slipped in the shower." Shauna leaned forward and glanced toward the garages, but saw no one. No shadows, no movement. "It's fine. Come in. Come in."

"You look *awful.*"

"Thank you so much, Kylie."

"Does it hurt?"

"I'm fine, honey. Stop fussing."

"You really need somebody to come stay here with you, Mrs. Bulger." Kylie's prattling began before she'd even stepped over the threshold. Her tone was of a mother chastising a child. "Your son should be here. What's his name? Harry? Why isn't he here doing things like starting the car for you, making sure you don't slip and hurt yourself like that. Jesus! That's some bump! Don, take your shoes off, goddamn it, this is a nice place she's got here."

Shauna shut the door behind the youngsters and followed them as they made their way toward the kitchen like they owned the place.

"I'll make coffee," Don announced. "Is there any food left over from the reception? I call dibs."

"You two go right ahead, make yourselves at home," Shauna said. "I'm just fixing up a few things in the back here."

She went to the bedroom and looked out the window, at the garden shed. She tried to keep her breathing regular, but every sound, every movement outside the house twisted the ball of tension growing in her chest. If the people she'd heard were still out there, they were well hidden. There was no point in alerting her young neighbors to the danger. Even if she managed to convince the couple that the voices she'd heard weren't concoctions of her defective, ancient brain, the people would be gone, probably regrouping for another attack. Shauna needed to find this safe they were all so determined to discover, assuming there was one, before they came back again.

From the corner of her eye, Shauna saw the huge pink fluffball of Kylie's furry jacket in the doorway.

"There you are!" Kylie said with the relief of a mother having momentarily lost her toddler in a forest of department-store clothing racks. "What are you doing, Mrs. Bulger? Can I help?"

"No, Kylie, I'm fine, really." Shauna nudged past her and walked into Mark's office. She went to the filing cabinet and pulled open a drawer. Hundreds of meticulously organized hanging files rattled on their rails beneath her fingertips. She scrolled through the labels. *Plumbing. Electrical. Certificates. Medical. Insurance.* In the distance, Kylie was blathering about her well-being, a parade of *shoulds*. Shauna should sit down. She should drink water. She should call a doctor. She should let Kylie take a look at her face, put ice on it maybe. Shauna found the folder she was looking for, marked *Renovation/Maintenance.* She emptied the contents onto Mark's desk and leafed through the documents. There were quotes and receipts for the knockdown and rebuild of the garage, and for the replacement of two rotting window frames at the back of the house, five years earlier. Shauna pushed aside a design sketch for a pair of gates they'd had installed in the driveway. Then she found what she was looking for. A quote from a company called Davis Security that had been filled in by hand.

1 x Davis Model 488 Combination Safe
1 x in-ground installation (external shed, concrete
  floor)
All labor $5,200 plus tax.

Shauna smiled. She might be old, but she wasn't befuddled. She knew her husband, knew his capabilities, his patterns, his logic. She'd been right that Mark would never have attempted to install something like a hidden safe himself, and that he'd have stowed away the quote and receipt, because he was a life-long pack rat for paperwork. Shauna also bet that when she found the safe, which she now knew to be hidden in the floor of the garden shed, she would discover that the security code was her own birthday. A lazy choice. It was Mark's code for everything. She puzzled momentarily over the date of commencement of work, written on the quote. It was the week that Mark had taken her to Florida for their anniversary.

Don appeared in the office doorway, armed with a brownie and a mug of coffee.

"Don, for God's sake, can't you use a plate?" Kylie said as she snatched the snack from his hand.

"What's with the suitcase?" Don asked, inspecting the suitcase in the hall by the garage door. "You going somewhere, Mrs. Bulger?"

"I am, as a matter of fact," Shauna said. "I'm off to Gloucester."

CHAPTER TWENTY-ONE

NICK DIDN'T SPEAK our entire ride back home to the inn. Neither did I. We'd left Karli Breecher with strained goodbyes, promises to be in touch when we'd had time to think. Thinking about what my friend had told me, about what it could possibly mean for him, me, the people of the inn, sent me into a daze. The highway before me melted away. I played Dorrich's message over and over in my mind.

They know what we did.

Somebody knows.

And they're coming for payback.

Our best-case scenario was that the "somebody" Dorrich was talking about was a journalist who had a tip about the massacre of the family in Afghanistan, that it had been planned and brutally carried out and was not a legitimate response to an act of aggression. In that terrible but nonetheless "best" case, Nick and his team would be exposed to the world as war criminals.

There would be trials, inquiries, the great military justice machine churning into action. I saw camera crews surrounding the Inn by the Sea. Nick, grim faced, wearing his dress uniform in a courtroom, trying to explain why, in the years since, he hadn't spoken a word about what happened. Trying to convince the world that in spite of that incriminating silence, he was not the monster that he seemed, but a good man and a faithful soldier tricked into witnessing and then covering up something obscene and reprehensible.

The worst-case scenario was that it wasn't justice for the crime someone wanted, but revenge. A relative of the murdered family, perhaps, who had tracked down the men and woman involved in the slaughter. I knew that the likelihood of this scenario was tightly bound to whatever the reasons were that Dorrich and Master had killed that family in the first place, why they'd chosen to trick Nick and Breecher into participating.

My experience as a cop in Boston told me that mass killings like this unfolded for three possible reasons. First, that the perpetrators were sick, twisted psychopaths who enjoyed senseless murder on a grand and violent scale—the work of active shooters and spree killers. Then there were the gangs who killed as a show of power—massacring whole families to establish their territory, or make a revenge statement, with intentional collateral damage because someone had ratted them out, or because there was a stash of drugs, weapons, or money in the house. And finally, there were those killings that occurred because the shock and horror of all-family murders was meant to disguise something far more mundane. I'd just made detective when I responded to a case like this, where a jealous teenager had wanted to punish his girlfriend for carrying on with another man, so he and a friend had donned balaclavas and come at the family with baseball bats. They'd tried, unsuccessfully, to make the crime look like a robbery gone wrong.

Was the massacre in Afghanistan the work of two monsters, two criminals, or two masters of deception? The hardest part in answering this question, I knew, would be summoning the patience required to get all the answers from Breecher and Nick.

Nick was staring out the car window at the pine trees and the sea beyond as we pulled up outside the house.

"I bet you feel like a ton of bricks just fell on you," he said.

"Yeah." I nodded. "Exactly."

"You have to decide what you're gonna do now," Nick said. His eyes followed a fishing trawler making its way slowly across the bay. "This is now your secret too. You asked for it and you got it. So you can decide to keep that secret, or you can turn us in."

"Keeping it to myself makes me complicit in what Dorrich and Master did," I said.

"Yeah."

"But turning you all in would mean losing my best friend. It would mean destroying your lives. You, Breecher, Master. It would mean disgracing Dorrich's memory."

"Maybe not Breecher," Nick said. "It would be tough, but she wouldn't take it as hard as the rest of us. Her dad would soften the blow."

"What do you mean?"

"Her father is a command sergeant major," Nick said. "That's half the reason she got to the front line. Not a lot of women make it there, but she passed the training and her dad gave her a nudge. I've always thought that's maybe why Master..."

"Why he what?"

"Never mind," Nick said, waving me off. "I'm tired, man. Whatever you decide to do, I can't hear it right now. I feel like if I don't get some shut-eye soon I'm gonna lose my head."

"Go." I nodded toward the house. "We can talk later."

Nick hung back at the passenger side door before he closed it.

"You wake me up by throwing more water in my face, I'll make you sorry you were born, Cap," he said.

"Try it." I managed a smile. The exhausted veteran slunk from the car toward the house. I exited the car to the sound of gentle rumbling waves and took a few steps into the bed of pine needles beyond the parking area to look out at the gray slab of water and the harbors to the south.

I didn't realize how hardened my facial expression had become until I turned at a sound and felt it crack into another smile. A small blond boy was approaching me, with some caution, a brown bundle of fur clutched in his small hands.

"Oh, hello," I said.

"Hi," the boy said and lifted the creature so I could see it. "I found this big mouse."

I recognized the fat rodent as Effie's pet.

"That's actually a rat," I said. "His name's Crazy. He belongs to one of the residents here."

"He might not be a rat. He might be a mega mouse."

"Ahhh, well, that's a good point." I laughed. "Could be. I'm not an expert."

I went over and straightened the tiny purple collar that Effie had fashioned for Crazy the rat so that the little bell, no bigger than a ball bearing, hung at the rodent's throat. "Where'd you find him?"

"He was sleeping in the big room with all the chairs." The child and I stroked Crazy together, one fingertip each, until the rat clambered up his arm, making him giggle as it settled on his shoulder.

"Crazy likes it in the sitting room," I said. "It's the warmest place in the house. You're a brave boy to just pick him up like that. Some of the people who live here are afraid of this little guy."

"Well, I have a hamster at my house," the boy said. "So I'm not scared of little animals. I really like birds. One time me and my mom saved a bird that got too wet in a storm. Its feathers got all spiky and we had to dry it off. We put it in a box and we gave it some water and in the morning it felt all better."

"Aren't you nice!" I laughed. The boy stifled a smile.

"I gueeeeess."

"You and your mom must have gotten here yesterday morning. Is that right?" I asked.

"Um, yeah."

"This inn is my place. I'm sorry I wasn't here to welcome you."

"That's OK."

"What's your name?"

"Um…" The boy tapped a finger on his chin thoughtfully, the mock detective pondering a clue. "Today I'm going to be Shannon."

"You have different names on different days?" I said. "That's a fun game."

"It's not a game." The child frowned. "It's very serious."

"OK," I said with a nod, trying to look stern. "So what's my name for today then?"

"Uhhh," Shannon said. He considered me, then took the rat down and cupped it in both his hands. He began laughing at his own joke even before it had left his lips. "Mister Butthead Man."

"Mister *Butthead* Man?" I roared in mock outrage, rising to my full height. "How dare you?"

The boy took off toward the house, repeating the nickname and leaping up the porch steps. He almost slammed into Susan's legs as he went through the front doors. Susan recovered and headed down the steps toward me.

"Have you come here to insult me as well?" I asked as she put a mug of coffee in my hand.

"If that's what you want, although I think Mister Butthead Man has a certain ring to it."

"Cute kid."

"Very outspoken." Susan nodded. "He just finished telling me that my hair is all wrong. I'd be better as a brunette."

"I don't see it."

"Not sure where his mother is," Susan said. She pulled her silky blond strands up into a ponytail and secured it with an elastic band. "The child just seems to have free rein. I saw him helping Effie change a tire earlier, and then I had to rescue him from hearing all about Angelica's brief but nonetheless illuminating foray into trading rare, discontinued shades of oil paint across southeast Asia."

"Wow."

"Yeah. I think Angelica's got writer's block. She's been at least 15 percent more insufferable lately."

I sighed. Susan patted my hairline, where the bump Nick had given me was receding.

"Trip was that good, huh?"

"I'll tell you about it later," I said as we headed toward the house. "Right now I'm going to finish this coffee and then I think I need to lie down."

"Got a hangover?"

"More like existential dread, I think."

"Well, you've got half an hour. Shauna Bulger's on her way over."

"What?" I stopped beside her at the bottom of the stairs. "She's coming here?"

"She just called." Susan shrugged. "Said she needs your help."

Desert Outside Bagram, Afghanistan, 2010

Nick might have looked at the bodies on the floor. The children. The women. He wasn't sure. Later, visions of them would come, push their way into his brain in the cold hours of early morning, but they were always different. Sometimes, in his visions, they were so perfect it was like they were all huddled asleep on the earth floor. Other times, he saw the deaths in all their gory specificity. Eyes wide. Blood coughed like black stars onto faded fabric. He was only in the room for seconds before Roger Dorrich dragged him out of the house and slammed him into the warm brick wall of the little house, his rifle shouldered and two hands clutching Nick's tactical vest.

"Oh my God, oh my God, oh my God, you—"

"Shut up, Jones. Shut up. Let me talk."

"You killed them! You killed them! You killed them!"

"Jones!" Dorrich snarled, grabbing Nick's jaw and shoving

his head into the wall. "There's no time for bullshit! We've gotta move fast!"

Rick Master was there, leading a stiff-legged and gasping Karli Breecher out of the house. Master was carrying a battered old farmer's rifle with duct tape wrapped around the stock.

"Listen up," Dorrich said as Breecher was thrown against the wall beside Nick. "What just happened, happened. Everything's under control. All you have to do is follow our lead. The scouts will have picked up the gunfire. There will be teams on their way here any second. We need to set this up properly and call it in."

"What the hell is this?" Breecher was huddled into Nick's side, her rifle gripped against her chest. "What are you *doing*?"

"It's what *we're* doing," Master said. "Look, everything's gonna work out. Just fall into line. Jones, you're going back up to the edge of the slope and fire on the house and car. Breecher, I'm sorry. But you're going to have to be the one who takes the hit."

"What do you mean?" Breecher asked. Her voice was quavering badly. Dorrich reached forward and grabbed the shoulder of her vest, pushed her sideways. Nick reached out to scoop her back against his side, an automatic reaction, but the shock had slowed him, numbed him. He would remember the sight of her there, silhouetted against the light of the house's interior, bent slightly as though bracing, as though she knew what was coming. Master stepped back, actioned the farmer's rifle and shot her in the stomach.

CHAPTER TWENTY-TWO

SHAUNA BULGER STOPPED just outside Gloucester, on a forested strip of side road dappled with sunlight. She waited ten minutes, her eyes on the rearview mirror, anticipating with dread the appearance of the two men in the battered truck she had spotted outside her home in Needham.

She'd hopped into Mark's pale-blue truck, leaving soon after she saw Kylie and Don off. She'd driven quickly past the two men, hoping against hope that they'd head into the house looking for the contents of the safe instead of following after her. Just in case they did, she had made a twisty, turny route through the suburbs as she headed for the highway. Nothing. They didn't appear now. But they knew what the truck looked like. She'd need to get rid of it.

She got out and went to the back of Mark's truck. She looked at the big suitcase lying on its side at the head of the truck bed, strapped into place between two similar suitcases loaded with

Mark's clothes and shoes. There was no blood seeping from the middle case. No ominous stains. Nothing to indicate what terrible cargo was curled within it.

Shauna got back into the truck and picked up the dead woman's phone. It didn't need an access code, which was an unexpected blessing. The device told her the flood of calls that had come in that morning were from a contact named simply "D." There were no messages from that number. Shauna flipped through the recent messages in the lead-up to the intrusion at her home.

Yo Mar, you bringing somethat good shit to Franks party on Sat? Will pay.

We need reup at Smithton house. 50caps.

Shauna had spent enough decades as a cop's wife to know what reups, caps, and bringing "good shit" to parties meant. It meant the female intruder and the one named Pooney were drug dealers. Shauna could have guessed something like that from their faces, their jittery movements, the terrible planning surrounding the break-in. All Shauna had to do now was find out who their boss was. She wanted to find the man who had sent them, the man who had set in motion this runaway train on which Shauna was now trapped, barreling down the side of a mountain. She again scrolled through the messages, each contact labeled only with a single initial. She stopped when she discovered texts from "P," which she supposed must have been Poon.

Where u? the contact labeled P asked.

Dunkies, was the reply.

I h8 to wake up and u not here!

Well Im bringin breakfast home so stop your complainin, Poon!!!!

We need to get there early. We at least 1 day late on batch.
Driver gonna kill us!!!! Get ur ass home!!!!

Driver. Was that "D"? Shauna went back to the list of messages but found none under "D," only brief or unanswered calls
in the recents list. She put the phone down and lifted the small
plastic tub she had retrieved from the safe in the floor of her
garden shed. (She was right about the combination code.)

She set the tub on her lap. This was it. This was what they
had come for. What these people were prepared to beat,
degrade, and humiliate her for. Possibly what they had planned
to kill her for. It was also something her husband of almost
five decades had wanted to keep from her so badly, he'd con-
structed an elaborate plan to ensure she never found out about
it. The safe. The secret commissioning of it. The weekend away
in Florida. It was all for whatever lay in the box on her lap.

There were five unsealed manila envelopes standing upright
in the plastic tub. Shauna lifted the first one and peered inside.
A small gray device lay blank and silent, its screen dark green,
lifeless, and marked with scratches. A single piece of paper
was wedged between the device and the side of the envelope.
Shauna slipped it out and recognized Mark's handwriting.

Michelle Dunbar, 1991. Richard Hannoy.

Shauna turned the envelope this way and that but found
nothing else inside. She picked up the device, examined it.
It was not a phone, but she didn't recognize what it was. She
picked up her own phone and googled the names and date from
the slip of paper, clicked on the first story to pop up.

The family of missing teenager Michelle Dunbar have
expressed their dismay at police mishandling of the

case, claiming a Palm Pilot belonging to the teenager has gone missing from police custody. The personal electronic organizer, they claim, was recovered from Dunbar's body and may hold the key to finding the girl after two years of investigative dead ends. Lead detective Mark Bulger refused to comment on how the crucial piece of evidence in the case was misplaced. Dunbar's boyfriend, Richard Hannoy, was released from police custody without charge yesterday following exhaustive interviews in which...

Shauna sighed. Oh Mark. While she was tempted to scroll further through the story, to look at the images of the missing girl and the strained, grief-stricken parents, Shauna decided not to torture herself with further evidence of how twisted and manipulative her husband had been. Shauna had known, deep down in her soul, that there were probably cases out there that went unsolved because bringing them resolution would in some way disadvantage Mark. He had been that kind of man. That kind of cop. She flipped to the next envelope, which contained a pair of black lace panties and another set of names. In the third envelope was a flick knife. In the fourth, a leatherbound diary. Shauna lifted the final envelope and reached inside. She found a dusty builder's glove, made of white cotton with protective plastic molding on the inside of the palm and fingers. On the back of the wrist was a reddish-brown stain that could have been old, dried blood. Shauna took the slip of paper from the envelope and read the names.

Georgette Winter-Lee, 1989. Norman Driver.

CHAPTER TWENTY-THREE

WHEN I SAW how frail Shauna Bulger looked as she exited the pickup truck just beyond the reach of the inn's porch, my natural instinct was to run over and catch her. Susan had told me Shauna needed help, but the woman I had seen only a day earlier at her husband's funeral seemed physically degraded, as though whatever had happened in the last twenty-four hours had deflated her, wrung her like a rag. There was an angry blue bruise spreading up her jaw, and a split in her lip, and she walked slightly bent, nursing an obviously battered frame.

"Jesus, Shauna," I said to her as I went and took her arm. "What *happened*?"

"I'm fine, I'm fine." She waved me off. "I fell, that's all."

"Are you hurt?"

"Just my ego."

I walked her to the porch and sat with her on a bench there. Effie came striding around the side of the house, toting a garden rake in one hand and garbage can in the other, and took in the sight of the truck and the suitcases strapped in the back as she passed.

"You said you needed my help," I said. "I'm glad you're here, but you should have called me earlier, before you drove all this way. I could have stayed in Boston."

"Oh, it's not like that," Shauna said. "I've just been rattling around the house, trying to make myself useful, and I needed a change of scene. The grief makes you restless. You can probably relate."

"I remember." I nodded. "I couldn't sit still after Siobhan. I lost a few pounds just walking around."

"Well, while I was trying to keep myself busy last night, I started going through all of Mark's clothes," she said. "I thought I'd donate them to Goodwill." She gestured to the three suitcases on the truck. "I loaded them up on the truck myself. Guess I over-did it and fell. Then I decided maybe I'd been overzealous with the packing. Too brutal. Perhaps there are things within those cases of Mark's that I'd like to keep. And then I...I drove here."

"Jeez," I said. "You're a bit muddled up, aren't you."

Shauna nodded, gazing at the sea beyond the horizon, and I noticed her mouth twitch just a little. I regretted my words immediately. The last thing she needed right now was to be patronized. I expected there would be plenty of that from her son, her friends and neighbors, the people who had been around her when Mark died. She'd come to me, I guessed, because she'd seen in me a friend, just the way that Nick had. Someone who would trust her judgment and not question her or try to direct her. As a widower myself, I was someone she could trust not to mishandle her grief.

"What can I do?"

"It's the truck." Shauna gestured to the vehicle. "It's a stick shift. I'm just not great with those. My little Honda is in the shop, and the Corvette is too fast for me."

"No problem," I said. "You can borrow my car. I'll drive the truck back, and—"

"I was thinking of staying at the beach house." Shauna put a hand up. "It's just too painful back home without Mark there. There are so many little reminders of him. I need fresh scenery."

"All right," I said. "Sure. You guys kept that place at Manchester-by-the-Sea, huh?"

"We did."

"Mark hosted a Christmas party there one year." I nodded, remembering. "If there are too many reminders of him at the beach house, you're welcome to come stay here."

"No, I couldn't possibly impose. But thank you. The Manchester house is my happy place. I chose it. I decorated it. It really has my stamp, rather than his."

"Nice place."

"Yes. Too nice for his salary. I'm sure he lied to me about the price." Shauna gave a mirthless smile. I didn't say anything. Her husband's obvious corruption lingered between us, silently, the ghost of sins neither of us wanted to imagine. "I don't know how to thank you for this, Bill."

"It's nothing." I waved her off. "It's a car. It's fine. With so many people living here, we have more cars than we know what to do with. I'll just get Susan—"

"No, don't," Shauna said. She put a hand on my arm and I noticed scratches and bruises on her knuckles. "Don't bother her. Don't bother yourself any further, either. If you just lend me one of your cars and toss the truck somewhere in a garage or—whatever you have here. I'd be so grateful."

"What about the suitcases? Want me to give them to Goodwill for you?"

"I think I'll need more time," Shauna sighed. "Could you just leave them in the truck, where they are?"

"Of course," I said. "I'll move your truck to the garage around the back. Stay here. Take a load off."

I jogged down the stairs just as Effie walked up to Shauna's truck, her hand reaching toward the truck bed's hatch.

"She's not a guest," I told Effie. "No need to unload the bags. We're just going to park the truck in the garage. Will you give me a hand?"

Effie nodded and pulled open the door beside me. I felt something hit my boot and looked down. It was a small silver chain that had apparently been caught up in the doorjamb. I reached down, picked it up, and walked it back to where Shauna sat on the porch.

I was heading up the steps, the chain hanging from my fist, holding it out to show my old friend, when I looked into her eyes and saw an expression that stopped me dead in my tracks. It was a look I'd seen a thousand times or more across my career, so familiar and so distinct that I felt my soul arrested in my body.

It was the look a person gives when they're caught.

The shocked, vulnerable, slightly frightened gaze of a perp cornered, presented with inescapable evidence. The cage door shut. The lies exposed.

"This fell out of your truck," I said.

Defiance flickered through Shauna, and her features fell into neutral.

I laid the silver necklace on Shauna's outstretched palm. We both looked down at the pendant hanging from it, a single cursive letter fashioned from scratched and worn silver.

It was the letter M.

"Oh," Shauna nodded, closing the necklace in her fist. "That's Mark's."

"Is it?" I asked. My incredulity must have shown in my voice, because Shauna gave a forced laugh. We both knew the letter on the pendant was so curly and delicate, it was obviously designed for a woman. And the chain itself was so thin and small, it was ridiculous to suggest it might have gone around the neck of the great hulking man that we both knew as Shauna's late husband. And yet Shauna sat there and lied to me, holding the necklace in her fist, her eyes locked on mine.

"Not *his,* I mean. Mine, but given to me by Mark. It's...it's a long story," she said. "He...he'd intended to give it to me for my birthday some years ago. He ordered it especially. Only, he didn't look in the box before he gave it to me, and..." She swiped at her brow. "It was the funniest scene: us sitting there at the restaurant, me opening the box and finding the...the complete wrong initial."

It was a good lie. A good recovery from Shauna, trying to pass off the pendant as Mark's, the whole story about the dinner and the mistaken gift. I stood there, stunned, wondering how long she'd been lying to me. And why.

But like Nick's secret, I knew Shauna's would unfold for me in time. I just had to be patient, vigilant, and watchful. I could only hope hers wasn't about to bring hellfire into my life, too.

CHAPTER TWENTY-FOUR

SOMETHING WAS GOING on in the house, Clay knew. There was tension and turmoil in the air. He felt it as soon as he stepped up onto the porch late in the afternoon. Bill was pacing the beach beyond the pine trees, which was something Clay had only seen him do in the months after his wife died. His hair was windswept and his face was hard, the way it had been back in those dark days. And then there was Nick, who Clay spotted sitting at the edge of the porch farthest from the beach, slumped in a rocking chair drinking a beer. That wasn't right, either. If someone was looking for Nick, they would search the running trails in the woods, or find him using the stairs behind the kitchen to do pushups. The tension in the household seemed to have infected everyone. Clay passed Vinny in the sitting room and found him reading a battered copy of *Little House on the Prairie*. Effie was standing in front of the refrigerator, eating ice cream from the tub. Upside-down world. Any minute now, Clay expected to run into the reclusive Neddy Ives, who barely anyone had ever seen, since the man stayed confined to his room on the third floor at all hours of the day and night.

But when Clay noticed the new arrival, April Leeler, in the dining room, he felt that same light, calming warmth that seemed to surround her. With his fingertips tingling weirdly— as they had whenever his thoughts turned to this beautiful, mysterious woman who had arrived in his life yesterday—he went to the kitchen and poured two glasses of red wine. He brought them back to the edge of the dining room and paused to ease a long, slow, confidence-invoking breath into his big lungs. April's back was to the door where he stood. Joe was lying on the carpet; Clay could just see the child's legs beyond the edge of the table.

"Hello!" Clay bellowed with all the breath he had mustered. April jolted hard in her chair at the sound.

"Oh, I'm sorry, I'm sorry!" Clay swept to her side. "I didn't mean to startle you. Here! Take this!"

Clay shoved the wineglass into April's hand, sloshing wine on her wrist. He was sinking desperately into a chair near hers, cringing at his bungled entrance, when he heard a laugh.

"This'll calm my nerves." April sipped the wine and smiled.

"I'm really sorry," Clay said. "I was just glad to see you."

"It's OK." She reached over and touched his hand in a way that made his stomach clench. "Did you just get home from work?"

"Yes. Two auto break-ins, a couple of drug overdoses, and a barroom brawl. Not a bad shift, all things considered." Clay looked down at the floor, where Joe was stretched out on his belly with his iPad, playing a game that involved choosing clothes for a series of colorful monsters. "How are you two set-tling in?"

"We're OK. At least one of us has been soaking up all the natural scenery," April said, glancing down at the child, who was putting a blue blazer on a green alien-like creature. "You know. Prancing in the woods. Climbing trees. Talking to squir-rels. Collecting beautiful seashells for his loving mother."

"I did all that stuff this morning before you woke up," Joe said.

"Yes, but you've been on your iPad ever since."

"I need to play the iPad."

"You *need* to?"

"Yes, otherwise it gets lonely."

The adults laughed. Clay could feel the wine warming his cheeks already. He quietly indulged in a momentary fantasy: this same scene repositioned in a home of their own. April urg-ing Joe to go out to play in their garden and make the most of those hours before bedtime. Clay and April falling exhausted onto their couch to debrief on the day, bare feet touching, maybe under a knee blanket, while a TV played, ignored, in the corner. The safety and security of mundane family routines, the fuel that ran Clay's heart.

With a little more nudging from April, Joe set down the iPad and leaped to his feet, running out to gather more seashells from the beach in the fading light.

"So where are you two headed?" Clay asked after a minute or two of mental rehearsing. "Joe says you're on vacation."

"Look, Joe says things," April said. "He's a talker. A lot of it is made up. You shouldn't pay much attention to it."

"Sounds like every kid I've ever met."

"Yes, it's just"—April gave an uncomfortable laugh—"you never know what Joe's going to say next, you know?"

"So you're not on vacation."

"We are! Uh. He's got that bit right, at least." April took a long draft of wine. "This is day three of our adventure."

"Where to next?"

"Oh. I don't know. We're just sort of winging it," April said as she smoothed down a lock of her dark silken hair and tucked it behind her perfect ear. "I like to pull into a town, get a feel for it. See what the motels are like. It's risky business, booking accommodation online. You can't capture the smell of a place in a photograph."

"You sure can't. Can't tell how noisy it is, either."

"In my dreams I'd do a vacation like this in an RV," April sighed. "Take our home with us. See the country one town at a time, just trundling along."

"Sounds nice," Clay said and smiled. "The open road. Just going where the winds take you."

"That's the plan." April nodded, smiling, looking just past him at the door to the yard into which Joe had disappeared.

"How long will you be away, all up?"

"Ah, a few weeks. Three? Three weeks?"

"So where's home?"

"Omaha."

"You came all the way from Omaha?" Clay frowned. April's wineglass was almost empty.

"Yeah."

"But you said this was only day three."

"Uh . . ." April set down her glass slowly. "Yes. It is. Day three."

"And you got here yesterday? From Omaha? That must have

been one hell of a drive," Clay said. "It's got to be—what? Fifteen hundred miles? Not much of a trundle. Sounds like you were hauling ass day and night."

April's mouth turned into a thin line. Her eyes traced the wood grain in the tabletop before her. "I must be confused," she said quietly.

"That, or you're lying," Clay said. April froze. Clay saw the muscles in the back of her hands tighten on the tabletop. He reached over and put a hand carefully on her forearm. It was warm and taut beneath his palm.

"Listen," Clay said. "I think I know what's going on."

"It's that obvious, is it?"

"Maybe not to everyone," Clay said. "But to me, yeah. I deal with this stuff all the time at work. A beautiful woman and her son, traveling alone for an indeterminate amount of time, during the school term, without enough baggage to last them a week. No mention of his father. Mom's got her eyes on the exits in every room, warning anyone who bothers to talk to her that the kid's untrustworthy and shouldn't be listened to. And this vague tale about a vacation to nowhere in particular. None of it makes any sense."

April's heartbeat was ticking through the muscle under Clay's hand.

"Unless, of course, someone's after you," Clay said.

April exhaled. She wouldn't look at him.

"Joe's dad, right?" Clay pressed. "You've fled. You're in hiding. Joe said something yesterday about being worried about being followed."

"I can't talk about it," April said, shrinking away from Clay's touch. "I'm...I'm...I can't get into it."

"You don't have to." Clay put his hands up. "I don't need to know the details. But you need to know something."

"What?" April chanced a look at him.

"You're safe here," Clay said. "I'm not going to tell any of the others what's going on. But you can't keep running. You've got no plan, and no direction. And that's going to lead you down the wrong road. Maybe tomorrow, maybe the day after. I've seen this before, women running off from their abusive husbands and ending up someplace bad, where that phone call—the one you make to him, saying sorry, begging for forgiveness, asking him to come pick you up—is the only option you have left."

April chewed her lips.

"You're safe here," he said again. Then he took a chance. "With me."

April looked at him and he tried to get a read on those eyes. She was calculating. Weighing. Clay hadn't felt the desperation to measure up so acutely in years. Joe banged on the glass doors beside them, startling them both. He was holding a hermit crab in his palm.

"Look!" he bellowed. "It's alive! See?"

They nodded and grinned until the kid went back to his exploring.

"Why don't you let me help you?" Clay asked April. He braced himself, expecting her to pull away again. But instead, she slid her hand up into his.

"OK," she said. "I think I will."

CHAPTER TWENTY-FIVE

SHAUNA STOPPED IN the middle of the sidewalk, stunned, it seemed, by an invisible force. Her feet simply slowed, and then were stationary, and her gaze locked on the muddled horizon of stores closing, restaurants opening, Manchester-by-the-Sea rolling gently toward night. All that had happened in the past twenty-four hours swept over her. The murder. The cleanup. The first close call at her home with the men who had come to her garage, and the second close call at Bill Robinson's house. She had been going through tasks mindlessly, in an exhausted haze. Dropping Robinson's car at the Manchester beach house. Going out to get supplies—food, painkillers. Now suddenly the path ahead seemed empty. There had been a plan, and now there was none, and she found herself staring at her own reflection in the window of a thrift shop. She looked impossibly worn, hard-edged and hollow. But there was something else there, too. Something new in her eyes. The last Shauna she had imagined had been a woman full of life and joy, sailing the coast, taking tourists along the glittering edges of the horizon. Before that, there'd been another Shauna in production: the nursing home version, boring long-suffering attendants with stories. Now she was looking at a Shauna completely unfamiliar to her. A wounded being, filled with fury. A killer. A liar. A criminal. The hopes and desires of those other Shaunas had been so clear. But this new one? There was no telling what she would do next.

Shauna lifted her eyes to the mannequin dominating the front of the thrift shop. It was a young woman's figure, ridiculously slim, like the woman Shauna had murdered. The mannequin was dressed in jeans that were torn at the knees, a T-shirt from some band Shauna had never heard of, and a dusty leather jacket. Shauna stared at that jacket.

When the shop attendant got it down for her, Shauna ran her fingers over the battered but strong stitching in the shoulders, the scratched zipper and purple satin lining. A faint smell of cigarette smoke lingered on the garment. The jacket was heavy, protective, loaded with a history Shauna could somehow sense was violent and dark. She pulled it on.

The shop attendant was hovering nearby, loading freshly washed clothes onto racks.

"For your granddaughter, is it?" she asked, glancing over.

Shauna didn't answer.

"No returns on sale items," the woman chirped. Shauna waited until the attendant had walked back to collect more washed items before she zipped up the front of the jacket, opened the door to the store, and walked out into the night.

CHAPTER TWENTY-SIX

NICK PARKED BY a playground outlined in blue moonlight and walked up the hill toward the lookout. All of Gloucester sprawled below him—the shipping yards and marinas reaching like gold fingers into the black sea to his left, and to his right a handful of scattered lights, houses, properties, sinking and disappearing as they were consumed by the distant woods. Breecher was sitting on the bumper of her rental car, watching red lights blink out on the sea. Nick went and sat beside her, and in the silence he remembered those long nights in the desert, when the two of them could go three or four hours without speaking, as they watched for planes overhead, or movement on the hills. There were no hellos or goodbyes. The four-man unit had functioned as a singular organism, sometimes stretched across the base, or across a slab of land, but always connected. Since the killings, he had felt Breecher, Master, and Dorrich's presence across the states and towns that stretched between them. Breecher had been the farthest away, in Chicago, the others closer in. All of them united, a circle of trust. What had happened linked them in a way that would never be severed. So it seemed ridiculous to greet Breecher. They were never really apart.

"Is Bill gonna tell someone?" she asked eventually.

"I don't think so," Nick said. He breathed warm mist onto the cold night air. "If he does, it won't come suddenly. He'll tell me first, and I'll tell you."

"Did he say anything this afternoon?" she asked. "After you got back?"

"He texted." Nick took his phone out of his pocket. "I tried to avoid him. But he's right onto it, as I knew he would be. He wants us to track down Master. He says he's gonna find out what happened with Dorrich. Whether there was a crime scene or whatever."

They watched the sea, the blinking lights.

"I can't believe we told someone outside the team," Breecher said. "It feels like . . . I don't know. Now that I've heard it told to another person, a regular person—"

"It's like it wasn't real."

"Yeah," she said. Nick could feel her eyes on him. "Have you ever told anyone else?"

"No," he said.

"What about your therapist?"

"No."

"Did you ever say anything to your shrink that they might, you know, be able to piece together—"

"Breecher," Nick said. "You're panicking. We can't panic right now."

"Hell yeah, I'm panicking," Breecher said. "Because if this hits the newspapers, the story won't come out the way it did in that diner today. We won't look like we were duped, you and me. We'll look like monsters. And when they find out the rest of it, the stuff we didn't say today, it'll be even worse."

"Hmm." Nick nodded.

Breecher rubbed her eyes hard with her palms, like she was trying to smudge out the memories. "Your friend Bill only really knows half of the story. But when he learns the whole truth—"

"I know," Nick said. "He'll turn on us."

The two veterans fell quiet. The cooling engine beneath the hood where they sat was quietly ticking, a sensation Nick could feel rather than hear over the breeze.

"We have to make sure he doesn't find out," Nick said.

CHAPTER TWENTY-SEVEN

NONE OF THIS Bulger thing made sense, and that worried Norman Driver. He stood in his kitchen, setting out the objects he needed to prepare his dinner, relishing the simplicity and orderliness of the task. Cutting board. Knife. Potatoes. Steak. His phone was propped against the edge of the window that looked out onto the lush driveway lined with sunset-lit trees. On the phone's screen, he watched two of his men, Chiat and Fuller, live-streaming themselves to him as they drove along a highway toward the Canadian border.

Driver toyed with the idea that Pooney had been telling the truth. That he and Marris had broken into Mark Bulger's house, beaten up the widow, and that she'd turned around and blown Marris's head off with a 12 gauge. Pooney said he'd hightailed it through a bathroom window after the lady was distracted by a knock at the front door. It all seemed credible. Crazy but credible. There were enough fine details—the bathroom window, the type of shotgun used—for Driver to believe Poon. But he'd checked the story out and there had been no calls to police that night, no bodies discovered in or around Needham. Two of his guys had checked out the house and found no crime scene. The woman had indeed been home. She'd even invited a couple of young neighbors inside, and after an hour or so all three had left, apparently calm and cheerful. When Driver's guys had gone in later, they'd discovered a safe hidden in the floor of the garden shed. It was unlocked, and empty.

So where was Marris? Where was Mark Bulger's wife? Where was his collection of incriminating evidence?

If Driver could find the evidence, he could relieve himself of a decades-old knot of worry in the back of his mind that one of these days, as Bulger had always threatened, the truth about what Driver had done to Georgette Winter-Lee would rise to the surface. That the glove he'd left behind in her apartment would find its way into a forensic lab somewhere, and Driver's life would be over.

Driver set aside the potatoes he'd sliced. He checked his phone. Chiat and Fuller were pulling up to the border. Driver heard the truck's breaks squeal. Chiat's face, pitted with acne scars, was cast icy white in the beam of the border officer's flashlight as Fuller rolled down the window. Driver listened while he rubbed spices into his steak.

"Evening, gentlemen."

"Hey."

"'Sup."

"What's the purpose of your visit to Canada tonight?"

"Just dumping a bunch of construction material." Fuller

sniffed as he dragged his nose across the back of his hand. "We'll be back through again in a couple of hours."

"Why do the job in America and dump the materials in Canada?" the officer asked. "That's a bit weird, isn't it?"

An itch worked its way up Driver's spine. He didn't like nosy customs officers. He washed his hands and listened to Fuller and Chiat describing the long day they'd had, the early start in the morning on a new job, the instructions from their overbearing boss.

Driver could see the officer's flashlight picking its way around the cabin of the truck. Driver's back teeth locked together, tension balling in his chest.

"We're dumping asbestos," Chiat said. "Nastiest shit on earth. It's basically cancer in a bag. Landfills get paid by the government to dispose of it. This place we're goin' to near Sutton cut a deal, I guess."

Driver watched the screen as the silence ticked by. He said a silent prayer that the whole notion of why the Canadian government would pay one of their own landfill operators to take US-born asbestos seemed too complicated for the kind of dunderhead who spent all day looking for smuggled fruit and vegetables at a customs checkpoint. For months, Driver's guys had been crossing back and forth over the border without being glanced at twice. Now this.

"It's a bit late in the day to be dumping stuff, isn't it? Couldn't it wait until morning?"

Don't ask to take a look, Driver prayed. If this guy decided he wanted to look in the back of the truck, he'd find enough fentanyl to kill an army of elephants.

"Can I take a look?" the guy said.

Driver stabbed the cutting board with his carving knife.

"Go ahead." Fuller shrugged, as Driver watched on his phone. "It's your funeral."

More silence. The officer's flashlight beam, which had settled on the dashboard, didn't move.

"OK. You can go on through," the officer said finally. "Take your 'cancer in a bag' with you."

Driver exhaled in relief. Chiat and Fuller nodded and waved as they drove on through the checkpoint. Driver tugged the tip of the knife from the cutting board and set it aside. After a few moments, the men in the truck looked at each other and started laughing.

"What are you two idiots laughing about?" Driver asked. "You just stared down twenty years in prison."

"Yeah, right." Chiat lounged back in his seat. "You wouldn't let us get all the way to prison, boss."

"You'd have us snuffed in the first holding cell we ever got to," Fuller said.

"That's the smartest thing I've heard you two say all day," Driver said as he started arranging the chunks of potato on a paper-lined tray. "Text me when you're back through the border."

Driver hung up. Darkness had fallen outside. His thoughts about getting a border-patrol officer on his payroll competed with the Marris puzzle. He tried to remember if Mark Bulger had a son. If so, perhaps the son had a hand in all this. Or maybe some cop friend of the old man. Driver was so distracted by his problems, he didn't see the distant light at the end of his driveway that appeared and then immediately snapped out as the cabin light of a car went on and off.

Then the window in front of him exploded.

CHAPTER TWENTY-EIGHT

DRIVER CURLED INTO a ball on the floor of his kitchen, listening to the sounds around him. Gas hissing out of the refrigerator at his back, which had been struck by the bullet that came through the window. Stray pieces of glass tinkling down from the upper edge of the window onto the countertop. Crickets and night forest sounds, suddenly louder now than they had been through the glass.

Most of what Driver felt in those first few moments was pure confusion, rather than rage. It didn't compute in Driver's brain that the gunshot had been deliberate. No one in their right mind would attack him in his own home. Not anybody from around here, anyway. Not after his murderous display upon arrival, and the whispers of his reputation that had almost certainly followed it. He decided quickly that the shot must have been an accident, a stray from a hunter.

Then another shot blasted out a window in the next room.

The cell phone on the countertop began to ring, breaking him out of his stupor and yanking the fury inside him up out of its slumber.

He crouched, slipped a hand over the counter, and grabbed his phone. The name on the screen sent another shot of adrenaline through his bloodstream.

Marris.

Driver pushed the button to answer the call and lifted the device to his ear, saying nothing.

"You want to know something crazy?" It was a woman's voice. Driver's brain started putting pieces together. Scenarios that were incredible but nevertheless apparently true.

"What?" he managed.

"I was aiming for your truck both times," the voice said. "Seems like I'm a terrible shot. At long distance, anyway."

Driver hugged the ground. Through the phone he heard a familiar sound: the slice and shunt of a rifle's bolt-action. He heard a shot and the *crunch* sound of his truck, parked just to the left of the kitchen window, collapsing as a tire was blown out.

"I'm getting better, though."

"You stupid bitch," Driver said. He heard surprise mingled with the anger on his breath. "You must be out of your goddamn mind. Do you have *any idea* who you're messin' with right now?"

"Norman Lucas Driver," the woman said. "Asbestos removal specialist. Drug kingpin. Murderer."

"You must be the Bulger wife."

"No," the woman said. "Not anymore. I'm on a bit of a journey of self-discovery right now, actually. I know how cliché that sounds, but it's true."

Driver crawled across the kitchen floor into the living room, hating who he was in this moment—unarmed, sweat-drenched, trembling uncontrollably as his body was flooded with fight-or-flight chemicals. He took a moment, a single second, to indulge in the pitifulness of it as he tucked his body behind the couch in the living room, where he could safely sneak a glance toward the end of the driveway. It was no use. She was parked in the moon shadow of a big oak tree, the license plate unreadable. Driver promised himself he would remember the feel of the humiliation burning through him, use it to fuel his revenge.

"People have been thrusting identities on me my whole life," the woman said. "You know? When I was a teenager it was: get married, have kids, be that person. Daughter to wife to mother, whether you like it or not. Then all of a sudden, here you come with your own version of me: murder victim."

"Lady, you got the wrong number," Driver said. "You should have called a shrink. What you're doing right now is ordering home delivery of the worst death imaginable."

"Oh yeah?"

"Yeah," Driver said. "I'm gonna get creative with you, bitch. Nobody gets to attack me in my own home. You just don't do that."

"I'm surprised."

"By what?"

"By the sanctity you attach to the home," the old woman said. "Georgette Winter-Lee was in her own home when you raped and suffocated her."

Driver smiled in the darkness of his living room. The puzzle was complete.

"Old lady," he said. "You're picking a fight with the wrong person."

"Young man," she replied. "I could tell you the exact same thing."

CHAPTER TWENTY-NINE

THE NEXT MORNING, I was in the kitchen serving up one of my classically terrible breakfasts when Susan came up behind me and put a hand on my shoulder.

"I know about Nick," she said.

The watery scrambled eggs tumbled out of the pan into the big china bowl I'd set out, a lump or two hitting the counter. I glanced through both doors to the kitchen, but no one was in earshot.

"So you cracked," I said. "You looked him up?"

"It was pretty clear to me yesterday that he'd told you something horrifying," Susan sighed. "You both looked shell-shocked. I guess I didn't like the idea of you having to take on this burden alone."

"Thanks," I said.

"I'm not happy about it." She shrugged. "I've broken an oath

I made to the public, and a promise I made to myself. But there it is. I can't go back now. This thing that he's involved in, it's spreading like a virus. And I've just willingly infected myself."

"So what did you find out, exactly?" I asked.

"The basics. His team was involved in a civilian shootout." She put her hands up in surrender. "On paper, it's all very neat. They were on a routine patrol, and they were engaged by a couple of men. They pursued. The men fled to a small dwelling. They exchanged fire with the dwelling and its inhabitants. A family of eight was unfortunately killed."

"But you know there's more to it than that," I said.

"Of course," Susan said. She leaned against the counter beside me and folded her arms. The morning light through the lace curtains over the window threw pretty patterns on the back of her neck. "It's too tidy. Dorrich, Master, Breecher, and Nick—they all gave the exact same version of events, down to the minutes between rounds of shots, the angles of fire, the positions of victims. Nobody remembers a traumatic event that clearly and correctly; especially not a whole group of people."

"So you're wondering why they did it," I said. "Why they killed that family. Because it was clearly deliberate. Calculated."

"Firstly, I'm wondering who did the calculating," Susan said. "Because if it was Nick—"

"It wasn't," I said.

Susan nodded. Her eyes searched mine, and I could tell she was looking for deception. Because she knew I would protect my friend, whether he was guilty of something this atrocious or not. I would lessen whatever harm might come to him, even if it meant shouldering the burden of what he had done. When

Susan was satisfied that I wasn't lying, she turned and opened a bag of bread that I'd set on the counter and started feeding slices into the toaster.

"What's the situation now?" Susan asked.

"Dorrich killed himself. He told Breecher that someone knows what they did. Master's missing. Breecher and Nick are trying to find him."

"So where are we going?" she asked.

"We? Who's 'we'? Just because you know what happened, that doesn't mean you have to get involved any further."

"In for a penny, in for a pound," she said.

"I'm going to find out what happened to Dorrich," I said. "Did he kill himself because someone told him they were going to expose him? Or did someone kill him, try to make it look like a suicide? The only reason anyone is saying suicide is because Dorrich's sister found him dead in the bathtub with a bullet in his head. That doesn't mean anything."

"Let's get this all served up then and hit the road," Susan said. I knew there was no point arguing with her. If there was one thing I'd learned about Susan since we'd been together, it was that once she had set a course, turning her off it required all the patience, will, and endurance of tugboats turning a great ship. I stood marveling at her, at her decision to get herself "infected" on my account, her willingness to open the door to darkness when she'd come to the inn in the first place to find peace and refuge. I supposed that was the nature of this house. It bred trouble, attracted trouble, gave it sanctuary. But so far, no darkness that had come knocking at the inn had outmatched us, and that gave me hope. Susan slapped my arm to knock me out of my reverie.

"Those eggs are getting cold," she said.

"I love you," I said.

"Just get moving," she said, rolling her eyes.

It wasn't until I opened the garage door that I remembered I'd lent Shauna my car. I told Susan as we stood looking at the row of cars, the older woman's pale-blue truck parked between Angelica's little VW Bug and Effie's black Mustang.

"When do you pick yours up from the shop?" I asked her.

"Monday."

"Let's ask Effie if we can take the 'Stang," I said. "I've been dreaming about opening this girl up, seeing what she can do." I stroked the hood. "Eff spends every spare second working on it. I bet there's a jet engine under the hood."

"We can't," Susan sighed. "I borrowed it a month ago and spilled a smoothie in it. She's never loaning it out again."

"Susan."

"Sorry, babe."

"I'd say we could borrow Angelica's car but I don't have a spare four hours to hear about its cultural origins."

We headed toward Shauna's truck, our decision made.

"Should we unload those suitcases?" Susan asked. I rattled the suitcase nearest to me, but it was strapped in tight against the rear of the cab.

"Let's leave them," I said. "They're just old clothes."

CHAPTER THIRTY

VINNY WAS SITTING on the porch in his wheelchair, using the blanket on his lap to shield his hands from view as he worked the piece of yarn clumsily with the bone needle. The physiology quack in Gloucester had spent a good ten minutes last session trying to talk the ancient gangster into knitting or crocheting as PT for his hands. Vinny, the onetime fish-gutter, boxer, standover man, and lifelong thug, now had hands that were basically bone and skin, the cartilage ratshit, no nice little nitrogen bubbles or pockets of fat to protect his bones from grinding against each other.

He'd whittled for a while but got bored. He refused to fill the household with lacy doilies and table runners to keep his pain at bay. Then Angelica, who for some months had been fluttering around him in a *will-I-won't-I* kind of way, had told him about Nålebinding. He'd sifted through Angelica's verbal garbage to decipher that the fabric-creation technique had maybe been invented by Vikings. So that was all right by him. Vinny suspected if Angelica caught him doing it, she might be nudged into the "will" side of her internal argument. But he was damned if anyone else was going to see him doing it.

He looked up when Joe burst through the door at a sprint and leaped off the porch, running into the woods like a wild deer. Adventure afoot, Vinny guessed. The mother, April, emerged more slowly, carrying a cup of coffee and butting the door shut with her hip. Vinny hid the yarn and Nålebinding needle under the blanket and took in the sight of her. She wasn't his type. He liked a woman you could get a handful of.

"Let me ask you a question," Vinny said. April looked at him the way a person looks at an unloved house plant.

"What the hell does a kid that age know about who they want to be?" Vinny asked, pointing after the child.

"Excuse me?" April cocked her head.

"Don't get me wrong," Vinny said. "I'm not one of these conservative types. I'm not a Bible-basher. I get that some people have ideas about—you know—about bein' born the wrong gender or whatever." He shrugged. "There was guys I knew back in the day, back in the business, who were a little ehhh . . ."

He waited for her to catch on. She didn't. April's frown had deepened so much it started affecting her whole head, so that her chin dropped and her mouth turned down.

"I think whatever you're trying to say," April said carefully, "you should stop it. Right now."

Clay Spears came out onto the porch beside her, brushing toast crumbs off his tie.

"I was just curious, that's all." Vinny shrugged again. "Forget about it."

"What?" Clay asked, sensing the tension on the porch. "Who's just curious about what?"

"That kid." Vinny pointed to the forest. "She's a girl."

"Who?" Clay asked. "Joe?"

"Yeah," Vinny said. "I wanted to know why her mom here's making out like she's a boy."

"Joe *is* a boy," Clay said.

"No, he ain't," Vinny said. "He's a girl."

'What?"

"That kid's a girl. What are you? Blind?"

"I'm not blind, I'm just…" Clay shook his head, tried to get his bearings. "Where is all this coming from? Joe's a boy. April said… I mean, he's a boy. Right?"

"I'm… I'm so insulted right now, I can hardly speak," April said, pinching the bridge of her nose. "Why are we discussing my child like this? Sir, I don't even know your name, and you're—"

"Look." Vinny gave a huge sigh. He felt heavy with regret at what he had started. "I was just trying to ask a question. Is it like, one of those—you know, those 'trans' things? And if it is—what the hell? Right? Because the kid's what—five years old? Who knows what they want to be when they're *five*? Today she's a girl. Tomorrow she's a boy. Day after that she's a freakin' squirrel."

"I think I'm just going to leave this conversation," April said. She set her coffee down on the windowsill beside her and put her hands up. "Joe isn't a girl. He's a little boy. He was born a boy. He always has been a boy. I'm not 'making out' like he's anything."

"Lady, I know a little girl when I see one." Vinny snorted. "I had three of my own. That kid's a girl."

"Vinny," Clay sighed.

"I shouldn't have asked." Vinny waved the couple off. "Jeez. You want to raise a weird, mixed-up kid? Go ahead. That's your business."

Clay and April walked off, not before the sheriff threw a look back the gangster's way that was as mean as the big ole softie could possibly manage. Vinny took up his needle and yarn again, but somehow the whole Viking thing no longer seemed enough to convince him that he wasn't straying into weird, mixed-up, gender-bending territory himself. He tossed the tool and the yarn aside and folded his arms. He decided he was done talking to people for the day.

CHAPTER THIRTY-ONE

DETECTIVE ELLOISE SHARMAN let me and Susan into Roger Dorrich's apartment in South Boston. She wasn't happy about it, pushing the door open with a pained look on her face. I'd known Elloise on the beat, had gotten drunk with her a bunch of times as a probationary officer, had once smashed through a plate glass window with her while pursuing a thief. But none of that removed the stink of my supposedly corrupt history. I hung back while Susan went in.

"Thanks for doing this," I told Elloise, trying to decide how I was going to convince her everything she'd heard about me in the past was untrue. I didn't get the chance.

"Whatever it is you're doing," Elloise said, "do it fast. Roger Dorrich's family thinks this has all been shut down and signed off on as a suicide. I don't need some grieving relative turning up and wondering why we're still poking around."

"We'll be quick," I assured her.

Elloise left to get a coffee and I went in. I stood in the small kitchen, looking out over the living room toward the view over Boston. The apartment was typical of military guys I had known. The view was expensive—army guys especially like to be high up so they can see the horizon, get the lay of the land. But the furniture was cheap, functional, mismatched, bought quickly and as needed by someone used to sleeping rough. Dorrich's fridge was empty except for condiments, and his cupboards were stacked with protein powders. I guessed he was so ravaged emotionally by his time at war that he had trouble keeping any potential romantic partners around long enough for them to have any effect on his living space.

Susan was leafing through a wallet she found on the edge of a flimsy coffee table. She pulled out some receipts and started flipping through them.

"Well, here's your first clue," she said, handing two to me. "When did Dorrich die again? Thursday?"

"Yeah. Morning," I said.

"Well, seven o'clock that same morning, he fills the car with gas," she said, pointing at the papers in my hand. "He buys a Diet Coke at the gas station and gets fifty bucks out of the ATM."

"What's this a clue to?" I asked.

"Dorrich not meaning to kill himself," Susan said. "Who fills the car with gas when they know they're going to go home and end it all? And what's the cash for?" She pulled the fifty out of the wallet and showed it to me. "And what's with the Diet Coke? Why not go full sugar? Come on. It's the last day of your life."

"I see where you're going with this. It's good. But it's not enough," I said.

"It's not?"

"You're ex-FBI," I said. "So you're going to try to use your behavioral science witchcraft to lock down Dorrich's mental state based on a few bits of paper from his wallet."

"Right," she said.

"Where I come from, people aren't columns in a textbook."

"Oh, I see." She folded her arms and cocked a hip, smug. "Please, go on then. School me."

"Outside the pretty offices and classrooms, on the street, where the *real* cops work," I said, "I dealt with stuff like this. Suicides. Mystery deaths. People do weird things, OK? Maybe Dorrich got the cash out at the gas station because he always got cash out. It was habit. Maybe he preferred Diet Coke to regular. Maybe he didn't want his family members to have to deal with a near-empty car when they were cleaning up his life after he was gone."

"OK. OK. Fine. So where's your razor-sharp, street-experience-hardened mind telling you we should look, then?" she asked. "Without a body, and without Dorrich's phone or laptop, we're scraping the bottom of the barrel for what actually happened here."

"Keep scraping." I shrugged. "Just keep scraping."

I went to the bathroom, where Elloise had told me Dorrich's body was found slumped in the tub with a bullet in the brain, entered through the right temple. The room was clean now. I leaned in through the doorway and tried to imagine Dorrich in his final moments, driven to the brink by some supposed threat to expose or punish him for the massacre that had unfolded in Afghanistan. But there was so much I couldn't know without a body, or at least pictures of it; whether he'd crouched there naked, as I'd seen many men do, trying to conceal the mess and shame of his ending. Or whether he had fallen there, fully clothed, as someone came through the door and snuffed him out of existence. I decided, as I stood there, that the priority was finding out who exactly had been threatening Dorrich. Maybe Dorrich had ended his own life in fear of this person, or maybe that someone had done the deed for him, but either way, I needed to know who I was dealing with. Who'd been coming to "make him pay"? I turned and was about to leave the room when my boot crunched on a piece of broken tile on the bathmat.

I bent down and picked up a tiny triangle of glossy-white tile, held it against the wall. It was the same style. I scanned the walls, first around the door, then over the tub, then against the back wall where a sink stood beneath a mirror cabinet. I went there and pushed aside bottles on the vanity, trying to match the shard with the corner of a tile just above the sink.

There was blue gunk in the grout of the cracked tile, more blue gunk in the rubber sealant joining the vanity to the wall. The spilled gunk had been wiped up hastily, leaving smears. I picked up the bottles on the counter, looked for something blue. There was tea-colored aftershave here. Yellow hair wax. Clear roll-on deodorant. I followed the side of the vanity down to a wastepaper basket. It was open and empty, lined with a clean white plastic bag.

I went to the kitchen and fished around in the cabinets until I found the trash can. It was also empty and relined, with a larger purple bag.

I found Susan sitting on Dorrich's bed, going through the contents of the nightstand drawer.

"You've got to come with me," I said.

"What? Where?"

"Downstairs. Parking lot, probably. We'll have to go together—I can't see Ell being happy with one of us hanging around up here and one of us hanging around down there."

"What's in the parking lot?" Susan asked.

"The garbage room," I said.

Susan's shoulders slumped.

"It's time to be a real cop now, babe." I grinned.

"I just bought these shoes," she sighed.

Within about ten minutes, Susan and I had set up a dumpster search system that functioned perfectly, as though it was something we'd done together a hundred times before. Being the athletic one, with the sure-footedness of a mountain goat and the work ethic of a mule, Susan clambered into the dumpster and began loading bags into my arms, while I placed them into piles on the cement floor. Among the bags were the random discarded items apartment-block garbage chutes tend to attract. Old shoes. A dead peace lily in a broken pot. Half of a broken broom.

I was interested in bags that matched the pale purple kind Dorrich used in his kitchen, and smaller, white supermarket-style bags like the one in his bathroom bin. Susan voiced her concerns as we worked, and they matched mine. We couldn't be sure, without asking Dorrich's family or another resident of the building, when the dumpster was emptied, and therefore if any garbage from Dorrich's apartment was likely present. We couldn't be sure Dorrich's family had even dumped his garbage here, or if they'd taken it someplace else. And we couldn't be sure the broken tile and mysterious blue gunk in Dorrich's bathroom even meant anything, or if we were interrupting a more useful search of his personal possessions to follow my hunch. But I had a feeling. A weird, unsettling instinct. I didn't like the chipped tile. I didn't like the blue gunk and its proximity to the chipped tile.

My stomach hitched, excited, when I tore open a small white bag and obviously bathroom-related content poured out onto the ground at my feet. I sorted through the tissues, used razors, clumps of hair and empty pill boxes, then seized upon a small plastic bottle of men's shaving gel. At the bottom of the bottle, a teaspoon or so of gluggy, bright-blue liquid remained. As Susan landed on the cement beside me, having climbed out of the dumpster to take a break, I showed her the bottle and the small but unmistakable bullet hole in the side.

"So what happened?" I asked. "He took a shot at himself and missed?"

CHAPTER THIRTY-TWO

IT WAS TWO in the afternoon before Susan and I were evicted from Roger Dorrich's apartment building by a surly Elloise Sharman, who'd become progressively twitchy about the time we were spending crawling through the remains of Dorrich's life. We slipped silently into Shauna Bulger's truck and coasted out of town, both locked in our own minds. There'd been no clue in the apartment as to who was threatening Dorrich. Not the name of a journalist scrawled on a slip of paper. Not the worrisome jottings of a man on the edge, written in a hidden diary. Nothing. Despite Dorrich's family having taken his phone and laptop, the hub of modern man's personal life, we'd been optimistic going in. But as we headed back to Gloucester, Susan's disappointment radiated from her body like a wave of heat, and I couldn't shake mine either. We drove almost all the way home in silence, Susan turning her watch around and around on her wrist, her eyes on the trees.

Though I'd made fun of her, Susan was right about Dorrich's behavior on the morning of his suicide. It was unusual. And the bullet that had struck the bottle and the tile in his bathroom didn't add up. But like the receipts in Dorrich's wallet, it wasn't enough to tell us what had happened that morning. The bullet casing from the shot to Dorrich's head had been recovered from the scene. There was no casing found for the other shot. Which might have meant Dorrich was murdered, and the killer took the first casing. Or it might have meant the shot happened at a different time, maybe days or weeks earlier, and the casing was disposed of then.

Loose ends. Unanswered questions.

Lies. Lies. Lies.

I had spotted the pickup truck that was following us as we pulled onto I-95 just after Stoneham. I'd quickly written off the pair of men in flannel shirts and caps as construction workers heading to Gloucester after picking up supplies in Boston, preferring to focus on the problem of Dorrich's death than on the road around me. The men came to my attention again as we started to see flashes of Sandy Bay between the trees on the home stretch. They were hanging back, maybe two hundred yards behind us. By the time we reached thick woods only minutes from the inn, a new disquiet was beginning to grow in my chest.

The driver closed the gap between us fast. Susan turned in her seat.

"What's the deal here?" she asked. "You know these guys?"

I didn't get time to answer. The driver slammed his foot on the accelerator, and the truck smashed into our tailgate. Susan screamed as our vehicle fishtailed and flipped, crunching and grinding on the empty highway, spraying sparks.

CHAPTER THIRTY-THREE

IT WAS A good hit. Precise. Effective. My thoughts slowed, only the hardest, most rational aspects of the crash coming to mind. It was a trick I'd learned in the academy. *Think about the crisis as though you're observing it from outside your own body.* The truck with the two construction workers in it nudged our bumper on the right-hand side, sending us into a fishtail. Our truck spun twice before we flipped and then crashed down the wide slope beside the forest. Two, maybe three seconds after impact, we were off the road, only a handful of glass and some skid marks indicating that we'd ever been there. That was the goal. We were under attack. The airbags smacked into us, knocking me unconscious. When I woke, I was upside down. Susan was unbuckling my seat belt, dragging me from the driver's side onto the wet grass.

The battered truck that had hit us pulled up beside ours. I was so buzzed from the concussion, I saw the lettering on the

side of the truck, but couldn't read it. Big red letters. A truck
bed full of rolls of black plastic and toolboxes. Susan was bleeding from the nose. I shook my head to clear the fog, but that
only made things worse. The two men in flannel shirts were on
us immediately, one grabbing and lifting Susan by the arms,
the other looping a big hand under my armpit and shuffling me
into the woods ten yards or so from the crashed truck.

"Where's the old lady?" my captor asked. He let me go and I
stood there, numb, taking in the sight of him. Big black beard.
Bucky white teeth. He shoved me, smacked me in the jaw to get
me talking. "Hey! Dude! Pay attention. Where's the old lady?"

I looked around. Had there been another victim of the crash?
A passenger in our truck that I didn't remember? The guy tried
to smack me again and I blocked it, pulled my gun out of the
back of my jeans. I didn't even get time to aim it before he had it
and was poking the barrel into my chest.

"I don't know what you're talking about!" I roared.

The guy shoved me again and I managed to maintain my
balance, arriving beside Susan. We were under the gaze of two
guns now, the second guy having pulled one from the waist-
band of his jeans. Susan stuck to my side, trembling gently
but quiet, trying as hard as I was to make sense of what was
happening.

"What's this about?" she pleaded. "Who the hell are you
guys?"

"Just shut it, woman." The smaller guy with bucky teeth gave
Susan a lazy look. "You're spitting blood everywhere."

I looked at Susan. She was indeed bleeding profusely from
the nose, the airbag punch to the face having really worked her
over. I lifted the hem of my T-shirt and wiped her face, holding

her head close to me so I could pretend to murmur comforts into her ear.

"You got a gun?" I whispered.

"Knife in my boot," she said. "That's all. You?"

"Nothing."

The big guy with the beard was digging through the cabin of our truck, now and then glancing up as cars passed on the highway out of sight of us on the embankment. I watched him take our wallets, check our IDs. He made a phone call, wedging the phone against his shoulder as he searched the glovebox.

I could finally make sense of the lettering on the truck.

DRIVER CONSTRUCTION SERVICES.

"Boss, your contact pulled through with the APB. We got the truck," the big guy said. "But there's no old lady. Just a couple of randoms."

A pause while the big man listened to his boss. Even with all that I was seeing and experiencing, I still couldn't make heads or tails of our situation.

"We got William Theodore Robinson," the big guy read from the license he had taken from my wallet. Then switched to Susan's. "And Susan Ann Solie...I don't know. They were just driving it. Maybe she sold it or gave it away or somethin'? Beats me, Boss. I'm asking them where she is, they're either acting dumb or they genuinely don't know...Could be...Let me try."

The big guy leaned out the open door of the car and looked at me.

"Where's Marris?" he asked.

I looked at Susan. She was blank.

"Who?" I shrugged.

The man listened on the phone call for a few seconds, then

hung up. He jutted his chin at his partner, which seemed to mean something, and the two of them came toward us.

"Listen, folks," the big guy said. "I'm real sorry. Seems like what we got here is a real bad case of mistaken identity."

"Yeah, no shit," Susan snapped. "Look, whoever this old lady named Marris is, we don't know her, and we've never met her. You picked the wrong people, the wrong truck, and the wrong mode of approach. You idiots just nearly killed an ex-cop and an ex-FBI agent. A world of trouble is about to fall on you right now. So put the gun down and back away."

The two construction workers looked at each other.

"Huh." The little one made a surprised noise at his buddy. "They're the law?"

"We better do this right, then," the big one said. "No cutting corners. We bury them deep, dump the guns, and burn the truck."

CHAPTER THIRTY-FOUR

SUSAN'S LAUGH BROKE a long moment of hard silence. We all looked at her, the sound absurd in the icy tension in the quiet forest at the roadside. She covered her mouth, shook her head.

"Sorry," she said and glanced at me, her eyes a little too wide, meaningful. "I just…Wouldn't that be just perfect? If they burned the truck."

I caught on quickly, gave a smirk I hoped was convincing. "Would serve them right."

"Why?" the big guy said. "What's…what's in the truck?"

I eased breath through my bruised chest, clenched my fists, tried desperately not to give the game away. I could see Susan doing the same, trying to rein in that desperate urge to plea, to fight, to run. *Stay cool.* The big man lowered his gun, gave a quick glance back toward the upside-down truck. Fuel was dribbling into the soil, and the crushed engine was hissing, easing a thin line of smoke. The big guy's boot crunched on a slab of safety glass as he took a curious step back.

"Looks like with all that fuel leaking, it'll be gone in a minute, anyway," I murmured to Susan. "By the time they've dealt with us, it'll be too late."

"Too late for what?"

"What's in the truck?" The smaller guy came over and pressed the barrel of his gun against my forehead. I fought the urge to knee him in the groin and slap the gun away. I knew I could disarm him before he could pull the trigger. But that would leave the big guy open to fire on us.

"What are these bags?" the big guy asked, nodding toward the suitcases. Two were still strapped into the truck bed. One had been flung into the forest, only feet away from him.

Susan and I remained quiet. Every muscle in my body was tensed, my thighs ticking, my knuckles cracking. I was waiting for that moment. That precious moment. When the big guy relented to his curiosity and went to the suitcase. The barrel of the gun against my forehead was warming with my body temperature. The little guy's eyes bore into mine. I heard the whiz of the suitcase zipper and the sound of the hard shell flipping open.

"Oh my *God*," the big guy said.

His partner turned at the sound. I reached up and grabbed the gun.

CHAPTER THIRTY-FIVE

THE LITTLE GUY pulled the trigger. I felt the gun buck in both our hands, the sound of the blast beside my eardrum like a punch to the side of the head. There was no time to react. In a world filled with a high-pitched ringing noise, I kicked out as hard as I could, landing my boot hard in the little guy's hip, sending him sprawling. By now the big guy was up and firing at Susan. I saw the flash but heard nothing but the ringing. I fired back, splinters of tree flying as the two guys took off toward their truck.

My heart was in my throat when I got to Susan. The broken nose had covered her in blood. I just about fell on her, searching with my shaking hands, the gun dropped, forgotten.

"Are you hit?"

Her tone was muffled, my hearing slowly returning.

"No! No! I'm fine! I'm fine!"

I crawled back to get the gun. More shots from the truck. I gave up, scrambled back, tucked myself behind a tree, made sure Susan was doing the same across the tiny clearing where the men had walked us. From my vantage point, I could see into the suitcase the man had flipped open.

A gunshot slammed into the tree behind which I crouched. I hardly noticed. I was so focused on trying to make sense of the object curved into the shape of the bag's interior. The naked body was in the fetal position, arms tucked into the space between the thighs and chest. There didn't seem to be a head. There was fluid, reddish brown, sunken into the creases and crevices of the figure's hips and shoulders, sucked into wrinkles in the surface of the vacuum-sealed bag that contained it. I'd seen plenty of bodies in my life. Never one housed so neatly in plastic, airless, white, unmoving, perfectly fitting into the bag as though it had been designed for her.

I put my head against the tree trunk and fought the urge to be sick. Susan ducked out from her hiding place, arrived beside me, eyes wild.

"No time," she said.

"Do you see—"

"Yeah, I see it." She glanced toward the body in the bag, grabbed my biceps. "We can talk about that later. Right now, we gotta run, Bill. We gotta run."

CHAPTER THIRTY-SIX

SHERIFF CLAY SPEARS leaned back in the seat of his cruiser, put his big arm on the windowsill and scanned the park. On the play equipment in front of his vehicle, Joe was hanging upside down, his knees curled around the monkey bars, the cruiser's second radio dangling from his fingertips a few feet off the ground. Clay watched the kid raise the radio to his mouth as a woman with a dog appeared on the little path that trailed into the woods.

The radio on Clay's shoulder crackled to life.

"Big Bear, this is Detective Joe. I'm gonna make a, um...a possible crime report, over."

"OK," Clay said and smiled. Beside him, in the passenger seat, April chuckled. "Go ahead, Detective. What's the scoop? Over."

"I'm seeing a lady with a dog," the kid said, his head turning as he followed the woman on the path past the play equipment.

"She looks kind of suspicious. I think probably she stole that dog. Probably she has lots of stolen dogs at her house."

Clay and April considered the report. Clay thought April's eyes looked happy behind her brown-lensed sunglasses. It made his stomach flip to think about those eyes, what they might convey as they turned on him in the coming days. Weeks. Months. Would he be looking into those eyes in years to come? The dreams were easier to conjure now that there was someone filling the empty space of the woman in them. A person with a name and a voice.

"Sure are a lot of suspicious characters around today," Clay mused over the radio to the boy. "Could be that a gang has moved into town, over."

"A crime gang?"

"Yeah."

"We better get more surveillance." Joe's tone was contemplative. "From all angles."

The pair in the car watched as the boy clambered across the equipment and took the slide to the ground, setting up again on his belly near the logs lining the edge of the play area.

"Listen," Clay said to April as they waited for more reports from the boy. "I'm really sorry about Vinny."

"Don't worry about it." April laughed uneasily.

"He's old-fashioned," Clay sighed. "Bullheaded. I mean, I see what he's getting at. Joe's pretty. But all little kids are pretty. Vinny's probably caught on to the idea that you're not being wholly truthful about something, the way I did, and he figures you're lying about Joe being a boy. But he's not going to question you about it anymore. Nobody is. I'll make sure of it."

April nodded, staring at her hands in her lap.

"It's..." She struggled, her lip trembling. "It's embarrassing, all of this. I mean, who lets it get that bad? So bad that you have to run away like a goddamn fugitive? There are women's shelters. There are...phone numbers you can call." She shook her head. "It just came out of the blue, you know?"

Clay nodded.

"He only started hitting me six months ago or so," April said. "And then, uh. Then he changed the numbers on the bank accounts. Locked up all the money. I couldn't leave the house without him wanting to know where I was going. Then one night, he just snapped."

Clay tried to quiet the anger but it rushed up inside him, fast and boiling.

"What's this prick's name?" Clay's jaw had become so tight he had to talk through his teeth. He turned the computer screen mounted between them toward himself. "Last name Leeler, right?"

April slammed a hand on top of the screen. "Wait—what? What are you doing?"

"This is the MDT," Clay said as he started tapping at buttons on the screen. "Mobile digital terminal. I can access criminal records for out-of-state suspects on here. I want to know if your husband has any outstanding warrants."

"No, Clay, I—"

"I know you want to move slow with this," Clay said. "Go at your own speed. Figure out how you want to divorce this guy and get custody of Joe and start your new life. And hell, I don't mean to be pushy. But April, we have to make sure you're not in danger. And guys like this? They usually have records. They usually have outstanding warrants." He tapped at the screen again, opened the search database. "If we can get him picked up, we can at least rest easy that he's not out there somewhere looking for—"

She was kissing him. It happened that fast. Her hand was around the back of his head and her lips were on his, and before he could even process what was happening, he was holding her cheeks and kissing her back, hard. And when they were done, he leaned his forehead against hers and felt a joy and excitement that was new and foreign and frightening, like it might get out of control and make him whoop and scream and punch the air like an idiot.

The two of them looked out the windshield and saw Joe standing there, watching them with an expression as disgusted as it was surprised. The boy held up the radio.

"Gross, guys," came his voice through the speaker.

The mounted radio in the dash blipped. Clay looked down at it.

"Sheriff, you about? It's Gidley here."

Clay grabbed the speaker, his whole face feeling like it was on fire as April sank back into her seat, smiling, daydreaming.

"Go ahead, Bob," Clay said.

"We got something weird down here at the marina," Gidley said. "South end, behind the sheds. Might be a sunken car."

Clay threw April an apologetic look, flipped his shoulder radio over to the police channel, and turned the car radio off. He got out of the car and shut the door. Half the time, sunken cars meant suicides, and his officers weren't polite about death on official channels. All efforts Clay had made to get them to use proper codes on closed channels around town had failed.

"OK." Clay's head was still spinning. He sucked in the cold air outside the car. "OK."

He looked into the car and saw April had turned the MDT screen toward herself, was tapping at the screen fast. His mind was spinning so quickly as Gidley talked, Clay noted the activity but didn't log it, couldn't interpret the warning bells going off in his head.

"We also got Rich and Warren out on the highway looking for a car crash, maybe," Gidley continued. "Might be a couple of shots fired. Not sure what's happening there. I know you've already clocked off, but—"

"I'll be right in," Clay said. "Over."

He slipped back into the car. April turned the MDT screen back toward him. He told himself he'd talk to her about that later, call her out on using his police resources covertly, hoping he wouldn't notice. He was here to help her. She had to understand that. But there was no time for all of that now. Clay smiled at mother and son, picturing himself saying what he was about to say next to the two of them every day as he left the house.

"Sorry, you two," he said. "Duty calls."

CHAPTER THIRTY-SEVEN

SUSAN AND I bolted through the forest. Strange thoughts penetrated the thick blanket of shock-induced numbness that had overtaken me. It occurred to me that I'd never run for my life beside my girlfriend. Any girlfriend. I guess I assumed I would outrun her, be the one stopping, slowing, looking back as the gunshots still popped behind us, now and then skidding off the undergrowth or hitting nearby trees. But it was her. Susan had to stop for me three times. Eventually the gunshots stopped, too. We emerged, panting, on the side of a dirt road. Beyond it, I could hear cars on asphalt. Wordlessly we headed there, crossing the flattened earth and entering the woods again. I was sucking in breath hard. Susan met my eyes and I shook my head, resigned.

"No more of those pies," I said.

She managed a smile, took my hand, and led me on.

CHAPTER THIRTY-EIGHT

NICK SAT IN his car in the parking lot of the imposing brick building in Providence, Rhode Island. To him, Chapel Street Homeless Services had the look and feel of a prison. Small windows, huge slabs of mirrored glass, people in uniforms with keys and lanyards walking busily about. He wondered if it was his paranoid thinking, making him associate a shelter, a center for charity, with threat and capture.

This was the fifth homeless shelter he and Breecher had hit that day. They were hoping to find Rick Master's sister, last heard to be homeless in Providence. Nick watched Breecher in the side mirror as she walked back to the car, looking tired and downtrodden. She'd only been inside five minutes this time. When she saw him watching, she shook her head.

She came and crouched by his open window.

"Never heard of her."

"Damn," Nick sighed.

"I might take a wander around the block, see if I can sniff her out," Breecher said.

"Shouldn't we give up for the day?" Nick asked, glancing at the setting sun. "I mean, we've got the faintest damn hope of finding her. Master mentioned to me that his sister was homeless in Providence maybe a year ago. Even if that was true at the time, you know what the homeless are like. She could be anywhere by now."

Breecher sighed, stared at the asphalt. Not for the first time since she'd come back into his life, Nick was struck by how beautiful she was. He knew it was weird to see her that way, now, as pain and uncertainty was dancing in her eyes. And he'd noticed her beauty before, on deployment, sitting across from a troop carrier for four hours, watching the vehicle jostle her gently into a semisleep. Maybe when Nick saw happiness, it just tapped back into that paranoid vein of his mental illness. Small streams all leading to the same river, the same great sea: to be happy was to be unsafe. It was just a state of suspension before an inevitable fall.

Distress was beautiful. It made sense to him.

"We have to keep trying," she said. "We know Master doesn't trust us right now. But a message from his sister might convince him to at least hear us out. He has to know we're as scared as he is."

"He's not going to be happy that we told someone," Nick said.

"We'll explain," Breecher said. "We'll show him that we had to."

Nick nodded, watching her.

"Hey, listen," he said. "Can you do something for me?"

"Sure."

"Can you smell these?" he asked. He took the keys from the car's ignition and handed them to her. She looked at the keys in her hand.

"What?" She squinted. "Can I *smell* your *keys*?"

"Yeah," he said. "You think they smell like soap?"

"Why in the hell would they?"

"Because someone's taken an impression of them," Nick said. He watched her eyes for deception but saw only confusion there. "If somebody wants to take a secret impression of your keys in order to make a copy, they press each key into a bar of soap. I think those keys smell like soap. You see if you do, or if I'm being crazy."

Breecher lifted the keys and smelled them, watching his eyes the whole time. He felt a loosening in his shoulders. Nick was indeed worried about the keys. He had been worried about microphones, email hacks, spy cameras, someone sneaking into his bedroom at night and messing with his stuff, maybe making impressions of his keys. But he had been quite capable of keeping those concerns to himself. Most of his crazy thoughts he kept to himself. But he'd decided to ask Breecher about the keys when he saw her walking back to the car, just to see how she reacted. And although she probably did think he was being crazy, she smelled the keys anyway. She indulged him. And Nick knew she was doing that for one reason: to make him feel better. She handed him back the keys through the window.

"They do a little, maybe," she said. "But you used the restroom back at that gas station. You probably used the hand soap, right? It's strong, that gas station stuff. Would have come right off your hands onto your keys."

Nick nodded, thinking.

"Plus, you can make much better copies of a person's keys from a photograph," Breecher said.

"Oh great. That's good to know."

"Just sayin'."

"Let me come for a walk around the block with you," Nick said. "It's getting late. This is not a nice area."

"I'm fine." She smirked. "They see you coming with that haircut and those biceps and they'll think you're a cop. Go back to that bar we saw with the purple lights out the front. We'll get dinner. I'll be twenty minutes tops, then I'll meet you there."

Nick watched her go, checked his sideburns in the rearview. Then he sent another text to Master in the same theme as he had been doing for days.

Dude, I need you to check in, he typed. **Me and KB are in Providence. We are all in this together. Holla back asap.**

CHAPTER THIRTY-NINE

BY THE TIME Susan and I arrived on the doorstep of Shauna Bulger's two-story brick house in Manchester-by-the-Sea, the sun was falling, reflecting as red orbs in front windows lined with pots of yellow flowers. Every curtain was drawn, every light off. My truck was nowhere to be seen—probably in the garage. I wasn't surprised. Whoever the men in the woods had been, they were after Shauna, and I could no longer believe the older woman didn't know anything about the danger she was in. She was obviously pretending she wasn't home in case they came looking for her here. I had to knock four times to raise her. She finally answered, carrying what I assumed was a big gun by her side, hidden behind the door. I could see the weight of it dragging at her shoulder.

"You've got some explaining to do," I said. Shauna looked us over—the front of Susan's shirt soaked in blood from her nose, both of us dirty and scratched up from scrambling through the woods. She backed up, pulled open the door, and let us in.

I wheeled on her immediately.

"What in the name of—" I barked.

"You guys want a drink?" she asked. "I was just about to have one."

"I'll have one," Susan said. I turned on her now. She made a soothing gesture and mouthed "Chill out" as Shauna headed for the kitchen.

I watched Shauna put the shotgun on the island benchtop. She pulled a bottle of scotch from a cupboard. The strange sensation struck me that I was looking at someone I didn't know, a stranger residing in the body of my friend. She was wearing jeans, boots, and a black leather jacket. Her close-cropped silver hair and cold, empty eyes contained a sort of war-weariness that didn't make sense to me. It was as though the Shauna I'd known until yesterday had gone off into another universe and come back scarred and possessed.

"Who's the woman in the bag?" I asked, the question seeming absurd as it left my lips.

"She was a junkie," Shauna said as she handed Susan a scotch, then poured one for herself. "A drug peddler of some sort. She and a man named Pooney broke into my house two nights ago. They wanted the contents of Mark's safe."

I looked at Susan, who was sitting on a stool at the kitchen island, her chin in her palm, listening to the words like she was listening to a bartender tell a wandering joke as he served cocktails in a fancy restaurant.

"I killed the woman," Shauna continued, wincing as the scotch hit her throat. "Then I went after her boss."

Shauna told us about the night of the break-in, the safe she hadn't even known about the existence of, and her eventual reprisal against Norman Driver. I stood in the middle of the kitchen and tried to imagine it, Shauna leaning on the hood of the car she had borrowed from me, firing potshots into the house and truck of the head of Driver Construction Services while he crawled across the floor of his home to safety. When she trailed off, I could hear the distant waves and boat lines clanging in the nearby harbor. I waited for a punch line. There wasn't one. This was really happening; my old friend had dragged me and my girlfriend into a deadly game of tit-for-tat with what sounded like a seasoned killer. I put my head in my hands.

"Who is Norman Driver?" Susan asked. "You said the people who broke into your house were druggies. Is Driver a drug dealer?"

"I think he may be the biggest drug dealer this side of Boston," Shauna said, nodding. "This afternoon I took a little drive-by of all of his current construction projects. He has a total of eleven houses between here and Ipswich having asbestos exterior cladding removed and replaced. That's a lot of properties that are completely inaccessible to anyone but his crews for days at a time. Great opportunity to get up to no good, and to keep your whole operation mobile."

"So not only did you use my car to go and shoot up Driver's house last night," I said. "You also went and drove it past every single employee he has working for him. Did you make sure you waved out the window as you went by? I should have given you my business cards to hand out."

"Bill." Susan made that placating gesture again.

"I don't know why you're being so calm, Susan," I said carefully, fighting the urge to scream. "Whoever this Norman Driver is, he has men working for him who are insane enough to think that putting an FBI agent and a cop in the ground is no big deal. You saw them. Those were experienced killers. And this is *their* boss we're talking about. We have no idea what Driver's capable of, and now we're *in a war with this guy!*"

"I know exactly what Norman Driver's capable of," Shauna said. "I've seen his handiwork." Shauna told Susan and me about the contents of Mark's safe. About what had happened to Georgette Winter-Lee. "Norman Driver is somebody who deserves to be taught a little lesson. And don't worry. I'm not asking you to do it. I'm going to do it myself."

"Oh, fantastic!" I wailed, the fury finally escaping. "Well, I suppose I should thank you for doing me and the whole world such a generous service. Thank you so much, Shauna. This is just great!"

"There is no reason for you to get involved." Shauna shrugged. "I'm handling things just fine on my own. Mark taught me some stuff over the years. You think a Boston police chief's wife would be completely incapable of defending herself? I don't need you, Bill."

"Good for you, Shauna, but this guy knows our names," I said. "He knows my car. His people just tried to kill us. We don't have a choice but to be involved. *You've* involved us!"

"Your truck will be fine. I'm leaving it in the garage and swapping into the Honda we keep here," Shauna said. She waved dismissively toward the garage. "I hope you don't mind that I swapped out the batteries."

"Shauna!"

"I'll be sure to let Driver know you mean him no harm," Shauna said. "Next time I chat with him."

"Next time you *chat with him*?"

Susan grabbed my arm and led me into the den. I shrugged her off me, harder than I meant to, and felt angrier still that I'd been forced into this position, blocked on all sides by a cage of loyalty and fear.

"Bill, listen—"

"No, you listen," I said. I took a long breath. "This isn't OK. Look at her. Look at what she's doing. Look at what she's done to us." I pointed to a mirror above the fireplace. Susan glanced at her battered and bruised reflection. "Most people, when they decide to have a late-life crisis, they buy a convertible. They book a cruise. They don't decide to go toe-to-toe with a murderous criminal overlord."

"You're right," Susan said. "They don't. So it's pretty clear that that's not what this is, Bill. This isn't a late-life crisis. It's something far more dangerous."

Susan sat on the corner of a couch near me. She took one of my hands, smoothed my knuckles with her fingers.

"I was married to a dangerous man for ten years," Susan said.

The little hairs on the back of my neck stood on end. Susan so rarely talked about her ex. All my senses were immediately on high alert, mentally recording, searching, decoding. Because I loved her, and I knew there was hurt and suffering there, something she carried around with her at all times, day and night. The opportunity to ease, or at least understand, that suffering awakened me. I watched her playing with my fingers, her voice soft, her mind elsewhere.

"It's a lifestyle," she said. "It's not something you pick up and put down. The danger is there in every interaction you have with him, from handing him his plate of breakfast in the morning to rolling over in bed beside him at night. You train yourself to be quiet. Compliant. Submissive. You monitor him constantly, taking his temperature, looking for clues to upcoming threats. For me, I was the object of my husband's violence. But Shauna, she could only guess who her husband was turning his violence on every day."

In the kitchen, I heard Shauna pottering around, rinsing the glasses in the sink.

"She must have known who he really was," Susan said. "From what you told me about Mark and Shauna on the drive to Boston, there was too much money around in this woman's life for her to believe Mark was legit. I've met plenty of wives of mobsters in my time at the bureau. There would have been too many secret phone calls and messages. Too many meetings with nefarious characters. Too many nights when she woke up and found all the lights in the house on and him nowhere to be found. I can't imagine how exhausting that would be, pretending you don't know you're married to a monster. And Shauna did it for what? Five decades?"

"But how does all that explain this?" I whispered, gesturing toward the kitchen. "Mark's dead. The danger is gone. She's free now."

"Yeah." Susan nodded knowingly. "And so is her rage. She has so much rage now for what she endured, and nobody to take it out on. Well, until Norman Driver came along and volunteered himself."

My phone bleeped in my pocket. I took it out, glanced at the message from Angelica without really taking it in.

Man here, possible new guest. Shall I assume responsibility for the transaction?

"Do you have that?" I asked Susan.

"What?"

"A whole bunch of pent-up rage at what your ex put you through, and no one to direct it toward."

She smirked. "Oh, probably. I'm probably headed for a late-life crisis myself. But I'll make sure I take the vacation cruise route and not the criminal overlord route, just to save your hair going any whiter than it already is."

"It's going white?" I stroked my temple.

"Let's get back in there," she said, nodding toward the door.

"Look," I began as I marched back into the semidark kitchen. "Shauna, Susan, let's just take a minute here. We'll make a plan, and—"

I stopped talking as soon as I realized the kitchen was empty. Two glasses were sitting draining on the edge of the sink.

Shauna and the gun were gone.

CHAPTER FORTY

ANGELICA HUFFED IMPATIENTLY, tossed her phone onto the dresser by the door. Bill wasn't answering. By the time she got to the porch, the man she'd seen through her bedroom window had pulled his truck into the lot and stepped out. He was standing by the garage now, looking up at the house appreciatively, his hands on his hips. He was a muscular fellow. A little older than her. Maybe in his early sixties. Sandy blond hair and stubble. Angelica went to the porch steps, squinted into the still evening ringing with the early music of crickets and the churn of the nearby waves. She could barely read the lettering on the side of the truck without her glasses. DRIVER CONSTRUCTION SERVICES.

His big dusty boots were crunching on the gravel as she waved him over.

"Good evening." She put a hand out with what she hoped was the reluctantly dutiful air of a responsible tenant and not the dreaded accountability of an actual landlord. "My name is Angelica Grace Thomas-Lowell. Vegan. Activist. Bestselling author. I'm a resident here at the Inn by the Sea or *Le Château au bord de la Mer,* whichever you prefer. May I assume I'm greeting a potential guest of this humble *auberge?*"

"This what?" The man tipped back his faded cap to get a better view of her.

"This inn. Guesthouse. Hostel. Bed and—if you're foolhardy—breakfast."

"Sure," the man said. He smiled and took her hand. His palm, like his handshake, was unpleasantly firm. "I'm Norman Driver. Is the owner home?"

"It's just me at present," Angelica said with a rueful flourish.

"But Bill Robinson owns this place?"

"Yes."

"So where is he?"

"I believe he went to Boston on some errand," Angelica said. "Please. Come in. I'm sure I can be of some service. I know there's one room available."

He followed her into the house. It was just as the door was closing behind him that Angelica got her first electric pulse of warning, a kind of biological strumming of the taut wires connecting her sensors with potential threats. She shooed the feeling away, telling herself it was a regretful harking from that corner of her brain that still housed redundant patriarchal hangups about unfamiliar manly men and frail damsels being left alone together. She led Driver into the small foyer and stopped by the guest book to resume her obligation as *hôtelier du jour.*

"I present our establishment for your perusal," she said. "Would you like a tour first? Or shall I tell you our rates and conditions? How many nights were you intending to stay?"

Angelica paused while she took him in. Driver's countenance strummed that wire in her again. Later, when she thought over his behavior that night, she would realize what it was—his eyes. Most guests looked over the establishment when they walked in. Noted the furnishings. Gave the atmosphere a subtle sniff. Leaned and looked down the hall. This man displayed no curiosity about the house whatsoever. His eyes were locked on Angelica.

"Sure," he said, his eyes unmoving. "A tour would be nice."

"All right. I'll, uh . . ." Angelica shook herself, trying to recapture her resolve. "I'll start with your room."

"How about we start with *your* room," he said.

CHAPTER FORTY-ONE

DRIVER WATCHED HIS words shred through the woman named Angelica. Fast, sharp, like a starting-gun crack. She flinched and her cheeks flushed red. Like Georgette had all those years ago, this woman was still trying to invalidate that growing sense of unease. Angelica swiped at her dark curls briskly, laughed, seemed to want to turn in place; but she was blocked from the front door by his body. Driver waited for a response. She bumbled over it, her eyes anywhere but on his.

"Ah, well, I don't think we really need to—"

"I want to see your room," Driver said again, his tone even.

"Well," Angelica said, "I suppose you could see what the-the-the permanent residents' accommodation standards a-are like. Um . . ." She was suddenly walking off down the hall enthusiastically. Driver guessed she had a phone in the room, and that she hoped to grab it and hold it politely by her side, a signal to him that she could dial for assistance at any moment. That she wasn't, in fact, completely alone. The phone was her weapon. But his weapon, his body, trumped it easily enough. He had thirty pounds or more on her. It was time to stop playing games, do away with the politeness, the ridiculous idea that she could keep hold of the phone and call someone and help would arrive in time to save her.

He followed her into the room, arriving a second after her, and pushed the door shut, sealing them in. She reached for the phone on the dresser, but he plucked it from her fingers and tossed it into the bed.

"You don't need that," he said.

He loved these moments. Those tremulous seconds before the violence, when both she and he knew what was coming. When he held off on the threats, held off on the pain, refused to show her what he could do until she acknowledged it by trying to escape. Maybe he just wanted her to see how good his disguise was. How he walked about the world like this, quiet and calm. But once again, he couldn't get the smile right. And the eyes. She kept glancing at his eyes, and every time she did her terror seemed to intensify. He backed her up against the dresser and she banged into it with her hip but didn't dare yelp.

"Open the drawer," he said.

"What?"

"The top drawer," he said. They were the same words he'd spoken to Georgette. He was there again in that apartment all those years ago, where he'd been hired to fix the drywall, feeling the weird urge for the first time, following it without even knowing what it was going to lead to yet. The young killer finally emerging from his shell. "Pull it open."

Angelica shrunk into herself a little, brushed at her hair again.

"We don't need to do this," she said.

"But we're going to," he said.

"Please, just," she said and straightened to her full height. "I'm going to go now. I'm going to leave."

"No, you're not."

She was starting to tremble. He didn't budge. Neither did she.

"Open the drawer, Angelica."

She turned and did what he asked. He knew what she was thinking. She was hoping that he was just some creep who wanted to look at her underwear, and when she complied, he'd go away. Soon she'd be hoping he was just some creep who wanted to watch her undress. Then she'd hope he was just some creep who wanted to feel her up. She'd hope and hope her way through the ordeal, until she was hoping he'd let her live. Norman stood by the end of the bed, folded his arms, and felt the delicious heat intensifying in his chest and crotch as she shivered, head to toe, waiting for her next instruction.

"Pull a pair of panties out," he said.

She did.

"Hold them up for me," he said.

She did.

"Pass them here."

He put his hand out, and so did she, but as they came together Driver's brain was seized by a sudden movement at the corner of his eye and a barked command. His body moved automatically, pivoting, the palm still out, as the man in the doorway stepped into the room and said "Catch."

Driver caught the object in a reflex movement. His fingers

curled around it, securing it tightly for the fragment of a second necessary for the man to tug back on the thin piece of string attached to the ring inserted in the object's neck. Driver watched the pin pop out of the hand grenade as though in slow motion. He was left staring at the device, his grip keeping the lever depressed, the explosive seeming to scream silently with deadly potential as it sat waiting to be allowed to blow them all to pieces.

"What..." Driver's lips moved involuntarily. "What the—"

The tall, long-faced man in the doorway wound the string with the ring on it back up into his palm. Angelica was still shivering by the dresser, seemingly as shocked by the appearance of the man as Driver was.

"You said you were alone," Driver said to Angelica. They were dumb words falling out of his mouth, the cataclysmic flipping of power relations in the room having rendered him momentarily senseless.

"I thought I was," Angelica replied. "I...you must be Neddy Ives."

"I am," the man in the doorway said.

"He lives on the third floor," Angelica explained, her voice flat, numbed. "He...he never comes out. I suppose I forgot he was there."

All three of them looked at the grenade in Driver's hand.

"I'll give you this," Neddy said to Driver, showing him the pin, "when you're back in your truck."

CHAPTER FORTY-TWO

THE DEPUTY LED Sherriff Clay Spears down the embankment beside the road. On the highway above them, after-work traffic was just tapering off. A dawdling line of cars still thrummed past the traffic cones set up by officers to section off one lane for the couple of cruisers and ambulance attending the scene. Clay stopped to examine the mud patterns in the damp earth, lit blue and red. He could see what had happened. One vehicle had bumped another off the highway, then followed it down to where it crashed on its roof between the embankment and the forest. The crashed truck was still there, a pale-blue pickup with two suitcases strapped into the back. Clay's boots crunched on grass as he followed the deputy to the third suitcase, which must have been wedged between the other two and popped free on impact. It was lying on its side at the base of a nearby tree. Clay went over and crouched carefully next to the bag so as to preserve a set of shoeprints in the mud at the front.

A woman's headless body was curled inside a vacuum-sealed bag, the flesh cream-colored and run with veins. From where he crouched, Clay could see a tattoo on the woman's hip, another on her collarbone. The body he'd seen at the marina only an hour before had been well covered in them. Clay had stood at the edge of the concrete ramp and watched the truck being hauled up slowly, water gushing from its open bed, a crab scuttling off the hood and making a run for it back down the ramp. The sight of the duct tape securing the man's hands to the steering wheel had flipped the first domino in Clay's mind, and now a veritable cascade of dread was ticking and ticking along, one aspect after the other.

The last time Clay had dealt with two bodies in one day had been when Mitchell Cline moved into town. Cline's brief reign of terror had brought gunfire and fear and pain to Clay's very own doorstep, but Cline was long gone, and Clay had thought it was safe. There had been a spate of disappearances a few months earlier, but in the absence of any witnesses willing to sit down and put their name on a missing persons report, Clay assumed those folks had just shuffled on. But maybe not. Maybe another monster had moved in. His thoughts went now to April and Joe. Their safety. The deputy was standing at his side, watching Clay chewing his lip, his hands on his hips and his face hard.

"I've asked my boys to hold off on picking up the shell casings," the deputy offered. "There's so many, we've run out of evidence bags. I've sent someone back to the station."

"Hmm," Clay grunted.

"They go back into the forest a ways," the deputy said, pointing into shadows where the forest thickened. "Four people total. Seems like two people got chased by another two through there, but not far. Must have let them go or lost them. There aren't any more bodies. We checked."

"Probably didn't want to leave the trucks and the body unattended for too long," Clay mused. "It was broad daylight. The two chasers thought it best to hightail it before someone got curious about the glass on the road or the sound of the gunshots and came down the embankment."

"You think it's a road rage thing?" the deputy asked. "The blue truck pissed off somebody, who bumped them down here, then had a shoot-out?"

"Doesn't explain the body in the suitcase," Clay noted.

The young deputy nodded, still pondering.

"Gang thing then."

"Probably," Clay sighed.

They parted. Clay took out his flashlight and walked on through the forest. Ahead of him, dozens of tiny yellow flags marked the locations of shell casings or footprints. He walked on past it all, until the light and activity faded and he was alone.

He was about to turn back when his flashlight beam glinted off something in the dimness under the canopy. He went over and picked up a sleek gold watch with a filigree-patterned face. He held it, trying unsuccessfully to deny the awful recognition blossoming in his brain.

It was Susan's watch.

CHAPTER FORTY-THREE

SUSAN WAS ALERTED to the atmosphere at the house before I was. She sat bolt upright in the seat beside me, as though she could smell the discontent on the wind. At the end of the long drive, I stopped the driver we'd hitched a ride with. Susan's hand was warm in mine as we walked toward the house, where Angelica, Vinny, Effie, and Clay were waiting for us on the porch. Vinny's mean eyes drew my attention first. And then I saw Angelica and noticed something in her eyes too. She'd been crying, but it was more than that. She was a woman who seemed blessed with an overabundance of confidence and self-worth—an intolerable amount at times. Now all that bluster had been stripped away. She looked vulnerable. Susan jogged up to her and took her by the arms.

"What happened?"

Angelica dissolved into tears. Susan hugged her tight.

"Some asshole came in here—" Vinny began.

"No. Let me say it. It happened to me," Angelica snapped, swiping at her eyes as Susan released her. The old gangster was silenced immediately. Angelica took a deep breath and grew a couple of inches as she did. I witnessed her resuming her usual regal bearing as clearly and deliberately as a person called upon to switch roles in a game of charades.

"A man came into the house," Angelica said, her lip trembling. "I let him in, having mistaken him for a potential guest and feeling it necessary to assume the temporary role of proprietor."

I glanced at Clay Spears, who was watching me knowingly. I got the sinking feeling he'd soon be taking me off to speak to me alone.

"The man intimidated me into allowing him to enter my private bedroom," Angelica continued, her chin raised in indignation. "He...he directed me and—and asked me to do things in a manner which made me believe he intended me physical harm should I not comply with his wishes."

"Oh God." Susan was still standing before Angelica, rubbing her arms. "What did—Did he—"

"He had assumed I was home alone," Angelica said, her chin rising higher still. "In my haste to assist our ostensible guest I forgot completely about our resident recluse. Mr. Ives arrived in the midst of my ordeal and encouraged the intruder to leave, with the use of a hand grenade. Reluctantly, and with much posturing, he did."

"A hand grenade!" I gaped. "Where in the world did Neddy get a *hand grenade*?"

I looked around. Effie's attention was suddenly completely consumed by the pet rat in her pocket.

"Effie, do you have hand grenades in your room?" I barked.

She sighed and slumped her shoulders.

"Effie, answer me."

She rolled her eyes.

"The guy came here looking for *you*, Bill," Vinny said and pointed at me, the tendons in his neck taut with rage. "He asked for you by name. Came in a truck with DRIVER CONSTRUCTION SERVICES written on the side. You know this guy?"

Susan and I met eyes. I didn't answer.

"Who the hell have you pissed off now?" Vinny continued. "Has all this got something to do with you looking like you were just in a car wreck?"

I said nothing, brushed the dirt off the front of my jeans.

"What have you done? Huh?" Vinny shook his head. "Last time, it was gangsters driving by the house, shooting machine guns through the windows. Now we got some psycho comin' in here trying to mess with our women."

"I'm not *your* woman," Angelica snarled. "I'm not anyone's woman. I'm my own woman. He messed with *me*. So if you are going to explain yourself to anyone, Bill, it should be me."

"I'm gonna find this prick." Spittle flew from Vinny's clenched teeth as he spoke. "I'm gonna put his head in a vice."

"No, you're not," Angelica said. "We're going to have him hauled into a police station and charged for being a sexual predator. Isn't that right, Clay?"

Clay Spears hadn't taken his eyes off me. He was leaning against the porch pillar, his huge arms folded across his chest.

"Probably not," Clay said.

"What?" Angelica said, squinting at him.

"From what you've told me," Clay said, "you willingly let

him in. He walked with you to your bedroom and asked you to show him your underwear. At no time did he touch you or overtly threaten you. I believe you, Angelica, about what happened. Of course I do. But I know how this would play out in a courtroom. You'd have to sit there and watch while a judge dismissed the charges against this guy for lack of evidence. Then you'd have to continue sitting there, watching while Effie is charged with possessing a deadly weapon. I bet there's a whole arsenal of illegal firearms and explosives in her room, which will be all the evidence a judge needs."

We all looked at Effie. She gave a resentful huff.

"Look," I said and put my hands out, trying my best to sound reassuring and confident. "I'm not going to sugarcoat this. Yes, there's a guy in town who's after me. A friend of mine got into a confrontation with him and she has roped us all into it. The situation is...it's escalating. We may also be in trouble on Nick's side of things, too. He's uh..." I held my head, suddenly exhausted. "There are guys from his past who maybe want to address some things that Nick's unit did back in Afghanistan."

They all waited for me to explain further. I couldn't.

"That is the thinnest, vaguest explanation of a potentially deadly predicament that I have ever heard," Angelica said. "There are *some guys* after you, and a *separate set of guys* after Nick? And they're all coming here?"

"I don't know," I said. "Maybe."

"Why?" she asked.

"I can't say."

Angelica stood there with her mouth open, appalled. Effie and Vinny looked much the same. Somewhere above us, I heard a window slide shut. Neddy Ives had probably been listening to my pathetic explanation and had decided he'd heard enough. The only person who looked unsurprised by it all was Clay. I let out a heavy sigh and turned to him.

"Shall we?" I asked, beckoning toward the beach.

He nodded, and we walked off the porch together.

CHAPTER FORTY-FOUR

"HERE'S WHAT I'VE got," Clay said as we hit the sand. It was dark enough on the beach that I could make him out only as a big round silhouette against the distant gold lights of Gloucester. "I got a truck that had obviously been run off the road and abandoned in the woods just outside town. I got a suitcase with a headless body in it. I got enough shell casings in the surrounding area to melt down and make a statue of myself to put in the town square."

"Why *don't* they make more statues of sheriffs?" I pondered aloud. "They're the backbone of municipal law enforcement. Some would say modern-day heroes."

"Bill."

"I know. I know. It's bad," I sighed.

"The abandoned truck is registered to Mark Bulger," Clay said. "That's your buddy who just died, isn't it?"

I said nothing.

"We did a welfare check on the son, Henry," Clay continued.

"He's been in Los Angeles with his girlfriend since yesterday. But the widow, one Shauna Bulger, is unaccounted for. Is she around town?"

"I just can't say, Sheriff," I said.

"Did Shauna kill that woman in the suitcase?"

"No comment."

"You were there in the truck," he said, putting something in my hand. I didn't have to look to see what it was. I'd noticed Susan rubbing her bare wrist in the back of the taxi, looking for the watch she twirled when she was nervous. "Or at least Susan was. Tell me why."

I shrugged. Clay shook his head and turned, and we looked at the black horizon. Finally he said, "You know, I do a lot of work with teenagers in town. Bored kids up to no good. In small towns, you get a lot of that. Marni was like that."

I tried not to think about Marni, a teen we'd lost to the last drug dealer who blew into town. A fishing trawler was coasting along the horizon toward the harbor. It let out a blast of its horn, which sounded to me like a mournful moan.

"Anyway, you know the expression 'ride or die'?" Clay said. "When like, you're so loyal to a person you'll ride out anything with them? You'd die before you bail out on a friend?"

I felt heavy with dread, standing there silently, knowing where this was going.

"You're ride or die for the wrong people here, Bill," Clay said. "Nick. Shauna. Whatever those two are tangled up in, you're risking everything that you have for them. Everything that *we* have, here, in this house. These people."

I thought quietly for a long moment, turning and looking back at the house, the lights beyond the trees.

"I have to," I said finally.

"Why?" Clay asked.

"Because someone has to," I said. "They're my friends. If I can just buy them time, maybe—"

"Maybe they'll come to their senses and let you rescue them?" Clay asked.

My words faltered. He put a hand on my shoulder. It felt impossibly heavy with his own certainty and my crushing trepidation.

"Some people can't be saved," he said. "And you're going to die trying."

CHAPTER FORTY-FIVE

I KNEW OF Nick's presence long before he arrived at the door of the dining room where Susan and I sat. Between Susan's clicking at her laptop, I heard the unmistakable *ca-chunk* of metal parts as Effie actioned her massive rifle somewhere upstairs, keeping lookout over the property. A car door shut out by the garage. Boots on gravel. Nick looked edgy and tired as he greeted us wordlessly and slid into a chair opposite me.

"You want the bad news or the worse news?" I asked.

He considered this, his eyes wandering over the scrapes and cuts Susan had suffered in the shootout in the forest.

"Start bad," Nick decided finally. "Let it get steadily worse."

I told him about Shauna Bulger, the headless body in the forest, the local crime lord who now lumped us in with the vengeful older woman. Nick's fists slowly clenched as I relayed Angelica's story about Driver coming to the house and humiliating her. Nick put his face in his hands and rubbed his eyes hard.

"Man," he growled. "We don't need this right now."

"We don't need this any time," Susan countered.

"Just tell him," Nick said. He lifted his face and shrugged, hard and angry. "Tell Driver what's happened. Just say, 'Look, dude. There's been a mix-up. We didn't know we were driving your dead girl's body around. Your beef is with Shauna Bulger.'"

"Well, it was," Susan said evenly. "But now it's with us. Driver's men ran me and Bill off the road. They shot at us. Driver himself came into our house and terrified one of our nearest and dearest. We're going to kick his ass."

"We're in league with Shauna, Nick," I said. "Whether we like it or not."

"But, I mean, whatever she does now, she's representing us," Nick said. "You don't think that's a major, *major* problem? This chick sounds like a loose cannon. Going and shooting up the guy's house? That's crazy. Driving around with a body in a vacuum-sealed bag, coming here and dumping that body on you, Bill? That's *crazy-crazy-crazy*. Yes, OK, we gotta kick Driver's ass. But we've also gotta disconnect from Shauna. Because we don't know what she's going to do next. She could be hiding under this guy's bed right now with a flamethrower, for all we know."

"A flamethrower would be an interesting addition to the narrative," I said and rested my chin on my palm. "Did you know about the hand grenades in Effie's room?"

Nick scratched his neck, his eyes on the ceiling.

"That's what I thought," I said.

"What do we know about this guy?" Nick asked. "What's his weak spot?"

"Well, we know he's powerful," I said. "An ex–FBI agent who

shall remain nameless at this time managed to pull his file. He's been investigated in connection with the sudden increase in drug traffic in several cities along the East Coast."

"The houses," Nick said. "You guys said he works asbestos. He must be using the houses as labs. It's obvious. If he's been investigated a bunch of times, how come he hasn't been picked up? Just raid the damn houses."

"It's not as simple as that," Susan said. "His operations are so big. So diverse. So mobile. He currently has eleven properties in operation that we know of. He'll have a couple of warehouses, too. He has a fleet of twenty or more trucks constantly moving between those locations, and suppliers and dump sites. His staff would be dozens of men strong, and he'll likely have some local law enforcement on his pad who can warn him if anybody tries to set up surveillance. Catching Norman Driver would be like trying to catch a rabbit in its warren. Too many tunnels. Too many escape routes. I sympathize with anyone who's tried."

"Guys like Driver usually know how to judge when it's time to move on and become somebody else's problem, too," I said. "I've seen it before on the job. You have a nightmare criminal like that, you're thinking it's going to take everything you have, personally and professionally, to bring him down. Then suddenly, just when you're reaching the end of your rope, he disappears. Moves on. It's a relief."

"When do you get to the weak spot?" Nick asked.

"Shauna," Susan said. "We have to find her. Firstly, because she is a loose cannon, just as you said. She's in over her head with this guy and she's going to get herself killed. And secondly because she's the key to shutting this whole thing down."

"She is?" Nick asked.

"Yes. She has something both we and Driver want," Susan said. "She has the evidence that could put him away for good."

She turned her laptop toward us. On the screen, a woman with a big smile and wavy, almost white-blond hair was sitting on a garden wall in the sunshine. She was midtwenties, staring right down the camera lens, fiercely full of life and potential. Or maybe I was just recognizing that in her, the way I did with most pictures of murder victims. How full of energy they seemed, now that I knew they were dead.

"This is Georgette Winter-Lee," Susan said. "She was twenty-three, living in an apartment complex in Lower Roxbury, when she was raped and strangled to death. Police believed she let the guy in, poured him a glass of water, then he took her to the bedroom and made her empty the contents of her underwear drawer for his perusal."

Nick's nostrils flared. I watched him trying to control the rage slowly building, drumming his fingers on the tabletop, his knees jogging under the table.

"Georgette had a hole in her drywall, and had told her neighbor the day before that she'd met a guy on the subway who said he could repair it for her. Crime scene techs logged the discovery of a construction-style glove that had fallen behind the bed after Georgette's body was found," Susan said. "The glove appeared to have blood on it. It was a masterful find. The glove would have had the perpetrator's DNA on the inside, and Georgette's DNA on the outside."

"But that glove never made it into evidence," Nick concluded.

I nodded.

"The boy messed up." Nick gave a mean smile. "He might be a very talented drug king but he slipped up as a scumbag lady killer. There's no hiding from that in your rabbit warren."

"So now we've gotta get to Shauna before Driver does," I said.

"And before he gets to us," Susan said.

CHAPTER FORTY-SIX

NICK HAD ALWAYS liked being on watch. The stillness. The silence. The slow pouring of one minute into next, hour into hour, a cup filling with time. He leaned on the windowsill of Effie's room, the best room for surveillance of the inn's driveway, porch, and garage. Effie lay sleeping in the bed, curled toward him, her cup filling with restful hours until she took over the watch again.

Almost everyone in the house assumed Effie was ex-military, but Nick knew better. He could tell because she didn't fall asleep the military way: the time-efficient, mechanical shutting down they taught at boot camp. He'd heard fifteen minutes or more of her tossing and turning, trying to fall asleep, while he'd scanned the property through the rifle scope. Nick's guess was that Effie was probably in a WITSEC situation of some sort.

Bill tapped a knuckle gently on the door before entering,

though it was open. Effie didn't move. Nick smiled in the dark as he took in his friend's striped pajama bottoms.

"Don't be jealous," Bill sighed. "You could head to Walmart and get a pair of your own."

"Or I could ask my grandpa if he's got spares," Nick said and went back to the rifle scope.

"All this stuff with Norman Driver," Bill said. "And there hasn't been a chance to talk about you." He recounted his and Susan's experience at Dorrich's apartment, the shot in the bathroom wall. Nick told him about the failed attempt to find Master's sister, Danielle, in Providence.

Bill stood pondering, watching the still blue night through the window. "If I was Rick Master and I thought someone was coming for me, I'd tell everyone I knew and loved to keep a low profile. Blow out of town for a few weeks."

"It was worth a try, though," Nick said.

"Yeah. Worth a try." Bill yawned. "Maybe tomorrow we can cajole Susan into using her FBI contacts again to see if Master has any properties in his or a relative's name that we don't know about."

"It is tomorrow," Nick said after glancing at his watch.

"Oh, right."

"Go to bed, man," Nick said. His friend went to the door, paused, looking toward the stairs to the attic. His and Susan's room. Nick felt a pang of jealousy, and maybe Bill sensed it, because he looked back and jutted his chin at Nick playfully.

"Where's Breecher?"

"I dropped her at her motel over in Essex," Nick said, refusing to bite.

"Somethin' there, maybe?" Bill asked. Nick could see his smile even in the shadow of the hall.

"You tryin' to make my watch feel longer or shorter?" Nick asked. Bill conceded and disappeared, but the damage was done. Nick's thoughts turned to his former teammate, and the smell of her body on watch in Afghanistan. He'd never got used to the smell of other men. The desert wind and days hauling equipment without hope of a shower or clean uniforms. Breecher always smelled good. Even when she smelled bad, she smelled good.

His fingers moved on their own. He took up his phone and texted, deliberately ignoring the consequences.

Lonely night without u.

Nick scolded himself immediately. He had come on too strong. Breecher had been in his life since 2010, and with one text, he saw himself destroying everything they'd ever experienced together. The triumph and trauma of war, their terrible shared sin, the return and the devastating plunge into uncertainty back in the US. Could one awkward text push her away, after all that? He started and deleted a series of replies.

That wasn't meant to sound...

It's just being around you after all this time reminds me of...

Sorry, I'm just saying...

With terror in his heart, he watched as three bubbles on the screen indicated she was writing back.

Her text appeared, and he smiled.

Be right over, it said.

Breecher arrived as he was handing his watch back over to Bill. Blessed timing, so he didn't have to explain, excuse, deal with stealthy smiles. He let her in the back door to the kitchen and led her silently to his bedroom. She was sliding her hands up under his shirt before he'd even shut the door behind them.

He knew her. Every inch of her body. He'd seen her bathing in a river in a ravaged village. He'd heard her crying in the tent in exhaustion and pain. He knew what she was like when she trembled and fought and laughed. But in his bed she was a complete stranger to him. New and exhilarating. He couldn't tell what was happening behind her eyes as she held him, what thoughts traveled through her mind in the warm, tired moments afterward.

She was asleep beside him, one of her legs twisted around his, when he reached over to grab his phone from the nightstand where it lay beside hers. He was thinking he'd screenshot the "Be right over" text. A shrink had told him once that good moments saved, recalled, relived, could be momentary oases in his troubled ruminations.

The phone buzzed as he touched it. Breecher's screen lit up as a text came through to her phone at the exact same time.

It was Master.

You'll regret this. Danielle was my sister. She had nothing to do with this. You're dead. Both of you: dead.

Nick felt a pang of terror rock through his body. He reached over, lifted Breecher's phone, saw the identical message written on her screen. He picked up his phone and googled Danielle Master's name. Breecher must have sensed the tension in him, because she woke and rolled over sharply.

"What-what-what?"

"It's him. It's Master."

"What's he say?"

Nick passed her phone over and watched her reading the

text. He felt the alarms begin to sound inside his brain, louder and louder as the seconds passed.

"What does that mean?" Breecher asked.

"You tell me what it means," Nick said. "You said when you left me in the car in Providence that you walked around the block and saw no sign of Danielle Master."

Breecher frowned at him.

"And that was true," she said. Her tone was hard.

Nick showed her his screen. The news headline that was the most recent match for Danielle Master's name.

HOMELESS WOMAN SLAIN IN PROVIDENCE, POLICE CALLING FOR INFORMATION

"Says here that she was found murdered in an alleyway last night," Nick said. "Happened around six. Two blocks away from the Chapel Street shelter."

"Jesus," Breecher said. She took the phone from him and scrolled the story. Nick watched her eyes. They weren't reading. Just looking at the story on the screen.

"What...what are you saying?" Breecher's voice was rising, her eyes narrowing. "That I left you last night, went and killed Danielle, and then came back to you at the bar and told you I'd found nothing? That you think I...*killed a person*...and then went and had dinner with you?"

"Don't give me that," Nick said. "Don't pretend you didn't kill guys over there and then sleep like a baby right afterward."

"Nick, this is crazy," Breecher said. "What are you saying? That this is me? That this...this whole thing. It's me?"

"Maybe," Nick said, his mind reeling. "I don't know."

"Maybe it was *you*," Breecher said quietly. Nick had to push aside the fury and confusion storming in his mind to look at her, to listen to her.

"What do you mean?"

"Well, you say you have these episodes." She shrugged. "You blank out. Do weird things you can't remember doing. Maybe when I walked away from you at the car, you went for a walk. You found Danielle and you killed her."

Nick's jaw was locked tight. The sheets squeaked as he twisted them in his fists.

"Maybe you went to see Dorrich," Breecher went on. "And he told you something that made you snap. How do I know?"

"Get out," he said.

"Nick, don't do this. I'm just saying, we can question this thing to death. But that doesn't help us." She reached for him. "We need to stick together. We—"

"Get. Out."

Breecher waited. Nick didn't budge. In time she gathered her things and pulled her clothes on. He watched her slip out the bedroom door into the darkness.

CHAPTER FORTY-SEVEN

MY PHONE BLASTED me out of a deep but troubled slumber at 8 a.m. I calculated that I'd had four hours' sleep, felt ancient and stiff. I grabbed the phone and answered before I even looked at who was calling.

Vinny's gravelly accent was unmistakable.

"You're gonna wanna get down to the Rusty Rabbit right now, Bill."

"The what?" I asked.

"Diner at the south end of Main Street," Vinny said. I could hear plates clattering and people talking in the background of his call. "Something here you should see."

I was approaching the Rusty Rabbit on legs that felt like rubber, my balance and coordination barely holding out, when I saw a truck parked outside with DRIVER CONSTRUCTION SERVICES written on the side.

From Angelica's description, I ID'd the boxy-headed and

small-eyed Norman Driver almost the second I walked in. He was sitting at the edge of a booth crowded with two huge men in construction uniforms: big, scuffed boots and sun-scorched caps. They weren't the same guys who had run me and Susan off the road, but they had the same mean, hungry look. They seemed to recognize me, which probably meant Driver had circulated a photograph among his men. Vinny's wheelchair was pulled up to a table across the aisle, and he was sitting with his elbows splayed over a half-eaten serving of pork ribs. Driver and his guys watched me, their eyes dark with menace, as I took a seat at Vinny's table.

"I love this place," Vinny said in greeting, sucking the barbecue sauce off a rib. "Ribs for breakfast. Urgh! You can't beat it. Great food, great company. Huh, fellas?"

No one at Driver's table answered. The man who had brought so much fear and rage into my life in the previous twenty-four hours sat sideways in the booth with one elbow on the table, his shoulders hunched and huge, scarred fingers knitted as his gaze bore into me.

"Vinny," I said carefully. "What the hell is this?"

"What's it look like? It's four guys shootin' the shit." Vinny shrugged, a rib in one hand and a slice of toast in the other. "Hey, they ain't your most talkative bunch. They're excellent listeners, though. I was just telling them what they should order from the menu. They're new in town, you see."

"Vinny—"

"Your buddy's got a hell of a mouth on him," Driver said to me. A weird, unsettling smile was playing about his lips. "Hasn't shut up since he wheeled himself in."

"Yeah, well, at least he's messing with someone his own

size," I sneered, immediately regretting losing my cool but too furious to reel it in. "I know who you are, Driver. I hope your mother kept your dental records, because the police are gonna need them to identify you if you ever come by my house again, you piece of—"

Driver's guys shot up in their seats. The boss settled them all with a single wave of his hand, like he was controlling well-trained dogs.

"Yeah, that's right," I said with a grin that was surely as fake as Driver's. "Not while you're wearing the company logo, boys. In fact, try not to commit any crime at all while you're wearing your work gear. Might get you in the kind of trouble that will haunt you for the rest of your life."

Driver's eyes flashed.

"Big words," he said to me.

"They're not just words, pal," I replied.

Vinny was smiling from ear to ear like a kid watching his favorite pro wrestlers go at it in the ring. Driver's phone began vibrating where it sat on the table. He didn't touch it. The squeal of a toddler in a high chair across the diner brought me to my senses. The room was packed, every table occupied with families and couples enjoying a leisurely Sunday breakfast. The bell above the door jangled as another family squeezed their way in. I had to take a few deep breaths to stop my voice from shaking with anger.

"Look," I said. "We're not going to do this here. We're surrounded by innocent people. Vinny, whatever you brought me here to see, I've seen it. We're leaving."

"Oh come on, I'm just having a laugh," Vinny said and wheeled himself closer to the table. I winced, expecting the gun that was almost certainly in his lap to fall from under his knee blanket onto the floor in front of everyone. "Just have a coffee. A bagel. Something. Read the paper." He shoved a newspaper from the corner of the table at me.

"Bill," Vinny went on, lowering his voice. "I got here first. These bozos came in after me. We can't leave now. We'll be submitting."

"Vinny, this is not a disagreement between dogs about who gets to piss on the best park bench. You're threatening a gun fight in a crowded café."

"Listen to you. So dramatic." He rolled his eyes.

The waitress deposited three huge plates of breakfast in front of Driver and his guys. Driver's men seemed to relax slightly, as though the appearance of food—rather than the presence of innocent bystanders all around us—meant there wasn't about to be a massacre here in the diner. No one ate. Driver's phone started buzzing again, remaining ignored.

"You know, I was just reading in the paper there, about the little drug crisis we're having in New England," Vinny said as he picked at his collard greens with his fork, his voice rising again for the benefit of Driver and his men. "Problem used to be that people were smuggling prescription painkillers into the States from China. Now that the cops have stamped that out, people have started making the pills themselves. Can you believe it?"

One of Driver's guys took up his fork, looking to his boss for permission to eat. Driver was too focused on Vinny and me. The men glanced at each other, undecided as to whether the mere presence of an enemy, even without violence, meant their eggs should get cold.

"Thing about these pills is," Vinny continued, "they're usually made in labs. By *scientists*. But out here, you got a bunch of *deficientes* throwing ingredients together like toddlers in a play kitchen. So the goods can turn out four, five times stronger than they should be sometimes."

Driver's guys had broken ranks and started to eat. The two men passed a saltshaker between them.

"Listen to me, huh." Vinny smiled when nobody responded to his lecture. "Trying to school everybody on this stuff. I should just shut up and let everybody enjoy their food."

He looked over at Driver's table. I followed his gaze. It was then that I noticed that the salt and pepper shakers on Driver's table didn't match. The pepper was round, plain glass with a silver top; the salt was crystal, with a square base.

The same kind I had in the dining room of my inn.

I looked around the tables, slowly rising out of my seat. The saltshaker on Driver's table was the only crystal, square-bottomed shaker in the room.

One of Driver's guys coughed and grabbed at his throat.

CHAPTER FORTY-EIGHT

THE BIG GUY closest to me gripped his neck and collar like he was choking on a piece of food. His face flushed red, the color spreading downward fast. I had just enough time to lunge forward and grab him as he collapsed sideways out of the bench seat. As I lowered him to the ground, I looked up and saw the other man beside him slump face-first into his plate of food, out cold.

Café diners were out of their seats all around me, chairs scraping, gasps of horror and surprise. As panic thrummed through me, I heard the innocent citizens of Gloucester offering up a gaggle of perfectly ordinary explanations for something I knew had come straight from the realms of impossibility.

"Oh God, he's choking!"

"He's having a heart attack. Someone call 911!"

"Does anyone know CPR?"

Others were making for the doors, their plates forgotten.

"OK, honey, let's go. Grab your toys. Let's give those guys some space."

"He's fine. He's fine. He's just playing a game. Grab your blankie. Let's go."

The man in my arms was convulsing and foaming at the mouth as I dragged him into the aisle and rolled him onto his side. Helplessly, I thumped his back, tried to clear some of the foam from his airway with my fingers. Even from my vantage point, crouched over the huge construction worker, I could feel the vicious, electric tension between Vinny and Driver as the two men were surrounded by helpful strangers.

Vinny backed his wheelchair into the next aisle. Driver exited the booth and crouched beside me.

"Get the other guy," I told Driver. "Check if he's still breathing."

Driver didn't move. He was so close I could feel his breath on the rim of my ear.

"What are you doing? Get help!" I yelled at him.

"I'm gonna kill everyone in your house," Driver said.

He patted my back, two hard thumps, and rose to his feet. As far as the people around us could tell, he probably looked like he was telling me he was going to go flag down a car, the pats a reassuring gesture. But I knew what they were. They were loaded with the certainty of a man who's as good as his word.

Norman Driver was going to kill everyone I cared about.

I had his personal guarantee.

CHAPTER FORTY-NINE

SHAUNA NOTICED THE car following hers as she headed out of a gas station in Ipswich, taking Route 133 back toward Gloucester. She'd spent the rest of the day before lying low, thinking and plotting, conserving her energy for what lay ahead. She imagined Henry had been trying to contact her, but she kept her phone off so that her mind was clear and her location couldn't be tracked. Then she'd spent the night in the car near Daniel Boone Park, sleepless, watching the still, flat water through the windshield and thinking about Norman Driver and his crew.

The man tailing her was young. He was close enough that Shauna could make him out in the rearview mirror; his short, scrubby beard and sunglasses. He held the steering wheel of his truck with one hand and dialed a cell phone over and over with the other, cursing and shaking his head when whoever he was calling didn't answer. When Shauna could see the spire of City Hall in Gloucester, the young man fell back a little, some half-formed instinct reminding him perhaps that the best kind of tail didn't involve the threat of running up the back of the mark if she stopped suddenly at a traffic light.

Shauna wondered how a man who looked to be in his twenties came to be working for someone as criminally advanced as Norman Driver. Did he see himself reaching "boss" status when he got to Driver's age, with a crew of underlings dealing drugs or running women or hitting banks or whatever? Or was working for Driver just a temporary gig, the same kind of desperate grab for good money at minimal effort that drove college girls to moonlight as exotic dancers? As Shauna led the young man into Dogtown Commons, the open view of the marshlands yielded to thick winter woods. She took a dirt road past a collapsed farmhouse and pulled over, watching as the young man's truck stopped a hundred or more yards back.

Shauna reached down and cranked the heater up. Warm air gushed over her, and soon the windshield was beginning to fog against the icy morning. The vehicle had a good heating system, just one of many features she knew cops valued in their vehicles, a desire born of long nights on stakeout. It also had good suspension, sound gas mileage, and plenty of cup holders—all requirements Mark had demanded of their vehicles over the years. Shauna gripped the wheel and watched the mirror, looking for her follower, wondering if the receiver of his frantic calls had finally picked up yet.

She unclipped her seat belt.

It was three full minutes later that she heard the faint crunch of his boots on the fallen leaves, perhaps twenty yards behind. Then she heard the shunt of his pistol action only a couple of yards beyond the driver side door.

Shauna heard the gunshots puncture the side of the car and smiled. He'd shot twice into the door, it sounded like, before even opening it. Seemed like he was indeed an ambitious baby-criminal hoping to rise through the ranks. Shauna pushed the trunk lid open and stepped out quietly, taking the shotgun with her. She stood behind the boy and, while he tore open the driver's side door of the car, she waited for him to put it all together: the empty driver's seat, the flopped-down panel in the middle back seat leading through to the trunk. The path through which Shauna had made her escape. Another cop feature. Bill would have attended enough road accidents in his career to know how useful an escape route through the trunk could be. The young man with the gun turned around just as Shauna was trying to decide if she should say something powerful, a movie villain's one-liner, like "See you in hell." Something that would make it all clear for him: how ignorant, selfish, and wasteful he had been to arrive where he was now at the end of his life, alone with her in these woods.

In the end, she said nothing. The boy opened his mouth in shock, taking in the sight of the gun in her hands, and Shauna could see he knew very well how stupid he had been.

She shot him in the chest.

Desert Outside Bagram, Afghanistan, 2010

Nick allowed himself to be pulled and shoved away from Karli Breecher. Some part of his mind couldn't comprehend that Rick Master had just shot her, that she lay writhing on the ground outside the goat farmer's house while Master tended to the wound he'd just created. Nick was walking in a nightmare, begging himself to wake up, his jaw clenched and step locked as Roger Dorrich pushed him back up the hill. They stood side by side, spraying their own truck with gunfire from the guns they found in the house, and Nick felt blinded by the flashes in the dark. Before he could catch up with his own mind, try to decipher what was happening and what would happen next, he was back at the house, standing alongside Dorrich, as Master applied field dressings to Breecher's stomach.

"You shot her," Nick panted, his voice sounding completely foreign to him. Numb. "I . . . I don't understand what's happening. What are you—"

"We need it to look legit," Dorrich said. "If we're going to tell them there was a firefight here, it makes sense one of us at least would get tagged. No one's going to question this. She's a colonel's daughter, for chrissake."

Breecher's eyes were big and wild, her bloody hand gripping Master's shoulder, her eyes on Nick, pleading as she fought to speak through the pain.

"I'm sorry, Breecher," Master said. "It'll all be worth it. I promise. It'll all be worth it."

"Come on," Dorrich said and grabbed Nick's shoulder and pushed him toward the house. "We have to keep moving."

Nick entered the house and walked through the room full of dead family members. His eyes were fixed on his own feet, and yet small clues to the horror intruded into the edges of his vision. A tiny hand flopped open, unmoving. A bare foot. Someone lying on their side, hair splayed over the stained rug. Dorrich led Nick into a large room filled with rugs, blankets, pillows. He shoved back a few, searching for something on the ground. All the while, Dorrich had one hand pressed against the radio on his helmet.

"Delta 6 receiving fire at a structure approximately five miles north-northwest of base, requesting immediate assistance. One man down, over."

Finally Dorrich's finger caught on a structure in the bare earth. He lifted a wood panel and flipped it over, then started dragging dusty duffel bags out of a wide hole in the ground.

They were faded camo-print bags marked with big black block letters.

U.S. ARMY.

Nick came when Dorrich beckoned him, receiving the bag Dorrich tossed him.

"Hurry up. Grab and go, Jones! Grab and go!"

Nick bent and opened the bag. Dirty, wrinkled bills, thousands of them, secured in bundles with elastic bands. American dollars. In his dreamy, disassociated state, he reached into the bag and felt the corners and edges of the stacks of cash creep up his arm. A depthless bag of money trying to suck him in by the wrist.

"Ghost money," he said.

Dorrich nodded.

Nick had heard rumors fluttering around base ever since he arrived, about CIA payments to village elders, local non-Taliban warlords, and agents who channeled money all the way to President Hamid Karzai's palace. Six months earlier, outside Tezin, he'd lain on his bunk listening to Dorrich reading a *New York Times* article aloud to his team. The article claimed that Americans were paying cash for safe passage through Taliban red zones. The reporter had described plastic shopping bags, briefcases, duffel bags full of cash being delivered in the dead of night. Army patrols were marking their vehicles with safe codes provided by the elders, so that rebels could see them with binoculars and know not to engage. Master had been in a fury as he listened, pacing the room, his fists balled and tucked into his armpits as though to stop himself beating the shit out of someone.

"I didn't come here to hand American tax dollars over to the goddamn Taliban!" he'd raged. "I came here to kill those motherfuckers!"

Dorrich was shoving another bag at Nick now, loading two bags onto his own shoulders.

"How much is here?" Nick asked.

"Should be about four million," Dorrich said. "There's been a bottleneck further up the line. One of the guys who's supposed to bring this money to the higher-ups in Kabul has been skimming off the top, so all the money's pooled here until they can figure out who the thief is. This represents nine months' worth of safe passage payments."

"Jesus," Nick said. Dorrich grinned and slapped his back, thinking, Nick supposed, that he was marveling at the money. At what a million dollars could mean for someone like him, a high school dropout from West Baltimore with few prospects back home except more deployments to this desert wasteland to fight in a war he didn't half understand.

But Nick wasn't marveling at that. He was marveling at the wastefulness of it all. The lives snuffed out in the other room. Breecher, and what a gunshot wound at close range to the abdomen would mean for her chances of survival. He marveled at Master and Dorrich's apparent complete disregard for the danger this would put Americans into in the coming months. Safe passages now unsafe again. He marveled at the years he saw stretching outward and away from him in this moment, years in which he would have to keep quiet somehow about what he was doing.

Nick could hear choppers on the wind.

"Let's go." Dorrich pulled at him. "We gotta stash the bags before they get here."

CHAPTER FIFTY

AT SUNRISE, NICK went to the second-floor bathroom in the Inn by the Sea, stepped up onto the toilet, and popped open the access into the crawl space beneath Neddy Ives's room. Effie was on watch across the hall. He was sure he'd heard Clay Spears's lumbering gait somewhere on the lower floors. If there was anyone else in the house, they seemed to be asleep.

Nick reached into the dark and dragged the old duffel bag across a beam to himself, then sat on the edge of the bathtub with it. He could still hear those choppers. He remembered showing members of Bravo 5 through to the room in the goat farmer's house with the empty pit in it. *Nothing here when we arrived. Just a hole in the ground.*

Probably drugs, someone guessed.

Nick unzipped the duffel bag and looked at the cash. His cut. Just under a million, so he was told. He hadn't spent a single dime. Hadn't unzipped the bag once since he'd retrieved it from an airport locker Dorrich had given him the code to, a month and a half after he returned from his last tour. It had been Masters's job to retrieve the bags from where they'd been stashed on the night of the massacre, not far from the farmhouse, in the desert, and get them safely into the US, hidden in the engine well of a broken-down troop carrier.

Dorrich's intel had been sound. Months later, as they sat side by side in a hall at some processing center in Arizona, waiting to describe the massacre to an inquiring committee, Dorrich had told Nick about the farmer he and Master had come across while walking by the side of the road to Kabul. He and Master had been on a supply run. They'd stopped and talked to the guy because they were bored. Dorrich told Nick about the nervous chitchat the man had engaged in with them, the suggestion that ghost money was being funneled through a nearby valley. It had taken months of research, Dorrich said. Months of lies, secret rendezvous outside the base; bribes to farmers, roadmen, bandits; sorting the rumors from the lies from the cover stories. Dorrich said he had wanted to bring Nick and Breecher in on the plan from the beginning. But it was Master who didn't trust them to go through with it. Nick was a soft touch, and convincing Breecher to risk her body like that would have been a hard sell.

Easier to beg for forgiveness than to ask for permission, Dorrich theorized, *and a million dollars bought a whole lot of forgiveness.*

Nick zipped up the bag and took out his phone. His thumb hovered over the green dial button below the name of his latest therapist. He put the phone down, bit his fist to try to stop the tears. He googled the tip line for the *New York Times,* tapped through to the blue-highlighted phone numbers, and again let his thumb tremble over the screen without dialing, playing the tape through to the end in his mind and trying to find something positive to latch on to.

But there was only darkness ahead.

And shame. Terrible, terrible shame.

He swiped the search page away and opened the phone's camera, turned it on himself. The phone gave a little musical sigh as he began recording.

"My name is Nick Jones," he said. "I'm a specialist E-4 veteran with the United States Army. I have something to report."

CHAPTER FIFTY-ONE

DRIVER STOOD OVER the dead kid in the forest and felt old. Maybe it was the vision of the young construction worker lying twisted in the leaves, the gaping hole in his chest and his surprised expression, that was making Driver feel the years he had under his belt that this kid would never have. Maybe it was the adrenaline draining from his system after a night spent madly organizing the stealthy shutdown and evacuation of four of his drug labs, a stash house, and a distribution center from inside properties being stripped and reclad.

Moving a drug lab was a lot of work. He couldn't risk just having his guys load up the packages and drive them off. Not now, while the heat was on. He'd had to arrange for other members of his crew to get into road accidents, pub brawls, violent domestic arguments to tie up the local cops and sheriffs, keep the roads clear of curious patrols. Then there was the decision he had to make about where to stash his operation until this

Shauna Bulger woman could be found. Driver had just been thinking he'd get a good breakfast in and catch a twenty-minute nap in his truck when the gimp in the wheelchair and the washed-up ex-cop had killed two of his men and ruined his morning.

Now this.

Driver's head hurt and his bones ached. Maynard and Doller, his guys from the dock, were standing nearby awaiting orders, cigarettes cupped in their palms against the wind.

"I don't even know this kid's name," Driver said.

"Spitts," Maynard said. He gestured to the corpse with his cigarette. "Regi Spitts's brother. Regi started him a couple of weeks ago, just watching over a couple of corner boys over in Georgetown. Must have come over when he heard you was looking for the Bulger woman."

"Well," Driver sighed, pulling out his own cigarette. "He found her."

Driver's phone dinged. He looked at the screen, which was still full of unanswered call notifications. Driver vaguely remembered the phone going off while his men collapsed from the drugs in their saltshaker. He opened the message. It was from a guy manning one of his houses in west Gloucester.

5-0, the message read.

Cops had arrived.

Driver sent a thumbs-up. Let the sheriff search the house. Sheriff Clay Spears was a resident of the inn where Bill Robinson lived. Driver imagined the sheriff would be hitting all of his properties that day, looking for drugs or paraphernalia. News would filter soon enough to the residents who had hired Driver's crews to reclad their houses. If Driver thought his phone was blowing up now, he dreaded the calls that were to come from concerned citizens hearing rumors that their homes were being used for criminal activity.

"This Bulger woman," Driver said, "is the biggest pain in my ass I've had in decades."

The men nearby listened, nodding, wanting to smirk but unsure if it was safe to. Driver bent and searched the Spitts boy's pockets for his belongings. He found a wallet in his back pocket, but nothing else.

A footstep in the woods behind them made all three men turn. Driver didn't pull his gun. He didn't need to. Both his men had the woman in the sights of their pistols far quicker than he ever could. He didn't recognize the good-looking Hispanic woman approaching with her hands up, palms out. But the buzzcut and the fact that she'd managed to get within ten feet of them without being heard said to Driver she was either military or a cop.

"I come in peace," she called out, offering a pained smile.

"Who the hell are you?" Driver asked.

"I'm a friend," Karli Breecher said. "I want something from inside the inn just as badly as you do."

CHAPTER FIFTY-TWO

CLAY SPEARS SEEMED filled with foreboding even before I'd explained my and Susan's plan to lure Shauna Bulger into the boathouse on the bay. The sheriff leaned against a pillar by a red kayak with his huge arms folded, watching me skeptically, trying to find an out. Susan perched on a workbench near him, chewing her nails. The silence while Clay contemplated our proposition was punctuated by small waves that whispered through the creaking boards at our feet. It was a beautiful night out there in Gloucester, the water calm and black and the stars peppering the wide skies. Susan and I had called Clay, and we'd all arrived at the marina almost simultaneously, slipped into the boathouse silently to talk about our plan.

Clay had heard what we wanted to do. He did not look enthused.

"You know," Clay said, "I'm busy. It took me just about all day to track down the phone number you wanted." He sighed and looked through the windows at the setting sun. "I was managing my team and some guys I borrowed from Ipswich, searching all of Driver's properties one by one. And here I am, at the same time, asking every scumbag in a Driver Construction uniform that I come across what phone number they were using to contact Marris."

"We're really grateful, Clay," Susan said.

"Marris was a sometime prostitute," Clay went on. "A drug cook's girlfriend. She was also a known thief, in and out of jail all the time for hocking stolen goods. You know how many phone numbers she's had in the last month? At least five. All burners. All untraceable."

"You're a saint, Clayton Spears." I nodded.

"Now that I finally have the number," Clay said, "I know that, according to you guys, it's probably the phone number that Shauna Bulger is using to contact Norman Driver."

"It makes sense," Susan said. "We're guessing Shauna would have found the phone on Marris's body. It would have had Driver's number in it."

"So, what I don't get," Clay said, "is why I shouldn't just put a trace on the number and locate Shauna Bulger myself."

"Because our plan is better," I said. "It's safer."

"It's *safer*?" Clay squinted.

"Yes," I pleaded. "Look. If you track Shauna down and try to approach her with a bunch of sheriffs, she might fire on you. She's really unpredictable right now. She's hell-bent on killing Norman Driver. If you find her, or a member of the public spots her and calls it in, someone could get hurt in a shootout or god knows what else. The best thing we can do right now is take care of this ourselves, Clay. Quietly and carefully."

Clay looked at Susan, tapping one stubby finger on his biceps, his scowl heavy.

"We don't have a lot of time for you to ponder this, Clay," Susan said gently. "If Driver gets to Shauna first, we're in big trouble. We don't know if he had contacts within the police who would do the exact same thing for him—track the phone to find her. And if Shauna dumps Marris's phone, our whole plan falls in a heap. We need to do this now. Right now."

Clay looked at me, his scowl collapsing into a defeated pout.

"Why do I have to hit you?" he asked me. "Why can't Susan do it?"

"Because she's my girlfriend, buddy," I said, smiling despite myself. "It's harder for her."

"You sure?" Clay asked. "I've heard you two argue over who folds the laundry."

Susan and I laughed. Clay took the zip ties off the workbench by Susan and heaved a huge sigh.

CHAPTER FIFTY-THREE

SHAUNA STOPPED THE car at the side of the road and turned the engine off. The gently descending evening sun only touched the outer trees of the woods on Norman Driver's property. Beyond them, Shauna could see only blackness. While the front of Driver's land, with the long driveway and the towering oak trees, was clear, the back half seemed dense. She wondered if there were bodies buried here. Shauna couldn't see Norman Driver bringing the victims of his drug trade to his own home for disposal, those nosy cops, dutiful citizens, or junkies about to flip that presented him with problems. But, knowing what he had done to Georgette Winter-Lee, perhaps there were other kinds of bodies here. Gloucester had only been Driver's home for a year or so. Had the same urge that had driven him to attack Georgette taken hold of him here, or was she his only ghost? Shauna didn't know.

She planned to find out.

The rifle lay on the seat beside her, the shotgun in the trunk, where she had placed it after killing the boy in the woods. She supposed she would need both, having only vague plans about what she would do when she got to Driver's home. If he was away, she'd lie in wait for him. If he was there, she hoped to prolong whatever scenario unfolded. Make him sorry. Make him confess things. Humiliate him again and enjoy herself.

She turned and reached into the back of the car, tested the lid of the box that contained the evidence that had the potential to bury Driver. It was shut tight.

She had popped open the driver's side door with two bullet holes in it and was about to step out when Marris's phone buzzed in the glove compartment. Shauna slid back into the car.

On the screen, a photograph. It was of her friend, Bill Robinson. He was lying slumped against the wall of an old, wood-paneled room. His lip was split, blood running in a steady stream from his mouth onto the chest of his white shirt. Shauna saw that his wrists were bound in front of him with thin black plastic zip ties.

A text message followed the photograph.

Twenty minutes, or I put a bullet in his head.

The number wasn't the one she knew to be Driver's, but she figured the text had to be from him. Shauna exhaled, heard the shuddering of her frightened breath. Another message came, this one with a pin dropped at the center of a map. She tapped the pin and the map spun out, revealing a blue, glowing path. She had a decision to make now. Follow directions into what was almost certainly an ambush and try to save her friend. Or lie here in wait for Driver, and sacrifice Bill. Shauna put the phone down on the dashboard and pressed her head against the steering wheel.

The old Shauna, the woman she had been until two days ago, when two intruders came into her house and put a gun in her face, would have rushed to Bill's aid no matter the consequences. But she was a new person now. Someone who got revenge. Someone who ran from capture. Someone who had killed, coldly and deliberately. What did friendship mean to this new woman?

She put a hand on the key in the ignition but didn't turn it.

CHAPTER FIFTY-FOUR

NICK SAT ACROSS the living room from Vinny at the inn. He'd known guys in the service who looked the way Vinny looked now. The old gangster was gesticulating with his battered hands, his speech steadily growing faster as he described the scene at the diner. Vinny's eyes were distant. Relishing. Reliving. Nick had played attentive audience to dozens of men like Vinny in his time. Proud killers. He was glad that Angelica and the woman guest with the kid had all moved to a motel in town to get away from the trouble at the inn. The way Vinny was talking would give normal people nightmares.

"So I'm tryin' not to look," Vinny was saying, his smile so wide Nick could see his blackened molars. "But I'm watchin' the plates, and I'm hoping these are the kind of rednecks who just add salt to everythin', you know? Without even tasting. And what do you know? Soon as the plate hits the table—*bam*. I got the one guy. He's *loadin'* up his plate. *Shicka-shicka-shicka.*"

Vinny made a shaking motion with an imaginary saltshaker. Nick rested his chin on his knuckles on the arm of his chair.

"And it's like I said." Vinny shrugged. "I don't know how strong this stuff is. I bought it for way too much from a pair of truckers, and they couldn't tell me. Every time they take this stuff, they said, it's a roll of the dice. Trial and error. Life and death. Kind of exciting, huh? And I mean, that's the whole point, right? Nobody knows what they're buying or what they're dealing. So I'm thinkin': *These guys are either gonna shrivel up like a pair of slugs or they're gonna get a little giggly like teenagers on mushrooms.* Who knows?"

"How long did it take them to die?" Nick asked, his tone even.

"The guy in the booth? He went out like a light," said Vinny, snapping his fingers. "But the one guy who Bill caught before he hit the floor: I don't know. I didn't stick around. When I left, Bill was trying out CPR. Man, Driver's face when the guy across from him started coughing."

Vinny laughed, pretended to choke, grabbing at his throat and rolling his eyes up in his head. Nick didn't move. Didn't smile. The older man hadn't seemed to notice that he was the only person enjoying this conversation.

Nick wasn't having fun but he wasn't angry. He felt numb, looking out at the darkness beyond the French doors. He wondered how long it had been since he'd become the kind of person who could sit listening to a man laugh about murders he had committed that day like he was reciting a beloved family anecdote. It felt like a lifetime. Nick couldn't find the lines that divided just and evil actions anymore, good and bad deaths, times to be silent and times to speak. So he just listened. He looked at his phone on the coffee table before him, thought about the recording it contained.

He'd just put into words memories that he'd kept inside since 2010.

And as he'd voiced them aloud, he'd experienced the same unquestioning paralysis. Like he'd already felt all that he could possibly feel about what happened in Afghanistan, and now he was hollowed out.

Nick heard Effie's footsteps on the stairs, and then she was in the doorway, pointing frantically toward the hall and the little foyer beyond it.

He went there and recognized Breecher's silhouette beyond the stained glass panels in the door. He opened it, feeling Effie crowding at his back, the enormous rifle in her arms pointed at the ceiling. Nick looked Breecher over, gave Effie the nod that it was OK.

"You gotta go," Nick said. He held a hand up before Breecher could speak. "It's not safe here. We've got all kinds of trouble headed this way from Bill's end of things and... it's just not a good time."

"I'm sorry, Nick," Breecher said.

For a moment Nick thought she must have meant about the timing. Some part of him assumed she was about to suggest they meet again in the daylight hours, when the unease that comes with night had lifted, and she could try to convince him that she wasn't lying to him. But another, deeper part of him was unsurprised as he heard glass breaking at the back of the house. Effie's sneakers squeaked on the floor behind him as she swiveled, desperately trying to decide if she should respond to the intruders at the back or stay with the intruder at the front.

Nick looked down at the pistol Breecher drew from her jacket pocket. She leveled it at his chest.

CHAPTER FIFTY-FIVE

THEY BACKED UP. From where he stood at the junction of the foyer and the dining room doorway, Nick saw what had to be Norman Driver and two of his men enter through the kitchen, glass crunching on their boots, the hard-headed construction boss at the lead with a pistol in his grip. Effie leveled the rifle at the approaching trio, but Nick put a hand on top of it, halting her. There was no telling whether Effie had calculated the odds of their situation or not. Maybe she had, and she was willing for them both to be blown apart rather than submit to Breecher, Driver, and the two crewmen. She was younger, hot-headed, and trigger happy. Nick took the rifle from Effie's hands and leaned it against the umbrella stand. He was silent and calm, hands on Effie's shoulders, as Breecher flicked her gun and motioned for them to follow Driver and his guys into the sitting room.

Vinny was motionless in his wheelchair, only his white-knuckled grip on the armrests indicating he felt anything more than he would watching another visitor to the house enter the room. Driver's men drew the blinds. Breecher pushed Nick and Effie into the corner of the room while Driver leveled his pistol at Vinny's head.

"You got any more talking to do, old man?" Driver asked the ancient gangster in the chair.

"Yeah, sure." Vinny smiled. "I want to tell you this: It's gonna be busy down there in hell. You might think you'll slip by me in the crowd. But you won't. I'm gonna be there, holding the door open for you."

Driver smiled. Vinny grinned back.

"I know I won't be waitin' long," Vinny said.

Nick and Effie gripped each other as Driver fired. Vinny's head bucked and he sagged dead in his chair.

CHAPTER FIFTY-SIX

NICK DIDN'T KNOW if his knees gave out and he sank onto the couch beside Effie, or if Breecher pushed him down. The room seemed to be turning slowly, ticking back on itself like the hands of a broken clock. Effie's hand gripped his own, drenched in sweat. On the coffee table near where he had been sitting earlier, his phone began buzzing. Probably Bill. The silence in the room and the smell of the gunshot pulled him out of himself, away from the screaming of his mind at Vinny lying dead in his chair.

Driver turned the gun on Nick as his two men left the room, heading for the stairs.

"The weirdo in the room upstairs," Driver said. "We're gonna bring him down. That leaves Bulger, Robinson, the girlfriend, and the bitch who talks too much. Where are they?"

"I don't know," Nick said carefully. He lifted his eyes to Breecher. "Bill and Susan have been out looking for Shauna

Bulger. She was never in this with us. She borrowed Bill's car. That's all."

"Save it," Driver snapped.

"Angelica got a room at a motel in town," Nick continued, the words feeling like razorblades in his throat. "She didn't feel safe here."

"What about guests?" Breecher said. "You mentioned there was a mother and child. Overnighters."

Nick shrugged. "Clay moved them. He's...he's got a thing with the mother. A romantic thing."

Breecher and Driver looked at each other. There were footsteps on the stairs, and Driver's two men shoved Neddy Ives into the room. The tall, hollow-eyed man folded himself carefully into a little armchair across the room from where Nick and Effie sat.

Driver smiled at Neddy Ives. He nudged the man beside him, gesturing to Neddy with his pistol.

"This is the joker with the hand grenade," Driver said. He cocked his head, took Neddy Ives in. "I bet you felt real powerful, didn't you? Making me walk all the way to my truck holding it, just so you'd give me the pin back. I bet you thought you'd made a real pussy out of me."

Neddy Ives said nothing. Driver lifted his gun.

"Who's the pussy now?" he asked. He fired. Neddy Ives collapsed and fell off his chair.

Effie tried to leap off the couch, to throw herself at Driver. Nick had to wrap his arms around her middle to contain her, gritting his teeth as she twisted and dragged her heels down his shins.

"Don't be stupid. Effie! Don't be stupid!" Nick cried.

"Yeah, same goes for you," Breecher said and turned to Driver, gesturing to the lanky man writhing in pain on the floor in front of his armchair. "Don't be stupid. You keep going and you're going to kill everyone in the goddamn house and leave us with no leverage at all. We need two things: your box and my money. And it's going to take some bargaining to achieve that."

"So start bargaining," Driver said, turning to Nick. In his eyes, Nick could see the mechanical turnings of a soldier's mind as they moved through battle; calculating, assessing, emotionlessly weighing one move against the next. He knew there was no compassion there. No room for subtleties, nuance. Nick knew that if he didn't respond correctly now, he was going to die. There was plenty of leverage left in Effie and Neddy Ives. "Start with the box," Driver said. "Shauna Bulger must've stashed it here. I know she did. It would have been the safest option for her. So where is it?"

"I. Don't. Know," Nick insisted. "You can trust me on that. I don't know. And you'd be wasting precious time trying to hurt me or my friends to get me to say anything else."

Driver clicked his teeth hard. He tightened his grip on the gun in his hand and glanced off toward the other rooms, the dark and silent hall and the yawning corridors upstairs. He seemed to decide, as Nick hoped he would, that he was wasting time here. That now he'd made entry into the house, the most efficient use of his time would be to search for what he wanted, find it, and leave before their window of access was closed by police arriving or residents returning home.

Driver nodded at Breecher, and he and his men left. After a few seconds, Nick heard drawers being ripped open in the dining room, shelves and cabinets smashing to the ground. The windows of the old house shook as furniture was overturned and shoved against walls. All the while Breecher watched him.

"Where's the money, Nick?" Breecher asked.

"Come on," Nick sighed. "Don't you think Driver's just going to pop you and take the money as soon as you find it? And what makes you so sure I didn't spend my entire share?"

"Because it's you." Breecher shook her head. She seemed suddenly, miserably tired. "You're the bleeding heart. The moral goddamn compass. That's the whole reason Dorrich and Master didn't let you in on the plan in the desert. Because you'd never have gone along with it. I'll be shocked if you've spent a single dollar of that money in all these years, Nick."

"You're right." He nodded. "I haven't. It's all still there."

"Where?" Breecher almost spat the word at him. "Tell me where, so we can end this."

He remained silent. Nick could feel Effie staring at him, trying to put his story all together. On the floor, Neddy Ives was gripping the carpet with one hand, trying to breathe through the pain.

"Where is it?" Breecher demanded again.

He just stared at her, and she must have seen something in his eyes that made her crumble. She turned away, and that was risky. Nick felt Effie's whole body tense, ready to leap at the other woman. But he held her back, shook his head. Their time would come. He could hear drawers of utensils smashing down on the kitchen tiles. Breecher seemed angry at herself for letting her emotions get the better of her. For letting her mechanical mind wander. Nick knew it was time to learn the truth.

"You knew, didn't you," he said. "About their plan."

Breecher nodded.

"I overheard them talking at the base," she said. "Dorrich and Master." Breecher drew a long breath, let it out slow. "I came back from chow unexpectedly and I heard them running through the steps. Divert off a routine patrol. Hit the house. Kill the family. Shoot up the vehicles." She shook her head, bitter. "What I overheard must have been an early version. They must have come up with a Plan B later on. Because what happened in the desert that night wasn't what they said they were going to do."

"So what was the original plan?" Nick asked.

"They were going to kill you," Breecher said.

Nick swallowed hard, trying to keep his mind in order. He couldn't react to this news now. Couldn't let it carry him away into the blessed rage that was waiting to envelop him.

"And you were OK with that?" Nick's voice broke as he tried to get the words out.

"I was OK with that," Breecher said, her gaze locked on his. "I could see their way of thinking. You dying out there would make the massacre look legit, and it would mean we'd each get a third of the money, not a quarter. And it would have made my own plan easier overall."

"Your own plan?" Nick said.

"I planned to take Dorrich and Master out as soon as they'd finished with you. That's why I didn't tell them that I knew what was going to happen. I was going to be the sole survivor," Karli Breecher said. "Winner takes all."

CHAPTER FIFTY-SEVEN

SHAUNA STOPPED THE car on a quiet curve of road north of the marina, stepped out into the long grass, and watched the cold lights, the stillness. Shauna saw no police cruisers. No construction vehicles. The place was lit up like a shopping mall: boat lights, road lights, markers on the pier, and lamps overhanging the closed office, all blazing yellow and icy-white into the evening.

Something told Shauna that the situation was wrong, but she had no choice now. Bill needed her. He was the one strand connecting her to the earth, a string stopping her from being swept away into dark winds. Because she had known, she supposed, that there would be other Norman Drivers in her future. That Pooney and Marris were the beginning, and the boy in the forest was a continuation, and Driver was going to be her next in an infinite line of nexts. Only Bill Robinson, and the photograph of him lying beaten and bound, had managed to ground her. She took the rifle from the car, locked the vehicle, and began to walk.

She took a shortcut off the access road and crouched in the bushes, her knees popping, watching for movement. Waves of exhaustion swept over her, the last couple of days like a cross-country journey awakening muscles she hadn't used in years, angering worn-down joints and disturbing her equilibrium. She told herself to push on. There was plenty of motion up there. Boats bobbling. Flags and sails being caressed by the breeze. By the time Shauna crept down the embankment and halfway along the little beach beside the marina in the blackness, her eyes were watering from the brightness of the lights. It only occurred to her that this had been the plan all along when she heard the hammer of a revolver click back right beside her ear. She turned, the rifle frozen in her hands, but saw only explosions of green and red light as her vision tried to recover from the lights of the marina.

"Put it down," a voice said.

Shauna lowered her rifle to the cold, damp sand. The cloudy color in her eyes dissolved, revealing a huge, hulking man in a sheriff's uniform. She might have felt some wave of dread or shame as the big guy drew her tiny wrists behind her back and cuffed her for the first time in her life, but there was no time. She was struck instead with a gut-punch of betrayal as Bill Robinson and the girlfriend, Susan, emerged from the shadows too.

"Wow," Shauna said and shook her head. She had to smile at the cleverness of it all. She looked at the split in Bill's lip. "So who bopped you, then?"

"Clay did." Bill gestured to the sheriff. "Very reluctantly."

"Well, I wish he'd left a piece for me." Shauna spat on the ground. "You're a betrayer, Bill. A Judas."

"I'm sorry, Shauna," Bill said.

"You know this is not the way it's supposed to end," Shauna said. Her throat was tightening with rage and regret. "All you had to do was look the other way for one more night. But I guess taking the law into your own hands is a privilege that's reserved just for you, huh?"

"Let's just cool it everybody, OK?" Clay's deep voice, full of authority, quieted them all. "You guys want to be nasty to each other, you can do it on your own time. I just punched a friend and now I'm arresting a lady, and neither of those things are my idea of a good time. I don't need to hear you sniping at each other as well."

Shauna gazed at Bill, shivering with fury.

"So where's the box?" the sheriff asked. "Mrs. Bulger, you gonna make my life easy and just tell me? Or are we going to do a dance back at the station for a while, first?"

"It's in the car," Shauna said. "Bill's car. I parked just around the bend there."

"Right," the sheriff said, nodding toward Bill and Susan. "Well, bad news, Bill. I'm going to have to confiscate the whole car. It's been used by Mrs. Bulger for a couple of days now in the commission of several crimes. I can't—"

"I get it." Bill held a hand up. "Don't worry. I get it."

"Come on, Mrs. Bulger." The sheriff moved her, pushing her sideways, his big hand gentle yet inescapable, an iron clamp locked around her biceps. Shauna went with him, and they walked into the darkness away from the marina. She spied the cruiser ahead, backed into a gap between dense bushes off the side of the road. Her footprints in the sand below her led nowhere, disappearing as he guided her up a set of concrete steps and onto the road.

Now the humiliation was coming on, heavier and heavier, like a series of blankets heaped onto her body. Her legs felt wobbly. She imagined the next few hours sitting in a cell, and then the inevitable meeting with a lawyer. The decision on whether to plead temporary insanity or some form of cognitive decline brought on by aging. She'd be in diapers in a locked ward within a month. Even faster than Henry had planned.

The sheriff guided her toward the cruiser. Shauna looked up at the barely visible stars, then at him. The big man was walking beside her now, her arm in one hand, the rifle in the other.

He had a kindly face. She'd seen regret flash there as Bill mentioned the punch to the mouth, the real and genuine squeamishness of a man who didn't like violence of any sort. An old-fashioned, warmhearted man who tended to think and expect the best of people. A man who put on the uniform every day because he was full of goodness, and it was bubbling up and over the rim of the saucepan, and he just didn't know what to do with it all.

This was a man who could be deceived, Shauna thought.

CHAPTER FIFTY-EIGHT

ON THE BEACH, Susan drew me back to myself, watching with guilt as Clay led Shauna away in cuffs. She ran a hand through my hair, and I was sucked back into this moment. Despite the pain and exhaustion there was an almost romantic lifting in my heart. The marina bathed us in a yellow glow, and the wind was tousling Susan's hair, and I told myself that no matter what had happened in the days before or what was coming, I had this moment. I had done my duty, and though angry and damaged, I knew Shauna would be locked up safe. My girlfriend kissed her fingertip and pressed it gently to my busted lip.

"Poor baby." She smiled.

"Baby? Are you kiddin'?" I snorted. "I took that punch like a man. It must have been hot as hell to watch. I don't know how you contained yourself."

"It was…" She thought, then conceded, "It was a strangely

evocative display. I'll struggle to contain myself at least until we get home."

I took out my phone and looked at the screen. When I saw that Nick had not returned my call, a knot of fear balled in my chest. I'd tried to call him almost an hour earlier, and he hadn't answered. While I'd waited for Shauna to come to the marina, my phone had been on silent.

I dialed again, stood listening to the tone, then gave up, figuring he was catching some downtime before his first watch of the house.

"Let's go," I said and wrapped an arm around Susan. "All I want to do is catch a couple hours of shut-eye before I go on watch."

CHAPTER FIFTY-NINE

KARLI BREECHER'S EYES blazed. Nick looked at his former teammate, friend, and lover, and felt cold inside, like the last embers of a fire were being unceremoniously stomped out. Breecher's grip was firm on the pistol, steady and tight. A single droplet of sweat would have given him hope. A tendon straining. But it was that dry, controlled grip on the gun that told him everything he needed to know, even before she spoke.

"I was OK with you dying in the desert," she said. "And I'm OK with it now."

"I believe you," Nick said.

"I'm broke," Breecher continued. She took a moment to look at Vinny, dead in the chair; Neddy, writhing on the floor; Effie, tucked into Nick's side. "I blew through my share of the money years ago. You know how it goes. I'd never had real money before. So I handed some out to family and friends. Spent some having a good time. Tried to chase my losses with bad investments. The rest drizzled away. So I got desperate. I figured I'd hit Dorrich first because he was going to be the biggest challenge. I needed to be fresh, ready for anything. But I spooked him on the approach. He left that message for me that he was being tailed. He knew someone was after him. He hid the money. When I finally came for him, he wouldn't give it up."

"He was always so hard." Nick smiled sadly.

"Never said a word." Breecher shook her head, hardly listening. "Even when I backed him into the tub. Even when it was clear, this was the end: tell me or die."

Nick watched her shake the regret off like it was dust on her shoulders.

"So now I'm even more desperate," Breecher said, composed again. "You understand?"

"I do," Nick said. "But you don't need to think about the money right now."

"What?" Breecher squinted at him.

"You've got bigger problems," Nick said.

Finally, that bead of sweat. Just one, at her hairline. She swiped it away. Nick relished in delicious, tenuous hope. He heard something thump in a room upstairs, a mattress being flipped off a bedframe, maybe, or a dresser being shoved over.

"The phone on the coffee table." He pointed. "Pick it up."

Breecher didn't move.

"You need two things," Nick said. "First, you need me to give you a code to unlock the phone. Then you need me to give you the password to my Twitter account."

"Why the fuck do I need to get into your Twit—"

Breecher's mouth fell open. She blinked at him, more sweat beading now on the smooth skin over her left collarbone.

Nick didn't need to explain it. But he did, anyway.

"I made a confession video," he said. "I tagged all the right people. It's scheduled to go live on the internet at seven o'clock."

Breecher's head whipped around, looking for a clock. She stepped back and almost fell over the coffee table. She caught sight of the black marble clock on the mantelpiece that read 6:25 p.m.

"You—" She picked up his phone, shook it in her hand as though to weigh it, to measure if the device itself was real. "No. This is bullshit. You couldn't have known we were coming here tonight. You wouldn't have set this up. You wouldn't have stayed in the house."

"Are you going to bank on that?" Nick asked.

Breecher's chest heaved with panicked breath. Nick winced as she raised the pistol and pointed it at Effie.

"The code," Breecher said. "Now, or I'll start putting holes in her."

"No," Nick said.

He looked at Effie, expecting her features to be taut with horror and betrayal. He was surprised by the smile he saw there. But he supposed Effie was calculating, as Breecher was calculating, the many exit routes now closed to the woman holding the gun on them. Because she couldn't kill Effie and Neddy Ives now, or Nick wouldn't give her the codes. She couldn't flee, because leaving Nick and his friends to Driver's men would be the same as killing them, and in thirty-five minutes her world would be destroyed no matter how far she ran.

When Breecher spoke, her teeth flashed brightly between her lips. She sneered the single word with so much malice, Nick winced.

"Go," she said to Effie.

Effie didn't wait. She dashed to Neddy's side, swung the tall man's arm around her shoulders, and helped him up. They limped out the door. Nick uttered six numbers, his whole body alive with exhilaration as he heard Effie slip out the rear kitchen door to safety.

Breecher's eyes were downcast to the phone screen, her gun still trained on Nick's face.

"You logged out of Twitter," she said.

"I did."

"So give me the password," she said.

"No," Nick said.

"I let them go," Breecher said. She was panting hard, and Nick could see the little girl in her for the first time. The child who had grown up under a star-spangled military father. The one who was an adult now, fearing the disgrace that would follow: the discharge, the prison time, the disownment. "Give. Me. The. Password."

"The moment I do that, you'll call those men back in here," Nick said, glancing toward the door. "And I'm as good as dead. You need to walk me out of this house alive. Then I'll—"

He had no time to finish. Breecher walked off, disappearing through the foyer to the dining room. He should have run, but, drawn by curiosity or simply by fear, he followed her instead. Driver's two men were in the room; one ripping books off a shelf in the back living area, the other crouched and poring over a pile of debris under a window. Nick could hear footsteps on the old boards overhead. It sounded like Driver was upstairs.

In three seconds, maybe less, Breecher had walked into the

room and shot both of Driver's men in the head. One in the back of the skull, the other in the temple as he turned toward the noise. Before Nick could react, bodily or emotionally, Breecher was with him again, the gun in his ribs as she shoved him toward the front door of the house.

"Go," she said again.

CHAPTER SIXTY

CLAYTON SPEARS WONDERED quietly if the little old woman he'd just put in the back of his cruiser was the oldest person he'd ever had back there. There wasn't much crime after a person hit seventy—either because they were dead, too dumb to stay out of jail, or too smart not to go legit by then. Sure, he'd had people of a certain vintage in the vehicle. Only a month earlier, he'd been cruising around town on a hellishly rainy day and had spotted an older man getting drowned on his way back from the supermarket. He'd given him a ride, but in the front passenger seat. The back was for the perps. He watched Shauna Bulger in the rearview mirror as he radioed in for updates. She seemed to be panting softly like an exhausted bird. He assumed this was her first ever arrest. Guilt clawed at his insides.

"Sheriff Spears back on the line," he sighed into the radio. "Dispatch, what's the lay of the land? Over."

"It's really kicking off here tonight, Sheriff!" the radio

crackled. "Boss, we got a possible drag race in Dogtown, minor assault in a hotel on Washington Street, couple of reports of prowlers over the north district."

"I'll be right in," Clay said. He tossed the mic back at the receiver. "OK, Mrs. Bulger. I'm gonna need you to get your mind around what's gonna happen over the next few hours. Seems like we got some dramas in town. The last couple of days have been madness all over Gloucester."

He started the engine and pulled out, taking the curved road around the marina toward where she had said she'd parked Bill's car.

"We're gonna get this box of evidence you've been toting around, and then I'm gonna have to drop you and it at the station," Clay said. He straightened in his seat, making the leather groan unflatteringly. "I would have liked to come in and process you. Get you into a nice comfy holding cell of your own. Maybe see if I could rustle up a cup of tea. But it's not that kind of night, ma'am. So you'll be stuck in the bullpen, I'm afraid, with the riffraff."

Only a cough sounded from the back seat in response. He glanced in the mirror. Shauna Bulger was red faced, still panting.

"Are you feeling all right?" Clay asked.

"Have you got any water up there?" she rasped. Clay started to get a sinking feeling in his belly.

"Uh, sure. Yeah. Let me..." He spotted Bill's car up ahead. "Let me just pull over here."

By the time Clay had pulled over and slipped out of the driver's seat, Mrs. Bulger was on her side, curled on up on the faded leather bench seat like she'd been sucker punched. Her rattling coughing filled the car as he tore open the door.

"Oh man," Clay said and lifted her out of the car like a doll and set her on the roadside. "Oh Jesus! What's goin' on?"

"My chest hurts." She sucked in shallow sips of air.

Clay had the cuffs off her wrists faster than he'd ever released a suspect in his life. The guilt was now thumping in his eardrums like a sonic beat.

He was bending over her tiny body, trying to roll her into the recovery position, when Mrs. Bulger's arm whipped around, her hand mashing a palm full of dirt into his wide, concerned eyes. Clay grabbed at his face, his yelp of surprise morphing into a yelp of pain as he felt her drive her knee into his crotch.

Clay hit the gravel at the side of the road like a bag of bricks. He gripped her ankle briefly as Shauna Bulger slipped away. He was only just clearing the dirt from his eyes when he was blinded again by the dust her tires threw up as she sped off in Bill's car.

CHAPTER SIXTY-ONE

I RECOGNIZED THE distinct headlights of Effie's Mustang zooming through the night as we drove back toward the inn in Susan's car. Susan must have seen her too, because she swiveled fast in her seat as I did, catching a mere glimpse of our friend in the other car. My heart lurched as my phone buzzed in my pocket. I pulled it out and read the message, every typed letter sending zings of terror over my skin.

BG x 4 @ inn w N

When I looked up, Susan's eyes were full of dread.

"Bad guys at the inn with Nick," I deciphered. "Four of them."

I didn't have to tell Susan not to approach the house in the car. My hands were trembling as I got out. Susan's breath in the night air was misting gold under one of few streetlamps lining the woods.

"We call Clay," Susan said. "We call in everyone we can."

"I can try," I said. I dialed and started walking. Susan was right by my side, unquestioning of my decision to head toward the inn on foot without waiting for backup.

We couldn't rely on help coming our way. If we were going to help Nick, we'd have to do it ourselves.

CHAPTER SIXTY-TWO

IT SEEMED EVERY light in the inn was on. Susan and I had come through the woods and along the narrow beach to the property, hoping to shelter from sight by the cars parked along the tree line. We crouched by the bumper of Vinny's sedan and watched the house for movement, but there was none. Blinds were drawn on the lower floors, and the porch doors were hanging open, being pushed back and forth gently in the breeze. I looked over at the open doors of the garage and counted cars along with those parked at the tree line. Angelica, Clay, and Effie all had cars missing from the lot, as well as April Leeler and her son, whose bronze van had been parked at the end of the garage. Neddy Ives didn't own a vehicle. Aside from Vinny's sedan and Nick's car, there was only one other car in the lot; a sleek black car parked right by the edge of the porch.

It took me a moment to recognize the rental.

"Karli Breecher," I said. Susan looked grave but nodded. Her instincts were as good as if not better than mine, and to her, too, it all made sense. Which meant that Breecher was either inside the house with Nick and in danger from the four "bad guys" Effie had mentioned...

Or she was one of the bad guys.

It's a hell of a thing to sneak into your own home. To try to be silent, and watchful and alert for danger, while at every step, signs of violence present themselves. There was glass on the pavement outside the laundry window. The frame bashed and shattered, muddy footprints on the windowsill. The mind wants to respond to each sign of defilement with a singular burst of rage. That someone would break *my* window. That someone would knock over *my* shelves. By the time Susan and I reached the hall, it was clear that someone had been injured and had fled—perhaps through the kitchen door. There were blood spatters, dark and heavy, on the floorboards. Smears on the walls. The kitchen was trashed. We stood and listened at the kitchen doorway, systematically discounting each individual chime of the strange music the house always played. Pipes creaking. Roof beams relaxing out of the warmth of the day, and the branches of those trees that could reach the house brushing against the weatherboards. Susan touched my wrist, and I met her questioning eyes. She and I seemed to understand simultaneously how bad this was, the silence. There were supposed to be at least five people here.

I slipped into the dining room and covered my mouth with my hand to stifle a shocked groan at the sight of Vinny slumped back in his wheelchair, a bullet in his head. His color told me he was dead, but I went to him anyway, put a finger into his cooling jugular and felt nothing. Someone had been lying, bleeding badly, by the foot of an armchair. Susan appeared in the doorway, her face a sickly shade of gray even before she'd taken in the sight of Vinny in the chair.

She had to gulp a couple of times to get the words out.

"Two dead in the dining room," she whispered.

I had the same kind of trouble getting the words out, myself. "Is it Nick?"

She shook her head. "Don't know them. Driver's guys, looks like."

"Breecher was here," I said, my mind racing. "And Driver. At the same time."

Susan and I stared at each other, each trying to understand. I didn't like the coincidental nature of it, the idea that Driver and his men might have been waiting in the forest for something to draw Effie's attention away from her watchpoint, and that very thing arriving conveniently in the form of Karli Breecher.

I didn't have time to think longer on that awful scenario, to try to fit the pieces together, before my life nearly ended then and there—in the doorway of the dining room in my own home, my girlfriend looking at me, my possessions and my world in tatters. But the bullet Driver fired from the end of the hall only nicked my left ear. The pain came afterward. Before I had a sense of what was happening, I was thrown sideways into the wall, the whole side of my head throbbing like I'd been punched.

Susan ducked instinctively, turned and whipped out her own gun. Two more shots peppered into the floorboards at my feet. Susan fired a couple of shots at Driver as he disappeared around a corner, heading for the stairwell.

We pursued.

CHAPTER SIXTY-THREE

SUSAN PAUSED WITH me at the base of the stairs. I heard signs of life in the house for the first time since we had arrived. I was surprised at Driver's stealth for his stockiness. As he retreated upstairs, I heard a floorboard or two creak. A piece of furniture moved slightly on a rug, pushed aside. Susan and I waited, silently plotting, trying to breathe through the adrenaline spike that the quick gunfight had inspired in both of us.

The stairwell was the most dangerous way for us to get upstairs. All Driver had to do was turn the corner and shoot down at us. We would have no cover whatsoever. Susan stepped close to me, her breath hot and damp on my face.

"We need to draw him away from the top of the stairs," she said. "You go back out through the laundry, climb the drainpipe, and get in through one of the upstairs rooms. Draw him to you, and I'll come up behind him."

"He'll see a move like that coming a mile away," I said and

shook my head. "If he hears a noise up there in one of the rooms, he'll be sure it's me."

"Not if he thinks we're both still down here," Susan said. She pointed, and I peeked carefully around the corner of the stairwell. I could just see the tip of Driver's shoe at the edge of the baseboard. It moved, and I looked up in time to see him duck back around the corner, having taken a moment to do the same thing—trying to catch a glimpse of the enemy.

I slipped my shoe off and crouched, positioning the toe of the shoe at the very edge of the baseboard so that it was visible to Driver from his position at the top of the stairs. As I backed away, Susan dashed across the bottom of the stairs. Two pops arrived from upstairs, the bullets puncturing the wall beside us, narrowly missing her as she arrived on the other side of the doorway. I heard the boards creek upstairs again as Driver leaned out to see if he'd hit her. Susan glanced at me and smiled, nodding.

For all Driver knew, we were both still positioned at the edges of the doorway at the bottom of the stairs.

I crept back through the eerily silent house to the laundry and slipped out the door into the night.

CHAPTER SIXTY-FOUR

NICK JONES WALKED through the dark forest. Between the whispers of his footsteps on the dry leaves came Breecher's footsteps from somewhere not far behind him and to the right, so that the rhythmic beat of their journey kept a quick pace in his mind. Crickets and night birds abruptly stopped their sounds as the two humans made their way further and further into the blackness.

The sea appeared beyond the reach of the forest, seeming to glow. No wave sounds. Nick watched it as he walked, trying not to think about the gun at his back.

"OK," Breecher said. "We're out. Tell me the password."

Nick stopped walking. He turned around, expecting the lights of the house to be a speck in the distance. But they were nowhere in sight. He decided he must have walked farther than it seemed he did, his mind twisted by worry and fear.

"If I tell you, you'll just shoot me," Nick said. "I'll give you the password when I'm safe."

"That doesn't work!" Breecher barked, throwing her hands up. "What—I'm supposed to just let you go and I—I just *hope* you'll shout the password back at me? Tell me the fucking password! We're running out of time!"

"You'll just have to trust me," Nick said. "You have to trust that I don't want the world to know what we did any more than you do."

"Oh, I don't know if *that's* true." Breecher snorted bitterly. "Part of me thinks you'd really love wallowing for the rest of your life in a military prison. You've been a miserable self-involved dope ever since that guy in the cornfield."

Nick balled his fists as he remembered. They'd been approaching a hostile village south of Bari Qol. He'd only been on the ground three weeks. He was young, unscarred, still flinching at the sound of gunfire. Nick and Master had been working their way through a cornfield, side by side, when they'd happened upon a man in dusty jeans and a sweat-stained shirt. Forties maybe. The guy had frozen at the sight of them, a stick in one hand and a ball cap in the other, just a man taking a stroll through a cornfield on a nice clear morning. Nick's training had kicked in. There was no decision. No weighing the danger of escorting him out of the red zone, only to have him come back and warn the villagers of their approach.

Nick had shot the man in the head.

It was his first kill ever. A civilian. Nick had held it together through the occupation of the village, back to the base, out onto patrol. He'd finally cracked in front of Breecher, only her, in the quiet of an empty mess hall in the early hours of the morning after his patrol had returned.

Nick had always believed his first kill would be the thing

that shut off the emotions, the pain. His "blooding." War was supposed to be easy after that. But instead, that had been the moment he became lost. Irredeemable.

"The password," Breecher growled. "Tell me."

Nick said nothing. She lowered the gun and shot him in the kneecap.

The pain didn't register at first. It was so extreme, so overwhelming, that his mind simply blocked it. Nick went down, clutching the limb, warm blood rushing between his fingers. Then the pain rippled around his body like a shockwave, a plunging into icy water. It stole his breath so that he gasped against the grass and leaves for a moment before he had enough air to wail.

"The password, or I'll put a bullet in the other one," Breecher said.

"OK," he breathed. "OK. OK."

He murmured the letters, the numbers. In the blackness of the night, she raised the phone and started to type. The phone bleeped as it accepted her login.

It was the moment of distraction he needed. Nick lunged sideways at her legs, defying the pain that wanted to seize every muscle in his body. Breecher fell on her backside on the forest floor, her lower legs encircled in his arms, both phone and gun flying from her hands. Nick scrambled for the pistol, dragging his injured leg behind him, Breecher's weight suddenly on his back, her fingers raking at his as he grabbed the weapon. The blood on his fingers made grip impossible. She took the gun from him easily, and he rolled over underneath her and looked up at her as she pressed the barrel to his chin.

The phone bleeped. A single high-pitched chime in the stillness of the woods.

"We didn't have to do this," she said. "You could have made it much easier on me."

"I guess I really am a glutton for punishment," Nick groaned.

The phone bleeped again.

And again.

Breecher shivered, her finger sliding in the blood on the trigger.

The phone bleeped again.

"What...what the hell is that?" she asked. Nick smiled beneath her. She got off him, holding the gun on his face as she backed toward the glowing phone screen sitting up against the base of a nearby tree. Breecher took her eyes off Nick for half a second to glance at the phone in her hand. She glimpsed all that she needed to. A mess of notifications springing up one after the other, a sea of sky-blue boxes and white birds, the phone vibrating as retweets went flying. The alerts wouldn't stop. *Ding-ding-ding-ding.*

"No," Breecher said, swallowing hard. "No. You said seven. You said *seven o'clock!*"

He listened to her panting as she put it all together. That he'd lied. That he had indeed wanted it all to come out. That he was the miserable, self-obsessed, guilt-riddled mess she'd said he was. That he'd scheduled the video to go live at 6:50 p.m., not 7 p.m., just in case. She threw the phone against a tree and came marching back to him. He felt the gun against his temple.

"You're gonna die now, Nick," Breecher said.

"Not if you still want that million dollars," Nick replied.

CHAPTER SIXTY-FIVE

NICK LISTENED, WAITING, hearing only her breathing. He knew what would come next. An enveloping *whump* as the bullet entered his brain, splitting his skull, closing him in blessed blackness. Or her voice. Her hips were on his, her legs straddling him. They'd been in this position before, a million years ago, earlier this same day. In Nick's bed. He put his hands on her thighs and remembered, relished the absurdity of it all.

"We can't go back to the house," she said finally. Relief, temporary but still delicious, washed over him, competing with the pain of his shattered knee. "They'll kill us. Driver will know I took out his guys. I—"

"You think I'm dumb enough to keep that kind of money in the house?" Nick asked.

She was silent. His head spun, pain and blood loss already dragging at him.

"You're bullshitting me," she finally said.

"You must have searched my room while I was sleeping, right?" Nick asked. "Didn't find it. So if I'd stashed it in the house, it must have been somewhere outside my own room. You think I'm that stupid? I'd leave it where it could be discovered by another guest? We have strangers coming in and out of the house every week. It would be too risky."

"You could have hidden it anywhere," Breecher said. Her voice was quivering. The phone was still dinging, insanely fast, as person after person discovered and shared Nick's confession video, the horror of what they'd done. "You...you probably stuffed the million dollars in a safe-deposit box somewhere."

"It's in these woods," Nick said.

"*Bullshit!*" she roared, jamming the gun in his jaw so hard his teeth clacked together. "Bullshit, Nick. Why in the name of God would I trust you now?"

"Because you have to!" Nick said. "You're done, Breecher. It's over. It's *over* for you! You thought you were desperate before? Try being on the run for covering up a goddamn massacre of civilians. By tomorrow morning, all our faces will be on every television screen in America. They will *never* stop looking for you."

"I don't trust you," she sobbed suddenly.

"Trust your instincts then," Nick said. "Why would I put the money in a safe-deposit box? Or a bank? Why would I put it somewhere it could be discovered by other people? I wouldn't do that. You know me. I'm not an idiot. I'd put it somewhere that I could access it quickly, in case you or Dorrich or Master ever did what I just did and told the whole world our little secret. I would put it in a bug-out bag here in these woods. You know that. It's the smartest thing to do."

She was quiet again. Calculating. Nick gripped her thighs and willed himself not to pass out.

"Is it far?" she asked.

"No."

"So show me."

"You'll have to help me up," Nick gasped.

"No way." Breecher got up and kicked him over. "You can crawl like the rat you are."

CHAPTER SIXTY-SIX

I TRIED TO remember the last time I'd scaled a drainpipe as I pulled myself, hand over hand, up the side of my house. I'd done it a few times on the job. Especially as a rookie. You always send the new guy up over the roof. New guys are disposable. I gripped the sill below Neddy Ives's window, thinking to myself how much easier it had been all those years ago. My socked feet found purchase on the window frame below, and I hauled myself up, praying Neddy's window wasn't latched. It wasn't. I inched it open, imagining the nose of Driver's gun edging around the curtain, the blast of light that would end me.

There was a clock ticking in the darkened room somewhere. I pushed the curtains all the way back to give myself some moonlight. I was stunned for a moment by what I saw.

The recluse's room was strangely orderly. I'd always imagined a hoarder's nest, but two walls were lined with filing cabinets, the drawers neatly labeled. EYEWITNESSES. CASE NOTES.

CRIME SCENE. Above the bed, the wall was completely covered with photographs, newspaper articles, little pink sticky notes. Trying to drag myself away from my curiosity, my eyes caught headlines as I headed for the door.

POLICE HUNT HUSBAND IN SHELLEY IVES DISAPPEARANCE

SPENCER EDWARD IVES SENTENCED TO THIRTY YEARS

I put my hand on the doorknob and froze. I'd been hoping to silently twist the knob, pull open the door, and check where Driver was in the hall, but as I gripped the cold brass in the dark I realized the knob was one of the old-style ones that had existed in the inn when I bought it. I'd replaced every knob the year before, but was unable to get access to Ned's room, so this one remained. It was likely squeaky or rattly, like the others had been. I had no choice but to yank open the door and hope I caught Driver by surprise, if he was indeed still standing at the top of the stairs.

I took my hand off the knob, lay flat on the floor, and tried to look down the hall through the crack in the bottom of the door. I couldn't see far enough. Taking the knob again, I filled my lungs with air, held my breath, and pulled open the door.

The door smacked against the latch holding it shut. I looked up, spotted the latch and bolt that I'd completely missed in the semidarkness, sitting at the very top of the door. It was a makeshift hidden lock, accessible from the outside, something Neddy must have installed himself. There wasn't time to do much more than fling myself sideways as Driver arrived at the other side of the door and started firing.

Gold light speared through the room from the bullet holes in the door. I fired back and heard a scream I recognized. In my terror, I saw a flash of blond hair through the bullet holes as Susan collapsed outside the door.

CHAPTER SIXTY-SEVEN

MY HANDS WERE numb as I ripped the slide bolt down, yanked open the door, and found her there. Nothing made sense. The hallway was empty except for Susan, who was crumpled against the wall, gripping the hole I'd put in her upper chest. Somehow, I was aware of the wail of horror that was coming out of me, but I was unable to stop it. I gathered up my girlfriend and held her against my chest. Down the hall, I spied the open window Driver must have slipped out of.

"I thought you were him!" I screamed. Susan's face was white and rigid with shock. Her hands were tangled in my shirt. She gave a little nod, like yes, she'd thought the same thing of me. That Driver had indeed anticipated our plan and gone into Neddy Ives's room to wait for me. I held her and growled in fury at myself, just for a second, unable to stop the regret leaving my body in a long, animalistic sound.

Then I picked her up and ran for the stairs.

CHAPTER SIXTY-EIGHT

NORMAN DRIVER EDGED his way along the side of the darkened inn, gripping a gutter with his stubby fingers and shuffling his boots along a ledge beneath the window.

He was out. He'd had enough.

Even before Bill Robinson and the blond woman had boxed him in at the top of the stairs, he'd decided it was time to cut and run. Whatever Karli Breecher's promise had been to him about a share in a million dollars cash hidden somewhere inside the Inn by the Sea, that seemed to be over. Driver had been searching a linen cupboard crowded with towels and sheets when he heard two pops on the first floor. He'd gone down and found his two men dead and Breecher and the others nowhere to be seen. Weird. He'd figured he would keep searching the upper rooms, at least until he heard tires on the road outside. But what he discovered in those rooms had only furthered his unease. The room with the obvious murder investigation going on in it had been followed by what looked like a psychopath's room: a pull-up bar, bed, gun case, and nothing else except what seemed to be an enormous rat wearing a pet collar. It was all too much. All too unexplainable. Driver had decided to hightail it, and deal with the problem of Shauna Bulger and the box of evidence another time, when he spotted Bill and the blonde sneaking up to the laundry door.

Driver got to the awning over the porch, clambered down onto the railing, and dropped to the ground. More gunshots upstairs. He didn't stick around to find out who'd shot who. He took off running through the woods, following the road but sticking off it by a few yards, just to be safe. With every step, his heartbeat eased. He was beginning to think ahead, to collect himself. The long, dark stretch of woods before him and the rhythmic beat of his boots on the earth lent itself to calm planning. He'd get out of town for a few days. Reevaluate. Sure, he'd lost guys. He'd underestimated the old woman and her loopy friends. But every boxer worth his salt took a couple of unlucky bops in the ring before they landed the big KO. It was just how fights went.

And then she was there.

It was as though his very thoughts had summoned her. Driver stopped running and stood in the dark like a rabbit in the crosshairs, gaping at her, the woman who had brought him so much trouble and pain and humiliation. She was like a ghost outlined in white moonlight, the rifle hitched against her shoulder confidently, her features set as she watched him approach like she'd known all along he was coming. Driver felt his entire body shrink into itself with terror as she dropped the forestock of the rifle into her palm, slid back the bolt with her other hand.

The *clunk* sound of the bullet locking into the chamber and the crunch of the slide bolt settling back into its housing seemed deafening to Driver. They were the brutal sounds heralding his final moments.

She didn't say anything.

She just eased her finger onto the trigger and pulled.

CHAPTER SIXTY-NINE

NOTHING HAPPENED.

Driver waited, his breath seized in his chest. The old woman lowered the weapon, clicked the trigger again, listened to something within the instrument grinding impotently. The gun had jammed. Driver released the breath trapped in his lungs and rushed forward as Shauna Bulger tried jimmying and shoving the locked slide bolt.

The rifle went off right next to Driver's ear as he plowed into her. He felt the bones of her rib cage crunching and twisting as their bodies came together, the air leaving her in a whoosh by his cheek as they hit the ground. Despite how small she was, she scrambled and twisted under him without even taking a second to recover from the blow. She was somehow unstoppable, unkillable, though her breath was rattling and her eyes bulged with pain.

Driver had heard people say their life flashes before their

eyes as they approach the edge of death. He'd always found a similar phenomenon to be true: when he took a life, the lives of those he'd already taken came to him, encouraging reminders of conquests past. There was Georgette there in the old woman's eyes, but also a string of other women and girls. Drug dealers and loan sharks who had crossed him, a couple of crooked cops who got too big for their boots. Shauna Bulger did what all the women he'd killed did: she reached for something, anything, to blind him with. He saw the handful of dirt coming and caught it, pinned her wrist to the ground. But a heavy boom and a flash in the distance distracted him, and he turned away at just the right moment, and didn't see the rock she'd clutched in her other hand coming at his face. Driver caught the rock in his left eye socket. His whole face clanged with pain, the agony seeming to shimmer and echo through him, like his bones were made of iron. He got up and stumbled back, wiping blood from his face. His boots hit the dirt road, and he turned in time to be blinded by a set of huge gold headlights only a few yards away.

CHAPTER SEVENTY

NORMAN DRIVER TOOK the full force of the car's bumper in the front of his legs. I caught a glimpse of his shocked face as I came roaring up the dirt road from the inn. I'd grabbed the keys to Vinny's sedan from a hook in the hall. The car was old and powerful and had a lot of weight behind it. Susan screamed in the passenger seat beside me, her strength failing and the life draining out of her, but not enough to disguise the crash from her senses. Driver's shoulder collapsed the windshield in front of us, and I heard his body tumble over the roof of the car, thumping onto the road behind. I slammed on the brakes, threw the car into park, and leaped out. But by the time I reached his body, I knew it was too late. His back was twisted unnaturally, his breathless, hairy chest exposed through his torn shirt.

I looked into the woods, spying movement. Shauna was standing there, a rifle in her hands, heaving with exertion. The urgency with which I'd moved since shooting Susan was still with me. I reached out to Shauna, even as I was backing away, retreating to the driver's seat of the car.

"Come on!" I called.

I was offering her one final out. A peaceful surrender. She could come with me and end this dark journey she had begun. Yes, it would mean jail time. It would mean facing her son, her friends, her family through the chipped and scratched glass in the prison visiting room, probably for the rest of her life. It would mean being punished for being a punisher, for taking revenge, for stepping outside the law just exactly as her husband had. I knew those were terrifying prospects for Shauna, or for anyone. But if she did not come with me now, wherever she was going could only be more frightening.

I left my hand hanging for a second, maybe two.

Shauna didn't budge.

I pulled the door of the car closed and drove away.

CHAPTER SEVENTY-ONE

NICK CRAWLED. THE sound of the phone dinging became more distant, but never slowed, a one-note piano tune stuttering through the night. In time he stopped and gripped his shattered knee, bit down against the pain for long moments as Breecher stood by silently, only part of her silhouette visible against the glowing ocean. He could hear the waves now. Tiny, three- or four-inch-high slaps of white foam illuminated in the moonlight. He stopped in sight of the tree.

He'd picked it because it stood alone. A young pine with a wide base, separated from its brethren by ten feet on all sides. He liked that about it. That it didn't fit in. He reached out, pointed, and lay his tired head on the ground.

"It's there," Nick said. "At the base, on this side. It's not deep."

Breecher paused, examined the tree at the edge of the forest, its roots half in and half out of the pale sand.

"When I dig it up, am I gonna need some other kind of

goddamn password or code to open it?" she barked. Nick gave a little laugh despite the agony he was in.

"I guess you'll find out," he said.

She went to the tree, dropped to her knees, and started digging with her hands. When Nick tried to roll himself onto his side to take the weight off his leg, she popped up, grabbing the gun and training it on him.

"Don't," she snapped. "Stay back. Well back."

"I will." He nodded. "I will."

He listened to her fingers digging in the sandy soil. The rustling of the duffel bag as she prized it from the grip of the earth.

Nick heard the zipper jangle and whizz as she pulled it.

He tucked his head beneath his arm and felt the explosion thump through the ground beneath him.

CHAPTER SEVENTY-TWO

THE MOTEL HAD been revamped since back when Clay had started as a lieutenant in Gloucester. As a rookie, he'd attended domestic disputes here, a couple of suicides, reports of suspicious activity. Now as he knocked and entered April Leeler's room, he found the crisp whiteness of everything almost unsettling. Laboratory-like. Joe was curled up on the small twin bed, playing with his iPad, his feet wiggling off the edge of the mattress. April was waiting for Clay, sitting on the edge of the bed, her eyes full of concern.

Clay went and sat beside her, and just like the supportive and caring wife that he'd envisioned in his fantasies, she took his head against her shoulder and played with the curls behind his ears.

"Urgh," he said, a single encore note to the miserable phone call he'd finished with her only ten minutes earlier.

"How long can you stay?" she asked.

"Not long," he said. "I just swung by to tell Angelica that Vinny's dead. I don't want her to hear it somewhere else. She's down in room seven."

He closed his eyes and counted off seconds in April's delicious embrace before he had to get back out there. In truth, he didn't even know exactly where he should go after he left the little motel at the edge of town.

Most of his officers were manning the inn, waiting for a forensics unit to come up from Boston to deal with the crime scene there. Three dead bodies in the house, one on the road leading in. And then there was the explosion and secondary crime scene in the woods. Nick had called Clay from the edge of the water deep in the forest to alert him to the explosion scene and to get him to send an ambulance out for a devastating gunshot wound to the knee. There was another body there, Karli Breecher. Nick had assured a stunned Sheriff Clay that the hand grenade he'd taken from Effie's room and rigged to the inside of the buried bag was the only explosive in the woods. But Clay had protocol to follow. More vans from Boston.

Neddy, Susan, and Nick were all in surgery. Clay had stopped by the hospital to find Bill tearing his hair out, with only Effie there to comfort him. Shauna Bulger was still out there somewhere, running around with a rifle that could take out an airplane.

Clay pulled away from April and held his throbbing forehead. Joe looked over.

"Shouldn't you be asleep?" Clay asked the child.

"I've been saying that for the last four hours," April said. Clay frowned at the boy, who paid them no mind.

Clay sighed again.

"What can I do?" April asked, one hand still lifting and twirling those curls behind his ear. "Is there some way I can help? I don't know Angelica well, but maybe I could go with you to her room. I'll comfort her after you have to move on."

"I wouldn't ask you to do that," Clay said. He had to laugh despite it all. "Man. You wait so long for a wonderful person to turn up in your life, and when she does, it's in the middle of a catastrophe."

She held him again.

"Dooooon't start kissing!" Joe warned from the other bed. Clay looked up. The kid hadn't lifted his eyes from the iPad yet. "It's gross-gross-gross!"

"That reminds me. Clay, I think I left a pair of sunglasses in the cruiser yesterday," April said, rising from the bed. "Can I just—"

"Sure, sure." Clay waved her away. He went and sat beside Joe as April left the motel room. There were pillow mints on the nightstand. Clay unwrapped one and popped it in his mouth, thinking he probably wouldn't get a minute to eat again before daybreak. Joe's index finger was dancing over the screen, helping a cartoon kangaroo hop over obstacles on an outback landscape.

"Isn't it a little past your bedtime, buddy?" Clay asked.

"Maybe," Joe said and smiled. "But don't tell my mom. I think she forgot. She's been waiting for you to get here. I've got a whole bunch of new games I haven't even played yet and I want to stay up as long as I can."

Clay sat and watched as the kid closed the kangaroo game and opened another. After the game designer logos appeared and dissolved, a scroll flopped down. On its surface were cartoon body parts. Joe started building an avatar, fitting a little girl's head onto a petite body. Clay watched him add a blond wig, a dress, Mary Jane shoes. When the game demanded "Name your character!" Joe tapped three letters.

ZOE.

Clay felt tingles roll over the surface of his scalp.

"They weren't there," April said as she reappeared at the door. Clay watched her cross to the bed, looking defeated, and curl up there again, taking the paperback novel she'd been reading from the nightstand.

With almost mechanical movements, Clay went to her, kissed her, and issued his goodbyes. He walked stiffly to his cruiser and sat in the driver's seat, tapping his fingers on the bottom of the steering wheel.

It was with a dread so heavy and so aching in his chest that he turned his head and looked at the Mobile Digital Terminal mounted to the center console of the squad car. The monitor was turned toward the front passenger seat, the way it had been the last time April was in the car. He hadn't left it like that. Clay turned it back. He awakened the machine, tapped through to the search history, and squinted at the top of the list where the most recent search was positioned. He put a finger on the screen and found the time of the last search.

11:47 p.m.

He looked at his watch.

It was 11:52 p.m.

Clay hit the search record and opened it up. The file related to a man named Thomas Oscar Savage. One conviction, four years earlier, for speeding. That was it. But there was a red alert on the name and a license plate linked to it. Clay clicked the alert.

WANTED—SUSPECTED HOMICIDE—POSSIBLE ARMED/HOSTILE

Clay took out his phone and googled the name Thomas Oscar Savage.

His phone screen filled with headlines.

OMAHA POLICE APPEAL FOR INFORMATION IN MISSING CHILD CASE

SEARCH FOR MISSING OMAHA GIRL SUSPENDED

MISSING ZOE SAVAGE PRESUMED MURDERED

SAVAGE PARENTS INTERROGATED OVER MISSING DAUGHTER

REGINA SAVAGE ARRESTED, HUSBAND THOMAS STILL AT LARGE

Clay opened up one of the articles. He scrolled down to a shot of a terrified-looking couple sitting at a press conference table, surrounded by police. Thomas and Regina Savage. Thomas was crying, wiping his exhausted eyes. Regina was holding up a picture of a small child.

Clay recognized that child.

CHAPTER SEVENTY-THREE

EVERYTHING EVAPORATED FROM his mind. The multiple crime scenes in and around his own home. The killer fugitive in the area that he personally had failed to keep contained. His three housemates in the local hospital, two of them fighting for their lives. Sheriff Clayton Spears even set aside his romantic disappointment, the most crushing letdown he'd experienced since his wife's departure. He could think of one thing only, which was that the little boy in the motel named Joe Leeler was, in fact, actually a little girl named Zoe Savage who had been kidnapped from her parents in Omaha and had somehow ended up here. All the stupid ideas Clay had been building up for years about what kind of hero he wanted to be in life went up in smoke instantly.

He had to be a different kind of hero now.

Clay felt the muscles in his shoulders bunching, his hands balling into fists, and his jaw locking tight. He got out of his squad car, slammed the door shut, and strode the six paces to the motel room door like a death machine lumbering robotically toward human prey. The lock smashed out of the doorframe as his boot hit the wood, the hinges popping, the whole door falling flat on the carpet with a breathy *whump*. Zoe screamed in shock and dropped her iPad, leaping up and scrambling to the bed beside April.

The woman wrapped an arm around the child. Clay felt his lip twist in fury. When he spoke, every word came out with a struggle, the syllables wrapped in pure, white-hot anger.

"Zoe," Clay said. He put out a hand. "Come here."

The child looked at April. April's hand tightened on the kid's shoulder.

"I'm going to take you home," Clay said. He put a hand on the butt of the pistol on his hip. "We're going to stay real calm. All of us. Nice and calm and quiet. You're going to come over here and stand by me, and I'm going to take you home to your real parents."

Zoe started crying. Clay eased a breath through his nostrils that was hot on his upper lip. April scooted the little girl closer to her, her other hand creeping up the surface of her thigh toward her pocket.

"I *am* Joe's real parent," April said. Her eyes held none of the warmth and light Clay had so fixated on when he first met her. They were almost unseeing, but glared into his own.

"Don't," Clay said. The hand that had beckoned the child was now turning, making a stop sign. His eyes warned her. "April. Do. Not. Move. I don't want to pull a gun in this room. Not in front of the kid. Not—"

"This is my child," April insisted, her hand still moving. Suddenly her fingers shot to her pocket. "I'm—"

Clay pulled out his gun and fired once.

Later, Clay would recall the sound of the blast and wonder if his own personal heartache had made him do it. Maybe it was because Shauna Bulger had already tricked him earlier that night. Maybe all his trust was used up; maybe the good nature that sometimes got him in a pickle on the job had been eroded to a point that it failed to launch. He didn't know. But Clay shot the woman who only moments earlier he'd considered the potential love of his life. A part of him hoped the reason he did it was his love, and fear, for the child she had abducted.

April flopped off the bed and onto the floor. Clay dropped his gun, ran forward, and scooped up the stiff and numb little girl.

He carried her out of the room, using the weight of her in his arms to fuel one last little dream about having a child of his own. He glanced back, and spied the handle of the knife April had been going for, butting out of the pocket of her jeans.

CHAPTER SEVENTY-FOUR

VENDING MACHINE. MAGAZINE stand. Row of chairs. Bank of payphones. I recited the names of the four points of my pacing route around the hospital waiting room. I didn't know how many laps I'd done, but I could see my endless route was starting to annoy Effie. She watched me going around and around from the back row of the room full of chairs. She fit right in there, her shirt drenched in Neddy Ives's blood and her eyes full of turmoil. To her left, three seats down, a father was clutching a wad of bandages to a blood-smeared toddler's forehead, and on her right, a guy with a possibly broken foot was lounging in a wheelchair, head bent forward, tapping at his phone.

I went and sat beside Effie, wringing my hands between my legs.

"Tell me again what happened at the house with Nick and Breecher," I said.

Effie rolled her eyes, handed me her phone. I could read for myself the story she had written out for me, unable to explain an ordeal that long and awful with her makeshift sign language. I pushed the phone away without reading it, thought about going back to pacing. Maybe I'd try going in the opposite direction. Effie put a hand on my leg and mouthed words that were clear, especially from the expression in her eyes.

Calm. Down.

"I can't do this again," I said, shaking my head, ignoring her direction. I pointed to a chair in the front row. "See that chair there? That's where I sat waiting for the doctors to tell me that my wife hadn't made it. Four hours I sat there. You see the sign out front when you came in? That's where they told me about Marni."

Effie nodded knowingly.

"I can't lose Susan," I said. "I can't do it again. I can't lose someone again."

Effie gripped my hand, tried to say something, but I didn't look. The words were tumbling out of me. Darker and darker, spiraling down.

"I stopped for Norman Driver," I said. My voice quivered. I paused for a long time, in case I lost it, only speaking again when I was sure I could get the words out. "I hit him with the car. He just came out of the woods really suddenly, and before I could slam on the brakes—*bam*. It was an accident. I stopped and went to see if he was alive, if there was something I could do."

Effie shrugged. *So?*

"So what if those few seconds make a difference?" I asked. "What if, you know, if she dies, and it turns out that she might have survived if I'd just got her to the hospital a few seconds earlier. I did a stupid, stupid thing, Effie. I shot her. And then I did *another* stupid thing. I stopped to see if some goddamn worthless, murdering, drug-dealing piece of trash could be saved. What if I—"

Effie grabbed my cheek with one hand and turned my face toward her, hard.

Cut it out! she mouthed.

I stopped. Effie tapped a message out on her phone, showed it to me.

You stopped for Shauna because you're a good man.

I wasn't convinced, so I went back to pacing around the room. Vending machine. Magazine stand. Row of chairs. Bank of payphones. I was trying to decide how many seconds I'd given Shauna Bulger to get into the car with me when a nurse came through the double doors beside the triage desk and walked up to Effie. I sprinted over to be at her side.

"Your friend, Mr. Ives, is out of surgery and is stable now," the nurse said. "But he's unconscious. He's had a difficult time. I'm afraid I won't be able to let anyone other than immediate family in to sit with him."

Effie nodded and the nurse walked away.

"They're not going to let me in to see her," I said.

Effie looked up at me.

"If she survives," I said. "Susan. I'm not her immediate family."

Effie hung an elbow over the back of her chair and tapped a message out on her phone with one thumb.

Better settle in, then. Could be here a while.

CHAPTER SEVENTY-FIVE

SHERIFF CLAY SPEARS walked up the ramp to Gate 12 at Eppley Airfield in Omaha at about midday, the little girl named Zoe Savage holding his hand. Clay was tired himself, but the kid was barely awake at all. For the whole flight from Beverly Regional, the girl had slept with her head against the window, her mouth hanging open and little snores coming from her now and then as she was disturbed by turbulence or the flight attendant's cart going by. Clay had sat and watched the child, thinking that now that he knew she was a little girl and not a little boy, he wasn't sure how he could have missed the distinction.

They'd talked a little back at the station in Gloucester, Clay stepping out of the little waiting room he'd settled the kid into to deal with multiple crime scenes. Mostly, though, Clay wasn't sure what to say to the girl. It was possible, he assumed, that he could make matters worse by trying to explain it all to her: how April Leeler had abducted her, how her parents had been charged with her murder, how her father was a fugitive. Clay thought he'd best leave that kind of thing to a child psychologist. He listened to what the kid said about her time with April Leeler, but didn't comment on it.

He'd almost known the kind of story Zoe would tell, even before the child spoke. That April Leeler had been a teacher at Zoe's school. That she'd been so nice and friendly. How she'd hustled Zoe into her car one afternoon, telling the kid wild stories about her parents not wanting her to be their daughter anymore. April had convinced Zoe that she was protecting her from her parents, who wanted to kill her. And that adopting a new identity, that of a little boy named Joe, would be their only safe option. April had shaved Zoe's head, bought her boy's clothes from the local Walmart, and driven the two of them out of the state as fast as she could.

What Zoe couldn't tell Clay was *why* April had done it; what sadistic malfunction in the woman's mind, or gaping hole in her soul, had made her abduct a child. And Clay didn't want to know. It hurt so bad learning that April wasn't the woman he'd thought she was. Learning more about that lie felt like unnecessary agony.

Zoe Savage waited silently, rubbing her eyes and leaning a little against Clay's leg, as two detectives from Omaha greeted them at the airport gate. They were standard police detective types—slightly overweight, world worn, dressed in wrinkled suits. They introduced themselves as Detectives Hanley and Erroldson and stood there for what must have been a full minute, gaping silently at Zoe.

"Well, Jesus," Hanley said and ran a hand over his bald scalp. "That's her, all right. I can't believe it. I'm standing here looking at her right now and I still can't believe it. It's like I'm looking at a goddamn unicorn."

Erroldson shook his head at Clay. "We had the parents dead to rights. I just feel like the ultimate fool."

"You rounded up the father yet?" Clay asked.

"Yeah," Hanley said. "Guy gave himself up when he saw the news report that you'd found Zoe in Gloucester. Boy, ain't he relieved. You found his daughter and you got him off the hook for murder. That man owes you a drink, Sheriff. Him and the mother both."

"I don't think so," said Clay. He lifted a tired hand. "I'm just gonna turn around and catch the next flight back home."

"What?" Erroldson laughed. "Hell, no. Sheriff Spears, you ain't going nowhere! We got a big reunion of this little one with her parents planned down at the station. Every news camera in the country is gonna be there. You've got to enjoy your moment."

"You're the hero here," Hanley insisted. "You can't just walk out on your time as a hero."

"Yes, I can," Clay said.

While the detectives stood there, gaping silently again, Clay crouched down and pulled Zoe Savage into a hug. He told her that she was a good girl. That she was brave. That everything was going to be OK. And then he shook hands with the detectives and walked down the concourse toward Departures.

CHAPTER SEVENTY-SIX

IN THE MOVIES, when someone might be dying, their loved one sits in a waiting room for a few hours, just enough time to slowly rise from the hard plastic chair at any sign of news looking slightly stale and tired. It didn't work out like that for me. For the first six hours after I drove Susan to the hospital, I did sit and rise and pace and wait, looking stale and tired and no more, and there were many possible signs of news. But the news didn't come. Eventually, Effie went away, and I was told that Nick was in post-op for his shattered knee. I didn't go and visit him. The emergency department waiting room seemed to be where the nurses expected to find me, so that's where I stayed.

When the news came, it was not the definitive "She made it!" of Hollywood movies. There was no one around to high-five and hug me. I'd been waiting eight hours, and they told me that Susan was resting from her first surgery and was about to go in for another round. They couldn't tell me if she would live or die, or under what circumstances either might happen.

After a day, my beard stubble was appearing and my clothes were reeking from worry sweat. They told me they'd had to remove half of Susan's left lung, as it had been torn to shreds by the bullet. They couldn't tell me if she was in or out of the proverbial woods.

After two days, my hair was crazy and my eyes were wild from lack of sleep and refusal of food. They told me Susan was in an induced coma, which was bad, but there was no sign of brain damage, which was good.

After three days, I was walking like a zombie from catching naps in corners, on chairs, on a bench outside the waiting room doors, and while Effie had brought me new clothes, I hadn't put them on. My skin was oily, and my teeth were furry, and my thoughts were fragmented from stress. When I was sleeping, I heard the hospital's alarm and announcement system in my dreams, and my eyes ached from the fluorescent lights. They said Susan was showing signs of waking.

On the fourth day, I was roused from a drooling slumber, propped against the vending machine, drawn there by its strangely soothing hum. It was a nurse who woke me. She said I was allowed to visit Susan.

I ran, forgetting that I'd taken off my shoes and tucked them under the chair in the waiting room. In socked feet I almost slid over as I was coming to a halt at the door of the room the nurse was pointing to. It was dark and warm inside. Sitting up in the bed, Susan was awake and waiting for me.

Her eyes were sleepy, but she still frowned as she took me in.

"Bill," she said. "Jesus. You look awful."

I fell into the chair beside her bed and took her hand, put her palm against my face. She made a sound that might have been a little laugh, had she been stronger, had it not hurt so much. I cradled her fingers against my face and just looked at her, thanking God or the universe or dumb luck or whatever the hell was responsible for her being alive with every ounce of my soul.

"I've got a question for you," I said eventually.

"Oh yeah?" she said. "Let me guess. You want to know if I forgive you for accidentally shooting me. You want to know if I'm that big of a woman."

She was grinning at her own joke.

"That's right," I said.

She paused, thinking. Took back her hand and tapped a finger thoughtfully on her chin.

"Sure, what the hell," she said. "I shot at you too, after all."

"Well, that's part one of my question answered, then."

"It's a two-parter?"

"Sure is."

"All right," Susan said. "What's the second part?"

"If you could go so far as to forgive me," I said, "would you marry me, too?"

CHAPTER SEVENTY-SEVEN

SUSAN'S SMILE BROADENED. I'd expected at least a little surprise at the proposal, but that's just the way she is. One step ahead of me, all the time. While she seemed initially taken by joy at my question, something flickered for a moment in her eyes. I knew exactly what it was. Doubt. Fear. Because if the last few days had confirmed anything for her, it was surely that I was a trouble magnet. It wasn't the house that sucked in ill fate, menace, and catastrophe. It was me. That malignant magnetism, and my loyalties, my sense of responsibility for the injustices that arose for the people I loved, my sheer dogheadedness: it was all going to make me a very dangerous husband.

And she'd had a dangerous husband before.

But I hoped, in that moment that she sat sitting there looking at me, that Susan could also see the fear in my eyes. I'd lost a wife before. I'd nearly lost her, too. And I knew my propensity to find myself surrounded by bad people and bad deeds didn't just exist because I couldn't walk by and let evil be done. There was something about me, too. Maybe I was cursed.

Being married to me would mean Susan was choosing to live the rest of her life in peril.

The doubt disappeared from Susan's eyes. I don't know what happy thought about me pushed her over the edge, but she seemed to decide then and there that whatever was coming, I was worth dealing with it.

"Go take a shower, and bring me a snack from the vending machine," she said. "Do that and you've got yourself a deal."

CHAPTER SEVENTY-EIGHT

EFFIE AND I got a bug into us in the weeks following that dark night at the house. We infected each other with the idea that we could expunge what had happened to us and our household by cleaning and repairing, so that was what we did. While Effie sanded, filled, and painted over bullet holes, I scrubbed blood from the walls and floorboards, hired a dumpster, and loaded it up with ruined rugs and carpet. On the day that Susan was due to return home from the hospital, I was putting fresh sheets on our bed in the warm light of morning, the sea beyond the round window making the slapping sounds of small foamy waves and the gulls crying happily.

As I breezed past, I spotted Effie through that little window. She was loading a slab of wood onto the rails of her circular saw, her hand flicking expertly as she marked the length for cutting with a pencil and steel ruler. She had commandeered a section of the lawn beyond the porch as her workshop, the grass around her powdered with sawdust and timber offcuts.

I went down from the attic and along the second-floor hall, going from room to room. Susan had been tired and sore when I saw her last, and I knew she would probably just want to go straight to our bed, but I wanted everything to be as perfect as it could be anyway. The new door to Neddy Ives's room was slightly ajar and still damp from a fresh coat of paint, so I pushed it open gently to slip into the empty room.

Over the days since I'd entered Neddy's room on that fateful night, I had returned a bunch of times to take in the investigation he was obviously conducting—into a crime he had been convicted of: his wife's murder. From what I could tell, he'd pled guilty and served almost the entirety of his thirty-year sentence, getting 10 percent knocked off for good behavior.

Spencer Edward Ives, convicted killer, had a couple days more to spend in the local hospital, having developed complications with the bullet wound to his stomach. I dusted his room and stood there under the corkboard for a while, looking at the articles, photographs, and sticky notes he'd assembled. It was tempting, so tempting, to dig into what was here, to use the opportunity while my most mysterious tenant wasn't around to discover more about who he was and what had brought him here. That he had spent twenty-seven years incarcerated for his wife's brutal murder explained why he felt so comfortable living in this tiny space, choosing to exist with only the walls as company. What wasn't explained was why he'd made this place a shrine to his obsession with his own case. I shook my head, forcing myself to look away from the wall of snippets, and left the room.

From the window of Nick's room, the door to which had

also been left ajar, I could see the troubled veteran returning from the woods. He was shambling slowly and awkwardly on crutches and yet was as drenched in sweat as he used to be when returning from a five-mile run.

No amount of new-paint smell, sawdust, or air freshener had been able to rid the house of the dark cloud following Nick Jones around. His Twitter post confessing to his part in covering up the massacre in Afghanistan had garnered national attention. He had stirred up urgent activity in a variety of online groups from QAnon to AboutFace, and every major news outlet had covered the story. I'd sat with him in his hospital room, expecting at any moment for the disgraced veteran to be hauled off by military police or CIA officials or someone, anyone, for interrogation about the incident. Men in suits did come, and they spoke to him alone, and when they left, my friend seemed even sadder and angrier than he'd been when I stepped out of the room.

I found out why soon enough. The US Army released a statement the following day discrediting Nick's story about what happened at the farmhouse in Afghanistan. Rick Master had stepped forward to act as the army's calm, collected, and thoroughly rehearsed witness, claiming that the official military account of the 2010 incident was true. Dorrich, Master, Breecher, and Jones had been fired upon by rebels and had responded within the parameters of their training, and while the killing of civilians was always unfortunate, in this instance it could not be avoided.

The CIA, in a joint statement, said any claims Nick Jones made about ghost money were untrue and likely inspired by his known schizophrenia. Roger Dorrich's death was ruled a suicide, and Karli Breecher's end in the woods near my inn was put down to an accident.

I watched Nick limp on his crutches from the edge of the woods to the firepit area and ease himself down on one of the benches there. Though I'd tried to broach the subject with him a couple of times since his release from the hospital, he'd not wanted to talk about his next steps in trying to be accountable for what he had done, if any. I assumed that the millions of fragments of singed American dollars that I was still finding scattered around the woods near the inn, and along the nearby beach, comprised all of the money in the duffel bag he'd used to blow up Karli Breecher. If Nick had saved any of it, or given any of it to another source, he wasn't telling me about it. I dusted Nick's room briefly too before moving on.

When I pushed open the door of Vinny's room, I found Angelica there. I was unsurprised, since the author, raconteur, vegan, activist, and grieving sort-of-girlfriend had been spending a lot of time in the deceased gangster's room. She didn't notice me as I entered, and I dusted the room silently, glancing up now and then to watch her poring over old photographs she was drawing, one at a time, from a shoebox sitting on the edge of the desk. No one had come to the house to claim Vinny's things, so she'd had unfettered access to his meager possessions, and seemed to be working on something on her laptop as she carefully examined each image. I knew that when Angelica wasn't working on whatever she was doing with the photographs, she was putting together a memorial for Vinny. I'd heard her making calls to florists and undertakers. But asking her what we as a household could do to help, or whether we'd be invited, only made her walk off in silence.

Though my inn was empty of short-term guests, and though those who lived there now included the survivors of gunshot wounds, hostage scenarios, public shamings, and brutal beatings, no character seemed to have taken the events of those dark days as hard as the man I found sitting in the dining room. Sheriff Clayton Spears was settled at the end of the table, idly tapping the side of a steaming mug of coffee with his palm, his huge back to the door through which I entered. Unlike the physical wounds of my other friends, Clay's heart seemed unhealable. I'd begun worrying about him when I learned that he had taken a leave of absence, and I noticed him wearing the same T-shirt and jeans around the house for days on end. As I entered the dining room now, he didn't move, his eyes transfixed on the dust motes swirling in the beams of light entering through the French doors.

"My fiancée's coming home today," I announced cheerfully, dropping my dusting cloth on the table and taking a seat to Clay's right. "You know the one. Susan. The blond babe with the mind like a diamond. You might remember her as my girlfriend, but she's my fiancée now. That's because I asked her to marry me and she said yes."

Clay lifted his weary eyes to me. I grinned back. My insistence on using the word "fiancée" upwards of five hundred times a day was driving everyone in the household nuts.

"You know who I'm referring to?" I pressed.

"Bill, please," Clay sighed.

"Hey, I was thinking we could get out of here later. You, me, and Nick maybe," I said and gestured to the doors. "Go down the pier with a couple of cold ones. I hear the yellowtail are biting."

"Maybe," Clay conceded.

"All right, it's settled. We're going. After my fiancée gets back."

Clay looked like he wanted to smack me. I heard a car

approaching the house. I was determined to get a half-smile out of the sheriff before I went to see who it was.

"You think you'll be all right on a public pier, dressed like that?" I pointed at his T-shirt. "Or should you go in disguise? We don't want the paparazzi bothering us."

Clay's single-handed solving of the kidnapping of Zoe Savage from Omaha, Nebraska, had almost eclipsed Nick's revelations on the internet. Footage of the little girl running into her exhausted parents' arms had become so familiar to me in the days I sat by Susan's hospital bed that I could have sketched the heartwarming scene from memory. Clayton Spears was being hailed as a hero from coast to coast, yet the attention only seemed to push the already shy sheriff further into his shell. I'd fielded a couple of phone calls from the Savages, and plenty from the media, but my friend had never accepted any of those calls and hadn't touched an enormous fruit-and-wine basket that arrived for him and landed in the inn's kitchen.

Giving up on injecting any cheer into Clay, I went to the windows and looked out, spying a good-looking young woman exiting a blue rental car at the end of the porch. I intercepted her at the front door, feeling weirdly flushed at the sight of her standing there straightening her crinkled business shirt and trousers. Auburn curls fell from a ponytail down the back of her neck, and she clicked a stainless-steel pen nervously as she glanced past me into the foyer.

"Hello," she said and flashed a set of perfect white teeth. "My name is Katie O'Leary. I was wondering if I could speak to Sheriff Clayton Spears?"

CHAPTER SEVENTY-NINE

I ALL BUT danced back into the dining room, shimmying to Clay's side and perching on the tabletop at his elbow.

"There's an incredibly attractive journalist here to see you," I told my friend.

"Uh-huh," Clay said and lifted his coffee mug, making no move to stand.

"She wants to speak to the Hero of the Inn," I said. "Sounds like it's mostly about the Zoe Savage thing. But she's also curious about you turning up in Boston with the missing evidence needed to solve the Georgette Winter-Lee cold case."

I'd let Clay hand in the evidence box Shauna Bulger had posted back to the inn from an unknown location, considering that my reputation with the Boston Police wouldn't help its already difficult chain-of-evidence situation. From what I'd heard, my former colleagues in the force had reopened the cases and were looking into the late Norman Driver's where-abouts in 1989 around the time of Georgette's brutal slaying. Convictions would be difficult, particularly without testimony from Mark Bulger about how he'd obtained the packages of evidence or from Shauna about how she'd retrieved the box from her husband's safe.

Searches for Shauna had been undertaken in all of the woodland from Crane Beach to Manchester-by-the-Sea, but no trace of her had been found. Wanted ads on the TV had dredged the bottom of the barrel, receiving the usual false sightings and rumors. But Shauna Bulger was gone. Whoever she had become when she was attacked in her home, she was living somewhere as that woman now. Forgetting day by day the life that she had lived as Mark Bulger's wife, and as my friend. Someone new, but not someone who would kill again.

That was my guess—my hope, anyway.

Clay sipped his coffee, and I nudged him so that he almost sloshed it over the edge of his cup as he set it back down.

"Come on, Clay," I needled. "You never know! That woman waiting out there might be your future fian—"

"Don't say it," Clay growled. He hid it well, but at the corner of his mouth, I saw the barest hint of a smile. "I'll go out there and get rid of her, if you *just. Don't. Say it.*"

I watched him go, and in a few moments, the sheriff and the journalist appeared beyond the French doors. While at first the young woman seemed to be wincing against gruff proclamations and that unbreachable stop sign of a hand, I folded my arms and watched as Clay's posture slowly straightened, and his lips grew into a smile while the two of them talked. Soon he was shrugging humbly and she'd dropped a hip, looked like she was teasing him, making him laugh so that his belly jiggled. It made me feel warm and hopeful to watch Clay giving love another chance.

I looked at my watch, calculating the hours until I needed to go and pick up my own second chance and bring her home.

TURN THE PAGE FOR A BONUS THRILLER
FROM JAMES PATTERSON AND CANDICE FOX!

BLACK
& BLUE

Single-minded detective Harriet Blue won't rest until she stops
a savage killer targeting female college students. But new
clues point to a predator more chilling than she
could ever have imagined.

CHAPTER 1

I'M AN EXPERIENCED hunter of humans. It's not hard, if you understand how they think. People have tunnel vision and are objective-driven. As long as you don't interfere with their goal, and don't make yourself known before you're ready to pounce, you can close in on a relaxed target pretty easily. It doesn't even require much stealth. Unlike animals, human beings don't use their alarm system of senses. Though the wind was behind me, Ben Hammond didn't smell me. He didn't hear my breath over the clunk of his boots on the pavement.

Hammond's objective was his late-model Honda Civic on the edge of the parking lot. So that's all he could see—he didn't notice me round the corner from the loading dock and fall into step behind him. He left the shopping center with hands full of groceries swinging at his sides and headed across the parking lot, already sliding into the driver's seat in his mind, shutting the door on the moonless night.

I followed with my head down, my hoodie pulled up against the security cameras trained on the few remaining cars. I let him pull his keys out of his pocket, the jangling sound covering the soft fall of my boots for the last few steps between me and my prey.

I closed the distance and attacked.

CHAPTER 2

"FUCK!" BEN HAMMOND grabbed at the back of his head where I'd punched him, turned, and stumbled against the car, dropping the bags. Glass cracked in one of them. He cowered in a half-crouch, trying to make himself smaller. Both hands shot up. "Oh, my God! What are you doing?"

"Stand up." I waved impatiently.

"Take—m-my—wallet," he stammered. "Don't hurt m—"

"You don't like the surprise attack, do you, Ben? You know how effective it is."

He realized three things very quickly. First, that I was a woman. Second, that this wasn't a mugging. Third, that he'd heard my voice before.

The man straightened almost fully and squinted into the darkness of my hood. I tugged the hood down and watched his eyes wander around the silhouette of my short hair against the shopping-center lights, the terror in his face slowly dissipating.

"I . . ." He straightened. His hands dropped. "I know you."

"You do."

"You're that cop." He pointed an uncertain finger at me, began to shake it as his confidence grew. "You're that cop from the trial."

"I am," I said. "Detective Harriet Blue, here to deliver your punishment."

CHAPTER 3

IT WAS A little insulting that my name didn't come to Ben's mind as quickly as I'd hoped. But I had just cracked him on the skull. What little gray matter was sloshing around his brain probably needed time to recover. I'd done everything I could to make him aware of me while he was tried for the rape of his ex-girlfriend Molly. When I took the stand to testify that I'd found Molly at the bottom of the shower where he'd dumped her, I'd looked right at him and calmly and clearly stated my name.

It hadn't been a solid case. Ben had been very crafty in getting back at his ex for leaving him: raping and beating her, but charming his way into her apartment struggle-free and sharing a glass of wine with her first, so it looked as if she'd welcomed the sexual encounter. I'd known, sitting on the witness stand and staring at him, that like most rapists he'd probably go free.

But that didn't mean I was finished with him.

"This is assault." Ben touched the back of his head, noted the blood on his fingers, and almost smiled. "You're in a lot of trouble, you stupid little bitch."

"Actually," I slid my right foot back, "*you're* in a lot of trouble."

I gave Ben a couple of sharp jabs to the face, then backed up, let him have a moment to feel them. He stepped out from between the shopping bags and came at me swinging. I sidestepped and planted my knee in his ribs, sending him sprawling on the asphalt. I glanced at the distant shopping center. The security guards would notice a commotion at the edge of the farthest parking lot camera and come running. I figured I had seconds, not minutes.

"You can't do this." Hammond spat blood from his split lip. "You—"

I gave him a knee to the ribs, then lifted him before he could get a lungful of air and slammed him into the car's hood. I'm petite, but I box, so I know how to maneuver a big opponent. I grabbed a handful of Ben's hair and dragged him toward the driver's door.

"You're a cop!" Hammond wailed.

"You're right," I said. I could just make out two security guards rushing out of the loading dock.

"My job gives me access to crime alerts," I said. "I can tag a person's file and get a notification every time they're brought in, even if their original charge never stuck."

I held on to Hammond's hair and gave him a couple of hard punches in the head, then dumped him onto the ground. The guards were closer. I stepped on Hammond's balls, so I knew I had his full attention.

"If I ever see your name in the system again," I told him, "I'm coming back. And I won't be this gentle next time."

I pulled my hood up and sprinted into the bushes at the side of the lot.

CHAPTER 4

I'M NOT A vigilante. Sometimes I just have no choice but to take matters into my own hands.

I'd worked in sex crimes for five years, and I was tired of seeing predators walking free from convictions. When I got close to a victim, the way I did with Molly Finch, I found it hard to sleep after their attacker was acquitted. For weeks I'd lain awake at night thinking about Hammond's smug face as he'd walked down the steps of the courthouse on Goulburn Street, the wink he'd given me as he got into the taxi. I'd managed to make a minor physical assault charge stick. But there had been no proving *beyond a reasonable doubt* that the sex Hammond had had with Molly that night hadn't been consensual.

That's how it goes sometimes with sexual assaults. The guy's lawyer throws everything he has at the idea that she might have wanted it. There was no physical evidence, or witnesses, to say otherwise.

Well, now there was no evidence to say Ben Hammond wasn't bashed half to death by a mugger gone nuts, either. If he went to the cops about what I'd done, he'd know what it felt like not to be believed.

But he wouldn't go to the cops and tell them a woman had given him a beatdown. His kind never did.

I rolled my shoulders as I drove back across the city toward

Potts Point, sighing long and low as the tension eased. I was really looking forward to getting some sleep. Most nights saw me at my local gym pounding boxing bags to try to exhaust myself into a healthy presleep calm. Smacking Ben around had given me the same delicious fatigue in my muscles. I hoped it lasted.

At the big intersection near Kings Cross, a pair of hookers strutted across the road in front of my car. Their skin was lit pink by the huge neon Coca-Cola sign on the corner. The streets were still damp from a big storm the night before. The gutters were crowded with trash and huge fig-tree leaves.

My phone rang. I recognized the number as my station chief.

"Hello, Pops," I said.

"Blue, take down this address," the old man said. "There's a body I want you to look at."

CHAPTER 5

MURDER WAS HARD work, but Hope had never been afraid of that.

She knelt on the floor of the kitchen of the *Dream Catcher* and scrubbed at the polished boards. She was trying to push her brush down the cracks and bring up the blood that had dried and settled there. *Deck,* she thought suddenly, dunking the brush in the bucket of hot water and bleach beside her. On yachts, the floor was not a floor at all but a deck. The kitchen was called a *galley.* She smiled. She'd need to get used to all the terminology. There was so much to learn, being a new boat owner. She sat back on her heels and wiped the sweat from her brow. She'd give the blood a rest for a while and work on the bedroom.

The young woman climbed backward down the little ladder and walked into the yacht's expansive bedroom, gathering up a garbage bag from the roll she'd placed on the bed. The first thing she did was take a framed photograph from the nightstand and dump it in the darkness of the bag. She didn't look at the couple's smiling faces. She threw in some reading glasses, a pair of slippers, and a folded newspaper. She opened the cupboard and started taking out the woman's clothes, grabbing great handfuls on coat hangers and bundling the shirts, skirts, and pants into a roll before she shoved them into the bag.

Jenny Spelling had awful taste, Hope thought, glancing at a turquoise skirt-suit before it went into the trash. Ugh, shoulder pads. So eighties. She felt a wave of excitement roll over her as she looked along the empty hanging rod, thinking about her own clothes racked there.

When she'd filled all the garbage bags on the rolls with their possessions, Hope walked to the back of the boat to check on her prisoners. The couple was slumped in the corner of the shower cubicle, Jenny's head twisted back against the wall so that her nose pointed upward and her mouth hung open. When Hope opened the door, Ken shifted up as much as his binds would allow. His wife was limp against him.

"I'm just heading out to get rid of some garbage," Hope said brightly. "You guys need anything before I go? More water?"

Jenny Spelling woke and immediately started shivering. She stared at Hope wordlessly, as though she didn't know what the young woman was.

"Hope." Ken's face reddened with desperation. "I'm begging you, please, just take the boat. Take everything. My wife needs to do her dialysis or she's going to die. Okay? It's only going to take a few minutes. That's all. That—"

"We've discussed this." Hope held up her hand, gave him a weary sigh. "It'll all be over soon. I'm not getting into this again. The last time I let you loose, you did this." She held up her forearm, showed him the bruise. "*Trust*, Ken. You had it, and you lost it."

"Please, please." Ken shifted. "You don't need to do this. Look at her. Look at her face. She's missed her dialysis for three days now. She's not right. She's—"

Hope took the duct tape from the counter beside the toilet and ripped off a length. She placed a strip over Jenny's mouth, but gave Ken a few turns around his head. He was the feisty one. She worked emotionlessly as the tape sealed off his words.

"She's gonna die!" the man howled through the tape. "Please!"

CHAPTER 6

HEADING TO THE crime scene, I drove through the quiet streets of Picnic Point and up through the national park. The dark hills were spotted here and there with the gold porch lights of suburban mansions. I'd spent some time out here as a preteen with one of the foster families who had taken on my brother Sam and me. That is, before their adoption dream had ended.

There had been so many young families who'd attempted to integrate us that it was difficult to decide which one it had been. All I remembered was the local school and the crowds of teens in green and gold uniforms, the curious glances we'd received as we entered midway through the semester.

As usual, Sam and I had only been at the school for a few weeks. As a pair of kids who'd been in the system since we were practically toddlers, we didn't make life easy for our foster parents with our bad behavior. It was probably me who had broken the spell by running away in the middle of the night. Or maybe it was Sam setting something on fire, or running his mouth at our potential new parents. We'd both been equally bad at school—fighting off kids who wanted to give us grief, trying to show our new teachers who was really boss. Once our new mommies and daddies realized we weren't grateful for being "saved," the fantasy usually died. In truth, Sam and I had always preferred the group homes and institutions they shipped us to between potential adopters. More places to hide. I dreamed as I drove by the lamplit houses of what it might have been like to grow up here, if I'd been a more stable kid.

The police tape started at the edge of the main road. I was stopped by a young officer in a raincoat and flashed him my badge, only then realizing that my knuckles were still wrapped.

"Okay, Detective Blue, head down to the end of this road where it turns to dirt and go left along the river. You'll see the lights," the cop said.

"The river? Shit!" I felt the fine hairs on my arms stand on end. "Who's the victim?"

The cop waved me on. Another car was coming up behind me. I stood on the gas and zipped down the slope, almost swerving on the corner where the dirt began. I couldn't wait to get to the crime scene. If the victim was a young woman, it meant the Georges River Killer had struck again.

And I was going to get him this time.

CHAPTER 7

I PARKED CLOSE, unwrapped my knuckles, and strode up to the crime scene with my heart pumping in my ears. I didn't even bring my scene kit. I had to know as much as I could, as fast as possible, so that I could get Pops to put me on the case. The Georges River killings were splashed all over the newspapers, and so were the idiots who had control of the case—a group of loutish guys from Sydney Metro Homicide who wouldn't give me so much as a whiff of what they had.

I didn't want the notoriety these cops seemed to enjoy so much. I wanted to be involved in catching what was probably the most savage serial killer in our nation's history. Young, beautiful university students were going missing from the hip urban suburbs around the University of Sydney campus. Their savaged bodies were turning up on the banks of the Georges River three or four days after they disappeared. My brother spent two days of his working week teaching undergrad design students at the university, and lived in their midst in the hip suburbs around Newtown and Broadway. I'd talked to Sam about it a lot, about how the girls in his apartment building were terrified, begging the landlord to put cameras up outside the block, walking each other to and from their cars in the late hours.

It might have been arrogant, or naive, but I felt as if there was something I could contribute. Though my conviction rate in sex crimes wasn't good, that was part of the culture of the court system. I was a good cop, and I could practically smell the Georges River Killer haunting the women of my city. When the police came knocking on that evil prick's door, I wanted to be right there to see his face.

The first thing I noticed that was wrong with the scene was the edge of the police tape. It was far too crowded. Half the officers who should have been in the inner cordon were standing at the outer cordon, talking and smoking in the dark. I recognized a photographer from my station loitering uselessly by the lights rigged up over the scene. A fingerprints specialist was sitting under a tree eating a burrito out of a paper roll. What the hell was everyone doing? I ducked under the tape and came up beside the only officer in the crime scene. He was crouched over the body.

When he turned around, I saw that the man by the body was Tate Barnes.

The walking embodiment of career suicide.

CHAPTER 8

THE EFFECT OF seeing Tate Barnes right in the middle of what I already considered my crime scene was like being maced. My eyes stung and my throat closed with panic. I'd never met the man before, but I knew the shaggy blond hair and the leather jacket from stories I'd heard. There were hundreds of variations on the story of Tate Barnes. It was a terrible tale about a crime the man had committed that he'd tried to hide from the bosses during his academy application. It was said that, as a child, Tate and a group of his friends had murdered a mother and her young son.

I turned away and grabbed at my face, tried to suppress a groan. I needed this guy out of my crime scene. Now. He straightened and offered me his hand.

"I'm Tox Barnes," he rasped. It sounded as though his throat was lined with sandpaper.

"You actually introduce yourself as 'Tox'?"

"I find it minimizes confusion."

I'd heard the nickname, but I hadn't expected him to embrace it. Officers called Barnes "Toxic" because any officer who agreed to work with him was essentially committing themselves to a lifetime of punishment from their fellow officers. General consensus was that Tox Barnes should never have been allowed into the force. Those who had worked with him were harassed relentlessly by their peers. He was the fox in the henhouse. Aligning yourself with him meant you were on the side of a predator.

I'd heard that there was nothing the administration had been able to do to stop Barnes from being a cop. He'd aced his application, and he'd committed the murders so young his record had been expunged. But that didn't mean the rest of the force was going to sit by and let a murderer operate in their midst. He was the enemy, and if you joined him, you were the enemy, too.

"Listen, Tox, I'm Detective Harriet Blue." I shook his rough hand half-heartedly. "I'm going to need you to clear out of this scene. Chief Morris has put me on it."

"Meh," Tox said, and returned to crouching.

I waited, but nothing further came, so I bent down beside him and glanced at the body.

"Sorry, I didn't catch that."

"I said, 'Meh,'" Tox replied. "It was a dismissive noise."

I was so shocked, so furious, I hadn't even taken in the sight of the girl on the sand before us. My eyes flicked over her naked chest, unseeing, as I tried to get my mind around the reality of the situation. She looked midtwenties, beautiful, dark-haired. She was wearing only a pair of panties. She was a Georges River girl. I knew it. I needed to get this parasite of a man off my case.

"You don't understand," I said, "this is my crime scene. This is my case. And I don't work with partners."

"Neither do I," he said, as if it were a matter of choice.

"Right." I sighed. "So you can give me a brief on what you've observed, and then I need you to beat it and take your dismissive noises with you."

Tox seemed to smirk in the dark as he stood and walked

around the back of the body. I couldn't tell if he'd heard me or not. At the edge of the police tape, twenty yards away, my fellow officers were watching carefully to see if I'd cooperate with their nemesis, thereby giving them permission to make my life a living hell. I noticed some journalists among the crowd. The uniformed patrol officers securing the scene were so interested in Tox and me that they weren't even pushing them back.

When I turned around, I saw that Tox had a pocket knife. He flicked open the blade with a snap, and slashed at the girl.

CHAPTER 9

"WHAT THE—" I stood up, tried to shield what Tox was doing from the press, who'd started snapping pictures. "What the fuck are you doing?"

Tox didn't answer. He flipped the girl onto her front and pulled the underpants he'd slashed from her hips off her body. I watched in horror as he poked at the corpse's backside with the butt of the blade. He leaned in close and examined the surface of her skin. Someone at the edge of the crowd sneered.

"Sicko," somebody said. "Someone say something."

"Nah, man. Leave him. Let him mess up all the evidence."

"Detective Barnes," I said, "I'm ordering you to stop what you're doing *right now.*"

Tox put both his hands on the corpse's back and pushed down hard, just once. He pulled the hair away from the girl's face and stuck his third finger between her lips, pushed it deep inside her throat. The dead girl's cheeks puckered obscenely to allow his finger to push down. He extracted the finger and looked at the tip in the torchlight, grunted thoughtfully. I watched him take the girl's wrist and give it an exploratory wiggle before he stood up and dusted off his palms.

"Mmm," he said, and strode away from me toward the riverbank.

I followed, grateful to be out of earshot of the vile things the cops at the tape were saying about him. I caught him at the water's edge and shoved him hard in the back. He stumbled in the sand.

"What was that for?" he said in his strange, whispery voice.

"Jesus, I don't know, for violating the corpse of a young woman in front of all the nation's leading newspapers and half the police force?" I snarled. "What is wrong with you, man?"

"I wasn't violating the corpse, I was testing a theory." He looked toward the mouth of the river. "The kids who found the body said they thought they recognized the girl from a party last night, a few streets back from the river. I wanted to find out if that was bullshit before we go off interviewing all the morons who attended the party. She wasn't there. So we can forget that."

I felt as if I were dreaming. This man seemed to have no idea how inappropriate his handling of the body had been. He was looking off toward the river and talking to himself as though I wasn't standing there.

"Of course she wasn't at the party," I said. "Are you *that* stupid? She's a Georges River girl. Right river, right age, right placement of the body. I could have told you that before you stuck your finger in her mouth."

"Are *you* that stupid?" Tox looked at me finally. "She's *not* one of the Georges River Killer's victims. No. She didn't die any-where near here."

"You're insane." I waved him away and turned back to the crime scene. "You don't touch a body until forensics is done with it. That's the first thing they teach you on the first day of forensics. You just...you've compromised the case."

I could hardly speak I was so mad. His passive stare made it worse.

"Forensics won't find anything," he said. "She's been in the water for hours."

"I'm not listening to you. I like my job too much."

"Heh," he said. "If you liked your job so much, you wouldn't insist on doing it wrong."

"Fuck you."

"She wasn't killed here. She was killed out at sea. She came here in the storm."

I stopped walking and stared at him.

He stuffed his hands into the pockets of his jacket and looked back with the ease and calm of a madman.

"Bullshit."

"Nope," he said. "She's got mottled livor mortis on her ass and pulmonary edema in her lungs."

He waited, but I wasn't going to give him the satisfaction of asking him to explain how he'd come up with that. He walked toward me and stood over me, as most men do.

"Livor mortis," he said. "The settling and pooling of blood in the veins after de—"

"I know what livor mortis is, asshole."

"Well, you'll know that if a corpse is being tossed around in rough water, the blood doesn't settle, so it never collects," he said. "Except in the ass. Fine skin. Lots of big juicy fat cells. I'd say she's been in the water at least twenty hours. With the storm blowing a westerly, she was likely dumped out there, in the ocean."

"The rigor mortis? Not set?"

"No."

"And the pulmonary edema," I said, feeling my hackles rise again. "The foam in her lu—"

"I know what pulmonary edema is, asshole," Tox said.

"She was alive when she went in," I whispered.

CHAPTER 10

I FOLLOWED TOX back to the body of the girl and stood facing away from the crowd. My mind was swirling. Sure, Tox knew his stuff. He'd already started developing a theory, helping my case enormously within only minutes of the scene being cordoned off. But as I glanced at the cops behind me, I knew I couldn't keep him around much longer or I'd never get the thing solved. Working with Tox Barnes wouldn't throw a wrench into the works. It'd throw a whole toolbox.

As far as I'd heard, people now and then were forced to work with him. But he was a burden that one took heavily, and offloaded as soon as possible. You found a way to transfer out of partnership with him, or soon enough you would begin to find your job almost impossible. People started avoiding you in the coffee room. Losing your reports, delaying your lab results. Accidents would begin to happen—someone would spill coffee on your laptop, bump your car on the way out of the parking lot, forget to include you in weekend get-togethers.

I'd just turned to him to ask him again to leave when I noticed he was smoking a cigarette.

"Jesus Christ," I said. "Put that out! You're in my crime scene."

He grunted.

"You've just had that hand in a dead girl!"

"That was this hand." He lifted the other from his pocket,

waved it, pulled the cigarette from his mouth with the clean one. "For a detective, you're pretty blind to details. Me? I've noticed everything there is to notice about your hands. Chewed nails. Swollen knuckles. No sign of a wedding ring, probably ever."

"Look." I leaned close. "I don't like you. I don't want to work with you. I've heard bad things, and they appear to be true. You should have waited for an autopsy to confirm your findings. There's a process, and it's in place for a reason."

"I don't like to waste time," he said. "And that's exactly what you're doing now, jibber-jabbering at me. What station you work at?"

"Surry Hills," I said.

"Right." He clapped me hard on the shoulder as he turned to leave. "I'll see you there first thing."

He wandered off, and the police officers lining the tape watched him go. When he was a good distance away they ducked under the tape and started setting up to do their jobs. I stood stunned in their midst, no idea what I should do next. The photographer snapped a picture of me standing over the body, my arms folded.

"That guy's a murderer, you know," he said, adjusting his lens. "Killed a mother and her young kid. Beat 'em to death. Tox was seven."

"Yeah, so I hear." I was badly craving a cigarette of my own now. I hadn't smoked in years. But no one around me was offering anything but hateful glances.

"Guy like that's gonna do it again," the photographer said. "You don't start that young unless it's in your bones."

CHAPTER 11

MY HEAD WAS a mess by the time I arrived at Surry Hills police headquarters. It was 6 a.m. and the sun was rising. I'd stayed at the crime scene and orchestrated the evidence collection, got rid of the press, and sent out a couple of detectives to bring the parents in. Within an hour we had preliminary identification. Until we could get the parents to ID the body, we weren't sure. But it looked as though the girl was Claudia Burrows: her description linked up with a missing persons report that had been issued a day earlier. She had a tattoo of a rabbit in a waistcoat on her hip that matched the report exactly.

I didn't like where this was all going, mainly because it was heading in the very opposite direction of the Georges River Killer. The killer we'd been hunting didn't drown his victims—he didn't put them in the water at all, but left them stripped to their panties, face down on the beach. His victims showed signs of physical and sexual abuse, while Claudia hadn't looked in any way battered. I'd checked her wrists and ankles for ligature marks but there were none, except for a rough sort of rubbing on one foot. For all I knew, she might have fallen into Botany Bay drunk and drowned there, the waves stripping her clothes off as she floated toward the mouth of the river.

Though it didn't look good for my entry onto the Georges River Killer task force, I wasn't going to let go. It was possible the killer had changed his methods to confuse us. He was a wily creature, as far as I could tell, and he might have recognized that he was being tracked. I went right to the door of the task force's case room and knocked, trying to shove my way in when no one answered. I came up against the thin and wiry Detective Nigel Spader just inside the door.

"You're not allowed in here." He pushed me back out the door before I could get a glimpse of their case board. "This is the last time I'm going to tell you, Blue."

"I'm allowed in," I said. "Chief Morris put me on a Georges River body last night. You'll need to debrief me and get me up to speed so we can start making connections."

"Your case is not connected to ours." He tried to shut the door on me.

"How the fuck would you know something like that? It's a dark-haired girl almost naked on the banks of the Georges. I'm ticking all the boxes. If I knew what other boxes I could tick, maybe the link would be even stronger. You're putting me on this task force, Nigel, before I kick you in the face."

"It's not the GRK." Nigel sighed. "Now piss off."

He slammed the door on my boot. I shoved forward, slid an arm into the gap, and tried to grab him. Pops's voice sent a bolt of electricity through me.

"Detective Blue!"

"I'm just helping, Chief." I pulled the door shut, gave the knob a jiggle. "Making sure the case room is secure."

"You've got the dead girl's parents in interrogation room six." He carried his coffee toward me. "I've put the paperwork in. You'll share the case with Detective Barnes."

"Are you kidding me?"

"He was the first responder," the old man said. "He's got some good theories. The media has got hold of the case already, so it'll be all over the news. And she's a bright, pretty university student. I want to have something meaningful to say at the press conference."

"University student?" My mouth fell open.

"She'd just applied and been accepted. Her parents told the patrol cops who picked them up," the Chief said. "Applied, studied—in the media's eyes, it's the same thing. She was full of prospects. We need to get something quickly."

"Well, you can tell them this is a Georges River Killer case, then." I counted off on my fingers: "Dark hair, Georges River, semi-naked, university student..."

"It's not," Pops said, and walked away.

I stood in the middle of the bullpen and looked at the officers all around me, some of them answering phones, some of them clicking away at computers. Had the whole world gone crazy? I felt as if I were speaking a foreign language, and everyone I talked to was pretending to understand and then brushing me off. I was concerned I was getting so frustrated I might be tempted to cry. I generally cry about once a year, so I wasn't going to waste it on this bureaucratic bullshit.

"This *is* a Georges River Killer case!" I roared. The men and women on their phones turned to look at me. "I need to be on the task force!"

"It's not," Pops said calmly as he closed the door to his office.

CHAPTER 12

THE *DREAM CATCHER* had been in a dry dock at Garden Island for two days. In that time, Hope had cleared it of almost all the Spellings' possessions. She did keep some things—a nice new laptop that had belonged to Ken, and some of Jenny's more modern jewelry. She was exhausted from constant trips to the shower cubicle to see if Ken was awake, and, if he was, to hold the chloroform-soaked rag over his face until he slept again. Jenny didn't stir at all. It was as though she knew her husband was lost in the land of dreams, and she'd chosen to join him there.

Between trips to check on her prisoners, Hope spent most of that morning lying on the bow in one of the deck chairs in her bikini, reading the yacht's operating manual and writing down questions for Ken. She needed a tan if she was going to fit in with the other yachties—she couldn't look like a newbie or they wouldn't accept her into their world. Sometimes she closed her eyes and pretended she was at sea, sailing across the Indian Ocean, the sun baking her pale skin a deep golden brown like Jenny's. She didn't keep her eyes closed too long, or she'd see flashes, electric zings of light that sometimes contained frightened faces, splashes of blood, clawing fingers. The images played about the corners of her eyes, made her chew her nails. They'd go, in time, these memories. She just had to focus on the plan.

It was almost funny, the way it had all come together one night at the Black Garter while she'd been sitting in the window watching the men outside. One of the girls had wandered in from the main hall with a sea captain's hat on her head, tipping the brim in the closet mirror and tilting her naked hips. She'd snagged the hat from the leader of a bachelor party, the pack of drunken boys hollering from the back courtyard as other girls danced around the lazy-eyed groom.

"What do you think?" The girl had taken the cap off and sent it sailing across the room into Hope's hands like a Frisbee. "Captain Hope, reporting for duty."

Hope had stared at herself in the mirror after the girl had gone, the cap too big on her head, a tiny girl playing dress-up. She'd remembered sailing with her father, those few times he had indulged himself over the years and rented cruisers for a trot around the harbor. Pretending he owned them. Lies and make-believe. Hope was so tired of all the games—the ones the men made her play, the ones she played with herself. Captain Hope, Master of Her Own Destiny.

It would take a miracle to achieve something like that, she'd thought.

Or would it?

What exactly *would* it take?

Hope walked the length of the vessel now, examining the newly painted surface, and then climbed down the ladder onto the floor of the dry dock. When she'd acquired the *Dream Catcher* it had been a hideous wine-bottle green, but the guys she'd hired for the makeover had finished the last coat of the new color—a chic, modern ash gray. Hope had started making lists of steps in her plan that very night as she'd huddled away in the back of the brothel, and once the list had been completed, she'd made a new one. She couldn't remember how many lists it had taken, how many crossed or canceled steps. Find a couple selling their yacht. Find an ally to comfort the couple as they inquired about the sale, someone cute and easy to manipulate, someone who knew how to act in a prescribed role. Hope had followed a recipe she found online for chloroform and cooked it in the brothel kitchen, whistling, as if she were baking a cake.

Picking out and commissioning the fresh paint job on the boat was one step she'd been looking forward to for a while. She stood now with her hand on the vessel and listened to the hull to see if there was any sign of the couple from within. Nothing. She wandered around the back of the boat in her sun hat and glasses and stood watching the men on the ladder as they applied the new name to the side.

"Just in time for the big reveal," the tall one said. He was a stunning young man in a cut-off undershirt, spattered all over with tiny spots of white paint. He looked as if he were covered in stars. He reached up and began peeling away the paper stencil around the lettering on the hull of the boat.

"The *New Hope*," she read. She felt a dark stirring in her chest at the sight of the words. She'd had the boys paint them in a deep crimson. Her dream, written in blood.

CHAPTER 13

TOX WAS ALREADY in the interrogation room with Claudia's parents. Not only was it one of the unfriendliest rooms in the station to speak to them, but I had no idea what he'd already said. I felt my stomach tighten as I spotted him sitting there in the cramped, musty room beyond the two-way mirror, their horrified faces. Mom and Dad had recently been crying. She was a heavy blond woman, and their daughter's lean features and dark hair came from her mustached father. I threw open the door just in time.

"...breast implants?" Tox was saying.

"What?" Mrs. Burrows frowned. She glanced at me, her mouth twisted.

"Yeah, what?" I sat down beside Tox.

"I was just asking Mr. and Mrs. Burrows here how long it had been since their daughter got those breast implants." He looked lazily at me. "You did notice the cadaver had breast implants, right?"

"Mr. and Mrs. Burrows." I put my hands calmly on the table beside the handcuff hooks. "I must apologize for my partner here. Detective Barnes has been under a lot of stress and isn't thinking clearly."

Tox folded his hands on the table beside mine, imitating me. "Look, your daughter was found deceased this morning, and that's very sad. But I'm sure that you'll get over that sadness and want to catch whoever did this, eventually. Well, you know what? *We* want to catch whoever did this *now*. It's our job, see. Now your daughter had fake tits—"

"Tox!" I yelped.

"—and I'm putting together the exaggerated size of those tits, and her petite figure, and the approximate cost of such a surgical enhancement, and your obvious middle-classness— I'm going to take a leap and say she was a prostitute."

"Jesus!" I clapped a hand over my eyes.

"Actually, it's not a leap at all," Tox confirmed. "She *was* a prostitute, wasn't she?"

The Burrowses sat stunned. I got up and grabbed Tox's arm and yanked him toward the door.

"I'll be back," I told the couple. "Just sit tight."

Tox turned on me in the hallway.

"What is it with you and wasting time?" he grunted, almost irritated. "I was on a roll in there."

"You were *not* on a roll," I snapped. "You were on anything but a roll. You were traumatizing the dead girl's parents."

"Jesus Christ!" Tox threw his hands up, flapped them dramatically, trying to imitate my voice with his gravelly tones. *"You're sticking your finger in the dead girl. You're smoking near the dead girl. You're traumatizing the parents of the dead girl.* You sure you're right for this job, Detective? You might find yourself better employed in undertaking. You're in love with the dead girl."

"You just... you can't talk to people this way." I was so horrified, the words wouldn't come. "These parents are grieving. No, they're probably not even grieving yet. They're probably still in shock."

"Is the emotional state of these people really your priority right now?" Tox shook his head in disbelief. "First you want me to slow down so that we can go through all the procedural bullshit surrounding the corpse. Now you want me to slow down so we can go through all the emotional crap with the parents. Do you actually want to solve this case or are you just trying to score overtime?"

"It's not crap, it's . . . it's life!"

"Not my life," Tox snorted.

A pair of patrol cops were walking down the hall toward us, carrying folders full of papers. One bumped hard into my shoulder as she passed, causing me to drop my phone. My punishment had begun. Nearby, an older officer I knew, Chris Murray, was fielding a call and glaring at us, taking in the figure of my new partner with obvious distaste.

"How long has the couple been missing?" Murray was saying into his mobile. "And what's the name of the boat?"

"Listen." I pointed at Tox. "If we're going to work together on this, there need to be rules. I think number one should be that I do all the talking, all the time."

"Geh," he grunted. "Sounds just like a woman. All the talking, all the time."

He went back into the interrogation room. I held my face in my hands for a long moment, relishing the darkness. When I lifted my head there were about five people in the bullpen staring at me, each set of eyes more hateful than the last.

CHAPTER 14

I CALLED MY brother Sam from the ladies' bathroom, leaning my forehead on the mirror. I knew that he'd probably be teaching his classes at the university, but I dialed anyway.

"What's up?" he answered.

"I'm in crisis mode," I said. "I need a friendly voice."

I explained the situation in a long, rambling stream. In the background of the call I could hear students rumbling through the halls of the university.

"Being partnered up with this guy—is it going to make solving the case difficult?"

"The case should be fine, but my social standing might take a hit."

He laughed. I'd never had many friends to begin with, and he knew that. I was a loner. Hardly a cheerful spirit. I forgot people's birthdays and didn't turn up to work drinks. None of my colleagues tried to set me up on dates. They knew a romantic train wreck when they saw one.

"If I stick with him too long, I might have to start chewing my lunch more carefully," I continued.

"Cops," Sam said. "All that ancient brotherhood bullshit."

"I can see where everyone's coming from." I sighed. "I mean, apart from what he's supposed to have done, the guy is also a world-class arrogant dickhead."

I told Sam about his treatment of Claudia's body, about how he'd spoken to her parents.

"He might just be out of practice on his behavior with other people, if he's such an outcast. He might have genuinely forgotten how people are supposed to talk to each other," Sam suggested.

"You always think the best of people," I said. "I don't know how. I'm about ready to kill him."

"Well, that might make things messier."

"You may be the only man I'm not prepared to strangle right now," I told him. "That detective Nigel Spader caught me at the door to the case room. I didn't even get a peek."

"Ah yes, I've met that one. He was here yesterday doing interviews of the faculty, trying to find out if we know anything about the Georges River girls," Sam said. "I think we're booked in for second interviews today. Two of the victims were students here."

"Second interviews?"

"A couple of us, yeah," he said. "I don't know why."

"Weird. Were the victims students of yours?"

"No." He sighed. "But some of my students were friends with them. A girl rushed out of my morning class yesterday, crying. It's hard to know what to say."

My stomach felt mildly unsettled. I put the phone on speaker and washed my face under the tap.

"Tell me how the second interview goes," I told Sam. I convinced myself it was just the stress of the new case and my new partner making me sick. If I kept on track, it would go away.

As I'd find often in my life, I should have listened to what my instincts were telling me.

CHAPTER 15

TOX SMOKED IN my car. As I drove, I tried to think of one thing about him that didn't annoy me. I decided I didn't mind Tox's leather jacket. I had a similar one. We stopped for coffee outside the station and then headed west toward Claudia Burrows's apartment on Parramatta Road.

"When you arrived at the crime scene last night, I saw you unwrapping your knuckles in your car," Tox said, putting one of his boots on the dashboard. "You box?"

"I box, yes."

"Who'd you beat up?"

"I didn't beat anyone up."

"Boxers spar. There's very little blood involved. Looked to me like you pounded on someone outside the ring, using your boxing skills to get the upper hand."

"See, this is what you do," I said. "You make microscopic observations and you blow them out into wild theories that make no sense."

"Like the tits."

"Stop saying 'tits'! Christ, you sound like a fat, sleazy truck driver in a highway bar." I imitated his quiet, gravelly voice, grabbed my crotch: *"Look at those tits! I love tits! Urgghh!"*

"Was that supposed to be me?"

"Yes."

"You want to know why I sound like this?" he rasped. I glanced over, and he pulled at the collar of his shirt, revealing a long pink scar at the base of his throat. "Drug dealer stabbed me in the neck during a raid. Went right through the windpipe and out the other side."

"Well," I said, "I'm sorry. I didn't mean to make fun."

He stared at me. "What kind of a horrible person makes fun of someone with a physical disabil—"

"Shut up!" I shoved him into the car door. "Goddamnit!"

"All right, so. Mom and Dad claimed Claudia was a part-time waitress," Tox said. "She wasn't paying for those knockers on a waitress's salary, and even if she was, you don't get them that size unless you're in the sex industry."

"Maybe she got a loan," I said. "And maybe she got them that size because she liked them that size. Look, I work in sex crimes, okay? So I'm going to need you to get your brain out of the Dark Ages and stop making misogynistic assumptions about our victim."

"Meh." He sat back and flicked his cigarette ash out the window. "What does your girlfriend think about you working in sex crimes?"

"My girlfriend?" I looked at him. "I'm not gay."

"Oh, right."

"What made you think I was gay?"

He waved his cigarette at my head. "Your hair."

We pulled into an old apartment block in Auburn and parked in the visitors' space. I didn't talk to Tox on the way up the damp concrete steps. If he was going to make me this mad every time we spoke, I was going to have a brain aneurysm before we actually discovered what had happened to Claudia Burrows.

Tox's sexism wasn't helped by Nigel Spader and his team rebuffing me from the Georges River Killer case. The Australian police force had always been full of boys' club antics, what Sam called the "ancient brotherhood bullshit." I was disappointed to see it creeping into my own station. Pops was a good chief, and didn't let even the most minor sexual harassment or favoritism play down between his staff. But I had the feeling Nigel and his boys didn't want me on the task force because I was a woman, and that even if Claudia did turn out to be one of the Georges River victims, they'd take the case off me completely. This was going to be a history-making case. There would be books about it. Nigel wanted his face on one of those books. He oozed heroic smugness.

Tox opened Claudia's door with the keys her parents had given us. He'd only prized it open a crack when it slammed back against him.

And someone inside yelled, "Go! *Go!*"

CHAPTER 16

HOPE ANALYZED HER reflection in the jewelry shop window, pulling the wig down slightly at the front and straightening her skirt-suit jacket. She'd kept only one of Jenny Spelling's suits in a hideous mustard yellow, the closest fit and the most modern piece she could find. It looked as though Jenny hadn't updated her wardrobe in decades. That irritated Hope. She couldn't stand people who'd been lucky enough to grow up in the lap of luxury who then refused to use the money they'd squirreled away. She didn't know much about Jenny, but she couldn't understand how anyone respected her, dressed like this. She felt awkward in the slightly too-big heels, like a child playing dress-up.

Her first stop when she got the money was going to be shopping, for herself and for the boat. The *galley* needed new curtains, and the *bridge* needed a lamp. Hope tried to contain the excitement bubbling up inside her, taking a deep breath before she walked into the bank.

She went directly to the manager's desk and sat down on the chair there. A young man with a big Adam's apple came wandering out, his face spreading into a smile.

"How can I help you?"

"Oh, hi." Hope extended a hand. "I'm Jenny Spelling. I'd like to make a transaction from my savings account, please."

"Of course." The young man glanced toward the queue waiting at the counters. "Is this a large transaction?"

"I'd like to empty the account and close it, actually," Hope said. "Nothing to do with your bank. You've been wonderful to my husband and I, but we're moving overseas and we'll be starting a local account there."

"Well, congratulations!" the young man said. "What an exciting time. Let me just get your identification, Mrs. Spelling, and we'll have a look for you."

Hope opened Jenny Spelling's clunky leather wallet and extracted her driver's license and credit card. She kept a hand up near her eyes, playing with the edge of her low, heavy bangs, as the young man looked over the cards.

It worked. He went to the computer beside him and started tapping. Hope could feel sweat running down the backs of her calves. She squirmed in the older woman's shoes, trying to keep a straight face.

"So it's your main savings account that you'd like to close? Or would you like to close your everyday account as well?"

"Oh, all of it," she said. "I'll take all of it, please."

CHAPTER 17

HOPE GLANCED AT the screen and noted the amounts in the accounts. The everyday was petty cash, but the digits in the main savings account made her heart twist in her chest. So close to her dream. So close to everything she'd ever wanted. She needed to play it cool now. She touched her eyebrow as a muscle began to twitch there.

"Um, so it says heeeere…" The young man frowned and clicked. "Says here this is actually a joint signature account."

"What?" Hope choked.

"Right here." The young man turned the screen toward her, tapped its glossy surface. "When you and your husband opened the account, you made a provision that you could only extract more than a thousand dollars from this account if you both came into the bank and signed for it."

"Fuck!" Hope blurted. She covered her mouth. "I mean, oh, dear. Um."

"You don't remember making that provision?" the young man asked. Hope scratched at her throat. "No, I don't."

"Where did you open the account?"

He turned the screen back toward himself while Hope shifted in her chair.

"Oh, God, it was such a long time ago." She laughed. "Look,

let me get a thousand dollars, and I'll get Ken down here to empty the main savings with me some other time."

"Right." The young man was looking at her very closely now. Hope turned her face away, glanced at the people waiting in line at the counter. "Would you like to empty the everyday as well? That account is yours alone."

"I know that," Hope snapped. She shoved her hands into her lap. "I'm sorry. Yes. I know that. I'll empty that account, too. Mmm-hmm."

The young man made some movements with his mouse. While he clicked and scrolled, Hope watched his face, until his eyes slid over and met hers.

"All right?"

"Yep." Hope smiled.

"All right." The young man got up and gave a cheerful smile. "I'll be back in just a minute."

Hope could hardly wait for him to count out the bills. She grabbed the money and her cards from the desktop and practically ran to the door.

In the street she paused and looked at the men and women passing by, their eyes on their phones. She'd hoped no one else would have to die for her plan to be completed. But something inside told her that more blood would be needed to wash away the life she was trapped in.

CHAPTER 18

I GOT OUT my gun and kicked in the door of Claudia's apartment, slamming it against the guy who'd just closed it on us. He fell into a coffee table covered in beer bottles, scattering them everywhere. There was another guy at the entrance to the kitchen. I pulled my gun up and shouted but he ran in there, hoping for an exit. There was none. Tox grabbed the first guy, picked him up off the ruined coffee table, and threw him into the television stand, crunching DVD boxes and splintering the screen of the cheap plasma. I went to the kitchen doorway and was narrowly missed by a flying frying pan. Two saucepans and a handful of cutlery came sailing out after it.

I put my gun away and grabbed the frying pan from the couch where it had landed. When I rushed into the kitchen the guy cowered into the corner near the blender as I wielded the pan above my head.

"How do you like it?" I yelled. His arm was raised against the weapon, eyes squeezed shut.

"Don't! Please! I'm sorry!"

I let him up.

"Shit, man! You're one crazy bitch!"

"Get out there." I yanked him toward the door. Tox had the other guy on the floor beside the glass heap that had been the coffee table. Bright red blood was pouring down Tox's chin and neck, making a neat column on his chest.

"Little prick kicked me in the face." Tox looked at the blood on his hand.

"What are you dickheads doing here?" I kicked my guy along the floor until he was beside his friend. "You know Claudia Burrows is dead, right?"

"We heard about it." My guy was holding his head of black dreadlocks, his eyes welling with tears of panic. "She borrowed some money from our boss three weeks ago. We were told to come get it before the police swept in and took everything."

The intruders had gathered a small pile of cash and electronic goods and put them on the couch, with some jewelry clumped into a Chinese takeaway container.

"How much did she borrow?" Tox asked.

"Not much. Five grand. It was a short-term loan. She said she was coming into some big money and she'd get it right back to us."

"Shhh, dude." Tox's guy nudged his friend. "Fuck, man. Who you talkin' to?"

"Pfft, they don't care." Dreadlocks waved dismissively at me. "They just care who killed her."

"How did you hear she'd been killed? Her body was only found last night."

"My brother's a patrol cop in Newtown." Dreadlocks waved again.

"Your brother's a cop and you're a loan shark's bitch?" I snorted. "No guessing who got all the hugs."

"What did Claudia borrow the money for?" Tox asked. "Did she say?"

"We're not talking any more. That's it. We're done."

"All right, well, it's down to the station with both of you for breaking and entering." I took the cuffs off the back of my belt. "And maybe assaulting a police officer."

"She needed clothes!" Dreadlocks wailed as I dragged him up and threw him on the couch. "Good girl clothes."

"What do you mean, 'good girl clothes'?"

"Shut up, Ray! Fuck!"

I cuffed Ray and left him moaning in regret on the couch, his face pressed between the pillows. In the bedroom, Claudia's things had been thrown about, drawers emptied onto the bed and her jewelry tipped onto the floor. I went to the closet and pushed open the doors, and immediately I could see what Ray meant. Claudia's clothes were scant—tiny tops and tight leggings, plenty of sequins and beads and the odd strip of gold leather. I pulled out a complicated black corset of velvet, the buckles jangling as I set it on the bed.

At the very end of the closet, there were three new outfits hanging, long-sleeved silk blouses and pencil skirts in plastic sheaths. Beneath them on the carpet was a pair of brand-new sensible leather pumps. I checked the brands of the outfits, tugged a price tag that was still attached to one of them. Damn. These were certainly "good girl" clothes. Against the rest of her wardrobe, these outfits seemed like a disguise. I bent down as one of the jackets slid off the hanger and gathered it up from the floor, spotting a dusty white powder on the wrist. I gathered it up and tasted it, expecting cocaine, but I was surprised. It was dry salt. Slightly fishy-tasting. Sometime recently, Claudia had worn these clothes by the sea.

CHAPTER 19

I NEEDED COFFEE. All the calm and contentment I'd managed to generate last night by giving Ben Hammond a pounding was gone now. My shoulders were as hard as stone. We stopped at a café on the way back to the city and Tox dragged out an ancient black laptop.

"Claudia's parents said nothing about her being a hooker." I rubbed my eyes. "Maybe she was just dipping into the industry briefly to raise some money to go to college."

"So why borrow the five G's then?" Tox asked. "Why spend them on conservative clothes?"

"I don't know. But while we're on the subject of clothes, you'll need to change before we go much farther."

The waitress was so distracted by the blood on the front of Tox's shirt that she hardly managed to get our order down. My new partner's eyes were steadily blackening and there was a graze above his nasal bone. Tox glanced at his shirt.

"Eh," he said.

"You're going to go to college," I mused. "Start fresh. Make something of your life. You're twenty-four years old, so you've left it late, but not that late. You've been accepted. What do you do?"

"You go out and buy textbooks," Tox said.

"Right. Textbooks, a laptop maybe. Not expensive clothes.

And where's this money coming from in the first place? The big money she says she's about to come into?"

An e-mail came up on my phone and I checked it. It was a brief summary from the medical examiner, a quick review of his initial findings before the full autopsy on Claudia Burrows. Tox had been right about the livor mortis, and the pulmonary edema, and the fact that Claudia had likely been dead a day, in the water about twenty hours. He was also right about the breast implants. I saw him smiling at his laptop screen. He'd probably just gotten the same e-mail.

"This is interesting," I said. "She'd had her hair dyed and cut no more than a week ago. And she'd taken a good bonk to the back of the head."

"Feet are showing blisters from the new high heels," Tox added.

"So whatever she needed to jazz up her appearance for, she's done it in the last week or so. Parents didn't mention any job interviews. Weird."

Our coffees came. I gulped mine and ordered another.

"'Skin slippage around the right ankle suggests ligature, ante-mortem, for a short amount of time, pulling downward over the front of the foot toward the toes,'" I read. "So she was weighed down when she went in the water."

"How do you figure that?"

"Well, weight goes into the water." I drew a circle on the greasy tabletop with my finger, a line rising from it. "Rope goes up from the weight, ties around Claudia's ankle. Claudia floats upward, pulling the rope down toward her toes. The rope doesn't bruise her too badly because it comes loose in the storm, letting her body float away."

We fell into silence to consider the images before us, the cold medical text detailing Claudia's horrific last moments on earth.

"This is a pretty nasty killer we have here," I said. "I can't imagine why throwing her in alive was necessary. By the time you've got her tied to the weight, she's under your control. Why not put her out of her misery? Why make her think about the journey down to the bottom of the sea? It's so vicious."

"I don't know about that," Tox said. "Think about it. Putting her out of her misery is extra effort. Extra *consideration*. What we might have here is someone who isn't even that thoughtful. Someone who never thought about what the victim would or wouldn't feel. I think we're looking for a killer whose priority is getting the job done, ticking the boxes. Just my opinion."

I pushed my phone away and studied his face as he checked through the rest of his e-mails. I couldn't help but feel an icy heaviness in my chest at his talk of priorities and getting the job done. He'd shown himself to be just that kind of man. Unconcerned with what people feel. I wondered if he was just talking about Claudia's victims, or his own ones, too.

CHAPTER 20

MY KNUCKLES STILL hurt from the impact against the back of Ben Hammond's skull, but I wasn't focusing on that as I smacked my opponent in his ribs, his chest. I surged forward and drove an elbow into the side of his padded head. Pops backed up into the corner of the ring. I didn't think of him as the old, squat man that he was. In the ring we were equals. I gave him a couple of jabs in the face and backed off to let him out of the trap he'd fallen into.

"Mind that back step." The Chief pointed at my foot with his red boxing glove. "Don't cross."

Pops had been training me since I'd arrived at Sydney Metro to take up the grand position of the only woman on the sex crimes squad. There hadn't been a female in my role for five years, but the department had wanted someone victims could relate to, someone who wouldn't accidentally intimidate them with their masculine hulk in the tiny station interview rooms. It wasn't long after arriving that I'd decided I needed some form of self-defense, my days filled with horrific stories of attacks in alleyways and empty parking lots, young girls ensnared walking home across darkened parks by fiendish predators. I was probably getting too swift for Chief Morris, who had been training boxers since before I was born. But I trusted his advice.

He'd made me strong, and he didn't take less than full commitment in his sessions.

"Tell me about the Georges River case," I said, batting away his swing at my face. "Why were your guys so sure my girl wasn't one of the victims?"

I'd given up on the idea that Claudia Burrows was a Georges River Killer victim. But something was nibbling at me about the certainty with which Nigel had shoved me away. Nigel hadn't even been called to Claudia's crime scene for a look. How could they know their killer wasn't responsible?

"Have you guys got a suspect?" I asked.

"Leave it, Harry," he said.

"You must be pretty set on this suspect if you're certain he didn't kill Claudia," I said. "Maybe because you were watching your suspect when Claudia was killed. Am I right? Have you got enough for an arrest?"

"I didn't even say we had a suspect."

"Well, if you don't have a suspect, I have to assume you're letting Nigel and his band of asshats push me away because they want it to be a men-only case."

I punched Pops in the stomach. He fell against the ropes.

"Harry—"

"I'm a good cop, you know." I thumped my chest with my boxing glove. "Being a woman shouldn't exclude me from anything."

"No one's excluding you."

"The Camden strangler? Dennis Yama? David Paris, that cannibal guy? They were all me, Pops. Homicide got the credit, sure, but it was the sex crimes side of those investigations that put them on track."

"Harry, no one's doubting your abilities."

"Then why the fuck am I being shut out?"

I pummeled Pops with a series of hits to the head. Without warning, he clutched at his chest and fell into the corner of the ring. I watched in horror as he collapsed.

CHAPTER 21

"OH, SHIT!" I tore my gloves off. "Shit! Pops! I'm sorry!"

I dragged the old man to his feet. He unclipped the padded helmet and let it fall to the mat. His face was red and drenched in sweat. He thumped his chest as though he had heartburn and shook his head.

"Are you all right?"

"Yeah, yeah."

"I'm sorry. I got carried away."

"You're too good for your old trainer, Harry." He batted me on the shoulder with his glove. "You're a good cop, too. You're not being shut out of the Georges River task force because of your abilities, or your gender. You gotta let it go. Okay?"

"Why?" I followed the old man to the stool at the opposite corner of the ring. I handed him the bottle of water sitting there. "I just don't understand. I feel like there's something you're keeping from me. And we've never been like this, Pops. We've never kept things from each other."

The old man sucked at the water bottle and regained his breath. He wouldn't meet my eyes. I ducked my head to try to see what was hidden there, whether it was guilt or shame or concern cutting him off from me. But he wiped his forehead on the back of his arm and turned away.

"It'll all come out in time," he said. "And when it does, you'll... you'll be grateful for all the time you *didn't* know the truth."

CHAPTER 22

HOPE NEEDED TO stay calm. It was rational planning and control that was going to get her through this. As soon as she had the Spellings' money, she was out of here. Off toward the sunrise on the gentle waves. She'd never look back on Sydney, on the feast of horrors the city had provided over her life. This town deserved to burn. She walked along the pier between the yachts and looked at the glowing city towers reflected in the black harbor. Soon she'd be underway.

Her plan was to leave behind the memories of what she had done to Jenny and Ken Spelling, along with the memories of her father and his sweaty, grabby hands. She'd try to replace the night beast he'd become after her mother's death with the man she remembered from her early childhood, his eyes set on the horizon, one warm hand on hers as he taught her to direct the helm, taking them out toward the edge of forever. She'd leave them behind with the memories of her almost skeletal mother curled up in the tub she'd died in, with the smoke-saturated bedrooms of the Black Garter hotel where she'd worked for almost all of her adult life. If she closed her eyes, she could still see the red lamplight out the front of the house of horrors, the men smoking there, looking at their phones, talking about the girls inside and which ones provided which services. Soon, when she closed her eyes, it would be the Caribbean sun burning red light there. Or maybe Key Largo. She hadn't decided yet.

As she powered the *New Hope* east out over the South Pacific, she'd jettison the images that sometimes zapped through her. Claudia's howling mouth as she'd sailed downward into the blackness of the ocean, the anchor yanking her soundlessly into the dark. Her confused eyes as Hope had come into the kitchen after they'd secured the Spellings in the bathroom, the hammer in her fist.

I thought we were in this together....

Her squeal of disbelief as Hope had raised the hammer above her head.

CHAPTER 23

HOPE STILL CARRIED the hammer with her in Jenny's cream Louis Vuitton handbag. She supposed she'd have to get rid of that, too. She was dreaming as she wandered along mooring number 17 and almost ran into the overweight man with the clipboard standing there.

"Oh! Sorry!"

"It's all right." He laughed. His name tag said STEVE. "Is this your yacht here?"

"Yes, it is, actually." Hope smiled. "It's just come out of dry dock. I signed in at the office."

"Yes, yes, that's all good." Steve glanced at his clipboard. "I'm actually just doing a safety inspection. The coastguard makes us do spot checks now and then on all the moorings."

"Uh-huh." Hope chewed her lip. She listened to the boat beside them. Was that thumping she could hear? Could Steve hear it, too?

"Everything's fine. It's just...it's so weird." Steve pointed with his pen to a red cone-shaped device strapped to the side of the deck. "I'm running checks on all the EPIRBs to make sure they're all registered and up to date, and this one isn't right."

Hope shifted her handbag on her shoulder. "An EPIRB?"

"It's an emergency position-indicating radio beacon." Steve looked at the sky, recited the words carefully. "Ha, that's what

I think it stands for, anyway. That beacon gets wet and it'll send a signal to the coastguard telling them you're in trouble. You'll want to chuck it in the water long before you start to sink, though!"

"Right." Hope laughed.

"They also kind of act like a microchip would in your family dog," Steve said. "They're registered to particular people, and particular boats, in case the boat gets lost. Or the people get lost! Ha! Now, I'm seeing that your boat here is the *New Hope.* But when I look up your EPIRB number on the computer, it says this boat should be *Dream Catcher.*"

Steve tipped his clipboard, which he used to balance a thin computer tablet. Hope hardly glanced at the numbers on the screen.

"Did you change your vessel's name, Ms...." Steve looked at the screen. "Ms. Spelling?"

"Uh, no." Hope wiped sweat from her neck. "No, this is...this is a different vessel. That we...we only recently purchased, my husband and I."

"Oh."

"I mean, I'm not even Ms. Spelling." Hope drew a long breath. "Whoever that is. I'm...uh."

Steve waited.

"Look, would you like to come aboard?" Hope gestured to the yacht. "Come on board and I'll show you the paperwork and we can sort all this out."

"Sure thing." Steve smiled. He turned and stepped across the small gangway to the deck.

Hope followed, sliding her hand into the darkness of her handbag and around the polished handle of the hammer.

CHAPTER 24

DESPITE THE EVENING gym session, I couldn't sleep. I desperately needed to. I called my brother and blasted him with complaints about Tox as soon as he picked up.

"What actually is the story with this guy?" he said. "How can he possibly be a cop if you're saying he's killed two people?"

"No idea," I grunted. "People are saying he was seven years old. If I had to guess, I'd say that because of his age at the time of the crime, he'd have been charged with involuntary manslaughter, if he was charged with anything at all. Apparently it was a group of boys, not just him. So his lawyers would have said he was influenced by the group, and far too young to know what he was doing."

"But you don't actually know any details about it?"

"No, the records are sealed. I tried to have a look before I left work this afternoon."

Sam scoffed. "So it's all just rumor, really?"

"What are you getting at?"

"Maybe he didn't do it."

"If he didn't do it, he'd have set everyone straight, right?" I said. "The bosses would have set everyone straight. He must have done it."

We fell silent.

"I'd like to think he didn't do it," I admitted. "But when I look in his eyes, I'm not so sure."

CHAPTER 25

I SAT IN bed all night on the computer after speaking to Sam, clicking around, looking for Claudia Burrows. She'd recently scrubbed her social media presence clean. There were suggestions that she'd once had a Facebook page and a Twitter account, but these were empty now, the links broken. I saw a couple of pictures of her on sites that must have belonged to her friends. She was a very different girl from the one whom I'd seen washed up on the shores of the Georges River. Her hair, which had been short and dark when she died, was long and bleach-blond, the roots dark and the ends scraggly. I learned that she sometimes went under the name Claudia Dee. Did multiple names mean multiple identities? Was it Claudia Dee who'd worn the skimpy clothes that filled most of her wardrobe, and Claudia Burrows who'd bought the more formal attire?

I didn't like the idea that Claudia had been pretending to be someone else, and that she'd recently told her creditors that she was coming into money. Had she been conducting a scam? If so, who was the victim? Had she been planning a robbery? I put the laptop away, discouraged by all the dead ends, and tried to sleep. Ten minutes later I had it open again, doing different searches.

At midnight I called Chris Murray, the detective from the Surry Hills station.

"Do you have any idea what time it is?"

"Murray," I said, "you've got connections in the records department, don't you? I want you to help me out. I'm wandering aimlessly around the Internet looking for anything I can get on Tox Barnes. Maybe they changed his name after the crime? Is that why I can't find any newspaper articles about him?"

"The fact that you're carrying on working with that monster without looking for an out is exactly the reason I won't help you," he said. "You should be trying to get away from him, not trying to understand him. I'm hanging up, Harry."

"Murray, don't go! I need help here, man."

"He *murdered* a woman and her kid," Murray said. "He and a bunch of other kids stabbed them to death."

"I thought they beat them to death."

"Is how they did it very important?"

"I guess not. What exactly am I supposed to do, Murray? I've got a homicide on my hands. You know how often I get homicides in sex crimes? I can't just walk out on this."

"Feign sickness and leave the case to him," he said. "He's good at what he does. He'll solve it himself in no time. Probably uses his killer instincts."

"This is what people do?" I shook my head. "They just drop him?"

"He's like a curse. You either find some way to drop him or shuffle him onto someone else. Otherwise you'll look like you're on his side, and you don't want people thinking that, Harry."

"This is insane."

"He's a disgrace to the force," Murray said. "He's a disgrace to what we stand for as police."

"But wasn't he only seven years old when the crime occurred?"

"I got a six-year-old," Murray snapped. "She knows it's wrong to kill people. Hell, my three-year-old knows that. I'm too busy for this shit, Harry. I got a couple of missing yachties from Queensland on my desk. I'm looking at hundreds of pictures of identical boats all day long. I'm seein' boats in my fucking sleep."

"What are you doing with a Queensland case?"

"Oh." He sighed. The wind seemed to go out of him suddenly. "Long story. It's bad. It's just one of those ones that gives you the creeps."

"Tell me about it," I said. I hoped by listening kindly to his problems for a few minutes, he'd take his fury down a few notches. It seemed to work. When he spoke again, his voice was softer.

"A retired couple in their fifties was last seen on their yacht heading south out of Brisbane. They travel a lot, so the woman does her own kidney dialysis on the boat. She's got some kidney problem, I don't know what. But she hasn't filled her prescription for the dialysate—the stuff she rinses her kidney with. By the family's calculation, the couple should have dropped into Sydney a couple of days ago at the latest to fill the prescription. If they did drop in, they didn't sign into the marina, and they haven't filled the prescription. Nobody on the East Coast has seen them. They were selling the boat. It's possible they swung in and picked up potential buyers. But we don't know."

"Jesus," I said, as sympathetically as I could. "Sounds complex. Why haven't I seen it getting much press?"

"It's early days yet. And these yachties go missing all the time. Decide to change direction on a whim and don't know their comms aren't working. Everybody's hoping they'll just pop up again in Indonesia or something. I don't know. I got a bad feeling about it. The coastguard is on the lookout."

"Anything I can do?"

"No, Harry, there's nothing you can do." His tone sharpened again, as though he'd realized I was only listening because I wanted his help.

"Look, Murray, I want to understand what I'm dealing with here," I pleaded. "What exactly is Tox supposed to have done? How many people were involved? I want to know exactly what he was charged with. I've got to find out what kind of man he is."

"I don't know, Harry, but I'm disgusted that you're even interested," Murray said. "We're supposed to be the good guys. He's an insult to us, and so are you right now."

The phone clicked dead in my ear.

CHAPTER 26

THE BLARING OF a horn woke me. When I looked out my bedroom window, Tox Barnes was sitting in the driver's seat of his black '69 Mustang, revving the engine. When I got in the car he tossed his phone into my lap.

"Check it out, zombie face," he said.

"'Zombie face'?"

He flipped the mirror down in front of me. He was right: I looked decidedly undead. I rubbed my eyes and raked back my apparently homosexual hair, slapping the mirror away.

On the phone screen was a video on pause. I clicked play, and the car was filled with the sound of deep-throated groaning and grunting.

"Urgh." I threw the phone back at him with barely a glimpse of the bare thrusting ass on the screen. "You're disgusting."

"I'm not sharing my porn with you. That's our victim, Claudia Burrows."

I took the phone back and watched. The camera panned around the ass and up the thighs of a petite blond woman. I'd seen that mouth before, with Tox Barnes's finger in it.

"Where'd you find this?"

"I was trying to figure out how she got those tits," he said, pulling away from the curb. "Her bank account showed she'd never been able to afford them. Then I got to thinking—adult film producers will sometimes pay for larger hooters for their actresses if they agree to appear in a certain number of movies. The films sell better if the girls have got a set of big juicy—"

"All right, all right, all right."

"She appears in that video as Claudia Dee." He pointed with his cigarette. "Had an old porn addict I know dig it up for me. It's about a month old. Straight to DVD, not available online."

"Nice work."

"Maybe that's where the big payoff was coming from," he said, roaring through the traffic like a lunatic, weaving in and out of the oncoming cars. "Maybe there was a feature film coming up."

"Yeah, and maybe she pulled out of the big film," I said, "and someone decided they weren't going to be messed with like that. I've met plenty of these porn guys. Women are just like horses to them. When they break down, or they go wild, you take them out the back and put a bullet in their brains."

CHAPTER 27

DIABOLIC VIDEOS HAD a studio on the upper floor of a building on bustling George Street, up a flight of carpeted stairs that reeked of gasoline. A huge pink neon sign at the top of the stairs blinded me as I arrived at the tiny foyer where a girl with too many piercings sat texting.

"What is that smell?" I covered my mouth and nose with my T-shirt.

"Some girl's ex-boyfriend came in here last week lookin' for her." The pierced girl yawned. "Poured gasoline all down the stairs. Said he was gonna light the place on fire if she didn't come out."

"She come out?" Tox asked.

"The place on fire?"

"We're looking for people who know this girl here." I showed her a picture of Claudia her parents had provided us with. Piercings hardly glanced at it. She only had eyes for Tox.

"You don't look like no cop."

"What do I look like?"

"I dunno." The girl leaned on the counter, wriggled her booty. "But I like it."

"This! Girl! Here!" I slapped the photo on the counter.

"Okay! Okay! Jeez!"

She pushed aside a curtain and led us through. The space

was divided into quarters by painted black partitions. I could hear whips cracking in the farthest corner. We passed an empty bed and arrived in the middle of a film set. Two huge black cameras were manned by men. On a satin-sheeted bed, an unnaturally hairless woman was propped, the hem of a blazing-white tennis skirt flipped back over her thighs. Her cotton polo shirt was ripped across the middle and tied tight beneath enormous breasts. She twirled a blond pigtail in one hand and licked the handle of a tennis racquet she held in the other.

Tox pointed. "What is she gonna do with that racquet?"

"Excuse me!" A man with a clipboard stepped out of the glow of the lights. "You're in the middle of a live shoot here!"

"I'm Detective Blue. This is Detective Dirtycreep. We're looking for someone who was close to Claudia Burrows." I flashed the picture. "We know she did a film here a couple of months ago. We want to speak to anyone who has any knowledge about her murder."

"I've never seen that girl before." The producer turned his nose up at the picture. "If she's dead, it's her own fault."

Someone tapped me on the shoulder and I turned around, only to be yanked face first into yet another pair of breasts. The girl hugging me was wearing six-inch silver sparkle heels, and nothing else.

"Harry!" she squealed. "Oh, my God, you little doll, what are you *doing* here?"

I'd handled Vicky Varouma's sexual assault claim at Surry Hills a couple of years earlier.

"Vicky!" I smiled up at her. "Hi! Tell me you know this girl."

"Oh, man." Vicky's face fell as she took in the picture. "Now there's a piece of bad news."

CHAPTER 28

"SHE WAS TALKING about everything changing," Vicky said. "She was outta here. She asked me for some money so she could get set up, and said she'd pay me back when she came into her big win."

"What was the money for?" I asked. We were sitting in the Diabolic Videos dressing room. I'd caught sight of myself in the mirror and realized Vicky's hug had covered my face and neck in body glitter. It was proving difficult to wipe off. Tox stood nearby, examining bottles of perfume.

"I don't know. But I saw her near Potts Point wearing some pretty flashy clothes. I was driving by and she was with another girl. Maybe she had a job or something."

"Who was the other girl?"

"I don't know that either. They were shopping for handbags. On *Macleay Street*. Damn, girl must've hit something good."

"Why did you say out there that Claudia was 'bad news'?" Tox asked.

"Oh." Vicky looked embarrassed, turned to the mirrors and started braiding her hair. "I feel bad now. She's dead. You shouldn't speak ill of the dead."

"You should if it'll help us."

"She was just a slimy character, our Claudia." Vicky sighed. "The kind of girls who end up in this industry aren't usually your silver spoon types. But I'd met Claudia's parents and they

seemed like nice, quiet people. Regular people. I couldn't figure out how she ended up the way she was. So deceptive. She
always had a scam on the go."

"Like what?"

"Oh, like she'd tell you she knew where to get cheap ecstasy
or something, you know, for the weekend. She'd take your
money and come back crying, telling you the dealer had robbed
her, smacked her around. She'd show you bruises that were
nonexistent, or days old. That sort of thing."

"Right."

"She lied like you wouldn't believe, so she made a good
actress for Diabolic. I think her parents thought she was a waitress or something. But she lied about things that didn't matter.
She exaggerated and exaggerated until you were basically being
asked to believe she had this crazy, wild, extravagant life. She
was dating movie stars and international spies."

"How sad," I said.

"She was always on the verge of a 'new life.' The big money
she was supposed to be coming into? I don't know." Vicky
shrugged. "Sounds like bullshit to me. I think she'd applied
to the university. She was going to buy an apartment, transfer up into a law-school program, be a criminal lawyer. She
kept watching clips from legal dramas on her phone, practicing
them out loud. I mean, *please*—girl could barely read."

"How'd she get into school if she could barely read?"

"I'd say she had a friend fill in the application form for her.
She'd have paid them to pack it full of lies about how she was
ready to knuckle down and study." Vicky looked at me. "I can
see why she was so determined to live a 'new life.' The life she
was living here was a total fabrication."

CHAPTER 29

HOPE'S PLANS HAD stalled. She knelt on the deck of her yacht, sanding the scratches in the polished wood, trying to keep her fury contained. The scratches went all the way from the anchor mount to a door at the side of the vessel, from where she'd dragged the anchor she had tied Claudia to.

In the first days, Hope had been sick whenever she'd thought about it. All that would go in time. Already she couldn't remember her face. Piece by piece, the memories would fall away. She just had to continue with the plan.

Hope heard a shifting in the bathroom. She got up and marched there, slammed open the door. Finally he was awake. Ken was just coming to his senses, shaking the chloroform fog from his head. He looked down at his sleeping wife, at the sheen of sweat on her skin. The woman was ghost white.

"So I had a magnificent time at the bank," Hope snapped.

"You got the money?" Ken's eyes widened. "Now you can let us go. You can—"

"Don't pretend you didn't try to send me into a fucking trap, Ken." Hope slammed the door again so that it banged against the shower frame. "The joint signatures? You were hoping to trip me up, and your plan failed."

"I wasn't," Ken panted, swallowed hard. "Hope, look, I didn't try to betray you. I just want to get my wife to a hospital. I just want this to be over. Jenny has got hours, not days, until her kidneys are going to fail and she's going to die. Do you understand that?"

"Do you think I'm a fucking idiot?" Hope sneered.

"No." Ken shook his head. "No, of course not. You're very clever. It would take someone very clever to pull something like this off."

"I've planned every aspect of this thing," Hope said. "Nothing is going to stop me. I deserve this, you understand? I've waited my whole life for my moment. You've got to make your own life, Ken. You've got to change your own destiny. Nobody's gonna change it for you."

"Imagine if you staged an incredible plan like this without hurting anybody." Ken nodded along. "Wow! You'd show everybody. You'd go down in the history books."

Hope sighed. She'd been enjoying Ken's praise, but he'd taken it a step too far. The man must know what had happened to Claudia. Two young, professional women had approached him about his boat. Those same two had accompanied him and his wife around the harbor, followed him down into the engine cavity to inspect the boat's inner workings. Now that their real purpose had been revealed, one of those girls was gone. Even from the bathroom where she'd locked them, Ken and Jenny must have heard Claudia's scream as Hope had brought the hammer down on the back of her skull. The scrape of the anchor. She felt exhausted as Ken launched into his tired pleas again.

"It won't take long. All you have to do is bring the machine in here," Ken said. "There might be enough dialysate left for one more dose. Just untie one of my hands, and I'll—"

"You're going to die, Ken," Hope said suddenly. The man before her stiffened, his eyes wide. Hope shook her head, bored, as she continued: "You're both going to die. You might as well just accept that now."

CHAPTER 30

TOX AND I settled in a bar on the strip in Kings Cross, sitting at the open window, watching the pimps and prostitutes wander up and down in the light rain. It seemed appropriate to head into Sydney's red-light district. What we'd learned of Claudia's life made me gravitate here, where the liars, cheats, and criminals came to play. The homeless crowding into corners to escape the wind and the hopeless slouching around the bars, tired from weeks of endlessly drinking away reality. Kings Cross was also just around the corner from my apartment. I hoped to wander back after a quick drink and get some much-needed sleep.

My phone calls and e-mails were ceasing to have any effect as word spread throughout the police force that I was working with Tox. When I called to see if the full autopsy on Claudia's body had come in, an officer at my station put me on hold for half an hour, and then hung up. I only got the report by calling back and pretending to be someone else. I couldn't get hold of the secondary detectives I'd tasked to look after the Burrowses, so I called their lawyer and asked if everyone was okay. I stared at Tox while I waited on the phone, trying to decide how the man himself ever got anything done without fabricating multiple identities and ringing around the world every time he wanted anything.

While I watched, I found myself trying to imagine him as a small child in a wild pack of other kids, pulling and grabbing and yanking an adult mother to the ground, stabbing her in a hurried rush, blood soaking their tiny clothes. I imagined him cornering her son, a boy his age maybe, holding the knife to the kid's throat. Why had they done it? Tox had a mean look to him, particularly with the bruised nose and double black eyes, the leather jacket that reeked of smoke. But I knew there was no "killer look." I'd known baby-faced preteen boys in school blazers and caps who'd assaulted girls so viciously they'd broken their victims' spirits for life.

Maybe it was all just a rumor and Tox was innocent. But if it was, why didn't he do anything to change the black mark against his name?

I was just starting to imagine him as a kind and gentle man wrapped in the shell of a dangerous one when he put his whiskey glass down, got up, and strode across the room with violent intent. I watched him take a pool cue from the rack, snap it over his knee, and roll the heavy end in his fist like a batter coming up to the plate.

"All right, buddy," he said, "let's go."

His target was a heavier, taller man who'd been playing a game of pool by the back doors of the bar. The heavy man and Tox lunged at each other.

CHAPTER 31

I WAS UP and across the bar before I'd really taken stock of the situation. My sheer bewilderment at the fight, and my own fatigue, had me diving into danger without a plan. I ran over and grabbed at Tox, but one of the heavy man's mates pulled me off him and threw me into the edge of the pool table. That hurt. My fists came up immediately, and I gave the guy a couple of warning punches to the jaw. But that only made him madder. He swung a heavy fist at my head. I ducked, surged up with an uppercut that crunched teeth and bone, and knocked him out on his feet. Before he could fall forward onto me, I shoved him back. He fell into a table full of glasses where two old men were seated. They hardly moved.

The room was suddenly full of people. I felt a hand on the back of my head, grabbed and twisted it, heard a man scream. I kicked his knee out and he flopped to the floor. I looked up just in time to see another fist swinging at me. It glanced off my brow. I ducked too late and shot the guy with a sucker punch to the gut that folded him in half.

Tox was holding his own against the guy he'd targeted originally. It looked as though it was all about to be over when five uniformed officers burst into the room, one of them leading a huge German shepherd on a leash.

"On the ground! On the ground!"

I flattened against the stinking carpet. The dog was standing right over me, barking in my face, slobbering in my hair. I realized I'd left my police-issue phone on the counter by the window when I'd run in to assist in the fight. As I lay being cuffed I saw a homeless man shuffle along to the window, pick up the phone, and continue shuffling.

We were dragged to a police van, which had been parked hastily on the street outside the pub. It was really raining now. Tox and I were shoved into the back of the van while the other fighters were herded up against the wall of the pub for a lecture about public brawls.

The lead patrol officer stood in the doorway and wrestled the keys into the lock on the van door.

"We're cops," I said. "We're both cops."

"We know," he replied, and slammed the door.

CHAPTER 32

WE SAT IN silence for a long time while the Kings Cross patrol cops drove us out of the city. Tox seemed genuinely unconcerned with our situation. He leaned back against the wall of the vehicle, watching me calmly as I worked through several levels of blinding rage.

"What the hell brought that on?" I asked eventually.

"We were in the academy together. Think he left the force a few years ago. He spotted me when we walked in. Started giving me the stink-eye. I thought he probably wanted a fight. So. You know." He shrugged.

"My life is becoming more difficult by the minute because of you," I snapped. "I can't even get people to answer the phone anymore. Now you've pulled this shit and I've lost my phone altogether."

"Meh. They'll issue you a new one," he rasped.

"Maybe!" I shrugged. "Maybe they'll just ignore me!"

"I'm hard to work with." Tox shifted, his cuffs clunking on the metal bench. "You must've guessed that."

"Well, I didn't know it'd be *this* bad."

"No one's forcing you to continue."

"Are you *kidding?*" I shook my head. "I'm supposed to drop the case completely because you're a murderer? This was my case to begin with, asshole!"

"You need to calm down," he said. "You're going all pink."

I tried to hold my tongue, but I was mad, and when I'm mad the words tumble out. If I get mad enough I start swinging. I was already imagining giving him a bop on that nose just to remind him how inconvenient he was.

"Did you do it?" I blurted, shifting to the edge of my seat. "Did you kill that mother and child?"

He looked up and held my gaze. "Yes," he answered.

CHAPTER 33

"WHY?" I ASKED.

Tox just looked at me. I wasn't going to get an answer that easy.

I shifted against the wall and sighed, let the rumble of the van rock me back into tired numbness. We seemed to be driving for an hour. I got up and tried to look through the slats in the door and figure out where we were.

"Where are they taking us?" I wondered.

"Not the Kings Cross police station," Tox said.

"Of course not the Kings Cross police station!" I sneered at him, fell into whining. "God, I should be in bed asleep now. I should have had a nice hot shower. I should have my lovely soft pajamas on."

"Pajamas?" Tox snorted.

The van stopped. I looked out the slats but could only see darkness, the occasional orange light. Two officers came around the back of the van and opened the door.

"Get out."

"I can't get down there with my hands cuffed behind my back."

"Get. Out."

I noted the names on their badges—Demper and Loris— and then gave up and let them have what they wanted, the humiliation they thought would make them feel like heroes. I made a jump for the ground, landed badly, and fell on my face. It sounded as if Tox didn't fare much better. I heard him slump onto his backside, try to slide off the edge and stumble.

One of the cops dragged me up. I'd bitten my lip. My mouth was full of blood. I sat on the ground as instructed, next to my partner. I was just getting an idea of where we were—some sort of industrial area near a canal—when blinding torchlight flashed in my face.

"Obviously you have no idea who this is." The cop flicked the light from my face to Tox's. My vision was clouded with green explosions.

"It's Tox Barnes," I said. "I'm well aware."

"Well, clearly you need an information session on who you're working with here, because you couldn't possibly know who he is—or you wouldn't be hanging out in bars with him. No one with any self-respect would," the cop carried on.

I sighed. Tox was squinting into the torchlight with one eye open. The light flicked between us, blinding us over and over.

"Tox Barnes and a few of his friends beat a woman and her young son to death."

"I know! I know!"

"Aren't you in sex crimes?" The second cop jabbed me in the shoulder with his boot, causing me to topple over. "How could you dismiss the gang rape and vicious beating of an innocent—"

I looked at Tox, thinking he'd jump in and correct an accusation as outlandish as this. He hardly seemed to be listening.

"Gang rape, too, now?" I struggled upright and squinted at the cop before me. I felt strangely defiant on Tox's behalf. "I can't keep up with all the versions of this story. What's next? Cannibalism?"

"She's on his side," one of them sneered. "I can't believe it."

"Where's your badge?"

"What?"

"Where's your fucking badge, bitch?"

I was shoved to the ground. The cop took my wallet from my back pocket and tore out the detective's badge. They took my cuffs off my belt, and my gun, too. Tox, they left alone. He watched, passive, from the dark beside me.

"You're an embarrassment to the force," the cop said, giving me a good kick in the ribs. He uncuffed me roughly and shoved my head into the dirt. "Have some dignity and leave this vicious dog alone."

They left us there in the dark, miles from the road.

CHAPTER 34

KEN SPELLING WASN'T going to die, not at the very moment he and his wife were beginning to settle into their well-deserved retirement. He was not going to die at the hands of some psychopathic freak who wanted to trade out of her shitty life the easy way.

Convincing her not to chloroform him had been easy—he'd simply not responded when she'd called from the doorway, having feigned a sluggish fever from around midnight. When he was sure Hope had left the vessel, he went to work. Ken kicked off his shoes and wriggled out of his socks. He stood in the middle of the tiny bathroom cubicle and stared down at his sleeping wife, trying to think of a plan. Jenny was sleeping for longer and longer periods now, and when she was awake she didn't make sense, her words slurred and delirious, her eyes unable to settle. Ken needed to act now, before it was too late. He took a deep breath.

All right, the door. That was a dead end. Though the bulkhead had wheels on either side, he'd heard Hope looping a rope through her side of the door every time she'd left them, probably tying it off against a pipe to lock them in. He experimented, turning his back to the door and shoving the wheel sideways with his bound hands. The wheel turned an inch or so and then clunked into place. Ken went to the wall beside the shower and kicked, listening to the sound ripple up through the iron hull. Yes, maybe he could signal someone by kicking. He lay on his back and kicked madly. Jenny barely stirred. In ten minutes he was drenched in sweat. He stopped and listened. There was not a sound from outside the vessel. He panted and stared at the ceiling of his prison.

Maybe if he kicked in a rhythm. Three fast, loud kicks, three slow ones, and three quick again. SOS. There had to be dozens of yachties wandering back and forth along the piers outside. Surely one of them would hear his signal.

But how long would Hope be gone? How long could he wait for his signal to be heard? Ken wasn't even sure all his racket was making it through the double hull of the boat to the outside world.

He stood again and looked at the porthole high on the wall behind the toilet. It had a single eye screw holding it shut. There was no way he could get it open with his hands tied. Or could he? Ken looked around the tiny room and spied the mop standing against the shelves of toiletries.

I'm not going to die, he thought. *I refuse to.*

CHAPTER 35

MY MAJOR BREAK came at midnight, but I ignored it. I was trudging up the stairs to my apartment block, scratching dried glitter and blood off my neck and trying to remember which key unlocked my front door. I'd lost my phone, but upstairs in my apartment I could hear the sound of my laptop jangling with a phone call. The ringing was finished by the time I reached the apartment. I ignored it and fell face down onto the couch.

I'd walked away from Tox in the dark of the industrial area without saying anything about the trouble he'd gotten us into. In truth, I was more horrified by his admission in the back of the van than I was by the roughhousing those idiot patrol cops had given us. It had taken fifteen minutes to find my wallet in the dark, up against the side of one of the warehouses where the officer had thrown it, and an hour to walk back to a major road. I'd stood there waiting for a cab for another half an hour, then had slept all the way home in it.

The laptop jangled again. I didn't know how long I'd been out. I crawled to the screen and tapped.

"What?"

"Harry? Vicky."

"Yep."

"I was telling someone here what happened to Claudia and I might have a lead for you," she said. I fumbled blindly in the dark across the cluttered coffee table for a pen. "One of the other girls said Claudia had been hanging around a prostitute from the Cross named Hope."

"Huh." I laughed. My instincts about Kings Cross and its connection to this case were right. The Cross was where dreams, lives, and promises failed. Claudia had been cooking up some kind of dream, and it had gotten her drowned at the bottom of the ocean.

"'Hope,'" I said. "That's all you got?"

"That's all I got."

"I'll take it. Thanks."

Almost immediately, an instant chat message popped up on the screen from my brother, wondering why I hadn't been answering my phone all night. I gave him a brief rundown of my experience out in the sticks, my fingers dancing over the keys.

> SamBluDesigner77: **Are you OK? Should you go to a hospital?**
>
> BlueHarry: **I'm fine. It was just a roughhousing. No worse than the guys used to give each other at the academy.**
>
> SamBluDesigner77: **You should report those cops! Not only is it assault, but if they didn't arrest you, dragging you out there against your will was probably abduction, right?**
>
> BlueHarry: **You don't rat on your colleagues in this business, Sam. No matter what they do. We deal with our problems in-house.**
>
> SamBlueDesigner77: **God, it's all so pathetic.**

BlueHarry: Speaking of abductions, how'd the second interview on the Georges River Killer thing go? What did they ask you?

I watched the screen for an indication that Sam was writing back to me. He started, and then mysteriously the speech bubble he was writing in disappeared. I waited for whatever was distracting him to go away, but he didn't start typing again. I had a strange urge to call him. My sisterly senses were in overdrive, but I told myself it was just fatigue.

CHAPTER 36

TOX DIDN'T HAVE any kind of desk. No police station would officially lay claim to him, so he would wander from station to station picking up cases as he liked. I'd heard his old department over in Auburn had started processing a transfer to North Sydney for him, and then the paperwork had "stalled." They'd been waiting for the police officer in the transfer position in North Sydney to transfer out, apparently, and then he hadn't. They'd filled Tox's spot in Auburn. So he existed in administrative limbo, not really Auburn's problem, not really North Sydney's. He might have complained and had the whole thing cleared up, but I got the sense that the wandering life suited him. He was basically a freelance detective, a consultant, but without the extra pay consulting detectives receive. Sometimes he would nab cases from the police scanner radio that he kept in his car. That's how he'd gotten onto Claudia's crime scene before me. He'd been out driving and had heard about the find.

When I arrived at Surry Hills station he was perched on the corner of one of the coffee-room tables, tapping away at that old, broken laptop. A group of my colleagues glared at the back of his head. I wondered if he'd gone home at all—he was still wearing the bloodied shirt. He didn't see me come in. Chris Murray was scrolling through pictures of boats. His computer screen was littered with CCTV footage of yachts. He looked at me guiltily as I went right to Pops's office and threw open the door.

"I need a gun, a badge, some handcuffs, and a phone," I said.

Pops glanced up. Detective Nigel Spader, whom I hadn't noticed sitting in the chair behind the door, burst out laughing.

"Oh, yeah," I said, slumping into the chair next to him. "It's really funny when police-issue items go missing. It's hilarious. Laugh it up."

"How did this happen?" Pops asked.

"How do you think? I'm radioactive from spending too much time with Tox Barnes. I'm practically glowing. Cops are coming out of the woodwork to mess with me."

"Who?" Pops asked. "Which cops?"

I sighed. Pops knew I'd never snitch.

"No one's forcing you to stay with him." Nigel shrugged. "Just drop him. He'll solve it himself. There's a new sexual assault on the case board this morning. Tell him you've got to prioritize that."

I closed my eyes and reveled in a private fantasy in which I thumped Nigel's head back into the wall behind him.

"Maybe I should just drop him," I said. "Maybe I'll give the sexual assault to one of the probationary detectives and jump over onto the Georges River task force. Oh, wait! I forgot! I don't have a penis!"

Nigel sighed.

"Did you seriously shut me out of that case because I'm a woman?" I asked. "Or do you actually have a reasonable motive? Like, do you have a suspect? Why don't you think you can trust me with your suspect?"

Both men were quiet. Again I felt that strange tingling up the back of my neck that told me something was very wrong here. That there was something very important being hidden from me. But one look at Nigel's face convinced me it was just him and his team being misogynistic assholes. He looked like one.

Soon I would know how wrong I was.

CHAPTER 37

IT TOOK FIVE minutes just to get the mop across the room, shuffling the thing with his knees and feet, knocking it against the walls, the shower cubicle, his sleeping wife. Another hour to get the handle through the screw loop over and over, turning the screw just a quarter-inch at a time. He sat triumphantly in the middle of the tiny room, exhausted, looking at the porthole propped open with the mop, the glorious blue sky outside. His face had swollen with pressure around the duct tape gag, sweat pouring down his neck. He tried to rouse Jenny. If he could get her to wake, try to slip her smaller gag off by rubbing her face against the frame of the shower, shout for help out the porthole. She woke briefly, blinked at him with uncomprehending, bloodshot eyes. No. It was up to Ken to save them both.

The big man stood, steeled himself, and climbed up onto the toilet seat. He looked outside and saw no one. Never mind. There might be people only yards away, out of view. He got down and kicked the second shelf of the cupboard down. Jenny's bathroom products scattered everywhere. Perfume bottles shattered. Shampoo and moisturizer and toner, all manner of women's things. Ken grabbed a shampoo bottle awkwardly by the neck between his big and second toes and hopped over to the toilet, almost losing his balance and falling by the shower. He climbed up, and with an agonizing stretch of groin and hip and thigh muscles he didn't know he still possessed, he leaned against the shower, raised one leg, and slid the shampoo bottle through the porthole.

He heard the gentle splash. Looked outside and saw no one. Ken hopped down, shuffled to the pile of toiletries, and grabbed another bottle with his toes. He had to work as fast as he could. He wanted a steady stream of floating debris, more than the usual marina junk. Someone would spot his breadcrumb trail. Someone would rescue them before Hope got back from wherever she was.

It was their only chance of survival.

CHAPTER 38

IT TOOK SOME serious cage-rattling through the strip clubs, bars, and brothels of Kings Cross to hunt down information on Hope. I heard fragments of her tale from homeless girls lounging in the back doorways of the supermarkets and kebab shops there. She was whispered about by conspiratorial old men in the upper rooms of Pussy Cats, Showgirls, and Porky's, where the rubber stairs glowed all day long with neon lights.

A crowlike old madam on Ward Avenue with a split lip told us her full name—Hope Stallwood—and where she'd been staying. But like most working girls, Hope moved around a lot. She pissed off her roommates with her drinking and drugs and her loud, late-night entrances. She was always broke, downtrodden, sullen, tired.

I'd known plenty of girls like Hope in my time on the sex crimes squad. Mostly they ended up dead in a bed somewhere, and I was brought in to assess whether they'd been taken advantage of before they expired. They all looked the same after a while. Bruised thighs tangled in the dirty sheets.

Tox and I didn't talk about the night before. But I'd stopped viewing our relationship with any kind of hope that it might be extended a minute longer than it had to be. When this case was over, I was getting the hell away from him. It wasn't the ill treatment I was suffering from my colleagues that disturbed me. It was the calm and gentle way in which he'd said "Yes" when I'd asked him if he was a killer. I replayed it in my mind, over and over, whenever I looked at him.

Yes. Yes. Yes.

It hadn't seemed possible that a man who'd done what he was supposed to have done as a child could be so normal. Well, normal-ish. I realized that I hadn't really believed he'd done it at the start. I felt shaken now that I could be so wrong about someone.

I followed behind him, lost in my thoughts as we moved from bar to bar and brothel to brothel. Everyone we spoke to about Hope Stallwood told us she was coming into money. Just like Claudia, she'd been on the verge of having it all.

I wondered if that meant we'd find her dead.

CHAPTER 39

WHEN HOPE GOT to Pier 14, she spotted two men standing by the edge looking into the water below them. Something about their fixed stare made her blood run cold. She walked by quickly and hazarded a glance at the gentle waves below, where a shampoo bottle and four other bottles floated.

"Where's it all coming from?" one of the men was saying. Hope looked, and saw he had a wet deodorant can in one hand and a bottle of styling mousse in the other.

"Let's go have a wander around," the taller man said. "See if we can see who's dumping rubbish."

"Oh, my God," Hope gushed, setting down her bag. "I'm so stupid. Those are mine."

The two men turned and stared at her. She took the bottles from the shorter man and shoved them into her bag. "I was cleaning out my bathroom this afternoon. I must have left the tub of products on the edge of my boat. Oh, this is so embarrassing. It must have fallen in."

"There's stuff everywhere," the tall man said, his face softening. "Couple of bottles floated over there, near Pier Sixteen."

"I saw a toothbrush." The shorter man laughed.

"God." Hope sighed dramatically and pushed her hair back. "Goddamn it. I'll clean it all up, I swear. This is so embarrassing."

She hustled away toward the *New Hope*, glancing back to see the men laughing and muttering to themselves. Hope's eyes were burning in her skull. If she didn't need Ken so badly right now, his end might have come much sooner and bloodier than she'd planned.

CHAPTER 40

AN OLD INDIAN woman answered the door to Hope's apartment. She was even shorter than me, and peered out angrily from the crack in the door. When she saw Tox, she started to close it again. My boot was in the way.

"We're lookin' for Hope Stallwood."

"What do you want? The drugs!" the woman howled. "The drugs, they ruin all of you! She's not here. That whore! She took her drugs and she's gone!"

Tox shoved the door open, almost knocking the woman over. We found ourselves in a tiny, filthy kitchen. My boots stuck to the linoleum.

"I'll call the police!"

"*We're* the police," I said. "Sit down. Tell us where Hope went."

"You're the pimps! Pimps with the drugs! Rotten drug dealers! I'll call the police!"

A young couple had appeared in the doorway to a short hall. I walked past them into a labyrinth of tight rooms divided into smaller rooms by hanging sheets. There were mattresses on the floor everywhere. Aluminum foil on the windows. Everything reeked of cigarette smoke and curry powder. A baby cried somewhere. I stepped on someone's foot and apologized. The owner of the foot was sleeping and hardly noticed.

I didn't know how people lived like this. Prisons were better.

There was black mold on the bathroom ceiling that could have been an inch thick. My mind was rushing with crimes as I looked around the ground. Possession of heroin. Possession of marijuana. Child endangerment. Child neglect. Rental fraud. Underage drinking.

Tox pushed aside a pair of damp towels and found a filthy, bare mattress in the corner beneath a window.

"Hope Stallwood was here?" he asked the young couple, who'd started following us around the apartment like wary dogs. They nodded.

Hope was long gone, but she'd left a couple of things behind. A plastic container of hair ties, some underpants and clothes that reeked of body odor, a few old, stiff pairs of shoes. I picked up a magazine and let it fall open. *Yachting Today*. There were yachts circled in the For Sale section of the magazine, the pages indented with scrawled red pen.

"What's this?" I showed Tox the circled boats. Was Hope lying here at night under the lamplight circling boats she dreamed of owning? Was it all fantasy, or was she actually making plans?

I held the paper close to my nose. She'd actually underlined some of the phone numbers for making inquiries. There were digits listed on the back page. I flipped forward a few pages and found a page was torn from the magazine. I ran my fingers along the ragged seam.

Tox and I realized what we were seeing at almost exactly the same moment. Goosebumps raced along my arms.

"We could call the magazine." He took out his phone. "Confirm which boat is missing from the mag."

"No," I said. "I know which boat it is."

CHAPTER 41

THIS TIME, SHE'D chosen the branch at Martin Place. The streets were flush with lawyers on their lunch hour gliding around in their slick suits. As their cab drove through the traffic toward their stop, Hope kept the gun pressed against the inside of the handbag in her lap, the barrel pointed right at Ken. She had to keep the fury in her heart contained now. This was the most important part of her plan.

The man beside her sat crumpled against the side of the cab. She might have broken a couple of ribs when she came at him with the hammer after his stunt with the toiletries. She didn't care. He deserved it. He looked pathetic sitting there, his eyes wandering over the people in the street. She could see on his face the desire to open the door and grab one of them, inform them that he was a hostage. His mouth fell open as the cab came to a stop at a set of traffic lights, right beside a police cruiser. Hope jiggled the handbag, reminding him of his situation.

"Try anything, anything at all, and I'll be right back on that boat with your wife before you can utter a sound," Hope murmured, glancing at the cabbie's face in the rearview mirror. "I'll shoot you, and before the police can work out where you've been, Jenny will be dead."

"I'm not going to try anything," Ken whispered. "You can

take the money. Take everything. Just hold up your end of the deal and leave Jenny on the pier unharmed."

"We'll see if your performance is convincing enough," Hope said. "I'm not making any promises."

They walked to the manager's counter, arm in arm. She shot him the loving look of a happy wife, slid her hand down and gripped his rough, warm hand.

What a lovely creature he was. She almost didn't want him to die.

The manager this time was an older, portly Asian man in a nicely tailored gray suit. He wore a small pink flower in his lapel and stuck his hand out for a shake a good ten feet away from Ken.

"Sir, madam. How can I help you today?"

They explained their business. The manager wore genuine regret on his face that they would no longer be customers, but brightened again when they spoke of their plans to travel the Greek Islands. He waved them into his small private office as though he were welcoming them inside his own home.

"So." He eased into his chair and turned the computer monitor toward himself. The nameplate on his desk read "Bai Yim." "What's the approximate amount of your holdings here, Mr. Spelling?"

"Eight hundred thousand," Hope answered for him. She felt a pulse of electricity run through her phony husband's body. Yes, Hope had seen their accounts, she just hadn't been able to access them. He must have been surprised at how far her planning went. He had no idea.

"So I imagine you'd like the amount in a direct transfer check?"

"No, we'd like cash."

"You're not concerned about carrying that amount of money overseas? International piracy is a real threat, you know."

"Oh, no, we've taken provisions." Hope smiled. "And we've got customs approval to take the amount out of Australia in cash, forgoing the ten-thousand-dollar limit."

Ken glanced at her. She was prepared. *Of course I'm fucking prepared,* Hope thought. *This is my one shot. I'm not going back to that life. I'm never, never going back.*

She pushed aside the flurry of images that swirled through her at the thought. Sweat-stained beds and needles. The crush and roar of the crowd on the strip. The hollering and laughing of men in the hallways. Money in, money out, money in, money out.

"I'll get our guard to escort you to your car, then," Yim said. "You can never be too careful!"

They all laughed. Hope put Jenny and Ken Spelling's IDs on the table. Mr. Yim hardly glanced at the cards. His eyes were on the computer screen as he tapped their names and numbers into the keyboard.

His expression changed in an instant.

CHAPTER 42

MR. YIM RUBBED his nose, glanced at Hope and Ken, and painted on a crooked smile.

"Everything seems to be in order." He rose unevenly from his chair. "I'll just—"

Hope grabbed the computer monitor and swung it toward her. The screen was blinking with a bright-red warning sign. She'd seen it reflected in the shiny buttons on the front of Yim's shirt, the light making the mother-of-pearl surfaces flash pink: NEW SOUTH WALES STATE POLICE ALERT.

There was a phone number, a brief message. Hope stood and whipped the gun out of her handbag. Yim threw his hands up.

"Did you press the button?"

"I—"

"Did you press the fucking button?" She actioned the pistol. Yim shook his head, but there was no telling if he was lying. She hadn't seen his hand move while he was sitting, but he could easily have nudged the silent alarm under the table with his knee. She'd seen him shift awkwardly in the chair before rising.

Time to initiate Plan B.

She turned and shot Ken twice in the stomach.

The man bucked violently at the impact, then doubled over. He didn't make a sound. Nor did the gun, thanks to the silencer. Hope shifted her aim to Yim, and the old man whimpered.

CHAPTER 43

HOPE WALKED STIFFLY toward the entrance, the gun tucked beneath her flowing silk shirt. The glass doors of the bank were only yards away, still opening and closing as people walked in and out. The silent alarm had not been tripped, or the doors would have slammed shut immediately, the bulletproof screens at the crowded counters flying up to the ceiling.

It was too late now to hope of getting the Spellings' savings. She'd have to settle for the yacht. If she could get into international waters before the police figured out where she was, she'd be fine. There would always be other couples to scam. Right now she was in flight mode. All that mattered was getting away.

She walked across the bank foyer to the doors. Hope didn't count on Ken's blood having run so quickly from his wounds in Yim's office. As Hope walked toward freedom, her stolen high heels left a series of red triangles in her wake on the huge white marble tiles. Hope looked up just as the teller at the end of the row noticed them, her frown deepening as she tried to work out how the customer could have walked in red paint inside the bank.

The two women's eyes met just as Hope reached the door.

"Excuse me, miss," the teller called. "Miss!"

Hope turned and ran.

She fitted through the glass doors as they snapped shut just at the last second, the edges catching her shirt, tearing the soft fabric. The crowd parted as she waved the gun in the air.

"Get out of the way! Move!"

There was a taxi on the corner. Perfect timing. Hope was going to make it through this. She was going to see that sunrise on the ocean. No one was going to stop her.

CHAPTER 44

ON THE WAY back to the station, stopped at the traffic lights at Elizabeth Street, three patrol cars zipped through the red signal in front of us, sirens blaring. An ambulance was hot on their tail. They were heading toward Martin Place at an incredible speed. I'd been trying to get Chris Murray on the phone, but he wouldn't answer. Finally I took Tox's phone and dialed, hoping Murray wouldn't recognize the number.

"Chris Murray."

"Murray, you asshole," I said, "you've been ignoring my calls!"

"I don't have time for your calls," he snapped back.

We yelled into the phone at the same time: *"I've found the yachties!"*

We were both panting with excitement, struggling through the confusion.

"What?" Chris said.

"I've—found—the missing couple," I stammered. "Well, I know who knows where they are. I'm tailing a suspect, a prostitute named Hope Stallwood, in my drowning case. I think Hope and my victim, Claudia Burrows, were working together to steal your couple's boat. Claudia ended up as excess baggage, maybe got dumped when the scam was over. Probably your yachties, too."

"Well, I'm hoping you're wrong about that," Murray said. "Because a young Caucasian female has just tried to access the couple's bank account in Martin Place. And they tell me that whoever she is, she wasn't alone."

"Jesus Christ! That must be her!"

"I'm on my way right now," Murray said.

"I'll see you there." I grabbed Tox just as we set off across the lights. "Turn the car around," I told him. "Head back toward Martin Place."

CHAPTER 45

WE RAN ACROSS the crowded square and pushed through the ring of people at the police tape around the bank. The alarms inside were still squealing, but the big glass doors were open and cops were running in and out. One passed me with his hands covered in blood, rubbing them on the front of his shirt, looking dazed.

I knew Hope was on the edge. Anyone who had lived for long enough in the kind of environment she had was probably pretty close to manic-depressive.

I spend so much of my job hoping I'm wrong. I hoped, as I pushed through the crowd, that somehow I'd made a mistake while joining the dots. Connecting the yachting magazine to the missing couple who had disappeared at sea. Maybe I was jumping to conclusions—leaping down a rabbit hole that would take me nowhere. I hoped I'd walk into the bank manager's office and find the missing couple there, safe.

I wasn't so lucky.

There was a man in his fifties on his back on the marble floor, bleeding to death in a huddle of paramedics. He'd been shot or stabbed, it looked like. The situation was so desperate that the paramedics had forgone getting him to the hospital and were trying to stem the bleeding right there, in front of everyone. There were female bank tellers in snappy red suits crying in each other's arms. I grabbed one and yanked her away from the tearful huddle.

"Who is he?"

"I don't know." She wiped her running mascara. "He came in with her, the shooter. They were a couple. Mr. Yim saw them in the office. We didn't hear the gunshots. They walked in together, and then she walked out. Someone saw blood and went in and found them."

I turned the corner and glanced into Yim's office. He was slumped against the back wall, his face gray, a bullet hole in his neck. Two men were holding a dark jacket against his wounds. But it was clearly over.

I heard the man on the ground struggling against the paramedics assisting him.

"She's still on board!" he cried, taking gasps of breath. "She's got her! She's got my wife!"

CHAPTER 46

HOPE LEANED AGAINST the bridge wall and kept the gun on Jenny, watched out the windows as the other yachties lounged and talked on their own vessels. Soon the cops would swarm the piers looking for her, a black and poisonous cloud rolling out over the water, stifling the afternoon sun. She'd be long gone before they arrived. Jenny was not in good shape. She clung to the helm shakily, her head nodding gently as waves of exhaustion rolled through her. Hope told Jenny to fire the engines and guided her on the throttle. The older woman's hands were so slick with sweat she could hardly grip the wheel.

"I'm sorry it has to be this way," Hope said. "This is probably going to be awful for your family."

"Where is Ken?" Jenny whimpered.

"Put on port five." Hope waved at the helm. "Bring the throttle back a bit."

"I have two grown sons," Jenny said. "They have children."

"I don't care."

"Just tell me if Ken is still alive," Jenny pleaded. "Tell me what happened. I have to know."

Hope hardly heard the sick woman at the helm. For many years, Hope had been thinking about people in terms of how they related to her "Circle of Care." A wide ring around her shut people out, or welcomed them in. It encompassed the people who were her responsibility, those she could trust, those it was safe to love. The circle had shrunk a little when she was a child every time her father had beaten her, so that the man had slipped out of it completely over time. When he'd grown old and mild, always moaning about forgiveness and mistakes, Hope hadn't been able to bring herself to pull the man back inside the circle. For a while, in her teenage years, there had been friends and boyfriends inside the circle, but they'd walked out steadily as she'd taken to drinking and partying. When she'd started working in the Cross, she'd looped that small but loving circle around the other girls in her brothel. Together they'd gotten through the long nights and sleepy days, pulled each other up from the depths when it all became too much, watched out for the telltale track marks that meant someone was losing control.

But when Hope had been kicked out of the brothel for hiding profits from her madam, she'd found herself and Claudia the only two people left in the circle. And Hope was so used to people walking out, or being squeezed out, that she had really just been waiting all the time for Claudia's turn to leave. And that turn had come when she'd fulfilled her role in taking down the Spellings. Hope had had no use for her after that. She wasn't part of the glorious plan.

The circle was closed. Strangers like Jenny didn't have a chance. Hope directed the older woman to rev the engines when the bow was pointing to clear, empty horizon. Behind them Hope could see cops arriving on the pier. They'd stopped the taxi driver before he could get out of the marina. It was a close call, but Hope was getting ahead of them. Maybe she'd make it. There were plenty of heavy things on board to tie Jenny to if she got in trouble.

CHAPTER 47

I PICKED A vessel close to the end of the pier and shuffled the old couple who were having tea on the back deck off it. The water police in Sydney Harbor were gearing up, and the coastguard was sending a chopper. The radio I'd taken from a patrol cop at the bank was roaring with dozens of voices coordinating things here and there. A hostage negotiator teaching young criminologists at the University of Sydney was being pulled out of a lecture and driven at top speed toward the coast.

I stopped Tox on the back deck.

"Maybe you should stay," I said.

"What?" he scoffed. "Fuck off."

"Look," I said, "this is our case. We don't want it fucked up by idiot water police guys who insist on ignoring us because you're on board. If you're not around, I've got a chance of having some pull out there. I want control of the situation."

"I'm not leaving this case." Tox pushed me away. "Get on the helm and shut up."

"They're going to fuck with us out there, and lose us our suspect," I said. "Tox, you're a murderer!"

"I'm a killer, not a murderer!" he shouted. "There's a difference, Detective Blue."

I stared at him. He was ignoring me. He worked the helm like an expert, bringing the boat out of its mooring and turning it toward the sea in a seamless glide while its owners railed at us from the pier. I didn't know what to say. He glanced at me.

"I don't care that people don't like me," he said. "I deserve some punishment. But I don't drop cases, and I don't lose suspects."

I opened my mouth to answer, but nothing came out. He gestured to the throttle.

"Get moving." He looked to the horizon. "We've got to catch up and talk her down before she does something stupid and kills the hostage."

The police radio channels separated. I got onto a channel with the water police and Chris Murray. The coastguard hung back and let us take charge, three boats behind a row of five police cruisers and Tox's and my commandeered leisure yacht. We lost sight of land quickly. The freshly painted *New Hope* grew larger as we inched closer.

It was an hour of slow, restless following before Hope finally answered repeated pleas to talk over the radio. She came through loud and clear on the channel reserved for the police.

"I've got Jenny Spelling tied to a compressor," she said. "She's going overboard if you get any closer."

CHAPTER 48

THE COMMAND TEAM, led by Chris Murray, said nothing about Hope's progress out to sea. As long as she was talking, Murray seemed happy to let her trundle on ahead of us. But I wanted Hope to stop. While she was underway, she thought she was shifting closer and closer to being free, and I knew negotiations would last longer while she felt she had the upper hand. Jenny Spelling was sick. She wouldn't last a twelve-hour siege. I shifted in beside Tox at the helm and pointed to the *New Hope*.

"Come up alongside her," I said. "Keep your distance, like she said. Don't get any closer."

I went out of the bridge and down the steps to the back of our vessel. There was a tarp to protect the deck from the rain, hanging over the rear of the galley. I tore that down. I dragged a net out of a box on the deck and then went inside, grabbed sheets and blankets from the bed, and lugged them out onto the deck.

Hope's vessel slowly loomed up beside me. All the lights were on. I could see the young woman standing at the helm, looking out. I couldn't make out her expression. Jenny was on the other side of her, just her feet visible near a gap in the wall outside the bridge.

"I don't know what this boat is doing out to my starboard side." Hope's voice was high with tension on the radio. "But I want them to fuck off."

"What are you doing?" Tox shouted at me.

"Go round the front!"

The engines roared beneath me. I copped a hit of sea spray in the face as the boat lurched over the waves. As we came across Hope's bow, I waited until the right moment and then began hurling the sheets, blankets, tarp, and net into the sea.

"What the fuck?" Hope screamed on the radio.

I hung on as we took a huge wave to the starboard side, crossing over to Hope's port side.

I didn't know if my plan had worked immediately. There was no discernible crunch of the propellers as they became tangled in the debris I'd put right in Hope's path. After a while, I noticed her boat was slowing. There was smoke on the wind.

I looked up in time to see Hope on the port side, standing over Jenny as she lay helpless on the deck. As I watched, Hope looked back toward the boats behind her and raised the radio to her mouth.

"You shouldn't have done that," Hope said. "Now I'll have to punish her."

CHAPTER 49

HOPE UNSCREWED THE silencer and threw it over the side. The gunshot cracked over the ocean, rolling and echoing on the waves. Jenny didn't move. Hope's voice was impossibly high on the radio, the screech of a deranged woman.

"You do not want to fuck with me right now!" Hope said. "This woman is really sick. It won't take more than a couple of shots to finish her off!"

"Fucking psychopath," I seethed. Hope turned and popped off five shots at us. One clanged off the roof of the boat, mere inches from Tox's head. I threw myself to the deck and listened. Tox veered the boat away.

"Good move with the tarps," Tox said as I crawled back into the bridge.

"Detective Blue, that was a damn senseless move," Chris Murray blasted on the radio. He wanted the water police to hear that he didn't agree with the risk I'd just taken, in case it caused Hope to kill her hostage. He also wanted Hope to know she had a good cop to trust, now that it was clear who the bad one was. I switched over to the coastguard channel to talk back to him privately.

"She won't kill her," I said. "Not yet."

"Your actions have caused the hostage injury!" Chris snapped.

"Jenny Spelling didn't move an inch when that gun fired," I

said. "I reckon Hope's bluffing. Probably put a hole in the deck. She can't risk the only leverage she's got."

Chris switched back to Hope's channel.

"Hope Stallwood, this is Detective Christopher Murray. The detective who disabled your engines acted completely without authority."

Hope's voice came over the radio: "Detective, your people are going to get an innocent woman killed. Is that what you want? Now you're going to have to provide me with another vessel. If you don't start listening to me I'm going to kill her. Okay? I'm going to murder her right in front of you!"

She was almost screaming. Murray needed to bring her tension levels down before she did anything stupid. I'd raised them to manic level, but it had been worth the risk. The water police and coastguard vessels were slowly maneuvering around the front of the *New Hope,* trying to box her in while she was distracted.

"Hope, we're going to need you to tell us what condition Mrs. Spelling is in," Murray said. "We can't see what's going on. Did you wound her just now?"

There was silence for a long time. Hope was focused on her victim. She wandered down the bridge a little, turned and paced back. Her face was taut. Jenny's legs were moving. I could see her knees jostling through the gap in the bridge wall.

"There's something wrong with her," Hope's voice crackled on the radio, frighteningly calm. "She's having some kind of seizure."

CHAPTER 50

"WHAT EXACTLY'S WRONG with her?" Tox asked.

"Murray said she's got some kind of kidney thing," I said. "I don't think she's had her medication. That's how the family knew something was up. Why they reported them missing."

My whole body ached to be on that boat. Though she wasn't giving us any details, I knew Hope could have wounded Jenny with that gunshot, just to mess with us. The shot could have tipped Jenny over the edge into a seizure.

Hope walked to the end of the upper level of the boat and looked at the vessels ringing her, paced back again and stared at her victim, now still.

"Hope, are you willing to let us send a medic on board?" Murray said.

Hope went to the end of the boat again, lifted her gun and started firing. I ducked, but she wasn't firing at us this time. Murray's boat had been carried forward a little farther than the others as we came to a stop behind the *New Hope,* and she was warning him back. I saw all three officers on board dive for the deck.

"Girl's gonna run out of bullets in a minute," Tox grunted.

He was right. Hope stopped firing and returned to the bridge. When she reappeared she had a hunting rifle in her hand. She pointed it skyward and fired at the coastguard chopper, which was hovering high above us. She only gave it one shot. This was probably her last gun.

"Move back!" her voice screeched on the radio. Murray put his boat in reverse and came into line with the rest of us.

Every second of growing darkness was agonizing. Jenny wasn't moving. A couple of times, rogue officers on the water police boats tried to creep forward into the circle we'd established around the *New Hope*. But she spotted them soon enough and forced them back.

I could see the air compressor she'd tied Jenny to. A third of the heavy, squat machine was hanging off the edge of the boat, just beyond the gap in the bridge wall. When she felt threatened, Hope would go to the machine and rattle it, push it farther over the edge and then pull it back. I waited for Jenny to move. She didn't.

I couldn't take it any longer. All of the vessels around the *New Hope* had their spotlights trained on the water around the hull. I got an idea, and flicked ours off.

"What's the plan now, genius?" Tox asked.

I switched radio channels onto the coastguard channel, so that Hope couldn't hear me. I radioed the three coastguard boats spread throughout the circle.

"Coastguard, coastguard, this is Detective Harriet Blue, over."

"Coastguard here."

"Can you guys wait a few minutes, then switch your lights off? I'm trying to set up a path in, over."

Hope had noticed I'd switched my spotlights off, and that the ocean in front of my boat was black. I played it casual, leaning on the top of the bridge, talking to Tox. If I was careful, she'd think I was just switching the big light off to conserve my boat's battery power. I could feel her watching me, but she said nothing to Chris about it as they negotiated over the radio.

My plan was working. After a time, one coastguard boat switched off its light. Then another. Hope hardly noticed. She was ranting and pacing.

"You don't fucking understand. You're a man. How could you? You probably grew up in some mansion in bloody Mosman or something. You probably went to private school, didn't you? You were a poor choice of negotiator, my friend. There's no way you could possibly understand me. All right? So don't say that you do."

"We had another negotiator for you." Chris sighed. I could hear his dismay over the radio. "He's been held up."

Half the ocean around the *New Hope* was in darkness. The police boats cut beams of light through the black waves. It was time to go.

"You coming?" I asked Tox. He looked bewildered, until I started taking off my shoes.

"Oh, shit." He sighed, peeling off his jacket.

CHAPTER 51

AS WE SWAM along the side of the *New Hope* to the diving ladder, the sounds of Hope's yelling from the upper decks reached
us. We'd dived deep from the back of our vessel, popping up
just once in the dark between the boats to breathe. The threat
of Hope seeing us and firing into the water made my jaw lock
with terror. I pulled my gun out of the back of my pants and
put it on the deck in front of me as I got to the top of the ladder.
I hoped that if I needed it, it would still work. I didn't know
how it would react to the saltwater.

The cold seized everything, made every muscle hard as
stone. I stood shivering on the deck as Tox climbed out. We
were near a dark, cluttered galley. Our socks squelched on the
polished wood. We listened to the voice above us, her footsteps
on the floor. Tox was sniffing the air. He went to the pantry and
pulled open the door. Leaning against it was a heavy man in a
white business shirt. Tox checked his pulse, but he was long
gone, his whole body a sickening purple.

"Water safety guy," Tox said. He pushed the limp body back
into the pantry and shut the door. "Probably caught on to her."

We crept around the back of the galley and up the stairs,
stopping when we were high enough to look across the deck
to the bridge wing. Jenny was on her belly now, unconscious.
She seemed to be breathing. There were no open wounds on

her that I could see, adding hope to my theory that the gunshot earlier had been a bluff. The compressor she was tied to was hanging halfway out over the side of the boat, its small wheels spinning. I could see Hope's leg by the entrance to the bridge. She paced, wandering over to Jenny and then back to the helm, never leaving her alone for more than a few seconds.

"We'll come up the other side," Tox breathed. "Get her from behind."

"We should split up in case she lunges for the compressor. I'll go up this side."

My partner's eyes glittered in the dark. He nodded and checked the magazine in his gun. We were set to go until Hope's voice rose in pitch and volume, stopping us in our tracks.

"Where are the occupants of that boat?" she screamed.

CHAPTER 52

I LOOKED, AND saw her pointing off the port side. It was our boat that had caught her attention. The water police on the vessel beside ours had seen us go into the water and lashed our boat to theirs, but hadn't sent another officer over to cover our absence. Hope had been watching our boat and noticed no one was on board.

"Shit," I whispered.

"The officers who were on that boat moved over to the next one." Chris tried to cover us. He didn't sound confident enough. "They're there, Hope. No one's—"

"Someone's boarded me," Hope snapped. "One of your officers has boarded me, haven't they? You people have no regard for life, do you? I'm going to kill this innocent woman if you don't get your officers off my fucking yacht."

She went to Jenny and actioned the rifle, pointed it at the woman's head. The wind whipped the young woman's hair as she stared out defiantly at the boats around her. I got up on my haunches and got ready to run.

"Hold your fire!" someone yelled on the wind. "Hold your—"

A couple of shots clanged off the edge of the vessel, just above Hope's head. She slid down to her backside and growled with rage.

"Fuckers!" she yelled.

I watched the fury tremble through her, down her chest and through her stomach like electricity in her muscles. It was anger that moved her, taking over and crushing her logic. She kicked out and toppled the compressor over the edge of the boat.

"No, Hope!" I yelled. "No!"

It was too late. I saw the heavy machine go over the side.

CHAPTER 53

THE COMPRESSOR HIT the water with a massive splash. The rope around Jenny's legs whizzed over the side. I sprinted along the deck and reached it just as the rope ran out and yanked the wounded woman off the side of the boat.

I dived in after her, the fifteen feet of free air between the deck and the water feeling like ten minutes of sheer terror before the blackness of the ocean swirled around me.

The water was so cold that for a moment I didn't know if I'd been successful in grabbing at Jenny's hands. I held tight, and as we sailed downward I realized that I had a death grip on one of her wrists. We were sinking fast. There was no sound. The woman in my hands had come to and twisted and bucked as we plunged toward the depths.

We sailed downward. The pressure on my chest and head was too heavy to bear after only seconds. A voice in my head began screaming.

It's over. Let go. Let go. Get to the surface!

But I refused to let go.

CHAPTER 54

HOPE WATCHED THE bubbles rise from where her hostage and the cop had disappeared into the black depths. A couple of officers from boats nearby leaped into the water, diving low to try to help, but Hope knew there'd be no saving them. The deaths were easier now. She hadn't meant to make the compressor go over the edge. The anger had zinged through her, taking possession of her limbs. She was surprised at how little impact the killing made on her psyche. There was a heat, a ringing in her ears, a pounding in her skull, but no regret, no paralyzing sorrow. That was good. If she needed to kill more now to get free, she knew it would be achievable.

"Is she coming up?"

The voice came from behind her. Hope turned and saw a man standing there, the rifle she'd been holding trained on her face. He was soaked through to the skin, blond hair plastered to his forehead, two black eyes and a bruised nose. His face seemed passive, but when Hope didn't answer, he snapped.

"*Is she coming up?*"

"No."

The man with the gun sneered. "I actually didn't mind that woman."

He turned the gun swiftly and slammed the butt into Hope's jaw. She staggered, and her legs went out from beneath her. She felt teeth wobble in her mouth, swimming in blood. The man must have been a cop. In the spinning world, she saw him go to the edge of the bridge wing and wave at the boats below.

"Suspect down!"

I'll never go down, Hope thought. She reached up while he was distracted by something below, her hand shaking. She slid her index finger into the trigger guard and pulled.

The gun roared, kicked out of his hand. The cop fell.

CHAPTER 55

I'D CLIMBED ALONG Jenny's body, pulling at handfuls of her clothes, and got to her ankle. It seemed years passed as I yanked at the rope. When the weight came free, we hung in the blackness. My eyes were bulging in my skull. She did nothing. The fight had gone out of her. I grabbed, clawed at her neck and head, yanked upward at her arms.

There was water in my lungs. My limbs were starting to shudder. I was drowning. I couldn't tell if we were rising or not. Jenny's hopeless eyes stared up at me. I needed her to kick. Do anything. Keep me down here with her, when every cell in my body was telling me to let go.

Suddenly, she started kicking. We grabbed at each other, pulled upward. The surface came unexpectedly. There were hands under my arms, wrapping around me, dragging me onto my back. I vomited water. Jenny was wide-eyed, being dragged toward the boats by cops.

"Let me go," I said. "I need to get to the boat."

"You're all right now." The officer who had me was trying to pull my head back, relax me, get me to safety. "Take it easy. Breathe."

This was no time to take it easy. I wriggled out of his grip and swam as hard as I could for the *New Hope,* kicking faster as I saw smoke rising from the back deck.

CHAPTER 56

SHE'D GOTTEN HIM in the face, it seemed. The cop rolled away, scrambled until his back was to the helm. He got up, grabbed at the bridge to try to steady himself and knocked the throttle forward. The engine roared and squealed, tugging at the tangled ropes and sheets. Hope went for the gun but he kicked it away and lunged at her, grabbing at her hands, the blood making his fingers slick.

They rolled, twisted, tumbled down the stairs into the galley. His face was a mask of blood, hideous and wet, two cool blue eyes bulging wild as he came for her. Hope grabbed a knife from the kitchen block and threw it, backed it up with a second one. He caught the blade in the air and kept coming. She fell beneath him, the blade inches from her face, and pushed upward with all her might. His blood dripped on her. Her hands slipped, and the knife shunted into the wood right by her ear.

The smoke was sudden, thick with burning chemicals. The wind picked it up from the deck and blew it inside the galley where they fought. The engine had ignited, pushed over its limit by the sheets and ropes tangled around the propellers. The burning fuel seared in their eyes. They both rolled, fighting through the pain, trying to climb to their feet.

Out of the glowing flames on the deck the woman cop emerged, the one who had gone after Jenny. Two other officers were close behind her on the ladder. The woman cop's whole body was shaking with adrenaline and exhaustion. Hope backed toward the stairs as the two officers turned, blocking her exit. She grabbed at the counter, tried to find a weapon. A bottle. A glass. Anything.

"It's over, Hope. The whole thing's going to burn," the woman cop yelled. "Put that down. You've got to come with us."

Hope thought about it. And a weary smile crept to her face at what she imagined, how similar it was to the life she'd lived before. Hands on her. Dark rooms and endless days passing the windows. A team of girls in the prison dorms who'd welcome her, who'd stick by her, cheer her on, try to keep her away from the needle. Sweaty sheets and thin pillows, and those faceless men wandering in the halls, never meeting her eyes, giving her commands.

No. Never again.

Hope went up the stairs and slammed the bridge door behind her.

CHAPTER 57

TOX AND I got off the *New Hope* just in time, falling into the water as one of the fuel tanks exploded and the back half of the yacht listed badly to that side. The water was slick with oil. I was so tired. My arms grabbed weakly at the waves, making no progress, the current trying to push me back against the hull of the burning boat.

Tox pulled my arm around his neck. I held on to his hard, broad shoulders as we swam to the nearest police boat.

As we climbed aboard, we turned to see the fire creeping into the bridge. I could hardly watch. There was no sign of Hope in the blackened windows.

CHAPTER 58

SOMEONE TOOK THE small boat we'd commandeered back to the marina while Tox and I rode home on a police cruiser with Chris Murray. I stood up at the front of the boat with the squat, ruddy-faced man while another officer commanded the helm. Someone had wrapped a blanket around me. But Tox sat unattended at the rear of the boat on a barrel with his own shirt clutched to the gunshot wound in the side of his face. He was watching the boat's wake disappear into the dark of the night.

"You did a sensational job out there," Chris kept saying. Shaking his head ruefully at it all. "You weren't coming up. I was willing to put money on it. You dived in, and you were down there too long, and I thought, *She's got herself tangled up with that woman. She's a goner.*"

"Cut it out." I jabbed him in the side. "You know I don't like it."

We stared at our feet. I knew the answer to my question, but I asked it anyway.

"The husband. Did he make it?"

"No," Chris said.

We shuffled away from the officer driving the boat. Chris's eyes wandered the coastline ahead of us, picking out the clustered lights of Bondi and Coogee and the dark patches where the cliffs met the sea.

"I did look up Tox Barnes," he said suddenly.

"What?"

"Yeah." Chris glanced at me. "After you called me. I felt bad. I knew some guys in records who could pull some strings for me."

"I *knew* you did."

"I thought I'd get the details, just to arm myself, in case you came at me again. I was ready to cut you down about it."

"I don't think I even want to know." I held my hand up. "I think he's all right. And if there was a time when he wasn't all right, well, that seems to have been a long time ago."

"That's the thing." Chris leaned in close. "He *is* all right."

Chris told me the story. It wasn't close to any of the ones I'd heard.

CHAPTER 59

I WENT TO the back of the boat and sat beside Tox as we passed through the heads of Sydney Harbor. Somehow he still smelled of cigarette smoke. One side of his hair was plastered to his head, while the other, where he'd been shot, stuck up in wild spikes. There was blood all through his chest hair.

"How bad is it?" I asked.

"Meh." He shrugged.

He pulled the shirt away. The bullet had carved a vertical line up the side of his face from his jaw to his hairline, burning the flesh on either side, a straight gouge that looked half an inch deep. It was a grisly wound. Something he would wear well.

"Wow, that's disgusting." I reached out. "Can I touch it?"

"Get off." He shoved at me. "Freak."

I looked out at the waves, and the words came easily. Seemed to flow out, unlocked by my exhaustion. I told him I knew about Anna Peake and her son. His victims. I knew that Anna had been heading west on the A32 highway toward Katoomba on a bright Tuesday afternoon when she'd driven under an overpass where Tox Barnes had been standing with a group of other little boys. He was the smallest in the group. Six years old. The oldest had been nine. The boys had been tossing pebbles onto the tops of cars as they drove underneath, cheering and laughing as the rocks clinked and bounced on rooftops and hoods, no idea that what they were doing was incredibly dangerous. They'd gotten over the thrill of raining pebbles on the cars when one of the boys dropped a pebble the size of a penny onto the windshield of Anna Peake's car. The crack of the rock on the glass had been so sudden, so startling, that Anna had swerved and gotten the afternoon sun in her eyes. She had gone across the double lanes and right into the path of an oncoming truck. The boys had rushed to the other side of the overpass and watched her car burn, the mother and her little boy inside.

The five boys had been interrogated by police. The town had called for the oldest boy on the bridge to face criminal prosecution. In the end, none of the boys had been charged. They were so small, and so terrified by the awesome power of their actions, that the police had taken pity on them.

All of the boys had changed their names legally at some point between the deaths of Anna and her son and their adult lives. Terrence Brennan became Tate Barnes. The name change had not destroyed his past completely. Though his involvement in the killings had been suppressed, it had arisen when he'd tried to become a member of the New South Wales state police. The panel of admissions experts who'd approved Tox for service had been obliged to keep his childhood horror a secret. But it had leaked, like all secrets do. It had grown in size, warped, twisted. People had added things. Some had said the boys had stabbed the woman. Beat her. Raped her. Kidnapped her. The boys had grown older. Younger sometimes. New versions of the story had been passed down every year from older cops to the recruits in their charge. Like all rumors, it had its own life. No one knew the truth.

CHAPTER 60

WHEN I'D FINISHED talking I looked at him, expecting something. But he just watched the glowing Harbor Bridge in silence.

"Well?"

"Well what?"

"I need to understand." I held my hands out. "You're innocent. Why do you do this to yourself? Why do you let the rumors go on? Why don't you fix your life?"

"My life's not broken," he said.

"Everybody thinks you're some kind of vicious psychopath."

"This isn't high school." He gave me a pitying glance. "You don't need to worry about what people think anymore."

"You said earlier that you deserve some punishment. Is that how you really feel?"

"A bit." He shrugged. "Mostly, I just let people tell their stories because it keeps them away from me. I've said it from the beginning: I don't work with partners. I'm better on my own."

I watched him, and slowly I began to understand. It was the same as my brother and me, the way we'd acted as kids, running away from the families that tried to take us in, behaving badly and shutting them out until they gave up on us. When we were on our own, we knew what to expect. We knew the rules of the game. Being "included" was risky. Because we didn't accept love and companionship, we couldn't be rejected. Sam and I had known all our lives that we could only rely on each other. Tox Barnes knew it, too.

I was sickened, suddenly, by how familiar I was with it all. Being the outsider. Pushing people away. I had to change his mind. I had to convince him to get his story out there.

"You take pride in what you do. Don't your victims deserve the best from you?" I said. "Your colleagues hate you. They throw up barriers every time you try to make a move on cases. If people knew the truth about you, you'd be a more effective cop."

He actually laughed.

"No, I wouldn't," he said. "I'd end up being a cop like you."

"And what's wrong with that?"

"Oh, man, you have no idea how ineffective you are," he said. "Waiting for autopsy reports. Calling the lab. Talking to colleagues. Hugging the victim's parents. You're a part of the system, mate. I'm outside the system. No one wants to take responsibility for me, so I do what I want. Skip the procedural bullshit. Makes me a better cop than you, I'll tell you that much."

I shook my head at him. It hurt, but I understood. He was pushing me away now, trying to annoy me so I'd leave him alone. I'd done the same thing all my life. Whenever someone uncovered the truth, made me vulnerable, I'd shut them down as hard and as fast as I could.

I walked back to the front of the boat and left him alone.

CHAPTER 61

I'D SLEPT WELL. The first night, it had been sheer physical exhaustion. Every limb had hurt. After I'd been checked over at the hospital, I'd gone home and crashed on my bed face first and slept until the next afternoon.

A couple of nights later I'd followed Matthew Demper and Alex Loris to a bar in Paddington and waited all night while the Kings Cross police officers got themselves nice and tipsy playing pool and betting on the horses. When they returned to their car, I'd given them a few seconds to remember me as the detective they'd made jump out of a police van with her hands cuffed behind her back. When their memory was jogged, I'd broken Demper's nose and given Loris a sound kick to the nuts. I slept even better after that.

I was all ready to take my place on the Georges River task force. It was the perfect moment, and I'd make sure Pops knew that. Nigel had called a press conference with the national media, telling them he had some big announcement with regard to the case. I walked into the station, planning to tell him that he could announce that he was adding me to the task force while he was at it. How could they refuse me now? The newspapers were lauding me as a national hero. For once in my career I was in a position to make demands. And I was going to demand a spot on the hunt for that killer.

I strode across the bullpen on the way to Pops's office, knowing Nigel would be in there being briefed about the press conference. I veered off my path slightly when I saw Tox standing by the coffee machine, half his face swathed in bandages, scratching at the bottom of a jar of coffee with a spoon. I marched up and slapped his arm.

"I'm about to burst in and put myself on the Georges River task force," I said. "Did you hear there's going to be some kind of announcement?"

Tox looked at me. His characteristic blankness had lifted slightly. There was a look in his eyes that was almost concern.

"You haven't met with the Chief yet? Does he know you're here?"

"No," I said. "What's wrong? Is it the announcement? Do you know what it is?"

Tox looked over my shoulder. The Chief was heading toward me, fast. The way he put his hand gently on my shoulder sent my stomach plunging. This was a man who'd broken my tooth in the boxing ring. He didn't touch me that way. No one did.

"I need to see you," Pops said. "Could you give me a few minutes, and then come sit down? We need to talk."

"In your office?"

"No," he said. "In the interrogation room."

CHAPTER 62

IT WAS THE hardest thing he'd ever had to do. And that was a hell of a statement, because what was "hard" in the job had changed incredibly over Chief Morris's career. When he had been a young patrol cop back in the seventies he'd thought the hours were hard, sneaking into the house late at night so he didn't wake the kids. When he'd first made detective, he'd thought finding the bodies of stupid young gang members with their throats cut was hard. It got to be so that the old man had seen such wicked stuff in his time...

But sitting his best detective down and telling her this news, now that was a whole new level.

Detective Harriet Blue sat across from him in the interrogation room, the lights making her look even more tired than she was, her angular head of scruffy hair balanced in one palm. She looked this way in the boxing ring. On the verge. Wired. Ready for the next strike, whether it was his or hers.

The Chief had a tough time trying not to think like her father sometimes. If he'd been her father he'd have kicked her out of the force a long time ago. Got her into something that suited that brilliant mind but wouldn't leave her a bitter, damaged old woman at the end of her career. He'd have dragged her out of the academy by her hair if he'd had to. But he wasn't her father.

The words came out slowly. He danced around the issue for a bit. Then he laid it on her straight, the way she deserved.

"We found the Georges River Killer," he said.

He looked at her eyes.

"It's your brother, Blue. It's Sam."

Harriet twitched, just once, the way she would do when he'd smack her good and hard in the boxing ring. She was trying to work out what had just happened.

Her sharp, cold eyes examined his.

Then she got up and left.

CHAPTER 63

HE FOUND HER in the Georges River Killer task force room, of course. She'd finally busted her way in. When Chief Morris came through the door, he saw exactly what he expected. The short, wiry Detective Blue was going at her nemesis Nigel Spader with all the blind ferocity of a Jack Russell terrier. Above her on the case board the evidence she'd been blind to in the months since the killings had started fluttering a little in the fray. All the officers in the room were silent. Some were half-heartedly trying to pull the woman off her victim.

"How could you be so completely wrong?" Blue howled. "How could you be so completely, completely *useless!* You pathetic piece of—"

"That's enough!" Chief Morris stepped forward, took Blue's arm. He felt her shaking. "Detective Blue, you get a hold of yourself right now or I'll have the boys escort you out onto the street."

Blue whirled around and looked at him. The shock and heartache of a betrayed kid, eyes wide, disbelieving, all the exhaustion of the former case now vanished from her features. Her cheeks were flushed and her teeth gritted. Just as she did when she came around from a near-knockout in the boxing ring, Chief Morris watched as she shook it off and set her mind to what she'd do next to survive. She shoved past him. He felt the gentle brush of her shoulder like the slam of a sledgehammer.

That's it, Blue, he thought. *You're not done yet.*

When she'd gone, the case room was somber. The men standing there looked silently at him, waiting for direction. Yes, none of them had ever been on the friendliest of terms with the little firecracker in their station. Harriet Blue was too determined, too brash, too obsessed with the job to fit in with these guys. But they still didn't like having to do this to her. How could anyone? A sex crimes detective's brother turns out to be the worst homicidal sexual predator in decades, maybe ever. Pops felt the humiliation. It was thick as smoke in the air.

He went to the case board and looked at the photographs there, interior shots of Samuel Jacob Blue's apartment taken during the search. Grainy surveillance images of the beloved brother walking in the street on the night of the first victim's murder, hundreds of meters down from her apartment, a dark ball cap pulled down over his face. The Chief absentmindedly pulled down fingerprint analysis from the first two victims. Turned it over and over in his hands, uncertain.

"We're right, aren't we?" he said aloud, his eyes wandering over the huge collection of evidence. He found that his throat was tight. This was really hitting him. It had been years since he'd felt this troubled.

"We're right," Spader said, taking the sheet from him and pinning it back on the board. "It's him. He's the killer. We checked and double-checked. And after we make an arrest, we'll get a confession. It won't take long. There's nothing you can say in the face of this stuff." He gestured to the board. "It's open and shut."

"It better be," Chief Morris said. If it was all a mistake, and they'd brought in an innocent man, the Chief was sure he'd have lost one of the greatest investigative minds he'd seen in his policing career. Blue wouldn't come back to the force that had turned against her. She wouldn't trust him anymore, his people. It had been enough of a mission to get her settled in the first place. She wasn't good with institutions. They'd mishandled her as far back as she could remember.

But worse than all that, all the embarrassment and mistrust, all the heartache and accusations and damage it would do to Blue and her relationship with the force, if they were wrong about Samuel Jacob Blue, it would mean one thing. That the monster was still out there. And they had no idea who he was.

Harry had taken down the central picture in the case board, a photo of her and her brother, their faces pressed together. It would be puzzling for her, how her brother could be such an evil being when every cell in her own body was inherently good. The Chief knew the answer. It wasn't about good and evil—it was about fire. It took a white-hot flame in a sick, terrible mind to drive Sam Blue to do what he did. So much energy. So much destruction. The Chief had seen that fire in the eyes of plenty of horrible men. He'd seen it most in the ghouls who lurked in the back of prison cells, those vicious dogs who were deemed unfit to ever reenter society. He'd seen it burning, too, in the eyes of heroes he'd worked with on the job, the cops who got up and rushed toward the sounds of screaming when everyone else was taking cover.

That same fire burned in Detective Harriet Blue. The Chief knew her brother's arrest wouldn't put it out. It would make it burn brighter.

ABOUT THE AUTHORS

James Patterson is the most popular storyteller of our time. He is the creator of unforgettable characters and series, including Alex Cross, the Women's Murder Club, Jane Effing Smith, and Maximum Ride, and of breathtaking true stories about the Kennedys, John Lennon, and Princess Diana, as well as our military heroes, police officers, and ER nurses. He has coauthored #1 bestselling novels with Bill Clinton and Dolly Parton, told the story of his own life in *James Patterson by James Patterson*, and received an Edgar Award, nine Emmy Awards, the Literarian Award from the National Book Foundation, and the National Humanities Medal.

Candice Fox is the coauthor of the *New York Times* and *Sunday Times* #1 bestselling novels in the Detective Harriet Blue series. She has won three prestigious Ned Kelly Awards for her novels *Hades, Eden,* and *The Chase,* and is also the author of several other critically acclaimed novels. She lives in Sydney, Australia.

JAMES PATTERSON
RECOMMENDS

JAMES
PATTERSON
AND BRIAN SITTS

CRIME HAS
A NEW ENEMY.

THE
NEW YORK TIMES
BESTSELLER

THE
SHADOW

A THRILLER

THE SHADOW

Only two people know that 1930s society man Lamont Cranston has a secret identity as the Shadow, a crusader for justice— well, make that three if you include me, and it is my great honor to reimagine his story. But the other two are his greatest love, Margo Lane, and his fiercest enemy, Shiwan Khan. When Khan ambushes the couple, they must risk everything for the slimmest chance of survival... in the future.

A century and a half later, Lamont awakens in a world both unknown and disturbingly familiar. Most disturbing, Khan's power continues to be felt over the city and its people. No one in this new world understands the dangers of stopping him better than Lamont Cranston. And only the Shadow knows that he's the one person who might succeed before more innocent lives are lost.

JAMES PATTERSON

1ST
TIME IN PRINT

and RICHARD DiLALLO

THE MIDWIFE MURDERS

I can't imagine a worse crime than one done against a child. But when two kidnappings and a vicious stabbing happen on her watch in a university hospital in Manhattan, her focus abruptly changes. Something has to be done, and senior midwife Lucy is fearless enough to try.

Rumors begin to swirl, with blame falling on everyone from the Russian mafia to an underground adoption network. Fierce single mom Lucy teams up with a skeptical NYPD detective, but I've given her a case where the truth is far more twisted than Lucy could ever have imagined.

From the Creator of the #1 Bestselling Women's Murder Club

JAMES PATTERSON

2 SISTERS

DETECTIVE AGENCY

FIRST TIME IN PRINT

& CANDICE FOX

2 SISTERS DETECTIVE AGENCY

Discovering secrets about your own family has a way of changing your life...for better or for worse. Attorney Rhonda Bird learns that her estranged father had stopped being an accountant and opened up a private detective agency—and that she has a teenage half-sister named Baby.

When Baby brings in a client to the detective agency, the two sisters become entangled in a dangerous case involving a group of young adults who break laws for fun, their psychopath ringleader, and an ex-assassin who decides to hunt them down for revenge.

JAMES PATTERSON

& J.D. BARKER

THE COAST TO COAST MURDERS

THE COAST-TO-COAST MURDERS

Nothing brings siblings together more than sharing a terrifying past. Both adopted, and now grown, Michael and Megan Fitzgerald trust each other before anyone else. They've had to. Brought up in a rarefied, experimental environment, they were sheltered from the world's harsh realities, but it also forced secrets upon them.

In Los Angeles, Detective Garrett Dobbs and FBI agent Jessica Gimble have joined forces to work a murder that seems like a dead cinch until there's another killing. And another. And not just in Los Angeles—the spree spreads across the country. The Fitzgerald family comes to the investigators' attention, but Dobbs and Gimble are at a loss—if one of the four is involved, which Fitzgerald might it be?

For a complete list of books by
JAMES PATTERSON

VISIT
JamesPatterson.com

 Follow James Patterson on Facebook
@JamesPatterson

 Follow James Patterson on X
@JP_Books

 Follow James Patterson on Instagram
@jamespattersonbooks